MW01677423

VOYAGI[illegible]S

BOOKS THAT EXPLORE CANADA

Michael Gnarowski — Series Editor

Dundurn presents the Voyageur Classics series, building on the tradition of exploration and rediscovery and bringing forward time-tested writing about the Canadian experience in all its varieties.

This series of original or translated works in the fields of literature, history, politics, and biography has been gathered to enrich and illuminate our understanding of a multi-faceted Canada. Through straightforward, knowledgeable, and reader-friendly introductions, the Voyageur Classics series provides context and accessibility while breathing new life into these timeless Canadian masterpieces.

The Voyageur Classics series was designed with the widest possible readership in mind and sees a place for itself with the interested reader as well as in the classroom. Physically attractive and reset in a contemporary format, these books aim at an enlivened and updated sense of Canada's written heritage.

OTHER VOYAGEUR CLASSICS TITLES

The Blue Castle by Lucy Maud Montgomery, introduced by Dr. Collett Tracey 978-1-55002-666-5

Canadian Exploration Literature: An Anthology, edited and introduced by Germaine Warkentin 978-1-55002-661-0

Combat Journal for Place d'Armes: A Personal Narrative by Scott Symons, introduced by Christopher Elson 978-1-55488-457-5

The Donnellys by James Reaney, introduced by Alan Filewod 978-1-55002-832-4

Empire and Communications by Harold A. Innis, introduced by Alexander John Watson 978-1-55002-662-7

The Firebrand: William Lyon Mackenzie and the Rebellion in Upper Canada by William Kilbourn, introduced by Ronald Stagg 978-1-55002-800-3

In This Poem I Am: Selected Poetry of Robin Skelton, edited and introduced by Harold Rhenisch 978-1-55002-769-3

The Letters and Journals of Simon Fraser 1806–1808, edited and introduced by W. Kaye Lamb, foreword by Michael Gnarowski 978-1-55002-713-6

Maria Chapdelaine: A Tale of French Canada by Louis Hémon, translated by W.H. Blake, introduction and notes by Michael Gnarowski 978-1-55002-712-9

The Men of the Last Frontier by Grey Owl, introduced by James Polk 978-1-55488-804-7

Mrs. Simcoe's Diary by Elizabeth Posthuma Simcoe, edited and introduced by Mary Quayle Innis, foreword by Michael Gnarowski 978-1-55002-768-6

Pilgrims of the Wild, edited and introduced by Michael Gnarowski 978-1-55488-734-7

The Refugee: Narratives of Fugitive Slaves in Canada by Benjamin Drew, introduced by George Elliott Clarke 978-1-55002-801-0

The Scalpel, the Sword: The Story of Doctor Norman Bethune by Ted Allan and Sydney Ostrovsky, introduced by Julie Allan, Dr. Norman Allan, and Susan Ostrovsky 978-1-55488-402-5

Selected Writings by A.J.M. Smith, edited and introduced by Michael Gnarowski 978-1-55002-665-8

Self Condemned by Wyndham Lewis, introduced by Allan Pero 978-1-55488-735-4

The Silence on the Shore by Hugh Garner, introduced by George Fetherling 978-1-55488-782-8

Storm Below by Hugh Garner, introduced by Paul Stuewe 978-1-55488-456-8

A Tangled Web by Lucy Maud Montgomery, introduced by Benjamin Lefebvre 978-1-55488-403-2

The Yellow Briar: A Story of the Irish on the Canadian Countryside by Patrick Slater, introduced by Michael Gnarowski 978-1-55002-848-5

Duncan Campbell Scott: Selected Writings, edited, selected, and introduced by Michael Gnarowski 978-1-45970-144-1

The Town Below by Roger Lemelin, introduced by Michael Gnarowski 978-1-55488-803-0

Pauline Johnson: Selected Poetry and Prose by Pauline Johnson, selected and introduced by Michael Gnarowski 978-1-45970-428-2

The Kindred of the Wild: A Book of Animal Life by Charles G.D. Roberts, introduced by James Polk 978-1-45970-147-2

All Else Is Folly: A Tale of War and Passion by Peregrine Acland, introduced by Brian Busby and James Calhoun, and with a preface by Ford Madox Ford 978-1-45970-423-7

In Flanders Fields and Other Poems by John McCrae, introduced by Michael Gnarowski 978-1-45972-864-6

Ringing the Changes: An Autobiography by Mazo de la Roche, introduced by Heather Kirk 978-1-45973-037-3

The Regiment by Farley Mowat, introduced by Lee Windsor 978-1-45973-389-3

God's Sparrows by Philip Child, introduced by James R. Calhoun 978-1-45973-643-6

Flying a Red Kite by Hugh Hood, introduced by Michael Gnarowski 978-1-45973-855-3

OYAGEUR CLASSICS

OOKS THAT EXPLORE CANADA

THE DESERTER

DOUGLAS LEPAN

INTRODUCTION BY SCOTT RAYTER

DUNDURN
TORONTO

Cover image: istock.com/kojihirano
Printer: Webcom, a division of Marquis Book Printing Inc.

Library and Archives Canada Cataloguing in Publication

LePan, Douglas, 1914-1998, author
The deserter / Douglas LePan ; introduction by Scott Rayter.

(Voyageur classics : books that explore Canada)
Originally published: Toronto : McClelland & Stewart, 1964.
Issued in print and electronic formats.
ISBN 978-1-4597-4326-7 (softcover).--ISBN 978-1-4597-4327-4 (PDF).--
ISBN 978-1-4597-4328-1 (EPUB)

I. Rayter, Scott, 1970-, writer of introduction II. Title. III. Series: Voyageur classics

PS8523.E67D4 2019 C813'.54 C2018-906349-1
C2018-906350-5

1 2 3 4 5 23 22 21 20 19

We acknowledge the support of the **Canada Council for the Arts**, which last year invested $153 million to bring the arts to Canadians throughout the country, and the **Ontario Arts Council** for our publishing program. We also acknowledge the financial support of the Government of Ontario, through the **Ontario Book Publishing Tax Credit** and **Ontario Creates**, and the **Government of Canada**.

Nous remercions le **Conseil des arts du Canada** de son soutien. L'an dernier, le Conseil a investi 153 millions de dollars pour mettre de l'art dans la vie des Canadiennes et des Canadiens de tout le pays.

Printed and bound in Canada.

VISIT US AT

dundurn.com | @dundurnpress | dundurnpress | dundurnpress

Dundurn
3 Church Street, Suite 500
Toronto, Ontario, Canada
M5E 1M2

EDITOR'S NOTE

MICHAEL GNAROWSKI

There is some ambiguity associated with the spelling of the LePan name. Douglas LePan (1914–98), the author of *The Deserter*, seems to have used different spellings, as evidenced in his personal archive at the University of Toronto. The record, of course, is in the way Douglas LePan approved the spelling of his name in his published works. The name is spelled as two words in his first two collections of poetry, *The Wounded Prince and Other Poems* (1948) and *The Net and the Sword* (1953) for which he won the Governor General's Award. Both collections of poetry were published by the distinguished London publisher Chatto and Windus, and the spelling is confirmed in Reginald Watters's authoritative bibliography, *A Checklist of Canadian Literature* (1959 and 1972).

Eleven years later, LePan published his novel, *The Deserter*, in which the confusion around the spelling of his name is marked. The name appears as two words on the front of the dust jacket, its spine, and on the hardcover spine. However, the spelling changes on the back cover of the dust jacket, where it appears as one word — capital L and capital P — as it does on the all-important title page of the book. However, this spelling is not found on the copyright registration entry; there, it is Lepan. He adopted a spelling for his name, with a single word with capital L and P, for later books published during his lifetime, including the particularly important memoirs *Bright Glass of Memory* (1979) and *Weathering It: Complete Poems 1948–1987* (1987). This is the spelling agreed upon with the copyright owners and used in this edition of *The Deserter.*

Douglas LePan had a remarkable and distinguished life. He attended the University of Toronto, Merton College, Oxford, and Harvard University. He served in the offices of Canada's High Commission in London during the war, then enlisted as an ordinary soldier in the artillery, where he fought in the Italian Campaign. In civilian life, he had a career in the Department of External Affairs, was an assistant to Lester B. Pearson, and was seconded as Secretary of the Royal Commission on Canada's Economic Prospects, the Gordon Commission, for which he edited a much-praised report. He also helped to develop the Colombo Plan for the United Nations. Later, he taught at Queen's University and the University of Toronto, where he was the principal of University College. In addition to the Order of Canada, LePan twice won the Governor General's Award for literature, held a Guggenheim Fellowship, and was awarded half a dozen honorary doctorates. He was elected a Fellow of the Royal Society of Canada.

INTRODUCTION

SCOTT RAYTER

In a piece entitled "A Bewildering First Novel" — a 1964 *Globe and Mail* review of Douglas LePan's *The Deserter* — Arthur Hammond confesses: "I remain baffled by the intent of the book, but very interested." Indeed, what can one say, even now, about LePan's only novel, which went on to win the 1965 Governor General's award for fiction (beating out the clear favourite, Margaret Laurence's *The Stone Angel*), but has been largely ignored and forgotten, remaining out of print for nearly four decades?

And what of LePan himself? Despite an impressive military record, a postwar career as a diplomat (working closely with Lester B. Pearson, for example), a position as professor of English, status as an award-winning and much-anthologized poet, all the more notable for a collection of gay love poetry he published late in life, LePan has largely faded from public consciousness and Canadian literary history since his death twenty years ago (1914–98).

In the 1960s, his long poem "Tuscan Villa" was for a few years so widely taught in Canadian secondary schools that a Coles Notes guide to the poem was published.[1] But that period was brief. Over the intervening decades there has been very little scholarship on his work — and hardly anything said about the novel. Nor, surprisingly, has anyone sought to undertake a biography, even though the carefully preserved, rich, and substantial archive of his papers (which includes professional as well as personal correspondence, the typescripts and notes for all his works, and even his daily calendars) speaks to a variety of research interests.

A fuller account of LePan's life seems called for, given the notable lacunae in his 1979 memoir, *Bright Glass of Memory.* That book tells of his military, diplomatic, and early literary career in London, where he found himself in esteemed company that included John Maynard Keynes, the foremost economist of the twentieth century; the writer and painter Wyndham Lewis;[2] and T.S. Eliot, the pre-eminent Modernist poet, playwright, and literary critic. Remarkably, however, he says very little about what seems to have been the most important formative experience of his life — the eighteen months (autumn 1943 to spring 1945) he served as a gunner during the Italian campaign in the Second World War.

LePan gave up a comfortable London-based position at army headquarters as an officer in order to enlist as an ordinary soldier. Those eighteen months with the Royal Canadian Artillery provided the fodder both for early and more decorous poems, such as "Tuscan Villa" and "Elegy for the Romanga" (the former

The author at about the time of the publication of The Deserter. *He was fifty years old.*

serving as the inspiration for Michael Ondaatje's setting in *The English Patient*), and for much blunter later war poems, such as "Below Monte Casino" and "The Haystack." And, importantly, that experience provided background material for *The Deserter* — shaping his views on such questions as the nature of heroism and of individual as well as national duty.

Yet he chose not to depict the war itself in the novel. In the introduction to *Bright Glass of Memory*, LePan briefly touches on this central period in his life:

> It follows that there are many sides of myself that are not represented here at all. Others may wonder whether I was accustomed to spend all my time with the great. You [i.e., his two sons, to whom the introduction is addressed] will know differently. You know me well enough to know that the time I spent in the ranks [of the army] meant more to me than any of the passages recounted here, and that the friends I had then in extremity were closer to me in crucial respects than any I have had before or since. One of them, a signalmen, is celebrated in "One of the Regiment." Another of them, an officer, is in his scout car, leading, in "Reconnaissance in Early Light." I will be remembering till my dying day all those artillery positions for the attack on [Monte] Cassino, and the crossing of the Rapido, and the breaking of the Hitler Line, and during the pursuit to Rome, when the regiment took up a new position almost every day and when the air was jewelled with the Italian light and the constant danger of death. That part of my experience is not touched on here.

The title of the introduction, "A Letter to My Sons," would suggest that Nick and Don LePan are the intended audience, but LePan nonetheless tantalizes a general readership with the complexities of his undisclosed subjectivity: "There is another part of me that is missing.... It is that hidden part 'which is death to hide,' that broods over secrecies and wildnesses and sometimes fashions them into poems."

LePan's novel likewise appears to take as its very subject the inexplicable and the unspeakable. It begins: "If the war had not been over, it would have been easier to understand. Then it could have been put down simply to cowardice. But the armistice had been signed two months before; and now the world, as the newspapers kept reassuring their readers, was slowly returning to normal." Here, the pronoun "it" lacks a clear antecedent, something previously mentioned that would make explicit what "it" denotes — something, very tellingly, that the narrator suggests cannot be understood. A reader might ask further, *who* won't understand? Everyone? Specific individuals, such as fellow soldiers, the top brass, or other characters who have yet to be introduced in the novel? And what is the nature of this thing that cannot be

Douglas LePan in his soldier's plain uniform circa 1943. His cap badge is that of the Royal Canadian Artillery, which he served in during the Italian campaign in the Second World War.

understood? Is it an incident, something that has happened? Or what someone has done, a particular act they have committed? There is, perhaps, an antecedent of sorts we can infer from the title of the novel itself. By replacing "it" with "desertion," the sentence and meaning become clearer, though we can't know for certain whether the narrator is referring to the act in general or an action taken by, let's say, the protagonist of this novel, a young Canadian solider named Rusty.

By remaining vague, the author intends not to baffle the reader, but rather to focus on the reasoning — the wherefore and why — which, as we learn, Rusty himself does not fully understand or accept.

The novel postpones the first use of the word "desert" for several pages, interestingly enough, until a detail about how in the infantry Rusty needed to be at the centre of the action — to "be in the attack company. Always closer to the moment's glittering sword-edge" — but "[n]ow that impulse seemed to have deserted him"; and so, we learn two pages later, "[a]s soon as the blackouts had been put up again and the lights were switched on, he knew that he was going to desert." His own desire for "action" — his raison d'être — having now deserted him (the military action having come to an end), he rejects the light of day and deserts his post to explore instead the darkness of both the nighttime world outside as well as the dark forces within himself.

Unlike in many other war (and anti-war) novels, Rusty, neither in his own views, nor as a symbol (think of Timothy Findley's 1977 novel, *The Wars*), comes to represent the horrors of war — the protagonist as either victim or perpetrator, or both. Rusty does not appear to carry the trauma of war with him, and it is important not to misinterpret his desertion as coming from a place of fear, protest, or trauma, particularly as he deserts *after* the war has ended and he is about to be demobilized. Rusty's growing ambivalence about the war and the army, and the ways they provide structure and give purpose and identity to his life, is made evident by the fact that we learn that he has been decorated with a medal for bravery, but are not given the details of how he came to earn it. Rusty states, simply, that it was "easy," "by the book."

By contrast, "the one thing that had ever fully pleased and satisfied him in action" was defying his colonel's orders and going out to rescue Spike, a fellow soldier who lay wounded in the battlefield. For that act of bravery and humanity, he is "reduced to the ranks … [l]osing his stripes." This kind of "logic" of war, which became the stuff of the absurdist and satiric novels such as the contemporaneous *Catch-22*, by Joseph Heller, makes Rusty begin to cast doubt on his identity and how to go forward when the war is over. Only in the upside-down world of war could the saving of a life be seen as a transgressive, even insubordinate and punishable act, while killing, the taking of life, is regarded as a moral and legal crime and is rewarded.

If, unsurprisingly, the world outside the military holds allure for a soldier whose spiteful and unworthy "superiors" have created and enforced his existence within a rigid and, what seems at times, nonsensical order, it also conjures up a sense of freedom from being responsible for others, from having to try and save a fellow soldier's life. To Rusty, desertion holds out the promise of no longer putting the communal above the individual, at once leaving him free to follow his own desires and, at the same time, potentially shielding him from the pain of love and loss, the routine offerings of war.

But this question of desertion and, by extension, loyalty — both to what and to whom — is the central conflict of the novel, which Rusty grapples with throughout. In deferring meaning, through the ambiguous use of the initial "it" pronoun, the novel offers a glimpse into Rusty's own mind, and what for him remains inchoate, unconscious, something that cannot be fully accepted. It is not simply the fear of arrest and punishment (which could very well include execution) that keeps Rusty from disclosing his status to others, even to those who've done likewise, it is also the shame, the inability to admit this truth about himself. Instead, he is forever qualifying his actions, trying to convince himself he is different from other deserters. However, it is only when Rusty begins to be humanized once more, an effect of the growing bond he develops with the young refugee Steve that he is finally able to speak the truth of what he is:

> "I am a deserter." The word came out nakedly. It loomed between them like a butcher-knife, hacking the darkening air and making Steve cringe back a little involuntarily, till what Rusty had intended as a rare attempt at baring his breast in sympathy was in danger of turning into a cause of offence.... [He was incapable of] admitting to the word himself. Recently he had become wary of using it about himself even in his own mind.... Now that he had brought it so painfully out, he felt it burning him like the great D that used to be branded under a deserter's arm after he had been caught and convicted....
>
> ... "It's because I trust you that I tell you."
>
> And with that Steve took his hand and held it in a grip of iron.

For Rusty to own what he has done, to claim that identity, is to admit his failure to follow the orders he swore an oath to carry out, even if it costs him his life. Instead of proudly wearing the medal for military bravery he received, he experiences the shame of his crime exposed for all to see, something akin to being branded with the putative scarlet letter emblazoned across the sinner's chest, a single letter standing in for the otherwise unspeakable word. Even the language used here suggests that Rusty is revealing some kind of sexual secret: "nakedly," "baring his breast," "offence," "burning him" with shame, something he couldn't "admit [to] himself."

With so much unnamed here, meaning operates on a number of levels. In his notes for the novel, LePan writes: "The city should be nameless. But if the reader assumes it to be London, there is no harm in that." To be sure, there is more than a whiff of that "unreal city" that his friend T.S. ("Tom") Eliot both depicted and imagined in *The Waste Land*.

Names, too, are at once significant and elusive. Characters lack surnames, while others sport nicknames, and in the underworld of criminals and deserters where our protagonist comes to dwell, people possess multiple identities and aliases. "Rusty," for instance, can be a short form of Russell, or it may have no connection to a person's name, and instead be a generic name for someone who has red hair. The word is used in other contexts, too, of course. It can refer (as it is used in the second paragraph of the novel to describe the barbed wire that circles the camp) to the ferrous oxide of age and decay that weakens and breaks down metal, stained as if with dried blood. Finally, the word *rusty* may also describe a state of atrophy that comes from lack of use. The name pulls in several directions, at once suggesting a simple, youthful innocence and a soldier unnaturally aged and damaged by war.

This wartime experience has made it impossible for Rusty to reintegrate into his family and the community in which he grew up — a daunting task compounded by his disdain for that world, which he directs toward his father (particularly since his mother's death); his sister, who castigates him for his treatment of their father and for his sense of entitlement; and "the girl back home," whom everyone expects he will marry. Indeed, his desertion just before he is to be demobilized and sent back home is a kind of protest against and outright rejection of what he calls "normal life": "Something had happened to him during the war which had so deeply affected his sense of reality that he couldn't stand a closed domestic life — or even believe in its existence."

This statement stands in sharp contrast to the observation made in the opening lines of the novel that Rusty's desertion appears inexplicable, because "the world, as the newspapers kept reassuring their readers, was slowly returning to normal." Rusty, we are told, has come to distrust newspapers, dismissing them as purveyors of what some today call "fake news." He believes them to carry invented stories and deliberate lies about deserters to whip up public indignation and the calls for a "clean up." In doing so, the press justifies the brutal police crackdown in the quarter, what we might characterize as a "moral panic" that allows the state to exercise power in ways it would not otherwise be able to carry out unopposed.

* * *

LePan's novel is in many ways a transitional work: it looks back to a number of modernist texts, both in form and content, particularly in its representation of war and desertion (e.g., Ernest Hemingway's *A Farewell to Arms*, or, even earlier, Hart Crane's *The Red Badge of Courage*), but it simultaneously anticipates the counterculture of the 1960s and the anti-Vietnam movement.

The Deserter echoes other Modernist works, some of which have been mentioned in brief discussions of the novel. For instance, LePan's treatment of the Hero's Journey, especially the hero's submersion into the underworld and ascent, brings to mind Malcolm Lowry's *Under the Volcano*, Albert Camus' *L'Etranger*, Joseph Conrad's *Heart of Darkness*, and, towards the end of the novel, with what seems like increasing paranoia that everyone is out to get him, Franz Kafka's *Metamorphosis*.

This is the front of the dust jacket of the first edition of The Deserter, *published in 1964. The author's name appears as two words but is one word on the back of the jacket.*

Although Virginia Woolf's novel *The Waves* is another text to which critics refer, I think the Septimus sections of *Mrs. Dalloway* and the effects of PTSD make for interesting comparison, especially because of the narrative focalization and the movement between third-person omniscient and the free indirect discourse that puts us right in the characters' stream of consciousness, in this case Rusty's.

Despite these Modernist preoccupations, however, the novel does not exhibit the radical experimentation of Sheila Watson's *The Double Hook*, Leonard Cohen's *Beautiful Losers* (published just two years later), or Scott Symons's scandalous *Place d'Armes* (three years later).[3] It is worth noting, however, that Symons did see *The Deserter* as a queer text and a forerunner to his own novel. Not only does Symons use the term "desertion" to describe his own character's sexual exploits, LePan's novel itself appears metafictionally as *The Traitor*, with the protagonist referred to as "a revolutionary without balls."

To be sure, *The Deserter* reads queerer than it once did, and LePan himself indeed thought queerly about the work, both before and after writing it. LePan's correspondence with publishers is very revealing here. McClelland and Stewart published the novel, but LePan was also communicating with Chatto and Windus, the U.K. publisher who had put out his first two collections of poetry, as well as with John (Jack) Gray at MacMillan. The former rejected it, and LePan decided not to resubmit to the latter after receiving a less-than-enthusiastic response outlining many "problems" and concerns with the text. In his first pitch to Gray, LePan tells him not to think of the work as a novel (something he reminds himself in his own notes); and in his correspondence with the marketing staff at M&S he asks that the word "novel" not appear in descriptions of the book. What did he hope to gain by avoiding that designation? What did he imagine it was or that people would call it instead? As a poet, was he hesitant about his first foray into prose fiction? Or did he see the work as experimental? While he initially may have conceived of a genre-defying text, by the time it was published and being marketed, it was pretty clear this was a novel. Perhaps he imagined or came to see the text as a different work altogether.

In LePan's obituary in the LGBTQ publication *Xtra!*, his friend Jeffrey Round writes: "He was more than happy to reveal that *The Deserter* was based on gay experiences in wartime England and that his only real regret was that he had never written a gay novel." There are certainly moments when the queerness does come out: the scene in the Plaza in which Rusty witnesses an exchange between a deserter/hustler and another man, an apparently not uncommon way for deserters to support themselves. Also telling are Rusty's (and the narrator's it would seem) multiple references to the pelt of hair running down the abdomens of Brandy and Dragon, two men he is rather taken with after first encountering them in the quarter. Sounding now like the homoerotic cartoon muscle-daddies in Tom of Finland's art, with their "masterful physique," the focus is on their animal masculinity: not only do they compare themselves to actual bears (Rusty even refers to the "cave" in which they live), they read very much and are recognizable as "Bears" — beefy, hairy, bearded gay men who seem the antithesis of the overly familiar gay man who is fashionable, urban, well-manicured, and coiffed. Moreover, these "bears" and "wolves" in the novel enact the freedom to do as they wish, we are told, as animals do, thinking nothing of guilt, shame, or morality: "They were misfits.... [But] how thin the line was between the misfit and the hero." Rusty struggles with his desire to live as they do, but is ultimately unable to give himself over entirely to such an existence.

LePan goes beyond subtext and mere connotation by portraying homosexuality directly, but not as some critics, such as W.C. Lougheed, mistakenly argue as evidence of animal depravity: "Dragon and Brandy, as well as the two guardsmen who are as willing to oblige a homosexual as a woman, reveal the hedonistic, immoral, irresponsible, egocentric, undiscriminating nature of the undisciplined essential animal vitality." By contrast, the actual scene to which Lougheed refers to reveals something quite different:

> "I deserted," said Bud, "because of crimson foam on my face. Always in action I was frightened — of being hurt or of seeing others hurt. The first time I saw a man lying dead I fainted. But I made a friend; and when I was with him, I went proud and happy. We even slept together once, but only once — that was all there was time for. Then one day he was caught by shrapnel and he broke all

> over me in a red froth that splattered my eyes and streamed down my cheeks. I screamed and ran and hid under a vehicle. I wouldn't come out. My whole body was stiff, I couldn't move it. And the first chance that I got after that I lit out."

Far from being "immoral" or "hedonistic," gay sex and desertion itself exist as affirmations of humanity in the face of the depravity of war, all the more striking in this passage for the variation on "pride" in this pre-Stonewall time of writing and the historical period depicted.[4] In fact, this brief description is unlike the far more troubling portrayals of Rusty's sexual encounters with women, including what he himself even admits is shameful treatment of his girlfriend back home, having ended things in his own mind, but not before trying to force himself on her, only stopping after she slaps him in the face several times.

Rusty's relationship with Mark, a former soldier and friend who now works for the government and with whom Rusty stays very briefly, also reads rather queer, particularly in the devotion he and Rusty seem to have for one another, and in the predilections they may share, which are only hinted at: "I have a taste for the dark, perhaps as brutal a taste as you have. That's why we're friends. We're in sunlight and in darkness to almost the same degree." Despite Mark's admission, or maybe precisely because he does acknowledge his dark desires (even if they remain unnamed, and, ultimately, unspoken between the men), he chooses the world of order over the dark underworld. Or perhaps, being significantly older that Rusty, he has already experienced that descent and has resurfaced, a journey Rusty must to go through himself.

Finally, it is the redemptive love of Steve, and not the women (some of whom are sex workers), that ultimately comes to humanize Rusty once more. And although he and Steve are the same age,

Steve is an innocent in need of protection, and who is unafraid to show emotion. That he is also Slavic brings to mind the queer yet problematic dynamic in Sinclair Ross's *As For Me and My House* (1941), with Philip, the repressed minister who only seems to come alive when he and Mrs. Bentley take in the Slavic orphan, Steve. These queer little echoes dot the text in various places, amidst Rusty's quest and love for the mythical Althea, with whom he has spent one night of paradise (that he wishes to regain), as well as the other sex workers and women he encounters, some anonymously, some whom he comes to know more fully.

LePan would go on to write openly gay poetry — notably, in *Far Voyages* (1990), a collection of love lyrics and elegies for Patrick Fabbri, his lover from 1972 until his death from cancer in 1985, and in some recent offerings John Barton has published.[5] According to Alberto Manguel, LePan wrote to him in 1995 lamenting how it was "slightly unfair that I must be preparing to take my leave at just the moment when the game here is beginning to get interesting." Manguel writes: "'Here' was, of course, Canada, which he had called in 1948 'a country without a mythology' and where he felt that at last an important literature was being written."

Interestingly, both "A Country Without a Mythology" and "Coureurs de Bois" — the two most-widely anthologized of LePan's poems, which were both long understood as being concerned primarily with Canadian history and identity, were, as LePan acknowledged to one of his sons late in life, "substantially informed by the experience of being a gay outsider in a heterosexual society, and the specific inspiration for the 'wild Hamlet' [who figures prominently in 'Coureurs de Bois'] was in fact not a Canadian at all, but a young American who had been a student of his at Harvard."[6]

LePan can be viewed as a transitional writer in the context of both Canadian and gay literature, arriving at once both too soon and too late. In his essay, "The Dilemma of the Canadian Author," which LePan published in *Atlantic Monthly* the same year as his novel, he takes up the choice that a writer such as himself faces:

> Instead of trying to refine the singularity of being Canadian, they may want to dive so deeply that what they have to say can be expressed in terms of what happens in an anonymous setting to an anonymous, or virtually anonymous, hero....
>
> ... [T]he advantages: it can produce a result of almost universal luminosity which can be understood anywhere. A strategy of this kind may also commend itself to some writers because of seeming to be congruent with contemporary critical views of myth and symbol.

If this explains his own "strategy of composition" for *The Deserter*, whereby anonymity and the use of myth and symbol emphasize Modernist "universalism," it can also be a way of evading or defying categories around sexual identity. In some handwritten notes in the archive, in a box marked "Notes and Articles on Homosexuality," LePan writes:

> I am not defined by my homosexuality.
> I won't slip or be pushed into a ghetto.
> My sexual orientation is part of my humanity.
> I have chosen to be a full member of society.

And if LePan came late to homosexuality, which is a complicated issue for the LePan biographer, it nevertheless goes without saying that he could not have had the extraordinarily successful life and career he did had he lived an openly gay existence.

* * *

The University of Toronto is a place that bookended, in a manner of speaking, LePan's career. He grew up with a father who was in charge of the buildings and the grounds at the university. During his high school years he attended the University of Toronto Schools (a secondary school operated in close association with U of T's Faculty of Education). He then became a student at University College (one of U of T's constituent colleges), where he completed his B.A. in 1935. He would return to teach at the university as a University College lecturer (1937–38), and, much later in life, as a senior administrator (he served as principal of University College from 1964–70), and eventually, to hold an honorary position associated with the university's Massey College (university professor, 1971–79), which carried with it some teaching responsibilities. Thereafter, as professor emeritus, he retained an office at Massey until his death.

Following his undergraduate degree, LePan spent two years studying on a scholarship at Oxford (1935–37) — years that marked out England as formative for his career in public life and as writer. He left Oxford to become a university teacher, first as a lecturer at the University of Toronto and then as an instructor and tutor in English Literature at Harvard (1938–41).

LePan was troubled by the isolationist views of some of his American colleagues; even before his move to Harvard, Hitler's invasion of Poland had made it clear to LePan that Canada would play a role in the war — and that he would be a part of it. In the early 1930s he had "disliked and distrusted the military," but the events of the late 1930s led to a change of heart. He first made enquiries about enlisting in the autumn of 1939, soon after war had broken out, and he applied again in 1940, but during the early stages of the war "the services were very choosy," and LePan, whose vision was poor without his eyeglasses, "couldn't meet their requirements."

In the spring of 1941 LePan made contact with someone he knew in the Canadian Army's education office in London, and was offered a position as an educational advisor; a year later he was appointed personal advisor on education to General McNaughton (who was at that time the face of the war in Canada). McNaughton was keen to usefully occupy the time of the more than 100,000 Canadian soldiers who would not see action until 1943 (during the Italian campaign), thereby keeping up morale and preventing desertion — a growing problem as the wait grew longer. It was also a way to keep young men in the habit of education, making it more likely they would return to or enter university after the war (since most who had enlisted were civilians). LePan oversaw correspondence courses and certificate programs as well as personal and directed reading amongst the men — activity that helped him maintain his own focus on literature and teaching.

In August of 1943, LePan was offered a position at Canada House — the Canadian High Commission — in London as a diplomatic officer. He was torn between accepting the position and taking his life in a very different direction:

> I knew that Canada House and External Affairs were seriously shorthanded. I knew they had important work to do. I knew that I would probably be put to better use there than in the army. But I had always been one of those who felt the War had to be fought. The army needed men. Why shouldn't I enlist, if I could? [Requirements regarding such things as the vision of enlisted men were now far less stringent than they had been two years earlier.] On the one hand were prudence, practicality, reason. On the other hand, something far deeper and simpler.... Inevitably in the positions I had held I had had to talk a great deal about the War

> without doing anything about it. I had some sense of how corrupting that could be. Inevitably, too, I had seen a great deal of Canadian soldiers. Why should they be going through shit and corruption while I was sitting at my ease in an office on Trafalgar Square?

LePan enlisted, and within six months was seeing active duty as a gunner in the First Field Regiment.

As the war in Europe drew to a close in the spring of 1945, LePan was again offered a position in the diplomatic corps, and this time he accepted, serving on the staff of the Canadian High Commission for the next three years, and remaining in External Affairs (as Global Affairs Canada was then called) until 1959. LePan held many important positions in the postwar period, including as Lester B. Pearson's special assistant when Pearson was secretary of state for external affairs. (In his memoir, LePan expresses the view that "Mike" lacked the sort of "passion" that characterized McNaughton, but praises Pearson "for his devotion to duty and to Canada, for all his assiduity, for all his kindness and humanity," and "for all the achievements of his minority governments [which will be appreciated more and more and more as the years go by, I feel sure].")

In his time at diplomatic posts in London, Ottawa, and Washington, LePan played a role in defining and shaping Canada's role in NATO, as well as in the creation and adoption of the Colombo Plan for Cooperative Economic Development in south and southeast Asia, in 1950. He devotes a large section of the memoir to a discussion of the Colombo Plan and its successes and failures. Though he acknowledges that the plan did not turn out as he and others involved in its formation "had hoped," he concludes that "it had results of which none of us need be ashamed." He cites the Colombo Plan as an early example of developed nations paying serious attention to the specific economic realities of many developing nations in the region — and of their acknowledging an obligation both to offer assistance and to help establish structures that could facilitate future development planning. Out of that work, LePan suggests, came parallel later programs to assist Caribbean and African nations, as well as international programs such as the Canadian International Development Agency (CIDA) and the Canadian University Service Overseas (CUSO).

During his time in London, LePan also served under Vincent Massey, who was Canada's high commissioner to the United Kingdom, and with whom he would later work setting up (and serving on) the Canada Council when Massey became governor general in 1952 (until 1959). Much as they spent years working together, LePan and Massey never warmed to each other; in *Bright Glass of Memory* LePan offers a commentary that is as revealing of LePan as it is of Massey:

> I never had anything but kindness from Vincent Massey. But he always seemed to me to be lacking in substance. Presence of a kind he always had, but not substance. In Canada House he very rarely ventured out of his own vast office, although the offices of almost all the other diplomatic officers were on the same floor. Whenever he did and appeared in one or another of our offices, he always seemed strangely diminished, a manikin in faultlessly cut shirt and jacket and carefully pressed trousers, almost like a piece of paper that you could easily put your fist through.

Other important positions LePan held in the postwar period included: special assistant to the secretary of state in Ottawa (1950–51); counsellor and later minister counsellor for External Affairs at the Canadian embassy, Washington, D.C. (1951–55); secretary and director of research, Royal Commission on Canada's Economic Prospects (the "Gordon Commission") (1955–58); and assistant under-secretary of state for Economic Affairs (1958–59).

All the while he was carrying out (and receiving national recognition for) his diplomatic work, LePan was making his mark in the literary world, first with *The Wounded Prince and Other Poems*, published in 1948 — the same year that he won a Guggenheim Fellowship for Poetry, and married Sarah Katharine Chambers (divorced 1971). His 1953 collection, *The Net and the Sword*, which draws on his experiences of (and takes as its setting) the Italian campaign, won the Governor General's Award for Poetry.

The fact that LePan was able to combine a successful literary career with a successful diplomatic career raises the question of why he decided to suddenly abandon that career in 1959. The suicide of Canadian diplomat Herbert Norman in 1957 is the best-known instance of the psychological toll that accusations involving alleged homosexuality could take on those in External Affairs who were suspected of tendencies that, in the 1950s, were regarded as invitations to blackmail. Did LePan's decision in 1959 to leave the diplomatic corps have something to do with the sexuality that he was then keeping a closely guarded secret? It seems plausible to imagine a connection, but no record of his sexuality playing a part in the move has yet been discovered. In any event, he took up a professorship in the English Department at Queen's University in Kingston, Ontario, in the fall of 1959, and taught there until returning to the University of Toronto as principal of University College in 1964. He remained in that post until 1970, though it took a toll on his health; it was a period of tremendous student unrest at the U of T, as it was on so many campuses throughout the Western world.

The Deserter was written during LePan's years in Kingston and was published in 1964. There was then a gap of some fifteen years before his next book. His later publications include *Bright*

Glass of Memory (1979), *Something Still to Find: New Poems* (1982), *Weathering It: Complete Poems 1948–87* (1987), *Far Voyages* (1990), and *Macalister or Dying in the Dark* (1995).

Among the many accolades LePan received were honorary degrees from the Universities of Manitoba, Ottawa, Waterloo, Toronto, Queen's, and York; the Blumenthal Prize (Poetry, Chicago); Fellow of the Royal Society of Canada, the Lorne Pierce Medal of the Royal Society of Canada; and Officer of the Order of Canada.

Despite these many honours and distinctions recognizing his literary achievements and his duty to this country, both during the war and later in his public service, LePan nevertheless had difficulty finding a publisher for his final work, *Macalister; or Dying in the Dark: A Fiction Based on What Is Known of His Life and Fate* (1995), a verse drama about the Canadian soldier John Macalister who was captured by the Nazis and executed in Buchenwald in 1944.

LePan believed he was being snubbed by the Canadian literary establishment for coming out as gay. Whether or not that is the case, the work has received little if any attention, despite the high praise extolled upon it in the few brief reviews that do exist. To be sure, for LePan, who had lived in a world that saw careers and lives ruined by the exposure of one's sexuality — through blackmail, police arrests, and the purges in both the civil service and the military — it would have been hard to ignore, despite the changes in law and social values, the insidious nature of homophobia still harboured by those who claimed they were more open-minded.[7]

The AIDS crisis made clear to LePan and others the attitudes of straight society toward LGBTQ people — indifference, fear, hostility. These are attitudes that we still see, not only in other places around the world, but in our own back — and front — yards. Still, despite all of that, LePan refused to back down or hide. He proclaimed himself to be proudly gay. It must therefore have been a proud moment for LePan to be asked to contribute to the *Church-Wellesley Review* (1991–2002), the annual literary supplement to *Xtra!*, Canada's LGBTQ news publication, alongside such notable queer Canadian writers as Timothy Findley, Jane Rule, and Shyam Selvadurai.

LePan's lifework extends beyond the printed page. He had a close personal, familial, and professional connection to University College throughout his life, and his legacy continues there today, not least in the Mark S. Bonham Centre for Sexual Diversity Studies, housed within University College and first launched as a small college program in the fall of 1998, the time of LePan's own passing.

In *Macalister*, LePan's moral imperative is clear, as it is in *The Deserter*: not to live or die in the dark — invisible, secret, and forgotten — but instead to choose the world of light as the only antidote to violence, hatred, and shame.

I would like to acknowledge and thank a number of the people I consulted while working on this project. Their expertise, insight, and suggestions for further reading have been invaluable: Paul Bowser, Russell Brown, Heidi Tiedemann Darroch, Margaret Fulford, Emily Gilbert, Dara Greaves, Andrew Lesk, Don McLeod, Nick Mount, Laine Zisman Newman, Allan Pero, Ian Radforth, David Rayside, Vikki Visvis, and Valley Weadick; Don LePan, for his editorial savvy and generous comments and suggestions for additions — all no doubt have helped make my work stronger; the staff at the Thomas Fisher Rare Book Library at the University of Toronto where the Douglas LePan papers are held; Margeaux Feldman, whose research assistance was nothing less than heroic; and Michael Gnarowski, the series editor at Dundurn for inviting me to the project and for his support, patience, and understanding.

NOTES

1. Thanks to Don LePan (son of Douglas, and himself both a poet and novelist, and the CEO and founder of Broadview Press) for pointing this out. Personal correspondence. June 1, 2018.
2. See the Voyageur Classics edition of Lewis's novel *Self Condemned* (1954; 2010, introduction by Allan Pero), set in a fictionalized version of Toronto.
3. See the Voyageur Classics edition of *Combat Journal for Place d'Armes: A Personal Narrative* (1967; 2010, introduction by Christopher Elsen).
4. The Stonewall Riots, which began on June 28, 1969, when patrons of the New York gay bar the Stonewall Inn began to demonstrate against the police raids on their establishments, are now seen as the moment of gay liberation in America. Annual LGBTQ Pride celebrations in New York and Toronto continue to coincide with that anniversary.
5. See *Malahat Review* 146 (Spring 2004). Also see Barton and Nickerson, ed., *Seminal: The Anthology of Canada's Gay Male Poets* (Vancouver: Arsenal, 2007), which includes a number of unpublished gay poems by LePan along with discussion of the work. The attention paid to LePan in these works put him clearly into the canon of this poetic tradition.
6. Personal Correspondence with Don LePan, June 2, 2018; and Don LePan, "The Original 'Wild Hamlet,'" Letter to the *Globe and Mail*, September 1, 2001.
7. Timothy Findlay's play *The Stillborn Lover*, based loosely on the Norman case, also exposes the hypocrisy and the chilling effect of anti-gay polices and laws during this era that indeed made one more susceptible to blackmail. As Gary Kinsman makes evident in his scholarship on this period, most of the blackmailing (of lesbian and gay

civil servants and those serving in the military) was being conducted by the Canadian government and the RCMP. During this period, three thousand Canadians were fired from their positions in government and in the public sector or were dishonorably discharged from military service, simply on the suspicion of homosexuality. See Kinsman and Gentile, *The Canadian War on Queers: National Security as Sexual Regulation* (Vancouver: UBC Press, 2009).

1

If the war had not been over, it would have been easier to understand. Then it could have been put down simply to cowardice. But the armistice had been signed two months before; and now the world, as the newspapers kept reassuring their readers, was slowly returning to normal.

At the depot where he was stationed, sentries were still posted immaculately, and during the hours of darkness additional precautions were taken against a surprise attack. But in spite of the commandant's efforts to keep everything running as though the war was still going on, some signs of relaxation were beginning to appear. The barbed wire around the perimeter of the camp had rusted away in several places and had not been repaired. The roof of one of the air-raid shelters had caved in and nothing had been done about it. And in response to grumbling, the adjutant had had to post a notice to the effect that it was hoped within the next few weeks to receive authority to lift the blackout restrictions.

Meanwhile, they remained in force, and it was in the atmosphere of a swamp that he lay on his bunk each night before going to bed and listened to young recruits boasting about actions they had never been in and to veterans from units that he didn't know calculating how large a gratuity their years of service would entitle them to and what they were going to do with it. A swamp where stale bubbles kept rising to the surface from dying vegetation. It surprised him how much more he resented the heavy closeness than he had only a few years before. He couldn't stand it for long; and if the time for lights-out went by without the sergeant coming in, he got up and turned the lights off himself, and then took down the blackouts. That didn't add to his popularity. From soldiers still reading or rolling dice on the blanket-covered table that stood in the middle of the room came shouts of "What the hell?" and "Who do you think you are?" But the protesting figures gradually melted into bed, still muttering, but not wanting to tangle with him. Partly it was because of the ribbon on his tunic, which carried its own authority, even though he had lost his stripes. Partly it was because they had seen him use his fists two or three times. He had big shoulders and a slim waist, and a body lithe as a sword. Mostly he kept to himself and wouldn't be provoked. But when occasionally he lost his temper, the room seemed powdered with diamond-dust, scored and slashed with it. So they slunk off to bed and left him to climb in and savour at last a few deep breaths of the air that was blowing in from the pine trees near the rifle range. Then a little later when everything was quiet in the block he would get up and stand at the window, looking into the sky as though it were the face of someone he had known, even of someone he had loved, but blank now, blank, he sometimes thought to himself, as though it had lost its reason.

The ceremonies of darkness and the ceremonies of the day were still being carried out. The guard was mounted, inspections were held, defaulters were marched into the orderly-room, the doctor kept his visiting hours, darkness and day were separated by bugle calls. But the camp had lost its function. Or rather its role had been reversed. The engines that had been used to turn out tank-drivers, machine-gunners, marksmen, signalmen, mechanics, cooks, were now revolving in the opposite direction in order to turn out properly attested civilians, free from clap, their teeth filled, with their documents in order and generously recompensed by a grateful government. It was a triumph of planning and organization for which the staff at headquarters, who had been responsible for the arrangements, could feel especially proud. They had some failures, of course; and, in those cases, they had to call on the assistance of the provost marshal and the psychiatrists and, in due course, of the jails and asylums and homes for incurables. But the wastage was surprisingly small. The assembly lines that had been used for so long to roll out military strength were now working on the whole very successfully to convert it back into civilian potential.

Why did he feel so detached from the whole process? It perplexed him. Always he had wanted to be in the thick of things. When he was in the reinforcement depot he made a nuisance of himself until he was dispatched to a unit. After he had succeeded and been in the artillery for a few months and had served through one campaign, he couldn't rest until he was transferred to the infantry. Nor was the support company good enough for him; he must be in the attack company. Always closer to the moment's glittering sword-edge. Now that impulse seemed to have deserted him. He knew that the focus of activity had changed, but this time he didn't seem to be able to change with it.

In the evening, as he sat by himself in the canteen, the conversation that frothed around him seemed as weak and unlikely as the beer slopped on the table-tops.

"Did you hear what the padre had to say about the need for welders? With all my experience I couldn't miss. In a year or two I'll have a machine-shop of my own. You just watch."

"I'm going to take my gratuity and buy myself a delivery van. I've been wondering about a name. What do you think of Spitfire Service? Or perhaps just Speedy Service — in gold letters on a green background?"

"Stay with a big company, that's what I say. They'll look after you, pensions, holidays, everything. I'm going back where I came from, and with a promotion. Look, here's a letter I've just had from the personnel office."

As a soldier at the next table took out a smudged letter from his pocket and handed it around, he saw for a moment this roomful of rogues and scroungers transformed into honest workmen and good husbands and fathers, leading their families to church in their Sunday best. What a hope! Surely the dogs of war were sleeping as savagely in these men's loins as they were in his. But for a while a merciful illusion clouded them. Even the talk of sex was expurgated a little, as though in anticipation of domestic bliss and propriety. It still suffered from some of the distensions of bravado. But now it dealt not so much with girls picked up anonymously for a night as with wives, either actual or prospective.

"As soon as I get home, I'm going to tell the wife to get up them stairs."

"No, I'm going to tell her to take a good look around first because she isn't going to see anything but the bedroom ceiling for days and days."

"That girl I've been kicking around with had better make up her mind. It's wedding bells or else. I've waited long enough to get someone to bring me my slippers."

He couldn't help smiling. He didn't have a girl. Not any more. He wasn't going to marry. At least not for a long time. He didn't have any post-war plans. The only purpose he was conscious of was to look for something he thought he'd been given. He didn't know what it was or where it had been put or even whether it would prove of any value if he could find it. But he knew he must look for it.

It was hard to tell when it was that he decided to light out. Looking back, he seemed to remember a restless, feverish night when he had dreamed of broken spars and an open boat with the planking clammy with sweat and with himself at the tiller, not knowing where he was bound but trusting to a great billowing sail that seemed to know its own way through the diffuse grey light that covered the ocean. Then just before daylight he was brought to the outskirts of a city where all the doors were shut and where no one was about except himself, trudging between cliff-like houses, all alike, high, with four or five storeys beneath a leaden sky, searching through bewildering crescents for the secret of the labyrinth while a thin drizzle sifted down and down, mingling with a fine white dust that was falling from the crumbling masonry and from occasional gaps where the cliff had given way completely. When reveille sounded, he found that he was lying almost naked. During the night he must have kicked off the blankets, and now they were tangled at the foot of his bunk with the rest of his gear, his heavy boots, his fatigue clothes, his webbing, his steel helmet, his two packs. His thick damp socks were lying by themselves, clinging like fungus to the concrete floor. As soon as the blackouts had been put up again and the lights were switched on, he knew that he was going to desert.

The day passed listlessly. The morning parade was short and lax and fragmentary. Five men were broken off to see the dentist, three were to see the welfare officer, another two had to report for treatment at the medical centre. The rest of the platoon was to provide fatigue-parties for work on the coal-pile and in the officers' mess. It didn't take much experience to tell which would be the easier of those two details; and he didn't object, it rather amused him, to wait on a group of officers most of whom hadn't seen half as much action as he had. So with the connivance of the sergeant (who was a little afraid of him) he soon found himself with a pailful of potatoes to peel. But when that was over he sat in the kitchen with the cook drinking mugs of tea and shooting the breeze about the Mediterranean. In the afternoon it turned hot and hazy. There was to be a lecture on "International Order in the Post-War World." But he could skip that without being noticed; and if there was any change in the usual routine he would have one of the other soldiers in the block come and call him. While they were all milling around waiting to go into the lecture, he slipped around the corner of the mess-hall and in a minute or two was in the tall bracken near the edge of the camp.

He took off his tunic and rolled it up and, putting it under his head, stretched out on the pine needles and dead ferns. He had a Western in his hip pocket and he pulled it out. He read for a while, and then lit a cigarette and lay back and looked up at the sky through the tops of the pines that were shimmering together in blue-green shadows. He felt easy and sensual. He might almost have been an animal, he thought, a deer curled up in the bracken, so unconcerned did he feel about what he was going to do.

He must have fallen asleep. For the soldier had to get quite close and call "Rusty! Rusty!" several times before he realized that someone was looking for him. When he opened his eyes and sat up, it took him a minute or two to recognize that this was the soldier he had asked to waken him if there were any change in the schedule. Apparently there had been. The commandant was to hold a kit inspection in the morning, and all webbing was to be blancoed by suppertime.

As he worked in his short-sleeves with the others at the blancoing troughs, he remembered that it was almost six years since the first time he had stood there and struggled to get his belt the proper shade of olive-drab. He had been only seventeen then, although he had told the recruiting officer that he was a year older. In one way he had been lucky, he realized: his nerves and tissues were so fashioned that he could keep most of the few commandants that anyone seemed to pay any attention to in practice; and that had stood him in good stead during these years while he had been shedding his childhood and getting to know what the world was like, cutting his teeth on it, biting on it like hard-tack. But in other ways he realized he had been deprived. There were things he had missed, clues perhaps that he hadn't been given. Sometimes he wondered what lay behind those filmy, intimate imperatives that were carried to him on the wind. If you traced them back, would you find that they were attached to some kind of order? Certainly that was what you would gather from the way people talked. But he didn't know one way or another. During the past six years his mind had gone on long marches and campaigns as well as his body, but what had happened to him there had mostly been hidden from him. His instincts had never forced him to any very strenuous questioning; and what he wondered and imagined had never been subject to schooling or discipline. For him the army had been church and school and city and family — all of them; and in the whirling darkness it had provided almost the only order that he knew. Its words of command came to him with ritual warmth and force. And not only because he had witnessed how they could hold a situation together and save it from chaos. With the fervour of a true believer he reverenced the words because they were an expression of inward essences, the essences of loyalty and courage, the military virtues that like an exiled beast had returned in the brave lechery of battle and had been seen rampant and bleeding on a thousand fields. Even a cathedral was chiefly hallowed in his eyes by the standards hanging at the level of the clerestory. And with the coming of victory, one of the most moving moments for him had been when the regiment had been paraded to lay up its colours. When smartly, lustily, the young sergeant of the colour-party advanced to meet the officiating canon and put the standard into his arms, it was as though the bleeding bodies of his comrades, ignorant and broken, were being given into the hands of wisdom for the wise to interpret and consecrate in whatever way they could.

Was it perverse to think that if he were going to desert, he should set out in proper style? It didn't seem so to him. After he had finished cleaning his webbing and had laid it out to dry and had come back from having supper, he sat down to sew fresh regimental patches on his sleeves. Then he spent almost an hour on his boots, first with a brush, then with a bone, then with a brush again and finally with a cloth. He polished his cap badge and his belt buckle. He gave his trousers a sharp crease and got dressed. Now he was almost ready. There were no good-byes to be said, since his friends were either in other depots or already discharged. All he had to do was to sort out his kit-bags and to arrange in the regulation manner the gear he was leaving behind. When that was done, he looked down at his bunk with satisfaction. It would be with the same kind of absent attention to detail, he imagined, that a suicide would make his final arrangements, tidying his papers, completing his will, and writing the few last letters that he was to leave behind.

Nothing could have been simpler than letting himself out. Instead of leaving by the main gate, he found a gap in the barbed wire at the back of the camp, strode through it in the dark, whistling and swinging a small kit-bag, and in a few minutes was on the road to the station.

When the train came in, he picked an empty compartment and stretched out. For a while — the wheels of the train insisted on it — he tried to think about himself and where he was going. But it was too difficult. He felt rebuked by the thin scalpel of light that dangled from a shaded reading-lamp (it was all that was left of the blackout arrangements) and slit the darkness around him. For his mind refused to focus like that. He was on his way, that was all he knew, and nature would have to take its course. It was an act of instinct, he thought, as he let up the blind and looked out; and that kind of act he had never regretted. The light outside had not yet entirely faded; it kept welling up palely behind the elms, whose boughs were beginning to melt into the clouds. An act of instinct, he thought. And this peaceful sky began to merge into the sky over the battlefield where he had done the one thing that had ever fully pleased and satisfied him in action.

Compared with it, what had won him his decoration had been easy and obvious. Anyone ordered to stay in a weapon-pit while the lieutenant crawled forward to reconnoitre would do as he was told. What else could he do? And if there was a local counter-attack that wiped out the lieutenant and surrounded the weapon-pit, it didn't take much intelligence to know that you had to keep firing so long as there was a magazine left. And if you were still alive by the time that reinforcements managed to reach you, that was just luck; and you couldn't complain if afterwards the unit kept pestering headquarters until they agreed to dole out a decoration. The whole thing had followed the manuals from start to finish.

But the night he was thinking of had been different. As soon as he heard what had happened to Spike, he knew what he had to do. On his own, instinctively, and no matter what the orders might be. The missing man was a signaller and must have lost his way in the failing light, for he had first been spotted crawling about fifty yards in front of the forward position with a coil of line over his shoulder. Then a burst of enemy machine-gun fire caught him and he went down like a dog, yelping. The to-do at the command post was terrific. Everyone had a plan and the colonel wouldn't authorize any of them. The medical officer wanted to go out in a scout-car under a red-cross flag and bring him in; the colonel said that too many M.O.'s had been lost that way recently. The signals officer suggested that heavy artillery fire be brought down and that a rescue team go out under cover of it; the colonel said that that would draw retaliation and anyway the artillery's ammunition scales might not permit it. Someone else suggested that a raiding-party be sent out and that stretcher-bearers follow in their wake; the colonel said that casualties from a raiding-party might be out of all proportion.

By this time it was dark. There was still a faint burnishing of green clinging to the tops of some of the trees, as there was now, but night was swirling higher and higher up the splintered trunks like an incoming tide. He let himself down into it and began to crawl, almost to swim, slowly forward. The cries had subsided a little, but there was still moaning enough to act as a beacon — moaning and occasionally a bloodcurdling wail. He stayed as close as possible to the earth and made whatever use he could of folds in the ground in the hope of not being spotted. As for mines, he would just have to take his chance. For the most part, though, he was numb and crawled forward hardly knowing what he was doing. When he reached Spike, he found him still conscious enough to recognize who it was and to mutter something stupid like, "I guess this is it, Rusty." Then providentially the wounded man lost consciousness, so that it was easier to hoist him on his back. The return journey was harder and longer. He was afraid that the extra weight might set off mines that he had perhaps passed over safely on his way out. And how could he avoid being seen now? He felt as though he were carrying a whole world on his back. And from somewhere deep within this world was flowing the issue of a dread imposthume — it was Spike's blood — that had long been gathering from the most distant and secret regions and, having broken now, was soaking his uniform and trickling down over his flanks as he crawled back towards his own front lines. He managed to get through them safely and kept right on until he came to the command post. The colonel didn't say a word while Spike's wounds were being dressed. But he didn't look jubilant, rather furious at something having been done successfully without any orders from him; and a few weeks later the rescuer got his reward by being reduced to the ranks. As though he would mind! Losing his stripes was nothing in comparison with having done what he wanted to do. The thought of it still overcame him with pleasure, with the searching, satisfying pungency of something extreme and difficult, the burnished, punishing odour of deserts and battle.

The train was now running through satellite towns within commuting distance of the capital. Wealthy stockbrokers had their houses here, set in gardens which gave out their freshness in the summer dark and smelled of innocence and of the money needed to make it possible. A dim harmony of white and gold. But in the darkness he was more conscious of the fragrance of innocence than of the money on which it was trellised — of roses, of new-mown grass, of kernels growing firm and milky. The air was heavy with the childish taste of milk. It stirred his memory with moony delights, with sweet things, sweetmeats, with everything that had been annulled for him by the pungent, leathery flowering of horror and virtue. He would have said that the only savours he could relish now were those with some dash of bitterness, of anise, say, or dill. How could he have any other taste after being suckled by a wolf?

As the train glided forward through a kind of milky way, giving off a faint phosphorescence in its passage between nurseries and small farms and mild estates, he thought of his own home, so much further away in the provinces, and of his last visit there. It had not been a success. It was as though the stalk connecting him to his childhood had been finally snapped, so that the milky juice (like that climbing inside a dandelion) could no longer travel up from the roots but oozed away on the ground. He was aware of the change and dimly associated it with his mother's death. She had died in the middle of the war when in many parts of the country the sky was boisterous with nightly raids. But she had taken her own way to the last. Characteristically, she had died quietly and in the course of nature, so that his image of her was not marred by anything grotesque or terrible. She was as natural in death as she had been in life, untainted for him even by the absurdities of burial, since he had not been able to get home for the funeral. Now she rested as becalmed in his mind as when he had been a boy.

It was only when victory was almost in sight that he was given leave and came home to see his father and sister. At first the visit went well enough. Although he wouldn't admit it even to himself, he was pleased by the flags over the porch and the hand-lettered sign that said, "Welcome home, Rusty!" He was pleased, too, to be in his own room again and to find that nothing had been changed. The same maps were still on the wall, his skates were still in the corner, and in the cupboard he found the cheap diving-helmet that he had seen advertised in a boys' magazine and had saved for and bought without ever being able to use. He liked being able to lie in bed in the morning and to spend the day as he pleased and to go out drinking every night if he wanted to. He didn't even mind very much being shown off to his father's friends. But it wasn't long before there began to be things that got on his nerves. He knew that he smoked too many cigarettes, but did his father need to take him aside and ask him whether he thought so much smoking "added to his efficiency?" And, hell, why did the old man urge him to invite some friends in for the evening and then complain the next morning because all the whisky was gone?

If his mother had still been alive, things might have been different. He had never got along well with his father, he didn't know why, perhaps because in some ways they were too much alike. But she had known how to keep them from galling each other. She had gifts of tact which she used unobtrusively to control the passions of her family, as another woman might have used them for tending a garden or arranging bouquets of flowers. Her son could seldom see the means by which her ends were achieved but knew who it was that had compassed them and was grateful. Her triumphs were as mysterious to him as those of a great hostess, even though the resources through which they were gained might be pitifully simple. After the once he had run away from school he had been almost too afraid to return home. But when he pushed open the kitchen door, she didn't say a word but just dropped what she was doing and made him some of the things he liked best, bacon and tomato sandwiches, and had him in bed by the time his father came home; and by the next morning the storm had almost blown over.

His sister did what she could to fill her mother's place, but her touch was not so sure. She was worried when she saw her father and brother falling out and one morning she spoke to him about the way they had quarrelled the night before.

"Why were you so hard on father last night?" she asked unexpectedly as she was going about the housework.

He was sitting reading the paper and he hardly looked up to answer. "I wasn't hard on him."

"Then why did you throw it up against him that he'd never heard a shot fired in anger?"

"Because it's true."

"That's no kind of an answer."

"Oh, I suppose because I couldn't stand any more of his advice."

"I don't understand you any more," she said, "You've changed. You always used to be so considerate." He knew she was speaking out of fondness for him and yet he hated it. He felt trapped.

She went on persistently. "Don't you see that he's getting older? I don't like to see him hurt. I know he hasn't done anything remarkable with his life. His marriage, his children, all these years working over the ledgers. Perhaps it doesn't come to much. But do you think he doesn't feel that as well as you do? And then you come back from the ends of the earth with a ribbon on your tunic and the world still before you. Wouldn't you be jealous?"

To avoid losing his temper he had gone on reading the paper, in the hope that following the type would help to blur what she was saying. Now he put it down. How could his father be jealous of him? His father was over fifty; he was twenty-three. They didn't live in the same world. But as soon as he had said it, he knew it was true just the same; the blood that coursed beneath his sunburn was witnessing to it in the very moment of his denial.

"I don't see what there is to be jealous of," he said as casually as he could. "And even if there is why should that make him watch me like a hawk? When I come in, he wants to know every place I've been and everything I've done. There's no way I can please him. If I don't talk about what I've seen, he complains of my being reserved. If I try to tell him what it was like, he doubts and argues until sometimes you'd wonder whether it was he who'd been there and not me."

"I know he irks you. I know he sometimes treats you as though you were still a boy. But he's nervous with you; and when you're nervous you get everything wrong. Try to understand him a little. No one is perfect, you know."

When he didn't say anything in reply, she added, "I sometimes wonder whether you realize that — that no one is perfect." The way she glanced up at him suggested that she was no longer thinking of their father.

"What do you mean by that?"

"You know just as well as I do. Not even the girl you marry will be perfect. But few people are as lucky as you are. I don't know what you're waiting for."

He didn't know either. But he knew he wasn't going to marry the girl who had so clearly been waiting for him. Every few months while he had been away she had sent him parcels with fudge and shortbread and occasionally a book or a pair of gloves, and he had written back to thank her and to say that the weather was hot and bright or gusty with rain. But he didn't really know her at all. When he left home he had been hardly more than a boy and had thought of her chiefly as a friend of his sister's. Whenever he was home on leave he took her out a few times, since it seemed to be expected of him, but he never had much to say to her. This time he had taken her to the pictures, and afterward they had had something to eat and had gone walking in the park.

She didn't resist as he led her deeper and deeper into the shadows, although she must have known what he intended. As they moved out from one darkness to another, the trees were drenched with moonlight and hung still and empurpled as though covered by great clusters of ripe grapes. He felt as though he were walking beneath a thick vine that was pulsing deeply among the leaves, pulsing and rippling like a serpent. It might be veined with blood so closely did it beat with his own urgencies. The flow through his veins and whatever it was that flowed through the world and showed in the splendours of the night sky seemed for once to move together, resting in peace in the purple blush that moonlight laid on the leaves. Or so he was about to say to himself in passionate silence when she spoke.

"What is it that a night like this takes you back to?" she said. "Is it to childhood? Or further back still, to God?" Her voice was high-pitched and awkward and uncertain.

He didn't want to reply, although he thought of saying something about water, and birth, and before birth.... He, too, was being summoned back to memories he could only dimly grasp, but that was something he wouldn't admit; and he preferred not to answer at all.

When they had walked on a few paces, she began again. "I love the moonlight," she said simply.

Her remark could hardly have been more innocent, but it made him shudder. With a click the scene in his mind was changed, and he found himself in a sunken road with a stalled convoy while a chandelier flare like a great moon floated gently down and illuminated every surface, every nook, every hiding-place, giving it all away to the low-flying reconnaissance plane that was going back and forth above the road, machine-gunning and dropping bombs.

They had now come almost to the end of the path and he took her by the waist and drew her down on to a bench. "I love the moonlight, too," he said, although it now all seemed to have been shattered and to be lying on the grass like hail. And he lifted his arm from around her waist and held her by the breast and began to kiss her, first on the nape of the neck where her hair was curling in delicate tendrils and then on the cheek. She whispered, "On my eyelids," and he kissed the rivulets of violet that covered her eyes while she lay back in his arms as still as a lake. Was it ready to receive the brandished sword? There was a sound from her lips like the first sighing of the night wind as he put his hand between her thighs. Then he put his lips to hers and his tongue went in like a bayonet. But now she was frightened. She was trembling and trying to push him away while he held her tighter and tighter. As they struggled, passion mounted in him and turned more and more into anger, almost into fury. Finally she got one hand free and slapped him three or four times with wan persistence. It hurt hardly at all, but at length the message got through to him, and he released her roughly and let her slump back on the bench as though she had been struck in return by his animal glare of impersonal hunger and by the words "Bitch, bitch" that he muttered as he let go of her. When he had straightened his hair and his uniform, he got up and walked away without saying another word or without even looking at her again. He felt ashamed, and angry both with her and more obscurely with himself for having been made vulnerable to shame. When he came to the park gates, though, he stopped and waited for her to catch up. She was crying and he let her clasp her hand in his. But he wouldn't talk to her even though she sobbed, "I'm sorry, Rusty," and added a little later, "I couldn't, I really couldn't."

She must have kept what had happened entirely to herself, because he heard nothing about it during the three or four days that remained of his leave, although his sister was a close friend of hers and continued to drop hints about people not appreciating their good fortune and living to regret it. Even his father managed to refer to the subject. It was on the last day before he had to return to his unit, and he had come to pay a visit to the large, old-fashioned establishment where his father worked as the head book-keeper. This was an observance that always made him feel like a small boy again since it hadn't changed in any particular since he was six or seven. They walked about the aisles and talked to the salespeople — elderly, all of them, now because the younger ones had been called up — and then in the hope of having a few words with the proprietor returned to his father's cubicle at the back of the store. It was a small office raised a few steps above the level of the floor and enclosed in glass so that the occupant could keep an eye on the salespeople while he was working at the ledgers or answering correspondence. His father always regarded it as an eminence of considerable importance and dignity and would point out that it not only commanded all the floor-space in the establishment but adjoined the doorway to the proprietor's private office as well and so allowed observation, albeit more deferential, of his movements, too. After they had waited vainly for a quarter of an hour for the great man to come out, it seemed hardly worthwhile to wait any longer. But his father wouldn't hear of his suggestion that they give up and go and have lunch.

"If you'll take some advice from an older man," his father said, "don't neglect your friends. If you do, you'll be the poorer. And I don't mean personally only, I mean financially, too. You never can tell when they'll come in useful."

Thinking of Spike and Mark and Slim and Sailor, he demurred a little that his father's employer, however estimable and influential, was hardly to be counted as one of his friends. But his qualification was brushed aside.

"You may not think of him as a friend," his father admitted. "But who gave you the first money you ever owned? He's almost been a godfather to you. And he could help you after the war."

"Oh, I think I'll be able to manage all right."

"That may be. But don't close any doors. That's all I want to say. We're all proud of you. But when the war's over, you'll have to make your way and you'll need all the friends you've got. So don't close any doors. I don't want to see you end up selling matches on the street corner. Have you thought what you're going to do? Have you thought what you're going to be?"

I am going to be, he thought, as if in sullen answer to his father's question. I am simply going to be. That to begin with. That above all. Isn't that enough? But all he said was, "I don't know."

"Well, it's not too soon to be thinking of it," his father went on, a little daunted but still dogged, as though he had mapped out in advance everything he intended to say and was not going to be balked either by his own nervousness or by his son's lack of response. "And you'll need a wife. Don't forget that either. If not the girl you're going with now, then someone else. You'll have to choose. But it seems to me you could easily go further and fare worse. Go further and fare worse." There! He had finally fetched up where he intended to. But he was so exhausted by the effort that he could do nothing but repeat himself, afraid either to go on or to conclude more definitely. And his son would do nothing to help him out of his embarrassment.

The train was melting these memories as it thrust through the blackness; it was as if its incandescent headlight was melting them, fusing them and casting some of them aside to sink back in his half-closed consciousness while he dozed in the empty compartment. Till all that was left of what he remembered of home was a store full of shop-worn merchandise. Overhead ran a network of wires where small containers clattered to and fro like spindles. There were no customers; but the faded salesladies, who stood as though propped up by the high chokers they wore about their necks, were kept busy merely tending the spindle-shaped tubes, stuffing them with bills and silver and speeding them on their way to the central cash-register. And then even that picture eluded him, and he was looking into a dusty attic with old furniture, old toys, old pictures, old disguises. Somehow the squirrels had found their way into it; and they were dizzily chasing hither and thither, garnering their treasure and at the same time ravaging and pillaging through the discarded ruined upholstery.

The brakes went on and at once he was wide awake, thinking that they might have arrived at the terminus, where he would have to be on the alert. But no. It was only a local station with a few soldiers standing about on a dimly lit platform. One of them got into the compartment. He had his full kit with him, rifle, large pack, small pack, respirator, two kit-bags. Rusty got up to help with the gear. As he did, he caught his own face for a moment in the mirror that ran above the seats. It was tanned and lined and leathery and difficult to imagine as the face of a young man of twenty-three. Only his hair, which was clipped short around the neck but rich and lustrous everywhere else and brushed thickly back across his forehead, stamped him with youth. That and a watery glance that glimmered fitfully at the back of his retina. But it was a glance so fugitive as hardly to signify, as hardly to attract his notice. For the most part he was satisfied with what he saw in himself. He looked hard. He looked like a soldier. Then, when the gear was stowed away, he looked at his fellow-traveller. They were remarkably alike. The newcomer was shorter and stockier and his hair had not the same chestnut glossiness. But his jaw was as square and his face as weatherbeaten. They sat staring at each other, as though they were both sure they were going to speak but were reluctant to begin, almost as though they felt there was something between them that others would not understand or might even regard as shameful.

At last Rusty said, "How long were you in for?"

"Three months. How did you know?

"Your webbing. The only place it's scrubbed that white is in the glass-house."

"Yes, I guess so." Then he was silent. He sat rigidly on the edge of the seat, his spine perfectly straight but tilted slightly forward, his two packs still on his back, his feet planted far apart as though to help support their weight, his fists resting on his knees but clenched like a boxer's.

After a minute Rusty offered him a cigarette and asked, "What was it like?"

But the newcomer, perhaps noticing the ribbon, was a little wary. Instead of answering, he said, "I don't suppose you've ever been in?"

"No, I've been lucky, I've never been caught. I've sometimes wondered if I could take it."

"You could all right," the newcomer said with a touch of admiration, which he at once redressed by adding, "You'd have to."

"How did you put in the time, mostly?"

"On the square. They shook us out about 6:30. We hit the square about 8:15 and they hustled us back about 11:30. Then we were out again all afternoon. You do everything on the double. You move on the double. You eat on the double. You piss on the double. You shit on the double."

"It sounds rough."

"It was. At night my legs felt like lead. For two years I'd been sitting on my ass driving a truck. How could I do pack-drill? I did, though. Oh, I was a fool. One night I got drunk and overstayed my leave and then I figured I might as well have a really good holiday. But it didn't take the provost patrols long to pick me up. That's what you always forget."

"I suppose so."

Their talk languished. The soldier from the detention-barracks sat immobile, while Rusty curled up in one corner of the compartment and closed his eyes.

His home had vanished, and his mother, and his father, and his sister. The army had vanished, too, and the war. The atmosphere he was wandering in was mild and featureless, a darkness softened by mist. It seemed a miracle that he had ever happened on a girl like Althea. When he first saw her, she was standing alone under the colonnade in the Plaza, her hair lifted a little by the soft breeze, her scarf fluttering out. At first he could hardly believe her being there, where ordinarily there were only creatures who were offering themselves for sale. He twice walked back and forth in order to be sure. But there could be no doubt of it, of how different she was, of how much she was herself. She had a look of passionate quiet, of tender intentness. She seemed to be waiting for someone; but when at last he spoke to her, she recalled her gaze and answered as though he was the one whom she had been expecting.

Looking back, he saw it all as floating quite free of time. But it must have happened about six weeks after the leave he spent at home and only a few days after the victory celebrations. It had been raining but had cleared, and the rain-clouds were scattering raggedly towards the horizon. As they walked towards the district where she was staying, some of the banners that had been put up for the celebrations were still flying from their standards, while others, brought down by rain or by the crowds and not yet cleared away, were lying in pools that in the dim light spread lavishly over the pavement. It was over these spoils — dragons, lions, blood-red crosses — that they made their way, treading confusedly on emblems of carnage, on trophies fallen from the tattered triumphant sky.

When they reached her address, she opened the heavy black door with a latch-key and they walked up three flights of stairs to a flat on the top floor. While she was mixing him a drink, she explained that the flat had been lent her by a friend who was out of town for a few days. But she had little to say about herself or where she came from; and he found no need to be more communicative about himself. Although there was no constraint between them, they came together in an air of almost astral quiet, an air steeped in the faint planetary light that came in through the window from over the roof-tops. It was an illumination that would have been inhuman had there not come with it a smell of the sea from the estuary to the east, that flowed, still tidal, fecund with brine and spawn. Either the stars had fallen into the sea or life's salt, secretive currents were twining among the heavens, so closely did flesh and blood seem to be intertwined with the starry stillness.

Then she gave herself to him. She did it as though for the first time and also with the ripe experience of the ages, of temple courtesans, of a goddess. She took his fury for granted, and how his fibres had been deranged by horror, his skin scarred and blackened by powder. Her suave delicacy made a refuge for his savagery till he ceased to know himself. He found his limbs expressive and controlled and yet astonished to the point of miracle, as though the longing in his loins were expanding like the nebulae, spiralling with the blue velocity of light, spangled, sophistical, surprised. But what he remembered most was not that miracle but the stillness afterwards. He who believed in nothing believed in this, the absolute stillness, the annihilation that lasted for minutes — for hours rather, for eternities — as they lay together. That lasted even as the world began its gradual merciless return. First a light skitter of mice behind the plaster. Then footfalls in the adjoining flat. Then further off a church-bell sounding, but muffled as though its clapper were striking through snow. Till the world gradually was reconstructed about them, but now turning on a new centre, sphere after sphere after sphere all whirling about that point of perfect stillness.

After a while he got up and went to the window. There was no moon. The last of the clouds had been swept away and the wind had dropped. The sky was vast and black and still, so still that it might have been tranced by some moon that he couldn't see. He was conscious of nothing but the print of her flesh on his and of her mouth still sweet on his lips. His mind had melted, he seemed to have been reabsorbed into the night sky; the night air seemed to wash protectively about him, bringing calm and nourishment and oblivion. As he looked back over his shoulder, she was lying on her side, glimmering like a half-moon, her limbs glimmering and glistening like magnolia petals, moist and open in the dark. He went to her, and as she put her arms around him he was aware for the first time of how her body was haunted by freshness, enveloped with a blossoming freshness, of honeysuckle, of new-mown hay. And his own sex, he noticed duskily, was as fresh and ardent as when it first trumpeted in wild orchids through his boyish flesh. So again they triumphed. And then perfect stillness again. And then the soft return of the whirling world, out, out, farther and farther until he could hear the stars tolling, tolling faintly like bell-buoys in the distant estuary.

How did he find his way back? He didn't know. All he remembered was walking back through empty streets, through woods, with her body still clinging to him, her fragrance. He had become a new land, a new map. Stars had fallen into his flesh, were seamed there in the grass. He was blinded. He walked gropingly. He put out his hand to the darkness and felt it swaying like a cloud or tree. Somehow he found his way back to the hostel where he was staying, but how he didn't know.

Where was the train taking him as it plunged through the darkness? He was neither awake nor asleep but sat with his eyes closed and his body slack, swaying slightly with the train. Was it returning him to that miracle of stillness? A faint smile creased his face as he thought of it. But that was impossible. She had never written to him as she said she would; and when he went back to the flat to look for her, she was gone and no one knew where she could be reached. No, it was all a million light-years away now. Still … he felt that if he put his hand to his breast he would be sure to find there something that he couldn't afford to forget, something of value that one day he might be allowed to open. He felt as though he were travelling under sealed orders.

2

The sun was glittering on the pavement as he came dancing down to meet it from the steps of the hostel where he had spent the night. The cleats on one of his heels were loose, and as he moved they clattered a little, like spurs. Let the onset begin! The capital, spread wide as a tournament, shimmered with opportunity that seemed to stretch endlessly before him, fluttering as gaily as pennons or pavilions. If the city had been hacked and torn, if there were still great gaps and holes in it, if for years nothing had been painted or repaired, in the light of this midsummer morning all that only added to its lustre and light-heartedness. The peeling stucco made it ripple like a tented city, impermanent, splendid, where a nomadic people had settled for a while, gathering their innumerable billowing caravans. A bazaar, a great bazaar, even though now there was little for sale, he thought, as he ankled out of the way debris fallen from the barrows that had stood there the night before. Yes, but a bazaar where almost anything might be secreted and rediscovered was the hint dropped by the pearl-grey sky, which comprehended so many truths and follies, so many wastrels and heroes and misers and searchers, such a confusion of riches and error. Perhaps the whole outspread city was based on corruption, perhaps it rested on a leprous swamp? But if it did, it was redeemed today by a hint of water, by a certain lucid watery raggedness that covered it with Venetian brightness. And redeemed, too, by its sacrifices and sufferings. They were still active in the air, adding to it sharpness, a glint of knives, distinguishing it with death and danger, so that nothing it surrounded could be entirely given over to sloth or to the certainty of gradual decay. It was a city where anything might happen. As he turned a corner, he came upon a troupe of middle-aged urchins who were performing acrobatic stunts before an audience of scattered idlers while one of their number tried to shuffle his way out of intolerable chains. A few pennies sparkled down onto the pavement, where a battered felt hat was resting. And then when the prisoner made good his escape and danced about in three or four heavy steps of earth-born triumph, the golden shower increased. The bright coins on the pavement were like water lapping, like water glittering far out in the sunlight along tracks that led — who knows where? To his eye the whole city glittered with adventure.

His first night in town had passed safely, even uneventfully. He got through the station without being stopped by the military police. Then he went and had a few drinks and thought about where to find a bed. The most natural place for him to go was to a servicemen's hostel, and although they always asked to see your pass, he thought, what the hell, he might as well chance it. And luck was with him. When he got there, a group of half-drunken soldiers were singing and clowning around the doorway. He followed them in, and in the confusion no one noticed that he didn't have a pass. As he was leaving in the morning he realized that he would probably never be able to go back, since in the meantime they would make a routine check with his unit and would find that he was absent without leave and would be on the lookout for him, should he come back, to turn him in. So what? Did he ever want to spend another night in that asylum with its tiny cubicles and its corridors that smelled of disinfectant like a public lavatory? He was more than content that those doors were closing behind him.

Now his strong relaxed stride was taking him towards the centre of the city, where he had been the day victory was celebrated. What a skirmish that had been! Matelots wading in the pools of the public fountains, their bell-bottom trousers rolled up to the knee. Bedraggled naiads being hauled up to gambol beside them and to fall hoydenishly in the shallow water. Despatch-riders who went scorching past with two or three girls clinging behind them till the rear of their motorcycles scraped comet-like over the roadway. That day he started drinking not long after he got up, and kept at it steadily. He happened to be on course in the capital for a few days and was staying with a friend who had been demobilized early in order to return to an important job in one of the ministries; and in spite of the general drought, there seemed to be no shortage with this type. They decided it would be a good idea to have a drink or two of gin and water as they were dressing and after that they never looked back. To follow the gins, they had a few beers with two sergeants who insisted that they join them. Then a glass of sherry or two in a saloon bar. Then some whisky. Then the fountains went on — for the first time since the war — and they strolled about them admiringly in a mist of cheers and spray. Then they fell in with a group of soldiers from his home-town who were drinking brandy from a water-bottle; and they had one pull after another and felt their chests being etched and arabesqued by its branching fire. They admired the decorations, the flags, the flowers, the thousands of hanging-baskets, and endless window-boxes to freshen the grimy walls that in so many places were still pitted by shell-fragments. But by this time the whole atmosphere was beginning to burst out in a vast bouquet, the phlox-blue sky, the rose-petalled banners, the white cadences of the bunting, all stemming out in profusion; and as they watched lightheadedly (being rocked by the same carnival motion) was beginning to tilt, yes, to revolve in the style of a great Catherine-wheel, faster and faster and faster. And now from the crowd figures began to appear and disappear inconsequently, as though they had been projected fro negro joined them for a while. Then a bald-headed r ing — wonder of wonders — an unopened bottle of his hand. He vanished to the sound of breaking glass and was supersided by a little ape-like creature flaunting an immense flag. But as unexpectedly as he had materialized, this monkey climbed up to a hotel balcony, waved his flag madly and disappeared into one of the bedroom windows.

As the day faded, there was a pause, the packed crowd swaying slightly, touched it may have been by hunger or the failing light or perhaps merely by uncertainty about where best to see the fireworks from, once dark had fallen. Then, there they were — the first rockets! Showers of sparks. As green as fishes. Then silver. Red. Acetylene blue. One shower leaping out of another. Like salmon laddering up the black sky. Or scattered and falling through a wide arc, scaly and scintillating. A sky so full of motes it seemed to be twangling with light and music. Again and again, bursts of metallic colouring. Their eyes could never have enough of these high huzzas and then of the slow silvery downward drift that left the low night over the roof-tops sleek and glittering with mermaids. They were held in a bright mesh that folded about their upturned eyes, a sheeny tent that ruled out the constellations and with sheer excitement made any cosmology unnecessary. The vast crowd was canopied under a fire of joy of its own making that, as it burst and fell, floating down above their heads, united them, held and directed them all in bonds it seemed that nothing could break.

Somehow in the press he was separated from his friend. He couldn't remember everything that happened later, whom he attached himself to, or even where he spent the night. That was the kind of party it was. It wouldn't have surprised him if, when the wave receded, some of the guests had been found a hundred miles away, wedged among rocks or washed up in the crotch of a tree. But he did remember one thing about the crowd's dispersing. In one of the streets along which he was carried by the ebbing flood, the curtains were not drawn, light streamed from the windows and, what was more, tall gas torches were lit that had not been used for years. Red smoke rolled from them, witless and rampant. In their glare flags bled over the street. It was as though the animal heart of the city, that had been almost extinguished but never quite, that had worked in concealment but for years had pumped out vigour far and wide, sustaining — long after he should have succumbed — a trooper with a leg blown off or a sailor adrift in an open boat; as though that animal heat at last was flaming out in wrath and joy.

Since then the temperature had fallen, of course. There were no torches or crowds or cheers or flags as he sauntered through the same streets this early summer morning. But was it mistaken to think that some of the excitement still lasted? He sensed it in the air, in the curl and ripple of the awnings, in the light breaking golden on a thick blue cloud that hung fleece-like over the east end of the city. There would be a time for routine and restraint as there had been a time for agony and suffering. But now let the tightrope-walker fare out over the dazzling gorge!

He felt the watery light run tingling through him. His muscles were striped the colours of the rainbow and his blood felt thin and frothy like water at the bottom of a falls. He might have been coming up from a great depth, his veins and arteries seemed so charged with bubbles formed in answer to the sparkle in the sky. The exhilaration he felt was acute almost to the point of pain. He would be changed. The infinite possibilities of this far-spread city would allow all his cramped cells to expand. He would be changed. And that will be disguise enough, he found himself thinking. Even someone from the town where he had grown up would pass him unnoticed. He would perhaps be unrecognizable even to his own family. And he found it pleased him to think that no one would know him, that he would move towards his purpose quite anonymously. In his home-town he was treated as a boy and had been confined and diminished. In the army he had soon stiffened into a new identity and found that he was expected to be consistently unmoved and brave and taciturn. Now he would be himself — or whichever one of his myriad selves any particular encounter happened to call out. For though he didn't know himself very well, he was dimly conscious of ruling over a wide city of impulse which could hardly be expressed by one stereotyped salute for every occasion. What was it that he had been told about saluting soon after he enlisted? That it started with knights raising the visors of their helmets? Well, he would be wandering far and wide and there would be many encounters, he supposed. But no one gesture could possibly serve for them all. That rickety general, for example, who was approaching now. Did he deserve a salute? He probably should have been retired years ago. But as they drew abreast, he felt his arm fluttering up automatically. Discipline triumphed, and his unreasoning pride in the ancient forms. Besides it gave him a bang to think that he was on the loose and yet was giving very soldierly salutes to every broken-down officer he passed. He liked the taste of the two flavours on his tongue, light and dark. Somehow it made him remember a soldier he had known, a wild bastard, who had had his prick tattooed with a jester's cap and bells because of the added pleasure the thought of it gave him whenever he was driving it home.

Light and dark. The city rippled with them. He thought of one night a few months before when he had been sitting with a girl on a park bench and fumbling with her bodice when a rocket had streamed in and landed not more than half a mile away. The earth quaked and the park seemed to be ringed with the crackle of breaking glass. But all he could do was to burst out laughing, laughing almost uncontrollably, there seemed to be such a disproportion between their ignorant romancing and the weight and precision of this elegant monster that now might nuzzle in any pasture. He amused himself as he sauntered along by trying to decide which bench he had been sitting on. Was it under that hawthorn tree? Or further along? Daylight made such a difference that it was hard to be sure.

As he ruminated, he came to a point at the edge of the park where a little crowd was gathered. A police van was drawn up at the curb and a man was being bundled in. He saw the sunlight glistening on a pair of handcuffs and on a trickle of blood down the prisoner's forehead. Then the door of the van was slammed to.

"What's up?" he asked of a scruffy little soldier who had got there before him and was now gazing stupidly at the patrol van as it drew away.

"Police. M.P.'s. Provosts. They're everywhere in this town. I hate them."

"But what happened?"

"Oh, just someone on the loose, I guess. They were looking at his pay-book when he tried to make a bolt for it. But they were too fast for him. One of them dived for his legs. The other one hit him over the head with a truncheon. Now he's on his way to the cooler."

"It looks more like he's on his way to the hospital."

"Oh, that's nothing," the scruffy little soldier said disgustedly, as the crowd melted and the two of them were left to walk on together through the park. "I've seen them go to work on guys with rifle-butts. The poor bastards were drunk, so the gestapo could really go to work on them. Really go to town. With their boots, too. They had to stay in hospital for a week, faces all swoll up. One of them had his jaw broken."

That might be, Rusty thought to himself, but he remembered provost types directing traffic for hours on a stretch at crossroads that the enemy had registered in with artillery fire and were shelling unmercifully. He contented himself, though, with saying philosophically, "I suppose they have their job to do like anyone else."

"Look at it that way if you like," muttered the little diehard, squinting at the bright sun with red ferret's eyes. "The way I look at it is, why did they join the gestapo? No one was forcing them."

"Well, some of them had a pretty rough war, at any rate," was his mild reply. But now he was lengthening his stride to shake off this hanger-on in a baggy uniform that looked as though it had been slept in. What was he driving at, anyway, this soldier who took the provosts so personally and smelled so unsavoury, what was he snuffing around for?

You couldn't stop him. "They may be soldiers, but they all have the soul of a flatfoot. And now they're streaming back. This town's full of them, I tell you. I hate them. I hate the whole boiling of them. And if you're wise, you'll be on your guard against them, too."

At the next fork in the path he struck off by himself so curtly that he might almost have seemed to be afraid of the little grouser at his elbow who was now left staring after him.

The park was being reclaimed for pleasure. Through leafy sunlight he saw workmen rolling up some of the barbed wire that had surrounded the anti-aircraft batteries and carting it away. The gun emplacements were being filled in, the huts were being dismantled, and even here and there flowerbeds were being laid out again. A little farther along, he stopped to watch a statue being restored to its pedestal. It was of one of the monarchs on a charger, with a spirited, flowing flourish in the horse's tail and in the way the rider held his hat; but now both horse and rider lay in bronze along the grass, as though capsized, while workmen fitted tackle about them and adjusted the blocks overhead in order to hoist them back into position. "How would you like to have balls as big as that?" one of the navvies called out, patting the horse's testicles appreciatively. And Rusty noticed that in fact everything was rather larger than life, of rather more than common mould.

Almost insensibly by this time he had circled around close to the spot where he had entered the park and, after crossing the street, was back in the busy central quarter of the city, with theatres, it seemed to him, dominant in one street, book-shops or wine-merchants or gun-smiths in another, while still another was given a brisk nautical air by shipping-companies with their house-flags fluttering from the roof-tops. In the older and more biblical cities that he had seen during the war, the dominance would have been complete; a street would have been given over entirely to makers of baskets or sickles or chairs. The texture of this city was looser and more open. Its order seemed to be little more than a probability elicited from the behaviour of very large numbers; it was derived not from fiat but from the indeterminate freedom of statistics, where some possibilities were more likely than others but where nothing, however obsolete, or novel or bizarre, was impossible. The coming and going of countless individuals had resulted in durable patterns, but their mesh was so loose that almost anything could swim through them. So to his eyes these streets undulated marvellously with chance as unpredictable as operated to produce living cells, the petals of flowers and the paws of animals. They were as alive with fortune as the palm of one's hand.

A dayspring! A miraculous draught! A shower of brightness! His head was full of fortune, he could not help admitting to himself as he turned aside into an amusement arcade to try the slot-machines. He knew they were only for suckers, but the idea of all the levers being released and of coins pouring out intoxicated him with the thought either of something that had already happened to him or of some miracle that was yet to come. Was it really a game of chance or a game of skill? he wondered as he put a coin in the slot and rubbed the rabbit's foot that he always carried in his pocket and pressed the plunger with delicate firmness. The machine that he was trying was decorated with a full-busted woman, who was dressed, as though to show that she had generous impulses, in black net stockings and black tassels. But she was unresponsive. He tried her again and again, putting in one coin after another and wondering whether it was his luck or his finesse that was at fault. Well, there were others. One showed a jockey in pink silk crouching over the neck of a racehorse and whipping it on to victory in a sweepstake. Another had a church spire with a rout of steeplechasers all making for it hell-for-leather. The ornament on another was a large emerald painted in the middle of the turban of a dark-skinned swami like an eye of wisdom. He went down the row trying each one of the machines and forking out more and more coins and going back to the cashier to get change and returning doggedly. Gradually he had sifted to the back of the arcade, where little light filtered in from the street and where the air was close and heavy. As he tasted its staleness on his tongue, it occurred to him that this was a place where pimps did their business, and receivers, and informers. Even now there were two men in the shadows not many feet away from him. But whether they were in communication with each other he couldn't be sure. The tentacles that hung from their eyes swung slowly around and seemed occasionally to meet, although neither of them spoke. Were they about to make contact? Or were they hoping to entangle him in some web they were weaving? Sometimes their antennae swept round towards him. But they slid off before engaging and left him uncertain whether they were wishing him away so that they could go on with some subtle, tentative negotiations of their own or whether for some obscure reason they wanted him as a partner. Whatever their purpose, he was sure, sure beyond any doubt, that they were eying him. Although he never caught their glances directly, he felt them clammy on his skin like the tracks of beetles or the moisture of spider-webs. Abruptly he pulled the plunger of the machine where he was standing as far out as it would go and let it fly back with a clatter and turned and walked out again into the sunlight.

Traffic on the pavement was almost at a standstill, he found, and heads were craning all in one direction to see whatever it was that was approaching along the path the police had cleared on the roadway. There was the thud of horseshoes. Then a jingle of spurs and bridles, growing clearer and clearer. Until it broke into view, a squadron of guards with the black manes of their horses flowing through the street like waves. They were mounting guard ceremonially for the first time since the war. But their archaic splendours of helmet and breastplate, of buckskin gauntlets and breeches, of crimson tunics, had not yet been restored; they shone with an authentic glory but it was dimmed by being filtered through khaki service dress so that there was some confusion as to who they were.

"The bird-catchers," cried one wrinkled old man in excitement.

"The blues," said another voice.

"The cherry-pickers," said another.

A middle-aged lady with a shopping-basket was so overcome that she cried out, "The dear creatures," and waved a lace handkerchief in the air and then had to draw it back quickly to wipe her eyes.

He sympathized with her emotion and yet was a little puzzled by it, too. He knew this regiment. It was wonderfully smart on parade. It was imperturbable. It was brutal. It was fearless, if a little sluggish, in action and as contemptuous of death as of any other enemy it had ever faced. Its members were simple and cunning, disciplined and anarchic, and not above eking out their pay with some earnings from male prostitution. It was odd to think of all that primitive carnal energy brought together and combed and kennelled, its coat made glossy to serve as an emblem of order, indeed as one of its supporters, as a kind of bear tethered to the court by a golden chain.

With animal courage gleaming in the standard that was carried before it and with animal ruthlessness in the farrier's axe that brought up the rear, the squadron — it had passed by in hardly more than a twinkling — would now be entering one of the forecourts of the palace. He had no desire to penetrate that labyrinth of courtyards, guard-rooms, antechembers, presence chambers, gardens, stables, mews, that great sprawl of buildings hutched one against another and hedged against the city. He had been there once to receive his medal and now he could take it or leave it. But it did contain one thing that he would like to see. He had read in the newspapers about how they were re-erecting the crystal sundial that had stood for centuries in one of the privy gardens. It seemed to be a large crystal sphere, banded by the zodiac and with all the signs — the bull, the ram, the crab, the lion, the scales, and all the rest — embossed on it. On the inner surface of the sphere moved the shadow cast by the gnomon. However it worked exactly, it lived in his mind as a great eye lying in the grass and absorbing as much of the heavens as the orb of the eye could hold. Silently marking the passage of time, it also drew together the architecture of the eye and the architecture of space, fusing them in a radiance that was bright and blue and powdery. That he *would* like to see, he thought, as he skirted part of the palace wall and wondered whether it was too soon to be making his way to the Plaza.

Hardly yet. He would wait until dark had fallen. But he knew that it was there he was being drawn. Its walls of symmetrical grey stone; its steeply pitched roofs; the shadows cast by the arches of its arcades; the tall windows round the upper storeys; and in the middle, towering above the traffic, the dark column continually furling and unfurling the measured space that fell in folds about it — why did all this hold such fascination for him?

It was only negatively that he could even try to define how it made him feel. It had been a centre of luxury and no doubt would be again; but it was not by any display of opulence that it attracted him. Some of the shops to be found beneath the arcades had not yet been reopened and of those that were again doing business few had much to offer. In any case, the square's dominant air was more reserved, even more severe, than could be produced by any commerce, however fashionable. It came rather from the ministries and chanceries that occupied the upper floors, where lights often burned late and where sometimes in a spell of particularly hot weather you could catch a glimpse through the partly opened windows of the high-ceilinged rooms where decisions of state were made. It was most severe in rain. Then the bronze-covered column shone black as a guardsman's bearskin, the streaming cannon at its base were no longer decorative but again seemed made for battle, the steep grey roofs rose grimly to meet the volleying storm. But for all the Plaza's martial sternness, it was not that that attracted him, he felt sure, congenial though he found it. For one thing, it hadn't suffered a single scar during the war. Nor was it deeply connected with any of his wartime memories. He remembered walking through it a few times during the blackout when it rose cliffed and cascaded in the moonlight. That had been eerie and superb. But its affinities were not really with the present at all; its rhythms harked back to earlier times whose tunes he didn't know.

Was he fascinated, then, by the Plaza because of Althea, because he had met her under one of its arcades? No … he didn't think so. It would be crazy to think that they would ever meet again. That had been something out of this world. It could never happen again. She had never written, and he had no possible way of tracing her. Besides he had begun to guess that it wasn't she herself that he was looking for. Even if he could find her, he had to admit that he wouldn't want to settle down with her — or with any other girl — and have children and earn money to pay the bills. No, what he was looking for, he was beginning to suspect, was rather something she had given him or had helped him to remember. It was as though she had sensitized a membrane, had made suddenly avid a deep craving which had always existed in him but which until they met had lived only underground and unaware of itself. Now it was resurrected and urgent and screaming like a forked root. But then why should he be so anxious for darkness to come so that he could haunt the place where he had first met her? Why, even now, did his eyes question every approaching figure that could possibly be hers? Why, when they were still distant, did so many deceive him by assuming so unimpeachably her image?

He gave up trying to unravel it and, turning in to have a drink, lost himself in a succession of bars and clubs that he had known during the war. Some were below the street level and had to be entered down a flight of stairs; some catered particularly to foreigners; some had their walls covered with regimental insignia; some featured a piano or an accordion. They were all exactly and gratifying as he remembered them, still frosted with discovery. A more searching observer might have detected that there was a little less uproar here or that the conversation there was slightly less abandoned or that the barman in a third was a trifle warier and less apt to serve drinks indefinitely to patrons who were too drunk or too outrageous. But Rusty hardly noticed these subtle differences as he sat with one drink after another and retraced the path of old excitements and wondered how long it would be before it was fully dark outside.

On his way to the Plaza he managed to conceal from himself for a while where he was going by following a roundabout route. In a few minutes, though, he found that he was standing at the very spot under one of the arcades where he and Althea had met. Her head had been framed by the stones of the archway, he remembered; her hair had softened them. Now in the gap left by her going he stood sullen guard, motionless minute after minute, staring at the barred windows of the jeweller's shop opposite (it was empty now) but, for all his immobility, noticing every face that passed, checking them off, "No … no … no." Occasionally he moved a few paces to one side or the other but always he returned to the same spot, like a sentry. He was so fixed that before long other eyes sought his and flickered about with languor or inquiry. His eyes dallied with no one's. Once they had identified a face as not being hers, their glance withdrew into itself, became self-absorbed. At first his self-absorption was unconscious and profound. But as time passed, it occurred to him to wonder whether, at least in part, it might not now be deliberate, whether it might not be something willed and assumed, like armour or a mask. Admitting that possibility seemed to make him more vulnerable. For it was almost immediately after it entered his head that he began to be accosted not only by eyes but by voices as well.

"Don't look so cross, lover-boy. Why don't you relax a little? I have a flat just around the corner."

He could guess what the flat would be like. From the level of his shoulder a cloud of scent swirled about him. He knew without looking down who it was, the flabby number in slacks and what might once have been a leopard's skin coat whom he had seen pass back and forth and try her luck with two or three other men. When he pulled his sleeve free from her grasp, she spat and hissed, "I don't wish you any bad luck — just wither with clap."

He found the next voice more ingratiating. "Something cheap and cheerful, dearie?" it inquired. He chuckled. She was almost old enough to be his mother. But the chuckle had been a mistake. Now she was starting to tell him all about a woman's problems in trying to be mother and father both to a ten-year-old son. He moved away a few paces and, when she had gone, moved back.

A few minutes later a guardsman came up and asked him if he had a light. In reply he struck a match and held it out. In its tiny glow he noticed that the guardsman, as he bent to light his cigarette, was looking up narrowly from beneath the visor of his cap as though debating whether to say anything further. Finally he asked, "You waiting for someone?" When there was no answer, he added after a moment, "You've been here quite a while." But when there was still no answer, he walked away.

After that he was left alone. The traffic under the arches had thinned. The arcades were almost empty. The vaulting barrelled dimly into the distance and, now that it was late, afforded protection mostly for those who were not prepared to brazen out their needs and importunities or who had not been hardened by estrangement. This was the hour when they appeared like glow-worms or fire-flies, fugitive unarmoured things. There was a slight young man, hardly more than a boy, wearing a long coat and patent-leather shoes, who was gazing into one of the shop-windows, clinging to it like a wet leaf, incapable of any motion of his own and waiting to be caught up and carried along by any gust. A girl came by with pride and style in her lustrous black hair and her rich black suit, but with a great tear in the skirt and with a look of despair in her eyes that tore the world to tatters. He was overcome by a feeling of loneliness, of how full of loneliness the world was. What concentration of pain had produced the diamond-hard glitter in her eyes? And the boy in patent-leather shoes — a waiter perhaps? — was there no one he could turn to, was there no better prospect for him than the mirroring blankness of a plate-glass window? Lonely and impenetrable particles, erratic, irreducible under any law or to any predictable course. Where were they going? What would become of them? And then as he remembered that the same questions could be asked about him, his mood unaccountably lightened and something in him fluttered overhead and gazed down with detachment, almost with amusement. Yes, to a dispassionate eye he must cut a ludicrous figure. Keeping watch here hour after hour when he might have been getting himself drunk, fucked, and tattooed (and all for a dollar — as the humourists insisted). And for what?

He strode out into the Plaza from the shadow of the arches. There was now little light from passing buses and taxis; the stars had reasserted their sovereignty. They were brilliant, merciless. Through a rearrangement of dominant points of light the square had been cast into another order of reality. Its own order had not been cancelled, but now it depended on the North Star and the Bear. In that light it seemed smaller, more like a village or even a stableyard. And he himself — he was changed, but was he diminished or magnified by the new relationship? Neither, he thought. It was too odd to admit of measurement. Rather in bewildering quietness he was stung into consciousness of himself as a burning particle; he was aware of the spark, the life, the god in him. There was something flaming within him which cast a wide radiance and could momentarily hold its own against the stars, which were everywhere and ruthless, like lance-tips. The radiance hardly more than glimmered — and was gone. But as it faded, there was left a pollen, the brushing of a moth's wing that afflicted him with more lasting strangeness. That brightness — and the stars in their frosty distances? It could be overcome by them. Yes. But what had it to do with them? How could they exist together? How did it come that there was this thickening, this clotting in space that could provide nourishment for life and consciousness? Often before going into action he had deliberately laid down his life in advance as it were; had taken it out of his own keeping and had laid it down, as you might a watch, to be picked up again if everything turned out luckily; or like a falcon from his wrist had loosed it, had kissed it good-bye, so that there would be no risk of his caring for it too much when he was in danger. And at those moments of deliberate surrender he had thought that he had been aware of himself with particular clarity. But that had been less estranging than this momentary shudder. Then he had looked at life only from the distance of his own death. Now he was seeing it from much farther off, from much higher, from the vantage-point of an order which excluded it altogether. If indeed it was an order, the maze of stars? Perhaps it was only the long-continued rout after a cosmic disaster with the scattered remnants fleeing ever outwards. But whatever it might be, it had no room for life or consciousness. He shuddered because it was steep and cold, because he was left with the mind thinking about itself thinking.... Up that stairway into the ice-cold heavens you could climb endlessly on and on....

On the other side of the Plaza two military police were finishing their last patrol of the day. As his glance, fluttering downward, caught them in its random descent, his pupils dilated and clamped around their rigid lockstep, left, right, left, right, over the echoing pavement. He stiffened. For a moment, as he stood motionless, he felt secretions flowing from his diaphragm and trickling down over his guts. The next thing he knew he was running, running as fast as he could. He didn't look back to see whether they were following but pelted on, twisting from one empty street into another, clattering with his cleated boots past the closed shop-fronts, racing from his invisible pursuers. When he came to himself, the first thing he heard was his own blood racing, and then, as he gradually slowed down, the deep indifferent pulse of a wide sleeping city. Finally he stopped in the shadow of a doorway and lit a cigarette. Where would he go? He looked at his watch. It was almost two o'clock. The only place he could think of at that time of night was Mark's. Perhaps he would still be up and would give him a bed.

In a few minutes he was standing in front of the block of flats where he had been staying on victory day. His friend's lights were still on. Yet he hesitated for a while in the ground-floor hall before pressing the bell and going up. How could he be sure that he'd be welcome? After all, the war was over. Mark again had a position in the world, while he was — what he was. In the regiment they had been inseparable, but their paths had diverged and would diverge farther and farther, he knew, now that Mark had returned to his own life and was back at his old job, doing Rusty wasn't sure exactly what but meeting people every day whose travels and opinions were reported in the newspapers and eating in expensive restaurants and wearing expensive clothes.

But he needn't have worried. As soon as his friend opened the door, it was as though they had never been separated and were back in the regiment together. He went in out of the dark to an arm being put around his shoulder and a background of light and comfort and security.

"God, it's good to see you," his friend was saying. And his half-formed apologies about the hour and about arriving so unexpectedly evaporated, and he grinned and let himself be drawn down a path that Mark was clearing through the books and papers scattered on the floor and ushered to a place on the sofa after a mass of records had been cleared away to make room for him.

"Now, what'll you have to drink? I'm sorry there isn't any marsala or cherry brandy. Will you settle for gin or whisky?"

He was wondering when his friend was going to ask him why he was in town and how long he was going to stay. He even felt a strong desire to confess that he was on the loose and see what Mark would say, perhaps even to ask for help in trying to discover what it was that he was searching for. For of all the people he knew, Mark was the one least likely to conclude straightway that he was out of his mind and to tell him to stop being a fool. Often this figure in the frayed silk dressing-gown with thick glasses and thinning hair seemed vague and ineffective. But he understood things. He might even understand what someone like Rusty was after.

The moment passed, though. He merely said that whisky would do fine. And his friend knelt down to open a case that was lying in the middle of the floor. That was like Mark. There was something at once elegant and sloppy about him. His name was really short for "the Marquis," a nickname he had acquired soon after he joined the army because of the amount of money he had and the kind of work he was accustomed to. But he didn't behave like a marquis. He could dig one slit-trench after another and still be cheerful. He didn't even mind teaming up with the company half-wit and spending the whole of a long, hot afternoon digging a beautiful, deep latrine. He was good for whatever came along, even though he often seemed to be thinking of something else while he did it. And perhaps it was because he was thinking of something else that his tunic, even on parade, was often stained, his boots scuffed, his trousers baggy. It was the same with his flat. There was plenty of whisky, but it was still in a case on the floor for anyone to trip over. Books spilled out from the bookcases over the side-table, the record-player, and down over the floor.

His desk was so littered with documents and scribbled sheets of something he had just been working on that you could scarcely see the red leather blotting-pad underneath or the silver inkwell and paper-knife.

He seemed to turn with relief from whatever it was he had been doing. "Now drink up," he said as he slumped back with a glass into an easy chair. "It's like old times to have you blowing in. Do you remember the night we had the party in the red house and we ran out of anything to drink and you went off to find some and just when we were about to pack it up, you came back and said you'd taken the colonel's scout-car and driven it into the ditch; but when we went out to see, there was a huge flask of wine safe and sound in its wicker covering on the back seat?"

Yes, he remembered all right, Rusty thought, as he unwound his puttees and unlaced his boots and unbuttoned his tunic and made himself comfortable, and then sluiced down a long swallow of whisky. He remembered all right. That was another time he had lost his stripes — when the colonel had learned about the scout-car.

Yes, those were the days," he replied dreamily, almost drowsily. He knew he wasn't going to tell Mark tonight. It was too good to sit in this warmth and comfort and forget the empty streets and the ice-cold questions and the sudden panic that had come over him so surprisingly. "I sometimes wonder whether they haven't spoiled me for anything else."

"You'd better drink some more of that whisky. That should make you more cheerful. What are you thinking of doing when your release date comes up?"

"I don't know," he answered evasively, as though his release date was still coming up automatically. "All I know is that I can't go home. I couldn't stand it. I wish I could find something really interesting to do; but I'm not fitted for anything. What I'd really like would be a job like yours — although I know that's silly. I haven't any education … anything."

"You've got plenty of things," his friend cut in vigorously, "energy, a good record, a good reputation, a good appearance. I'd back your prospects anytime. And why do you think that what I do is so fascinating?"

"Well, you travel. You move around. You meet interesting people. You deal with interesting subjects."

"Would you like to know what I was dealing with before you came in?" Mark reached over and fished out a thick folio document from the litter on the desk.

Rusty took it and read, "Sir, I have the honour to forward a memorandum prepared by my commercial counsellor on car-loadings in Trieste for the month of July."

"Or perhaps you're interested in petroleum production in Rumania?" He fished out another despatch and handed it over. "That's the kind of fascinating subject I deal with. Someone I knew once went for a holiday in Capri, and he told me about going to swim in the blue grotto. He said the water was a wonderfully deep blue, almost purple, and clear and mysterious. As he gazed down before diving in, his head was full of that imperial colour and of memories of Tiberius and others of those swindlers. Then he dived, and the water closed round him, dark and luxurious. He opened his eyes on a world of sapphire. It was so magical he could imagine himself being sensitized to a whole new existence where there could never be suffering or boredom or routine. But when he came to the surface, he felt something sticking to the crown of his head and put up his hand and pulled away a piece of used toilet-paper. That's what it's like being in the Ministry. You start with images in your mind of an ambassador being borne floating along to present his credentials at the palace; or of a young second secretary making such a witty retort to the Princesse de Polignac that the salons ring with it for weeks; or of a wise and ingenious formula that brings peace for a generation. But when you actually dive in and come to the surface you find that what you're involved in is the statistics for car-loadings in Trieste and petroleum production in Rumania and abortion in Japan and suicide in Stockholm and pain, tyranny, torment, madness, everywhere. The crap from the whole wide world comes flooding across your desk. I'd far rather clean out a latrine every now and then."

Rusty wondered whether his friend (who was usually more laconic) was being so voluble in order to avoid raising the obvious question of what had brought him to town. No, he wouldn't say anything tonight.

"But you move around at least, you go to interesting places," he heard himself resuming.

"Oh, yes. To international conferences. Which invariably are held in the most fashionable resorts, but in the off season when the hotels are empty and need the business. So that all you have for diversion is to walk along the deserted esplanade and admire the waves under a November rainstorm or to imagine how fine the public gardens would be if only it were spring and all the tulips were out. But it *isn't* spring, and the tulips *aren't* out, and so you go back to a chilly bedroom to try to draft a statement for the head of delegation which will be ambiguous enough to please everyone."

"Well, you ought to know. But I always thought it was different. I always thought of you as doing something rich and important."

"I suppose it is important. At least somebody has to do it. And I mustn't exaggerate. Occasionally a moment comes," he confessed sheepishly, "when all the information you've gathered becomes suddenly coherent and you seem to be able to see a long way down through it, you might be gazing into a forest that for all its foliage was still perfectly lucid or along the aisle of a cathedral that made perfect sense in spite of all the memorials. In those moments you can even have the illusion there might be something you could do about it."

"I always knew your future would be worthy of you," Rusty responded simply. He wasn't envious. He only sensed a perfect blankness when he tried to think of his own future.

"No, it won't be," Mark replied. "Nor yours either. Whose is? But don't think you'd find things clearer or easier if you had a position like mine. You'd hate it. And those moments never last. The telephone rings and someone wants a report on whether it's true that Signor Casanova is trying to corner the market in sugar. Or you have to turn back to the dreary chit-chat of some self-important head of mission who doesn't know whether his arse is bored or punched."

But they both confessed that they were beginning to feel tired. "And I have to have a memorandum ready for the Minister by noon tomorrow," added Mark, as he went into the next room to see that everything was ready for his visitor, whom he insisted should sleep in the bedroom while he slept on the couch; he wouldn't hear of anything else.

As Rusty climbed in between the monogrammed sheets in his coarse khaki shirt, he felt grateful all over again for having some place to sleep and a roof over his head and warmth and welcome. Who could have a better friend? Bless him for not asking why he was here or how long he was going to stay, for just looking after him and making him feel at home. He stretched out and closed his eyes. But as he tried to sink deeper into the warmth and fall asleep, something was blowing bright prickly motes against the back of his eyelids. The particles stretched out almost illimitably, like sunlight over the sea, but were broken before they reached the horizon; now it was darker, and the scintillation seemed to be moonlight reaching up to an orb that was hidden, over a pathway flawed and treacherous; now the motes were phosphorescence, clambering, lightening, up a ship's rigging but never quite reaching the top. Before he fell asleep, they had turned red, deep coppery red, and were glittering like knives.

3

It must have rained during the night. For, although it was bright by the time he got up, there were still bracelets of rain sparkling here and there on the roadway, and the air seemed washed and pure. Before leaving for the office, his friend had wakened him only long enough to tell him what there was for breakfast and where he could find it. Then Rusty had turned over and slept a little longer, a light, dreamless sleep where he seemed to be sheathed in coolness, as though he were lying face downward in a bright shallow stream or in grass that breathed and rustled round his limbs. Then he stirred and lay on his back, half-awake, watching the light from the street that was turned green and watery by passing through the leaves outside the window and glimmered and rippled on the ceiling. Who was the hero that Mark had mentioned who liked three things above everything else — reading plays, lying in bed, and watching the flight of birds? He didn't care much for reading, except occasionally an adventure story to while away the time. But he liked lying in bed; and it was good to watch the pigeons fly up from the street every now and then, when they were startled by the traffic, and flutter about the roofs for a little and then glide down again.

After he had had breakfast and taken a leisurely shower, he went to the window and stood for a long time looking out. The colour of the buildings opposite, pale washes of pink and cream and blue, floated against the clear, mild sky. There was a flower shop across the street and, in spite of the passing vans and taxis with their horns and fumes, it seemed to give freshness to the whole morning, making him think of cool buds cut and lying in fern. Or of blossoms falling from a bough. He had a feeling of weightlessness that made him remember what a paratrooper had once told him about the calm there was after the parachute had opened, when the fear of jumping was behind you and the jolt of the harness, while the impact with the ground still seemed far away, so that you floated airily for a while over the battlefield as though you were out of the world and time. The freshness of the morning tempted him to feel rather like that. If he were to stand on the window-sill and jump out, naked and glistening, his senses were persuaded that he would drift slowly down, innocent and uninjured.

Then he padded around the flat, examining the prints and rows of books, but mostly exulting in his own hard, tanned body. He didn't have any possessions or position or prospects. But that at least was something he could claim and glory in. His belly was hard as a board. There wasn't an ounce of surplus fat anywhere. It was all good hard muscle. On the calves of his legs. Along his arms. Around his shoulders. Where his chest spread like a cuirass. Who in the apartment block would believe it, he thought, if they were told that a panther was housed in one of the third-floor flats and was prowling hungrily? If he had a flat like this he wouldn't use it for working in late at night, struggling to draft an official memorandum; hell! no, it would be a hideaway where he would bring his partners night after night to make them accomplices in his hunger, working them up, making them cry out in pleasure, and then subduing them utterly as he rode them to a fare-thee-well. He felt excited as he thought of it. The green-gold light from the street grew thick and jungly, huge leathery leaves sprung up and blotted out the bookcases, the sleek racehorses in the sporting prints took the bit in their teeth and seemed to become the masters of their riders. It was his friend's flat no longer. It was his. The light was tawny as it flowed speckling round his flesh. It lionized him as he stood staring, heavy-lidded, naked, in the middle of the room, his brain revolving a thousand images of innocent outrage.

But it was time to be dressing and to be making for the Ministry, where he had agreed to meet Mark before going out with him for lunch. What would he say to him? It wasn't fair to leave him in the dark any longer, wondering but unwilling to ask. He debated with himself, as he walked toward the Plaza, how he would phrase it and whether he would wait for an opening or just blurt it out. He had better not put it off any longer, he decided. He would tell Mark as soon as they met.

It was by now well past noon. The common ragamuffin sun had robbed the Plaza of all speculation and of every thrust of unease. It swirled dustily about the base of the central column, spilled over the curb and, frolicking in the gutter, poked gentle fun at the severe facade of the Ministry with its correct architrave and heavy pilasters. In that light no one could be intimidated even by the stiff facade of the Ministry portico. Still, he had a moment of agitation when he presented himself to the security guards who were stationed just inside the door. But it was all right; Mark had told them that he was to be expected, and he was cleared and passed over to a frock-coated messenger, who conducted him along to his friend's office. On his way, he saw through a half-opened door what must be another office but which seemed to be the size of a throne-room, with a row of windows overlooking the Plaza. He had a glimpse of a vast expanse of red carpet, of mirrors, and of a chandelier as large as a pool. That was all. The next moment he was safely delivered, and in only a few minutes more he was back in the street again with his friend at his elbow. But the colours of that room still glimmered in his head, tantalizingly, mysteriously, as though sometime he were to see it once again.

As they walked to the restaurant, Mark seemed preoccupied. Not angry, although he was frowning a little in the bright sunshine as though he had just been released from shadows. But preoccupied and silent. Perhaps he was worried about some problem in the office. Rusty knew that most of his work was secret and that he mustn't be questioned about it unless he mentioned it first himself. But the weather was too fine to be spoiled by silence, the air was too full of freedom. So he spoke out of his own lightheartedness, about the city seeming this morning like a circus, with clowns and performing animals, with a multitude of tight-ropes netted across the sky, and with thousands of acrobats balanced precariously. "It seems a place where anything might happen," he said.

He didn't know whether Mark had been listening. But his friend replied, "Yes, anything might happen." And then he added sardonically, "Someone I knew was standing just about where we are now one night early in the war. A land-mine came down, and exploded not many yards away. Miraculously he wasn't killed, merely stunned by the blast. He seemed all right to the rescue-squad when they came along. But he had lost his memory. He couldn't remember his name or even what he had been doing fifteen minutes before. He couldn't remember that he should get up in the morning or put on his uniform or go on parade. So the Army sent him to a neurological hospital. They tried everything; but it didn't do any good. He was just the same. The only thing they could do was discharge him on a pension and send him home. But as he was travelling from the hospital to a depot to be discharged, he had to wait in the station for the train to come in; and while he was waiting, there was a raid and a stick of bombs straddled the platform. That did the trick. His memory came back. He knew who he was. His mind was as clear as a bell."

"And what became of him?"

"Oh, he was sent back to his unit as though nothing had happened. I've rather lost track of him. But he survived the war all right. Now I think he's in his old job again, preparing the young to make their way in the world — by teaching them the romantic poets or something like that."

The restaurant was cool and dark, with so many waiters in white ties and tail coats and so many bus-boys in white aprons that for a moment he was afraid he was being drawn in out of his depth. But as Mark ordered, he relaxed and remembered what he had to do. They were beginning on vodka and smoked salmon and thin slices of brown bread and butter when he said, with his eyes on his plate, "I should have told you that I'm on the loose."

Then he lifted his eyes and smiled. "But I imagine you knew that anyway?"

But his friend didn't smile in return. "I don't think I wanted to know it. I'm not sure that I want to know it even now," he replied evenly. "When did you light out?"

"The night before last."

"So you have until tonight to get back?"

"How do you figure that out?"

"You know as well as I do that so long as a soldier isn't away more than seventy-two hours, the matter rests with the unit. If you're back by tonight, you'll probably find that someone has covered up for you. Or at the most you'll be docked a few days' pay or be confined to barracks for a few days. Tomorrow morning it will be a different story."

"But what makes you think I'm going back?"

"I know how wild a character you are, and that's fine. But I never thought you were crazy. We'll check on the trains after we've had lunch."

"Check on them if you like. But I'm not going back."

Mark looked weary and baffled, as though this was one problem too many for him. "I'm beginning to be really worried about you," he said. "Do you know what happens after you've been on the loose for more than a few days?"

"Sure, they set the military police on your trail. I can deal with those bastards."

"It's not only the military police. All the police forces in the country are alerted. They're all linked by teletype and they get all the details. Soon every police station in the country has your photographs, your fingerprints, as well as a full description — six foot one in height; weight, one hundred and seventy pounds; well built; brown eyes; thick brown hair parted on the left; a snake twining around a dagger tattooed on the left forearm (if I remember correctly); civil occupation, none. And all that's put on cards in the central registry here in town so that the machines can produce every fact about you at a moment's notice. Then they start checking everywhere you might turn up — with your family, your neighbours, your relatives, your friends."

"I see. You're afraid you're going to get into trouble by having a friend who's a deserter." As soon as the words were out of his mouth, he knew from Mark's eyes how wounding they had been, and he wished he hadn't said them; but he had never been able to apologize except indirectly, and often only when it was too late. It was a weakness he was ashamed of and yet seemed helpless to do anything about.

But Mark rallied and said steadily, "It's not myself I'm afraid for. It's you I'm afraid for, son. I see you in the sun and then I see you going down, down, I don't know how far, I can't see how far. And I can't understand it."

He was being drawn in out of his depth after all, although not in the way he had anticipated. He had never realized how deeply his friend cared for him, and now he felt that concern flowing around him; it troubled his clearness of heart. He was glad that the waiter came up at that moment with the next course and that the gap in the conversation was lengthened by someone from another table coming over to speak to his friend, excusing himself first and then going on in another language. When he had gone, Mark said under his breath, "A counsellor from one of the embassies. I wouldn't trust him further than I could throw him." And then dropping the mask of vivacity he had worn while he was talking to the diplomat, his face seemed tired and his eyes again seemed to be questioning an unfathomable downward vista.

He seemed to be searching for light — and for further words like bright pebbles to hurl against the giant shadow he saw looming over the future. But Rusty prevented him from saying any more by putting in, "Forget what I said a few minutes ago. I know it isn't true, and I ought to be ashamed of myself for saying it. I'm a clumsy bastard, so don't take anything I say too much to heart. But try to look at it this way. You say you can't understand me. Is that so very surprising? I can't understand myself either. And you're how many years? — seven years? eight years? — older than I am. Your blood runs slower. You're closer to settling down. I still feel the blood racing in my veins. It's carrying me on to some destiny of my own that I haven't a clue to. I can't help myself."

With every syllable he said, his friend seemed older and more defeated. "It was the war that put the taste for extremity in your mouth," Mark replied. "You were trained for it and you came to delight in it. Now you can't give it up."

"I don't think so."

"Yes. Listen to me. In some tribes they used to think that to make a hero you had to heat him into a fury. He had to be initiated step by step like a sword being tempered in the fire. But then when his work was done he had to be cooled back into sanity or he'd destroy himself or the very people he had been defending. So they plunged him into one cold bath after another until the fury was cooled out of him."

"I still don't think so. I liked danger. I liked being trained to extremity. I admit it. But my fury comes from further back than that."

At last Mark smiled. It was the smile of someone who was courteously admitting defeat — but for this encounter only. The battle would be resumed when they met for dinner.

After they had agreed when and where they would meet and Mark had left to walk back to the Ministry, Rusty turned to saunter down towards the harbour. It was a long way. But he had the afternoon before him. And he was disturbed by how his friend had responded, by the unspoken questions that lay only a little below the surface of their talk, and felt that he must take them up and see if he could find answers to them. Why was he on the loose, why was he resolved not to go back? That was the question that had so baffled Mark. Well, why, why was he? he asked himself. He held the question in his mind minute after minute as he walked on down the busy street. But he could do nothing with it. It slipped from his grip. And its place was taken by another question, "Who am I?" And then by another, "What am I looking for?" One question succeeded another like the streets turning and flowing into one another. He couldn't answer them, hard as he tried; he could only keep on walking, although the effort to grapple with them clouded the afternoon for him and made him miss the ripple in the awnings, the sun glittering on clocks and signs, the newly minted chimes that plashed sparkling down. Then the questions vanished. In their place came images — of a diver falling freely in space, of blossoms falling, white hawthorn blossoms they might be, of a gnarled bough left naked against a wide distant sky. And then, with a musical return, the blossoms floated upward to rejoin the bough; the bough grew smooth and supple as a wand, and with all its blossoming foam rose and drew down the sky and was dissolved there. The images were not to be questioned, and seemed to require no answers. They were still, inevitable, commanding. He was hooded by them; he walked enveloped by them, musing.

It was only when the first of the vessels in the harbour came in view that the cloud about him parted and he saw masts and pennons pinnacled above the roof-tops. He felt his eyeballs fluttering like humming-birds and then darting out to sip the sweetness from those sunlit, honeyed spars. From the crow's nest he imagined the antennae floating away aft, the rope ladders curving gracefully down to the bulwarks, the ship's red entrails open to receive new cargo, the whine of the winches, the slings swaying and plummeting down, the matelots swearing as they worked to fit the hatch-covers in place or, if they were off duty, washing their clothes and hanging them out to dry. He hurried on, aware now of the ship chandlers' shops he was passing with their windows full of blue woolen jumpers, rubber boots, sheath-knives, chronometers; of the tattooists' establishments flaunting designs of full-rigged ships, flags, half-naked women, and more slyly hinting at displays of indecency within; of the bars and dives and brothels. It was as if at the very edge of the sea every human need was recognized so that the savour of the emporiums that catered for them would cling to the cargoes being shipped to the ends of the earth. As they sailed out into the blue, these ships would bear the taint of impossible cravings, of intoxication, of nights spent in unlicensed, inordinate embraces. Rockets might soar more absolutely into space. But the parabolas these ships would follow still seemed a more exact figure of the total venture, since sailing alone on their far courses they yet went spiced by memories; however stripped by extremity, they would still always reek with lust and failure.

In a moment or two the buildings that had been shielding the harbour from him divided and he was standing by a dock where a large freighter was being loaded. Beyond it stretched the estuary broadening towards the sea and marked by spars and bell-buoys. Gulls wheeled, lit on the masts, wheeled off again. A light breeze, mingling sun and salt, quickened the harbour, ruffling it into shallow white-caps. He loitered. He idled. He was content with the joy of looking. Images and questions sank from his consciousness. He watched two sailors painting the hull from a stage floating in the water. He wandered around to the stern to see what port the vessel hailed from. He sat down on a crate that was standing ready to be loaded and felt the sun warm his shoulders. All the engines in his body seemed to be idling. If he sometimes half-wondered how he would meet the questioning in Mark's eyes, his doubts had scarcely time to bubble to the surface before they were reabsorbed by the warmth and by his sense of well-being. Was there some challenge that he could rise to? As though in answer, as though this might be the only answer he could give, his glance roved up the varnished mast, up to where it impaled the sky. From there he could possess all the towns and steeples of the world and set them ringing through his flesh and out into the golden air that was becoming deeper, richer, as the sun swung lower. The afternoon was growing late. The light, so thin and fine and constant before, was now beginning to thicken and ripple like a watermark. He would have to be on the move, he realized, if he was to get back to the west end and have time to get spruced up before meeting Mark for dinner.

As it turned out, he was at the rendezvous before his friend arrived. Waiting in the lobby, he felt self-conscious about his private's uniform and his heavy boots, although he had given them a high polish. The club servants were polite enough; but as they passed back and forth in their green liveries, carrying messages or serving glasses of brandy or port, they had the air, he thought, of doubting whether he could really be a guest of one of their members. But then Mark arrived — he had been kept late at the Ministry — and they went in to dinner.

They took up the conversation from where they had left off.

"Everyone has some fury in his veins, you know," Mark continued, as though he had been holding the thread of the conversation in his mind all afternoon and had been meditating on it. "That's true even of someone so old and bald as I am. But it doesn't absolve me from doing a day's work."

"It isn't only that you're older than I am," Rusty replied ruthlessly. "You're more respectable. Or put it this way: you sit at the centre of things, I'm away off at the edges. Look at how you live. You eat at places like this. You have a nice flat. You have a good job that will carry you on and on. You couldn't be fixed more comfortably."

"I don't see what that has to do with it."

"Don't you? You can dull your fury with good living. You can feed it caviar and smoked salmon and other tidbits until it becomes as tame as a pet poodle. You can take the edge off it with luxury. There may be fury in your blood, all right, perhaps a whole river of knives, for all I know. But you can blunt them any time you like with money and comfort."

"I don't think you understand my life — or me either. You don't know enough about it. You see only the outside and you judge from that. On the outside perhaps it seems frosted and exciting. But it's really a jungle, where I work; with its roots going down into torment. The problems of people who have lost their homes and can't go back, people torn apart by divided loyalties, people ravaged by memories of hardship, persecution, torture. That's what I have to deal with. Is that so difficult to understand? I wish to God I could make you realize what it's like to be cut off from everything you've known, to be homeless, wandering. You were speaking of how free and airy and open this city seems. And yet you want to outlaw yourself from it — and from everything else!"

"No, I don't want to be an outlaw," Rusty replied calmly. "All I want is to be an explorer. I want to explore this city, I want to enjoy it."

"Perhaps you'll find more than you bargained for. What do you think this whole performance, that looks so light and speculative to you, is resting on? You ought to know because you helped defend it. On force. Yes, and that's just as true now as it was in wartime. The whole structure, billowing out so freely and so unsupported in appearance, is anchored to one central point. It's a bazaar that is balanced like an inverted pyramid on one point, on a single point — on the glint of hand-cuffs. That's what it all comes down to, everything that makes it the tantalizing show it is."

"You may be right in what you say. But I don't seem to mind." His glance wandered adrift like the eyes of a lookout uncertain whether he was gazing into the sky or into the sea. "Or, perhaps it is that I'm searching for some order that doesn't rest on the police."

"I don't think you know what you're searching for. I don't think you know what you are." He pressed home what he took to be his advantage, as though determined that someone whom he valued so highly should not be allowed to slip away from him and be lost. Then he went on more gently. "We've both been talking as though we were so different. Are we? You tell me that I'm respectable. But you have a greater feeling for decorum than I have. You're on the loose, but your uniform looks as though you were about to mount guard. In the very way you walk, there's crispness, the snap of laurel."

"I know that I love style and smartness. I know that we have things in common. But you're right. I don't know what I am. I am so many things. I love bugle-calls, but I love prowling in the dark, too. Sometimes I think I'm an animal from a coat-of-arms, a bear or a stag, who wants to leave his post and go back to the woods. Or further back still. How can I explain it? Do you ever have the feeling when you look at the mast of a ship that it's been made so smooth so that you could climb clear into heaven? I sometimes feel as though I had fallen a long way, as though I had fallen from a bough. But there's still the scent of blossoms about. I sometimes get a scent so strong I feel I must trace the spoor right back to its lair. Or … how shall I put it? A taste comes into my mouth of cherries, of ripe cherries. I am standing in an orchard. The light mottles my skin as it comes through the green leaves and the sleek scarlet fruit. A unicorn could come out of the wood and gore me and I would hardly notice, I am so much part of the orchard, of its blood-stream. Then the trees begin to lift, as a mist might lift, and they lift me with them. And as I rise, there is still the juice of cherries in my mouth. But now it isn't sweet, it's salt, it tastes more like blood, it tastes more like the sea."

There was a silence. He didn't know quite what he had said. Or, at least, he didn't understand it. Twice Mark began, "I can't …" as though to prevent something that seemed to be passing above their heads from escaping utterly. Twice he got no further. He raised his hand almost episcopally but let it fall, and it sprawled clumsily on the table. The silence between them was so heavy that Rusty felt he had to say something, almost anything, to break it.

"And don't think it rests only on force," was what he said. "There's night, too. It rests on that as well. That's what I mostly want to explore. The night city."

"Yes, there's the other hemisphere … and the fascination of water … of drowning … of destruction." Again his friend seemed to be peering down a deep, baleful vista.

"Perhaps. But why should you think the dark is so destructive? How could the city ever go on if it didn't have its wick dipped and be doused night after night and go wandering in its sleep?"

"It's not the city I'm talking about," Mark cut in, "it's you. And I don't see how any night-wandering can be fruitful unless it's counterbalanced — yes — by duty. If you have spent the day working in the fields or as a ruler, you may be able to explore the night city without being destroyed by it. Perhaps. I don't know. But to do nothing except walk through the dark streets …"

"You sound as though the only person you would allow to wander about after dark would be someone like the king in the Arabian nights — I forget his name — who used to disguise himself and walk through his own city at night, poking into odd corners, talking to thieves and runaways and visiting the wine-shops as well as the mosques."

"I wouldn't go that far. But I always sympathized with Harun al-Rashid, I always admired him."

"Ah, I knew you felt the same fascination as I do. You say that I love order and ceremony without knowing it. You love the dark without knowing it."

His friend hung his head. "I have a taste for the dark, perhaps as brutal a taste as you have. That's why we're friends. We're in sunlight and in darkness to almost the same degree. But what makes you think I don't know it? I know I'm split into two hemispheres, light and dark. I try to bind them together, though, so that I won't be destroyed. Sometimes I'm cunning, sometimes I'm clumsy. But I try. And the world, too. I can't do much. Nobody can do much. But to bind it together, isn't that worth trying? I don't believe there's any order to be found in the world, or in the ridiculous small world of the state. Still, I think it's worthwhile to try to give it one, and an order as free and generous as possible. I don't believe in social order but I want to sustain it. You admire it, you see it billowing out lustrously in this city, and yet you want to escape from it."

"I'm not trying to escape from anything," Rusty insisted.

But Mark ignored his denial. "That's why I'm afraid for you. I see you cutting yourself off from everything, going off into the shadows, growing dimmer, vanishing, disappearing."

"No."

"I see a figure I knew as a hero being tarnished by shadows."

"No."

"And it's all the worse because what I see disappearing is a part of myself."

They got up and went into the coffee-room together, both tall, both erect, with a kind of formal gravity as if they knew that one word more and something might snap between them that never could be mended. Over coffee they gossiped about what was in the evening paper. Another shipload of released prisoners of war had arrived from the other side of the world. There was trouble among a cantonment of refugees who were unwilling to return to their homeland now that it was under a radically different regime. Plans were announced for the meeting in a few months of the new world organization. Gradually the tension between them relaxed. They even began to laugh and joke a little as they discussed what they would do for the evening. In the upshot they didn't decide. They merely set out and found that they were led from one bar to another, their steps becoming more unsteady as the night wore on, their voices louder, their stories more highly coloured. When they rolled home after midnight, they were both so well away and in such good humour that before they went to bed Rusty gave an imitation of Mark receiving an aide-memoire from an ambassador ("Yes, your excellency.

You may stick it up your ass, your excellency") and Mark replied with an imitation of Rusty in a detention barracks (the prisoner laughing to the point of hysteria as he tried to make his mess-tins shine like silver) — and they swore eternal friendship.

Not that it could last. He knew that it couldn't and he thought that his friend did, too. But the end came sooner than he had expected. A few nights later, while Mark was dressing for an official reception, he couldn't find his best cuff-links and called out casually to Rusty to ask if he had seen them. Somehow he thought the question insinuated that he had borrowed them or stolen them, his temper flared up, he began to shout that he wasn't going to stay where he wasn't trusted, and a few minutes later he was throwing his few things into his kit-bag. He wouldn't stop to listen to reason or even to say good-bye. He walked down the stairs without turning to look back. But as he descended, over his shoulder he heard Mark's voice saying, "If you ever need me, I'll still be here."

He didn't know where he was going to go. He shouldn't have lost his temper, he was ready to admit to himself before long as he sauntered through the evening air and cooled off. It was stupid when he didn't have anywhere else to stay and a miserable way to behave towards a friend, into the bargain. Yet he couldn't conceal from himself, either, that it was a relief to be out and completely on his own again. All day it had been hot and he had stayed in the flat until he had been beginning to feel almost stifled, stifled and prickly all over with heat and confinement and a sense of obligation. Now it was cooler. He felt refreshed, invigorated. Although the light would soon fade, it was still strong and decisive and fell slashingly, purposefully before him. He welcomed it with open arms. But what he was only half-conscious of was its mild rebuke, as though the city with its shadows of rich sibilant purple was steadily asking him just above a whisper where he was going, where he was going.

He was going first to the Plaza. He would stay only a few minutes, he told himself. Of course Althea wouldn't be there. But because of her it had something of the savour of what it was he was seeking. If the scent ever went cold, he could pick it up again there. Black and greasy as they were, its stones reminded him of her, of meeting her there, of her limbs, of what she had given him, of how he had been confounded; and what he had known that night was somehow allied with what he was searching for. The colonnade was grimy with assignations. They covered it, silting it over with a rich, dark loam. But out of that marsh had sprung one perfect orchid, delicately veined and coloured and — a great rarity — with a most subtle perfume. A flower flushed with rose and white and of the texture of the evening sky. Why could he not hope that once again the heavens would open and he would be drawn up, that once again his deepest longings would be satisfied?

He waited. Sunset was beginning to possess the sky. The clouds that had been moored and almost motionless all day were coming adrift and were being flushed a deep rose. But the square itself remained untransfigured. It was still rectangular and unilluminated. The faces that he watched flowing through it were heavy with the heat of the day and many of them ugly with worry or fatigue. There seemed to be a ragged procession flowing by of glass eyes and bad teeth and goitrous necks and flat breasts and sagging stomachs and thick ankles and falling arches; a procession without any distinction of face or figure and blotched with almost every human infirmity and deformity. And all of them different: one with a neck as long as a crane's; one round and waddling; one stooped, bleary-eyed, heavily veined; one brittle with years and dry cheeks and bony hands. All of them different, but all of them flawed, imperfect, irredeemably marked with the coarse clay from which they had been made.

Then twilight fell, tilting the square aslant, softening the profiles of the passers-by and making it easier to believe that one of those shadowy figures approaching him under the colonnade might be the one he was hoping for. But none of them yielded that answer to his interrogation. Soon he was aware of little more than a stream of disembodied eyes being blown beneath the arches, vagrant and yet imperiously compelled like a great harvest of locusts being brought to judgment. No, she was not to be found in that wavering and indiscriminate multitude. Perhaps if she were to appear again, it could only be as a disembodied spirit? With the thought of that possibility, he relaxed. Called home from the quest, his gaze grew slack and swung limply, idly, about him. The street lamps had been lit and on the curb not many feet away from him he saw a girl standing by herself. He moved a few paces towards her. She made no answering move in his direction. But she didn't move farther off, either. She was allowing herself to be approached. Did she know it, though? Now that he was closer, he could see that she looked diffident, even a little frightened. If she had been at ease, she might have been almost pretty. Her complexion was good, but her eyes were strained and her lips were compressed. He sidled over a few paces more and stood beside her.

"It's been hot," he said, wondering if she would answer.

"Yes," was all she said, and her tone was as non-committal as the monosyllable itself.

There was a pause, and then he said, "Do you live here or are you from out of town?"

"From out of town. And you?"

"I am, too," he said. He still couldn't be sure. She was wearing a light flowered dress and had a charm-bracelet dangling from her wrist.

There was another pause. But then it was she who spoke, and in a rush and in a voice that sounded on the verge of tears. "Oh, I'm so worried. I was to meet a friend here more than an hour ago and he hasn't turned up. It isn't like him. But I can't wait forever. Oh, it's so lonely being by yourself in a big city."

Rusty took her gently by the arm and said, "Would you like to walk on a little way with me?"

She went with him, obediently, like a child. After they had gone some distance, she asked, "Where are we going?"

"I don't know," he answered. "What part of town are you staying in?"

"I haven't any place to stay yet." She looked slight and young and unprotected.

"Nor have I."

She told him that her parents didn't know that she was in town for the night and would be furious if they ever found out. He told her that he was on the loose. Her look, when she heard him say that, was meditative, almost calculating; but she said with forced gaiety, "Then we're both deserters."

"But you must be serious. Where could you find a place to spend the night?"

At last she said, "I think I know a boarding-house that would take me in." And it wasn't too far away. When they were near it, she said, "If you'd like to, I think you could come in for a little while. But wait till I see whether they can give me a room."

As she stood in the light of the door, silhouetted against it, waiting for someone to answer her ring, again he had the impression of innocence, as though she were a child standing there after singing a carol. In a moment someone came and let her in. Then in no time she was back at the door and beckoning him to come in, too.

The room she had been given was dim and fusty. It smelled of scalded milk, and dust, and dirty towels. It was haunted by dried sweat and dried sperm and the ghosts of half-washed bodies. The floor was covered with cracked linoleum, which in some places had so worn away that the deal boards underneath showed through. The roses in the wallpaper had long since ceased to flower and, like rose-leaves in a country parlour, were brown and crinkly. The bed had brass rails and knobs at both ends and was covered by a faded coverlet which was flesh-pink, except in the many places where it was stained and torn. The only other furniture was a washstand and an upholstered chair pitted irregularly with cigarette-burns.

She sat on the bed with her legs dangling over the side. He took the one chair. But they made hardly more than a pretense of resuming the conversation they had had on the street where their souls had seemed as naked as buds and had been blown about in the dark by loneliness and for a moment had touched. She had the air of waiting for something, while he felt in every vein, in every pore, a storm gathering that had been brewed out of too long continence till his eyes were blinded with cataracts, his horizon seemed livid with cloud-rack, his blood was betraying him into a battlefield or a cauldron that, as it whirled and whirled, could have utterly disintegrated into chaos had it not been anchored by the weight of a heavy shot-tower that, looming out of the dim landscape, dominated it, mastered it more and more. But in every quarter of his body he felt heavy. Each of the muscles at the back of his legs and along his shoulders seemed to weigh as much as a whole ham strung up to smoke. And the fumes had penetrated so that all his sinews were deeply tanned with the frenzy of smoke and powder. A trumpet was speaking not only to his ear but to the swirl of animal excitement that was drenching him through and through. His brains had dissolved. They had spread and scattered their riches through the rest of his body, giving it added gravity. He felt gorged and taut. He was like a panther ready to spring.

As he undressed her, she was unresisting; she seemed concerned most of all that he shouldn't tear her dress. Then she lay back and opened her legs and he entered her, deeply, ravenously. At first she recoiled and withdrew the little that she could from his ferocity, whether in apprehension or indifference it hardly occurred to him to wonder. But he thrust more deeply, more deliberately, even more brutally, pausing at the end of each thrust, staking her to the bed, and only then releasing her momentarily to drive down and impale her once again. After four or five such strokes her reluctance vanished, she became part of the storm, she joined him as part of the storm-torn landscape, of the scud, of the bruised, threshed sky, of the reverberation, of the imminence of deluge. Clasping her legs about the small of his back, she rode with him through thunder, through the drumming rain, into harbour and release.

He lay back, bathed in sweat, and let the darkness cover him. In a minute or two she put out her hand toward him and said, "That was wonderful." Then, when he didn't say anything, she added, "I'm so glad my friend didn't show up. I would have missed you." Her fingers curled about his, but his hand lay heavy and inert so that her fingers were like vine-shoots twining round granite. He was breathing the thick darkness in and out, his lungs were heavy with it, he was beginning to exhale a dark sheltering dream in which he floated, hardly moving. "Now my loneliness is all gone," she murmured. But he felt like a dark world, a separate world, a separate death. And she with whom he had just collided must be another world, another death. The atmosphere that was being recreated about him was lightening a little, there was some shade in it. He could discern outlines, gestures, memories. Was that Althea reigning so mildly among the shades? He didn't know. But he shut his eyes and turned aside from his bedfellow and must have slept a little.

When he awoke it was because she was exploring his body with her hand, dabbling in pools of shadow and returning and going on. Almost at once he was roused and ready. Without a word, he swung himself over and, vaulting like a rider into the saddle, fitted himself to her and was astride and away. Ah, it would be a long course this time, he knew as he settled into a long easy pace. Soon she was shuddering beneath him. But on he went. Twice, three times, it was as if his mount shuddered and sunk under him. But he went on relentlessly till she was moaning and biting and calling on him to finish and he was grasping her by the hair and was coming in strong in a tangle of salt and sea-weed to explode like breakers on a beach.

Then immediately he was asleep. In an oceanic night that nothing could lighten or penetrate. Once he was half wakened by someone moving about in his room; but before he could open his eyes he remembered that the door was firmly locked from the inside and, reassured that no one could have got in, again fell dead asleep. When he next awoke, it was early morning and a light as thin as paper was twisting in through the window. She was moving about, but she called softly to him to go back to sleep because he needed his rest, as she said.

And so he did. But he wanted a cigarette and there was a pack in his tunic pocket, he remembered drowsily. She had gone out by now, he supposed to the lavatory. Half-asleep he got up and walked over to where his clothes were scattered and found his tunic and fished out the cigarettes. As he lay back and watched the smoke twist up from between his fingers, he was reminded of all the reconnaissances he had been on in this ashen zero light and of how cold it had been and of how, even so, his tongue had always been burnt by the first cigarette of the day — or was it by the taste of danger? But something else was moving in his mind as well. Finally he got up and reached out for his tunic again and unbuttoned the pocket. It wasn't there. In a flash, though, he knew where it was. He went over to where her clothes were piled and quickly sifted through them until he came to her purse at the bottom and opened it — and there was his wallet.

At first he was furious. He felt his throat tightening and his fists clenching. Almost at once, though, his passion began to ooze away and he began to think of it differently. Poor kid, she must have been too frightened to ask for money, but before long she would be playing a different tune and saying with a smirk "Well, if you would care to give me a little present ..."; and a few months more and she would be so hardened that she would quote her own price quite brazenly. But now she was too frightened or too ashamed. Well, it was early days ... and a long hard life to look forward to. He took up the wallet and, after counting over his money to see that none was missing, put it back in his tunic and began to get dressed.

When she came back, she was surprised to see him already buckling his belt. She had to take an early train in order to preserve the fiction she had told her family, she explained, but there was no reason why he should leave so early, too. His only answer was to go on dressing with cheerful persistence. In a few minutes she was almost ready and turned to the mirror above the washstand to put on some lipstick. He could see her face in the mirror as she opened her purse to get out her lipstick and compact. Her lips went taut and she let out a little cry.

"Is there anything the matter?" he asked innocently.

"Yes, there is. I've lost something important."

"That's too bad," he grinned. "It wouldn't be my wallet by any chance would it?"

"You dirty skunk!" As she whirled around, veil after veil of dissimulation slipped from her, and her face turned ugly with anger.

"Well, listen to that! You'd think you were the one who had been robbed. What have you to complain about? If you'd only asked me for money, I would have given you some."

"What do you want me to do? Behave like a common street-walker?"

"Well, that's what you are, isn't it?"

She bared her teeth like an animal. "I'll make you pay for that, you rotten no-good bastard. I ought to have known the kind you are. I ought to have clawed your eyes out while I had the chance. I ought to have torn your prick out by the roots."

"Just mind your language," he answered stolidly. "I said that I was willing to give you some money. But another word or two like that and you won't get a penny."

"Oh, yes, I will. You'll give me what I ask for or you'll be picked up by the police within fifteen minutes, lover-boy. And I'll laugh and laugh as I think of you doing time in the glass-house. So hand it over; you know what the charge is. And you're lucky I'm not asking for your ring or your wrist-watch."

"And you're lucky I'm not taking the boots to you, you little tramp," he countered roughly. But he felt more shaken than he could admit: by telling her he was on the loose, he had put himself completely at her mercy. It was the first time he had ever had to pay ransom; and as he took out the money crisply from his wallet and handed it over, the thin early morning light seemed to be seething and hissing around it. Day was breaking like spray against the zero of some icy, unimaginable horizon.

4

He had disposed of his uniform and had replaced it with some civilian clothes he had bought on the black market. They were poorly cut and didn't fit very well, but at least they had the effect of making him less of a mark for the military police and of blending him in with the swelling number of men who had been discharged. He had also found that the black market could supply him with ration-books and an identity-card. With that discovery, his kit was complete and he was ready for a new life.

Now that he had finished shedding one skin and acquiring another, he was freer to look about and to observe the surroundings he had moved to. He had taken a room in a part of the city where foreigners had always gravitated and he began to notice how foreign it was still. Originally, it had been settled by weavers and paper-makers who had migrated here from overseas. They and their families had vanished long ago. But the streets still had foreign names; the restaurants served foreign sauces and exotic drinks, arak, tequila, rice wine, ouzo; on the streets were occasionally to be seen black faces, yellow faces, brown faces as well as white; and every tongue spoken anywhere in the world could be heard here at one time or another. It was only gradually that he began to realize that beneath this surface babel spread a deeper resonance. For all its foreign air, most of the inhabitants of the quarter were native-born. Neither negroes nor bondmen, they had been born free and in temperate latitudes. But entering these precincts, they became aliens. About almost all of them, he noticed that there was something a little furtive and ill-at-ease, as though they were creatures of a forfeited or rejected patrimony. Here they were living like foreigners in the bosom of their homeland.

More and more he came to speculate by what route and with what passport they had made their way to this enclave. In the house where he had taken a room, there was a middle-aged man with closely cropped iron-grey hair. He stayed in his room most of the day and only went out toward evening. As he passed through the hall (picking up a cane from the umbrella-stand before he went out), his bearing was so impressive and military that it was difficult to believe, as Rusty learned in a few days, that he had been dishonourably discharged and now made a living, a meagre living, as a confidence man. Why had he become a petty criminal? Why had he lost his commission? For he must have had a commission; he looked like a retired colonel. And so he had been — or almost. He had been a major, it turned out, and had been discharged for being drunk on parade. But why? Hundreds of officers sometimes appeared drunk on parade and nothing came of it. It was hushed up, finessed, forgotten; indulgent friends took care of it. Why had he lacked friends to cover up for him? Or why had his drunkenness become so flagrant that such friends as he had were powerless to help him? Was there some disappointment that had destroyed him, some fundamental and undying resentment over the terms of enlistment under which his cells had been called up at birth and commanded to do their duty? So Rusty wondered as he watched him swagger out with an air of false authority.

In the case of the girl who had the room at the back of the second floor there was no need to wonder. One night she took an overdose of seconal and the doctor arrived only in time to save her life. When she had returned from the hospital and was recuperating, although still wan and listless, she used to come up to Rusty's room and smoke endless cigarettes and tell him why she wanted so much to die. She had been engaged to a young officer in the navy who had gone down with his ship; and every word she said was an effort to resurrect him from the deep or to join him there. He had looked so handsome in his blue uniform. He had a shy way of smiling and pushing back his cap and slapping his leg with his gloves whenever he was pleased. Whenever he tried to grow a beard it came out red, although his hair was the colour of Rusty's, a glossy brown. But she couldn't stop with details like that. Lying back like a foiled implacable goddess, with cigarette smoke coiling about her, she must try to seize the mortal she had lost, the mortal who had eluded her, more completely, more intimately. When he was stripped, his skin had a reddish glint, she remembered. There was something celtic and coppery and smiling about it, for all his seriousness. When he was lying satisfied above her, she loved to run her fingers along the runnel down his back and through the fine crisp hair curling over his buttocks. Then she could feel his heart beating, sometimes so wildly that it made her anxious. Sometimes she even thought that he had been born to an early death. But not that! Good God, not that! Lying fathoms deep — and still ravaging her, ravaging her! "I don't know what to do. I want to die. I want to die!" she would finish in a paroxysm contorting the square peasant features that should have been almost beautiful.

Then there was the young man on the same floor, pleasant enough looking, who might have been taken for a happy-go-lucky bank clerk, keen at games and likely to get on, had it not been for something loose and devious in his smile and for some tell-tale vanity in what he had to say. In fact, he was a dip, a hook, a pickpocket. The moment always came when he couldn't resist telling you himself, even boasting about it. That was the trade he had taken up when he left the army. And he made a good living from it, or so he claimed. At least he wasn't fool enough to have a steady job. He worked when he liked, he pleased himself. Of course there were some drawbacks to the life as there were to any other. It meant a good deal of night work, because the pickings were fatter and easier after dark when you could go around from one bar or club to another and find many of the clientele in a mood not to worry too much about their wallets. But he liked being abroad at night. And as Rusty listened, he reflected, yes there were many reasons for haunting the streets after nightfall. That was the peculiar season for every one of the lodgers where he was living, that was when they came into their own. They were all nocturnal creatures, night-walkers all of them, moon-men, anglers in the lake of darkness.

But night or day, as he went back and forth, treading the rabbit-warren of alleys, courts, tenements, and passageways that made up the quarter, he had the feeling that it was a separate principality. One in which everyone lay in bed until noon, like royalty. In which there was no industry — and little commerce, except traffic in the pleasure of the senses. In which there were no settled occupations: the labour force consisted of pimps, barrow-boys, out-of-work actors, trumpeters, prostitutes, and — linking them all — underworld runners, who conducted their business merely by sauntering and gossiping, walking a little way and then dropping into a bar, coming out again and going on, sauntering and gossiping. There was milk delivered, and bread, and other commodities; but these things came in from outside and were paid for with money either filched from the good burgesses who lived on the other side of the wall or earned by catering to whatever palate they had for food or drink or lechery.

As the days went by, he came to know the whole quarter more amply, its boundaries, its customs, its liberties. He learned where cigarettes could be bought even when supplies had run out everywhere else, where it was possible to get liquor after hours, which barmen and waiters could be trusted and which had the reputation of being informers for the police, the doorways in which plainclothesmen sheltered after dark and where their patrol-car was usually drawn up, the houses which pandered to this craving or that, the passageways by which you could escape from one to another in the event of a raid, the hours at which the coffee-stall was frequented by street-walkers, then by musicians after finishing their last performance, then by guardsmen before returning to barracks, the whole circuit of the hours between the time when it was wheeled up at evening until it was trundled away as night was paling into the morning twilight.

It stood in a side-street alongside a ruined church, and whenever Rusty stopped there before going to bed and looked out over the area where the nave was flattened and on toward the filmy tower that still hung against the sky at the furthest outskirts of the quarter, the bareness of the space surrounding and isolating a few tiny jets of light (in the street-lamps and underneath the coffee-urns) made him think of a courtyard, a courtyard for travellers, for arabs stopping with their caravans in the middle of a desert journey, a caravanserai that with its momentary comfort only illuminated the immensity and hopelessness of the journey.

It might almost have been another race that lived within this quarter, it sometimes seemed to him, a people so different that they should have been distinguished by a separate pigment, who had more in common with the beasts than the machines, who were accustomed to lie down at night not far from goats and camels and got up with something goatish still clinging to their skin, whose heads instead of being full of figures (of insurance premiums, dividend payments, export earnings) were coloured with images of animal delight-couplings in the forest free from contingency or consequence, lizards mating in the blaze of absolute noon — and whose lives, by mocking the tables, seemed to fall quite outside the meshes of probability. The city enveloped the quarter where they lived, washing round and through it but unable to obliterate it. It might have been a reef or shoal where a different species was still managing to exist. Or a casbah in the middle of a modern city where an alien race lived on uninflected, almost even untouched, by the progress sprawling, brawling, proliferating around it.

Merging in his mind with other quarters, other cities that he had seen during the war, it would sometimes shimmer in the heat till it became the citadel of a different religion, where believers in another faith had migrated, bringing with them their own idea of what was holy. They might have been hemmed in, he fancied, by a more powerful orthodoxy and forced to defend these narrow limits against persecution. Time after time efforts had been made to dislodge them. A crusade would be preached against the outcast faith, and the believers who held it would be put to the sword — men, women, and children. A few months afterwards, though, there would be a rumour that the sacred tablets had been preserved, that the forbidden rites were being celebrated in a cellar; and before long the faithful would grow to something like their old numbers, the walls would be rebuilt, until everything was much the same as before and the fortress of the persecuted faith looked out scornfully over the multitude who beleaguered it.

Gradually he came to realize that many of the denizens of the quarter were deserters like himself. Sometimes in a bar he would find himself in conversation and the talk would flow on casually until he noticed a slight discrepancy in the stranger's story, a slit not very gross but wide enough to admit a knife-blade just the same, and he would lose interest since what he was listening to wasn't true; or he would ask some questions that made the stranger gaze into his drink and bring the conversation fumblingly to a stop. Once when he asked an innocent but particularly incautious question, his companion for the moment hurriedly put down his glass, picked up his raincoat, and walked out. It took him a minute or two to guess that he had been mistaken for a plainclothes detective. He smiled to himself and thought little of it and went on drinking.

The time passed carelessly. He slept late and then, if he felt like it, walked to the palace or in one of the parks. It was beautiful summer weather, almost cloudless day after day. He liked to watch the swans and the children sailing boats and then to stretch out and drowse under one of the elms. During the daytime he avoided the Plaza because he didn't want to run into Mark hurrying to or from the Ministry with a brief-case in his hand. But he often haunted it idly at night when he couldn't be recognized so readily and when it was easier to imagine that Althea might possibly reappear.

Although he wandered at will through the summer streets, he was tethered to the special aromatic quarter where he had a room, and he returned there not only to sleep but to eat and drink as well. He tried almost all the inexpensive restaurants and was in and out of almost all the bars, snuffing their individual savours. In time, though, he took one restaurant down a back street as his own and became habituated to one particular bar. He chose it because the barman seemed friendly and because there was usually a table in the corner where he could sit by himself and spread out a newspaper to read if he wanted to.

The heat wave was accompanied by a crime wave. The papers were full of indignation about the rising totals of thefts, armed robberies, burglaries, and of appeals to the authorities to take effective action. "Rid our streets of these wolves!" demanded one editor. "Yesterday morning a bank messenger was robbed in broad daylight and left bleeding on the pavement. The previous day an elderly woman was held up at the point of a gun and knocked unconscious by thieves who escaped with her purse. The day before, the gangsters attacked a delivery van and got away with a rich haul of furs. In none of these cases has any arrest been made. If this is allowed to continue, our streets will revert to a state of savagery where no law-abiding citizen can feel safe. The police excuse their ineffectiveness by claiming that the city is full of unapprehended deserters and of unregistered firearms. That may be so. But the time for excuse is over. What is needed now is action."

He put down the paper and lit a cigarette. He could imagine the kind of man who had written that tirade. He pictured him as a pot-bellied journalist who had spent the war assuring the public that our forces had "retired to prepared positions" when a brigade or two had been so cut up by shell and mortar-fire that half of them were lying mangled in the open while the rest were cowering anywhere or fleeing for their lives. He had seen too much to believe the newspapers any more, and he didn't believe them now. There was no reason to think there were so many deserters in the city as all that or that any but a very few of them were criminals. His own case was different. But most of those who were on the loose had deserted because they were afraid to go into action and had been hiding out ever since. If they were afraid of action, were they likely to have the guts to rob a delivery van or hold up a bank messenger? Perhaps a few of them might have been driven to crime when they had run through their money and had found difficulty in establishing a good enough identity to get them a job. But most of them were probably as innocent as he was. Still, he felt glad that he had drawn so much of his back pay before he lit out.

A few days later when he was sitting in the same accustomed place, he couldn't help overhearing a conversation that confirmed him in what he thought. Two young men of about his own age had come in and had taken the table next to his. What first attracted his attention was one saying to the other, "What will you do when your money runs out?"

He lowered his paper so that he could see who it was that was speaking. It was a thin young man with light downy hair and such a scrawny appearance that he might well have been pigeon-breasted beneath his suit. His companion was more fully fleshed and looked slackly out in the world with inoffensive watery eyes.

"Oh, I don't know," came the reply. "I guess I'll go and work in a brewery. They don't ask any questions there. And they give you all the beer you can drink as well as your wages."

"What about working in the market? I hear they need men there and don't care where they get them from."

"Yes, that's a good go, too. But I think I'd rather work in a brewery. The hours are better. And I'd like the beer. Or I might go to work for a few weeks hauling crates in this exhibition they're setting up, 'Homes for Ex-Servicemen.' But I don't intend to work long. Just enough to get a little money to tide me over."

"Perhaps by then there'll be a general amnesty."

"Perhaps." But the echo didn't sound very convinced — or very concerned either.

The scrawnier of the two was less complacent. "I sometimes wonder what I'll do if they don't declare an amnesty soon. I want to go home. I hear my own name so seldom I sometimes wonder who I am. I'm afraid, I'm afraid of losing myself."

"If you want to get your name back, all you have to do is hand yourself in," his stolid companion replied ruthlessly. "Then you'll get two years in the glass-house. But you'll have your own name all right. And a number into the bargain."

The slighter of the two defaulters seemed so nearly ready to cry that Rusty put up his paper again and turned over the pages to look at the football scores.

That night he dreamed of a mild, featureless landscape with clouds through which he moved effortlessly like a swimmer through moonlit surf. Over it reigned a figure with suave, undulant flanks. Although he couldn't see her face, he knew perfectly who it was — and was pleased. It was a landscape naked of all striving or desire and he dolphined through it as though he were native to it and at home. Then the grey mildness convolved into a labyrinth that was pearly and resonant as a shell. Then different figures appeared — or was it only one? — a football player leaping into the air in a coloured jersey, an acrobat superbly lithe and balanced, treading out over the frothy waves, an athlete banded around his waist with gold who was about to spring and vault triumphantly over a bar or bull. When he awoke, his heart and limbs were still calmed with the brightness from the figure whom he had seen and recognized. So he had dreamt of her several times. Yet he knew that the more he dreamt of her, the less intently he tried to find her, even the less he believed that finding her might ever be possible. He lay quietly in the early morning light, desiring nothing, anxious about nothing. He wasn't concerned that his identity-card bore a name other than his own or that he could never get an insurance card under his own name to allow him to seek a job. He didn't want a job and he didn't care about his name. Anyway, it was engraved on the back of the medal in his kit-bag; that was enough. Nor was he afraid of losing himself. If that was the cost, he was ready to pay it. But he was not losing himself, he was finding himself. He felt now as though nothing could touch him.

In the afternoon as he walked in the park, his flesh seemed crusted with gold. Full and perfect as the sunlight was, it was broken by the tall shade trees and fell waveringly through the leaves on the lovers and the children and the old. But wherever he chose to move, it was continuous and unflawed. He was his own sun, a sun generating so much brightness that it could not all be absorbed by the already heavily laden air but accumulated on his flesh in thin layers, banding him like a ceremonial athlete. Where it wasn't protected by shade, the grass had been scorched by day after day of continuous heat, and there were bare patches where the children had been playing all summer. In spite of the cloudless sky, the dust created a haze which suggested the thin smoke rising from some kind of arena, a bull-ring or an amphitheatre, where at any moment ceremonial beasts might be loosed for combat. Under the trees along the palace wall it was as cool as though an awning had been spread for privileged onlookers; but in the open the heat rose like a jungle. Coarse red lilies assailed the light with animal cries, flaunting their praise of lust untrammelled by duty or affection, wrestling angrily with the sun, coiling a whole barbarous empire around them. Their leaves rose stiff and leathery and cactus-like, shaping themselves into a clump of crude, primitive broadswords. Frowningly he walked through the heat, welcoming it with sovereign answering energy, half expecting that wild animals might appear (as though this were still a park of royal beasts gathered from all over the world) and wondering whether, if they did, he would find himself as their destined antagonist, vaulting over them, goading them, destroying them, or else as their brother and ally. It was a light for lions and leopards, for animals that a king might keep, and his own animal heat exalted in it.

By the time dark had fallen he felt a great thirst in his throat; but whether it was for drink or company or contact, he didn't know. Since leaving Mark's he had kept more and more to himself. He passed the time of day with the owner of the little shop where he bought newspapers and cigarettes. Occasionally the drowned sailor's fiancée would knock on his door and come in and talk for fifteen minutes, and always on the same theme, while he listened sympathetically but hardly saying a word. The barman in the bar he frequented was a gross, amusing ruffian who had been everywhere and seen everything, and sometimes when business was slack they would lounge on opposite sides of the bar and swap stories. But whole days passed when he hardly spoke to a soul. He didn't feel superior to others who lived in the quarter, but he couldn't entirely conceal from himself that he felt some distaste for many of them. They had their own problems and predicaments, and he was no one to sit in judgment. But after he had been speaking for a few minutes to a type whom he suspected had convicted himself of cowardice by what he had done or had fallen to a point where he would do anything for money, his honour felt subtly affronted. So he withdrew more and more into himself and became warier of chance conversations. Perhaps, too, he was becoming warier of giving himself away.

Anyway, tonight he needed noise and company. Well, there were always the catacombs, all the dives that spread through the vaults and cellars of the quarter, as many as a thousand of them, someone had told him, although that was difficult to believe. The one he chose was already as packed with bodies as the hold of a slaver. And almost as dark: except for the tiny stage it was lit only by candles thrust into the necks of bottles, one for each table. He found a place at last at the back and after a few minutes his eyes became accustomed to the gloom. Some of the clientele were familiar to him as residents of the quarter. He spotted the young pickpocket, for example, whose room was on the same floor as his; and after catching Rusty's eye he was so disconcerted that he got up and left. But others of the audience were from the other side of the border, from the world of schedules and obligations, and had come on here in dinner-clothes in a momentary mood of licence for furtive, half-acknowledged instincts.

A sallow pianist was banging out a blues tune to which he fitted new words.

Pick my pocket
Comb my thicket
Steal my wallet
You can fill it
In one ear and out the other
I don't care which way you hunt
In and out and through ...

(and then spreading out his legs from the piano stool and leaning back and leering at the audience)

What's a word that rhymes with punt?

After the applause died down and the waiters had had time to take new orders and fill them, the pianist came back, and bending over the piano with an air of romantic absorption, began a melody in a quite different tone and rhythm.

Blow, blow, soft breezes blow
Ever so softly, sweet and low,
I have a dandelion, want to blow?

The music went on imploringly, one verse after another as simply as a folk tune, but with rising fervour till it ended in a great burst of passion that with the final chord brought the pianist bolt-upright to his feet, shivering and shaking stiffly all over, like a tree shedding its leaves, with his hands fluttering helplessly at his sides. Huddled anonymously in the gloom, the audience thundered out its applause, calling and stamping; and the slave-ship seemed to be wallowing darkly, almost awash.

A man at the next table, already far gone and glassy-eyed, reached out and offered him his flask; and Rusty took a long pull from it gratefully in place of the watered whisky that the waiters had been serving him in the conniving twilight. Almost for the first time that night he felt a lift from what he had been drinking. In a few minutes a willowy negress made her entrance, followed by a drummer, a trumpeter, and the pianist. At once a savage din broke out from the three musicians as the dancer tantalizingly undipped and let fall the flimsy bra and panties she was wearing and threw out into the audience the roses she had pinned in her hair, and then, writhing and rippling, pouted forward with her torso, gyrating to the music, driven back by imagined pleasure, coming back for more, gyrating faster, till the moist lips that she half-opened with her thighs were the centre of a red vortex in which all the audience was involved, a Venus fly-trap that none of them could entirely escape, a tell-tale pathway to delirium. Body and soul, she was endeavouring to draw the whole audience up inside her, to be impregnated with them enormously; and the music was assisting fiercely, implicating them, working to dilate their pupils, to quicken their pulse-beats, to make them participate with her impossibly. And in the dark they could be felt responding, with glazed eyes and an occasional hiss of indrawn breath. But she had hardly finished and the applause had not yet died down when the man at the next table held out his flask again and murmured huskily, "Not much if you've seen the donkey-ride at Alexandria, eh?" Rusty took another long pull from the flask and felt it scorching the membranes of his throat and knew how full of frustration the air was. It reeked with defeated desires. It was blue with the stale breath of impossibility. As the performance became more abandoned and approximated more closely to imagined felicity, the darker loomed the moat. The pinnacles on the other side still gleamed delectably, but they were as remote as ever and more heartbreaking. It was the taunting distance they maintained like mountain-peaks that seemed to vein with icy flaws the close underground air, warm from tightly packed bodies, and make it so unexpectedly chill and lonely.

Now a slight young man, not much more than a boy, was coming out to sing some songs unaccompanied. With one part of his mind Rusty wondered whether it was the youth he had noticed under the arches some weeks before peering dazedly into an empty plate-glass window. It might have been. He was wearing a black turtle-neck sweater and brown corduroy trousers. There was a big mop of fair hair falling over his forehead that he shoved back before starting to sing. His voice was uncertain but pure and clean, and he sang as though to himself, forgetful of the audience. Rusty was so engrossed with the fading peaks of his own private heaven, so bowed down with their disappearance, that he hardly heard any of the first song, a ballad about a wanderer. But as the boy began again, the spotlight shifted to keep him in focus, and Rusty lifted his head to listen.

Last night I got a letter
Telling me to come home....

But it was only a dream
A prisoners dream
I wish that I were dead

The last time he had heard that song, a soldier was singing it to a guitar. One evening before going back into action. The regiment was in rest but was on twenty-minutes notice to move. Grumblingly the pup-tents had been rolled up and stowed away. The kitchen had been dismantled, and the orderly room. The signals trucks were lined up and ready to roll. A few drivers were still gassing up the last of the vehicles, but for the most part there was nothing to do. Soldiers were wandering about aimlessly, with time on their hands and yet not free, confined to a few fields like convicts in a prison yard. Then Sandy went over to the back of one of the trucks and got out his guitar and sat down on an ammunition case and began to play. It was a little while before his strumming had any effect, the company was so edgy and irritable, the new reinforcements wondering what it would be like in action and how they would acquit themselves, the old hands gloomily canvassing their chances, convinced that the odds against their coming out alive were lengthening with each additional time they went under fire, while everywhere there was murmuring that it wasn't right for the regiment to be called back into action so soon. But one by one soldiers began to stroll over to the music. And then a voice caught up the tune, caught it and hurled it cleanly into the air, sparkling and leaping. And then other voices joined in, not so clear and true, but strong, and gaining in confidence and volume, until in the radiant evening air there was a bonfire blazing, a bonfire of spirit and defiance, that went on and on, from one tune to another, as though there could be no end to the resinous stuff that was feeding it, as though there was an inexhaustible courage that blazed out the more fiercely the more it was buffeted and confined. At last

Sandy had to ask for a rest. While he paused, the mood passed, the fire burned down, everyone could see that the gold in the late evening sky was darkening. When he began again, the tune was slower and sadder and no one would join him, so he went on singing to himself, drawling over his guitar.

Last night I got a letter....
But it was only a dream
A prisoner's dream....

Two days later, he remembered — he had seen him, he had helped bury him — Sandy was found lying face-down in the open, his big awkward limbs contorted, the shit still oozing from a wound in the small of his back as big as a stove-lid.

I wish that I were dead.

Now the song was curling up in the gloom, bright, elusive, final, floating like a wisp of bright hair in the heavy smoke-filled atmosphere, reminding the prisoners of their isolation, of their shackles, of how they were shackled to brightness and despair. In spite of the spotlight, few in the audience were looking at the singer. They were either sunk in on themselves, groping for a paradise that must exist but that baffled and eluded them, or else were gazing vacantly at the low, murky ceiling. The air was like vinegar. There were grey shapeless things growing in it. It was clouded with failure. He took another long pull from the flask that had been held out to him again and paid his bill and went out.

On the pavement the crowd was still thick and close. It seemed to be moving aimlessly round and round like a slow, sad sargasso in the midst of a larger ocean, whose murmurings could be faintly heard further out. But he hardly noticed. He was conscious of little more than the whisky signalling hoarsely through his fibres and of the thrust of his bones and muscles, rapacious as a gladiator's. The network of nerves and brain-cells slung over his frame might have spoken to him differently. But excitability was crackling through his synapses, his nerves were electric, they enfolded him like a scarlet coat that was burning, burning. And his bowels of pity, of sympathy? He might have taken different counsel from them if they had not seemed haunted by worms, enflamed, gnawed to desperation by unending parasites. He was drawn on by the momentum in his own heavy limbs, by loneliness, by the gleaming pinnacles that he knew existed but that he could no longer reach, enticing, unapproachable, but never to be surrendered. He was drawn on blindly. He needed to be slavishly awash and adrift and drowned. He needed to be gorged and drenched with night.

Till he was lying face downward in a pool of sweat, exhaustion, slime. He didn't remember how he had got there and he hardly cared. He had noticed so little about who it was he had picked up that she might have been a mulatto for all he knew. She lay beside him in the pouring dark, but he was so little aware of her that she might have vanished. Vanished as completely as he had himself. He had slipped into another element. He heard nothing, saw nothing. Appearances were gone. They had been stripped away as the flash and then the bang of artillery firing were stripped away by a flash-spotter, watching them carefully and measuring them with a stop-watch in his hand, peeling them off one after another like a rind and throwing them away, until he had the essence he was looking for. All that was left to him now was fume, smoke, an element that might have existed before creation, before the continents were formed, before the dry land was separated from the sea. He had descended into the fumes of an ancient, oracular cleft, into the sacred dark that he had always surmised must lie at the heart of this beleaguered quarter, its tablets of law, the vapour on which the whole fastness rested. Sometimes he seemed to be gazing through great pillars, as in a frontispiece, on a wide sea; but it was a sea without any shore, without any currents, without any stars to steer by. And then again he could see nothing, nothing at all. There were no distinctions, no differences, nothing picked out by light or shade, no marks, no signs. And time was gone, too. It was in rags, it meant nothing. How long did this phase of darkness last — twelve hours? twenty-four? thirty-six? two days? three days? He didn't know. Nor how he got food or drink. For certainly he went on drinking: alcohol was part of the slippery ambiguous haze in which he lived. Occasionally it parted, but only enough for him to see the clots like mulberries on his chest where she had bitten him or, a little further off, the coiled snake tattooed on his forearm, his snake and dagger still guarding him; and then the mist closed in again. Familiar as he grew with the dark, he was never allowed to make out the far side of the room or even the outlines of so much as a chair or a wardrobe. In time images were to come to him, but they were furnishings brought by the night itself, shapes that it had spawned, things created, it would seem, out of nothing. Lying on his back, he saw a shower of rays as actinic and intense as from the sun blazing down at midday on the sand of an August beach, but a shower not of light — of darkness — a shower mastering him, filling all his pores with darkness, burning him black. Or another image of droves of beasts on the beach ramping by with black manes. Or — it may have been hours later — a peak glittering with ice that in the doom of light was eerily iridescent, with violet, blue, green, even a few veins of crimson here and there, the pillars of rock, black, jagged, volcanic, the ice stretched taut between them, taut and flying as a sail, drumming in the wind, and slippery as a membrane; and then a whole jungle of peaks, range after range, impenetrable, unscalable, with no hint of any habitable valley below them or any vegetation or succour. Then darkness again, total darkness, as though the climber had slipped and fallen. He didn't know how much later it was — he might have slept a little — that he wakened to gaze down at himself from a great height. He was there and yet not there. He recognized himself, but there was no substance to what he saw — in any of the shapes it took. Now he seemed, far down there on the grey sandy beach, to be lying like the carcass of a fish, his bones picked white by the gulls; now there was nothing left of him but a thin grey network of nerves, the light reticulations hardly showing on the sand; now he was an empty tattered fishnet stretched out to be dried and mended; now he was merely the netted mackerel ripple left by the waves in the sand itself, hardly visible in the owlish light and soon to be washed away by the incoming tide. Then again complete darkness. What time was it? He didn't know. There was no clock ticking anywhere. Even the ticking of his own pulse seemed to have been suspended. He couldn't tell whether it was night or day. If someone had brought a clock-face a few inches from his eyes and shown him the hands standing at two o'clock, he wouldn't have known whether it was early morning or afternoon. He was as adrift as a patient in a fever who has been asleep a long time and wakes in a darkened room to wonder whether it is the middle of the night when the crisis is most likely to come or still day with help close at hand. He could hear nothing. But then out of the silence he seemed to be conscious of a voice, a woman's voice, a voice crying, "Rusty, Rusty," softly, imploringly. It wasn't from anywhere in the room. That was as still as a vault. After the last furious bout she had passed into a profound sleep. No, it came from somewhere out of the grey world of shadows. He couldn't recognize it but he was touched and moved by its pleading, by its repeating his name so softly, so imploringly, with so little reproach. He was awake, now, broad awake, and almost weeping.

He hardly noticed that he brushed his eyes. Then he glanced down at his outstretched body on the bed. It was lucky he was strong enough to stand all that punishment, he thought with a wry flicker of amusement; and he remembered, how a tough little soldier, a real little scrapper, had said to him once, "For a poor boy, all he's got is his body." How right he was, he thought grimly as he prowled around the room collecting his watch and his wallet, making sure it hadn't been rifled, seeing that the money he had given her was still lying on top of her dress, and then quietly letting himself out.

It was night. There was no one on the streets. The quarter was deserted. His watch had stopped, but he knew that it must be late, very late, for this was a part of the city where there was coming and going almost all night long. But now there was not a soul. The restaurants were shut and padlocked; there were no lights beckoning down cellar stairs or through swaying curtains; bins of refuse were stacked gauntly at the edge of the pavement waiting to be collected. In the still night air a faint odour was given off by the quarter. After their long heavy frenzy, his senses had awakened preternaturally alert and acute; and what they caught was an odour of decaying fish, or crushed and fly-blown damsons, of spilled cinnamon and nutmeg. It might have risen from a city built on shoals and around lagoons, from a city whose fortunes had been founded on the trade in spices, whether brought overseas in great carracks or by desert routes overland on camel's back. And the fragrance, subtly compounded and decaying, that hung in the air was imbedded in a sea of bitumen, in the heat still rising from the matrix of softened asphalt on the roadway. He snuffed the air. He seemed to be coming back from a long journey, and he kept looking for landmarks — like the spire of the ruined church. His mouth was dry. He felt weatherbeaten. It would be good to see something familiar. As they hunted for the spire, his eyes went roving above the rooftops and, not finding it, slid into the skirts of the sky and engaged with the lowest stars and fell back, wincing, as though those fires held a rebuke not only for him but for everything human, for everything that had been broken from the stem of unconsciousness, for the memories wakened by the tang of cinnamon, for the sense of loss, and for the frenzy to recapture what might be unattainable.

Then the silence opened out, and he was by the ruined church with its tower branching over him. Its own delicately contrived and suspended astronomy seemed to be falling in a cascade of blossoms, blanched and melancholy, that made the empty streets more lonely. He hurried on, hoping that the coffee-stall might still be in its usual spot and still open. It was not only open, he found when he reached it; it was the centre almost of a tiny carnival, a five-pointed star of light and hilarity. There were two guardsmen and two civilians and a young man in a white shirt and a soiled apron serving in the stall; and they were gathered and riding in mirth like a carousel.

"Jesus, I'm telling you," one of the guardsmen was saying as he came up, "when she said she wanted me to wear my riding-boots and my spurs, I couldn't believe it. I thought she was daft. She was serious, though, dead serious. I tried to put her off by saying that that would cost extra. But she said she didn't mind. I think she was loaded with it anyway. So there I am mother-naked, except for my riding-boots, hard and shiny, coming up over my knees and my spurs jingling out behind me, and wondering all the time what would the sergeant say. Hell, why should I care! Ride 'em! Ride 'em!"

His crackling laughter stopped for a moment as the newcomer came up and was silently interrogated to see whether he was abandoned enough to be trusted with those confidences. Rusty must have easily passed this reverse inspection for the guardsman went on with hardly a break.

"And when I was leaving, she gave me a packet big enough to keep me in drinking-money for two or three weeks. Now let that be a lesson to you! That's what comes of always being smart on parade. And don't you forget it. Never once on charge. Boots spotless, breeches and tunic pressed, belt pipe-clayed, spurs sparkling. The pride of the regiment!"

"You mean that's what comes of always being as randy as a stallion," the other guardsman put in good-naturedly.

"Well, listen to who's talking," shot back his mate sarcastically. "You'd think you spent every evening poring over a hymn-book."

"Oh, I do all right. I get along."

"You get along. I'll tell the frosty, fucking world you do. How much did you rake in tonight?"

"Enough. But I had to work for it. I was done like a dinner."

"I feel sorry for you. My heart bleeds." He took off his cap with a flourish and passed it around like a collection plate. "Wouldn't you like to help a poor destroyed veteran, survivor of twenty-five campaigns and untold battles, including eleven rapes, thirty-three seductions, a hundred and seventeen fornications, and God knows how many unnatural offences. So what was it tonight?"

"Well, if you want to know, I really did have to work for it tonight. In more ways than one. I finally had to slug him to get any money."

"But you came away with the loot. I never doubted it. So what are you complaining about?" And then turning to the two civilians, one ginger-haired, the other thick-set with a broken nose, who had been joining in the hilarity but hadn't been saying anything, "Don't you wish you were back in the army instead of being on the loose? With three square meals a day, all free, and a free bed and free clothes and plenty of juicy pickings to be had after dark?"

"Yes, and getting up at six in the morning," replied ginger pertly, "and cleaning out the stables and scraping the barrack-room floor with old razor-blades and polishing, polishing till everything is like a mirror and you could scream. That's all for the birds!"

Rusty was only half listening. He took a few sips of watery coffee and turned and leaned with his back against the bare wooden counter and looked out and wondered how soon it would be day. Were the stars beginning to pale a little? Not yet, he thought. And the faint, hooded light from the coffee-stall was still as ruthlessly clipped in by the dark as ever, it ventured out as weakly and pitifully into the ruined surrounding space, the tiny star in which he stood was still completely lost and engulfed. Yet there were some signs of morning. A few birds that would never be noticed in the daytime could be heard rustling in the dark leaves and shaking the sleep out of their throats and rehearsing a welcome for some great appearance that hadn't yet been announced to anyone but them.

His attention drifted back to what was being said. Now it was the heavier and more thick-set of the two civilians who was speaking. "So I climbed in through the kitchen window and slipped along the hall and up the stairs and found the money just where I'd been told it would be. I was checking to see I had got all there was when the silly bitch woke up and turned on the light and was about to scream. I stopped that. She was sitting up in bed with her mouth wide open but not a sound coming out. She was paralysed, I think, because she couldn't see me although she knew I was there. I was standing against the wall just a little behind her; and I reached out and covered her mouth with one of my gloves and then with my other hand I hit her on the back of the neck, not hard, about as hard as you'd hit a fish you had dangling over the side of a boat; and then she went limp. She'll be all right in a few hours, though. And she'll never know what hit her. That's the beauty of it. Oh, there's plenty you can do and get away with it if nobody knows who you are."

Yes, there's plenty you can do if nobody knows who you are, Rusty reflected. But he felt like moving on, he didn't know why, whether it was because he was tired, or because what he had heard was sitting uneasily on his stomach. He wanted to move on anyway and be by himself and get home and get to bed.

That evening, after he had spent most of the day sleeping, he went out and made for his usual bar and sat down in the corner by himself with a drink and the paper. Sure enough, there was a report of the robbery. He caught the headline, "Victim of Brutal Assault," and read on:

> A middle-aged woman is lying critically ill in Our Lady of Mercy Hospital as the result of a brutal attack by a cat-burglar in the early hours

> of this morning. The victim, who is still unconscious, sustained multiple fractures of the skull and may also have suffered damage to some of her upper vertebrae. According to a spokesman at the hospital, the full extent of her injuries will not be known until further x-rays have been taken. Her identity is being withheld until the next of kin have been informed.
>
> Apparently the burglar gained entry to the house through a back window which was found pried open when the police examined the premises this morning. The victim was sleeping alone in the house … conjectured she was wakened as the burglar was searching her bedroom … considerable sum of money believed to be missing. No clue … which might lead to the assailant's apprehension … police investigation still continuing. Detectives on the case … inclined to think the crime was the work of a deserter.

His eyes slid away from the last sentence and wandered evasively through the rest of the news. An angry quarrel had broken out at the first meeting of the new world organization. The frontier of Persia was threatened. An increase in the butter ration had been announced. An official enquiry was being instituted into the death of a prisoner at one of the detention barracks.

He knew that the savagery he felt in himself was different, it came from different sources, it was moving towards different ends, it was different, different. But he wanted desperately to be reassured. The scene around the coffee-stall had now turned a deep red in his imagination. Those great red mouths grinning and baring their fangs were haunting him; they were like animals that had come out of the jungle and were gloating around a water-hole, replete and sated with carnage; and he remembered they had accepted him as one of themselves. He was blind enough, God knows, but not so cruel and blind as that. There was some star reigning over him that drove him on to frenzy — and not so much a star as a great full moon. He was not utterly abandoned, not utterly bestial. But they had taken him in and welcomed him! What if his blindness should thicken? What if it were thickening at this very moment? And could he be sure that they had always been so different from what he was now? Perhaps they had once felt, too, the estrangement from something perfect; perhaps everyone in the world had suffered at some time and in some degree from the lesion he was suffering from now; perhaps that secret lay coiled at the core of the world as it whirled and ruined on, at the heart of a soldier murdered in prison and at the heart of his murderers, at the heart of turbulent frontiersmen in Persia; perhaps it was that that was preparing new wars in the very bosom of the squalling peace?

He couldn't resolve it. His fantasy swirled before him, vague, indistinct, but vast and frightening as a nebula enlarged and brought close by the lenses of a telescope, a wild, angry crab or tarantula. Through its flailing claws he could hardly see what he was reading. The print was blurred, almost blotted out, as he leafed through the pages abstractedly. But however filmed his eyes might be, they couldn't entirely avoid the impress of a single word that stood out starkly just under the masthead. "Intolerable," the editor was fulminating. "The police know the quarter where most of the deserters are harbouring. Then why don't they act? Are they afraid?" There was no need to read on to the end; he could fill in well enough the rest of the protest.

He got up and went to the bar for another drink. Business had slackened and the regular bartender, who had been too busy to serve him when he first came in, moved down to the end of the bar to fill up his glass.

"Well, where have you been all of this time?" he greeted him jovially. "But don't bother answering. I can see for myself. All I need to do is to look at those pouches under your eyes, they tell me everything I want to know."

Rusty tried to smile back genially, if non-committally, in response to the barman's broad wink. But he didn't feel like smiling. What was still swirling out in front of him was hurting his eyes. They felt bloodshot. And on the other side of the counter the barman loomed through the haze as gross as a butcher. His huge, freckled hands might have been stained with gore, his leather apron might have been splattered with entrails and offal.

"So, you're not talking, eh?" the barman rallied with friendly gruffness, standing back with his hands in his pockets, a towel draped over his bulging forearms. "All right, have it your own way. Probably just as well." And then as a particularly succulent recollection overcame him, his big beer belly began to shake and the ripples spread slowly up to the folds of his thick neck and to the sparse red tufts of hair on the top of his head. "Believe it or not, but I knew a young punk once who managed to get his discharge that way. Kept at it night after night till his nerves were so shot that he had himself paraded before the M.O. He baffled the poor M.O. to a standstill, and after a few days he was passed on to the trick-cyclists. They put him through every test they could think of, took him back and forth over his life history till they knew more about it than he did himself. The only thing about him they didn't know was what he was doing every night behind the lilac bushes. It's dogged as does it. And he was dogged. Every night with a little slut behind the bushes, and every morning as meek as milk with the trick-cyclists questioning him hour after hour, trying to find out why his nerves were screaming like piano-wires. It's wonderful what you can do if you stay in the groove. At last they knew they were licked, and he was given his discharge. Stout fellow. But that was a discharge that was really earned. With palms. With bar. Should have been mentioned in despatches. He told me it took more out of him than a dozen campaigns."

Under cover of the bartender's final gust of laughter, Rusty tried to escape and move back to the corner. But as the giant rumbled to the other end of the bar to serve a customer who had just come in, he called in a stage whisper over his shoulder, "Don't go. I have a little proposition for you."

When he came back, he lowered his voice and leaned over the bar confidentially, almost conspiratorially, if anyone so massive and obvious could ever be taken for a conspirator.

"I wondered if you'd like to make a little money?" he asked.

"I suppose almost everyone could do with a little more money," Rusty replied. He wasn't in the mood for talking with the bartender tonight. He wanted to move away and be by himself.

"But how about you? It's you I'm interested in. Would you like to make a little money?"

"I suppose so. It all depends."

"Depends on what? I rather fancied you probably needed some money."

"Maybe. Maybe not. It all depends on what your proposition is." He was growing tired of all this fencing. "What would I have to do?"

The barman leaned even closer, so that Rusty noticed for the first time the wiry red hairs growing out of his nostrils. "It wouldn't be much. Just a few light taps with a hammer." The barman paused for that to sink in, his great bulk swaying uneasily over the bar, his eyes narrowed, as though he wasn't sure whether he had gone too far or not far enough.

A few light taps with a hammer? Was that supposed to mean something to him? Rusty wondered. The swirling cloud in front of him had disappeared, but it had left his eyeballs aching and strangely unfocused. They were searching for something that had surrounded him and had now moved out into the far distance where he couldn't find it. He was having difficulty in grasping what the barman was saying. His attention kept trying to circumvent the figure looming on the other side of the bar and wandering past him to the shelves of bottles and the cut-glass mirror at his back.

"A few light taps with a hammer?" he repeated. "And what would I be paid for it?"

"Your fair share. You'd get a fifth of the total haul."

Now he had come to the point. And now Rusty felt all his senses sharpen to a hard tip of anger. He was aware of his fists beginning to clench and the muscles in his upper arm beginning to contract. A second more and he would have knocked the barman's teeth out — and have hardly known what he had done. It had happened a hundred times before, that immediate reaction to something he considered an affront, and the air had been scored and cleansed by his naked fists. But this time a restraint fell on his tense muscles and he gradually relaxed them. There was now somewhere in his folded brain-cells a slight inhibiting stain that made him realize he couldn't afford to express his anger. The barman must know that he was a deserter, he couldn't help but know. That was the reason he had made his proposition. And it wouldn't be hard for him to take his revenge if he found himself too proudly spurned and refused. Rusty felt his arms go limp. And he heard himself answering, "I don't think that's my line. But I'll think it over."

For the next few days he hardly left his room. He didn't walk to the palace in the afternoon even though the weather remained golden and superb. He didn't lounge in the parks. He didn't appear at his usual restaurant or go back to the bar. It wasn't that he was afraid that the proposition would be repeated. He wasn't thinking it over and he knew that the barman knew that he wasn't thinking it over. His reply had been a refusal. But he had been shaken just the same. It shocked him that he could be considered for any kind of crime or violence, and for a while he wanted to be seen in the quarter as little as possible. So he stayed in his room, only going out to get food — bread and sliced ham and salami, that he bought from a little delicatessen with connections on the black market, and fruit from the barrows.

He seemed to be alone in the midst of a jungle or a wilderness. He ate only when he felt hungry, with no regard for what time it was; and then he wolfed down his food as hurriedly as though he must be off again and was miles from the last settlement and the last traces of law and order. With the door of his room closed and the windows shut, there were few sounds that filtered in from the outside through the old heavily built house, and those that did seemed so twisted and inhuman they might have been the calls of animals to be heard in some far distant part of the world, apes chattering or the caw of parakeets. In the silence he was reminded of an explorer whom he had read about as a boy who had travelled thousands of miles down a great river only to find himself at the end in the middle of endless swamps and creeks and savannahs with no outlet to the sea; and then as he tried to find the channel he was murdered by his desperate and half-crazed companions. The foliage on the peeling wall-paper, grey-green and faded, was like snake-infested vines or creepers; and sometimes as he sat in the stillness, smoking, they seemed to be hemming him in. Before long they might close in and coil round and crush him. And yet the furnishings of his room were so anonymous that he knew it would be useless to try to move. To move to another room in the quarter would merely be to move to another thicket as enclosed and sunless and impenetrable as this. Sometimes he felt so solitary that he thought of Robinson Crusoe, cast away on a desert island. But this island of his was hardly larger than a cell, he reflected, and there was nothing in it to do and nothing to build. He hardly knew how he spent the time. He read a little in books he found on the mantlepiece, westerns and detective-stories; but he seldom started at the beginning and almost never went on to the end. He slept a great deal. He sprawled on the only chair or lay on the bed in his shirtsleeves, smoking and staring up at the ceiling. Sometimes it occurred to him that he himself might be the desert island where it had been his fate to be cast away.

Yet he was grateful for the stillness. He knew that he had been wounded, or at least bruised, and time and quiet were needed for whatever it was that had happened to him to be covered with new tissue.

He slept well each night and woke refreshed and felt that his hurt was healing. He thought that it might assist the healing process if he established some routines for himself, however slight. He had become careless about shaving and about his clothes. Now as soon as he got up he shaved carefully and washed as fully as he could with the antiquated facilities that were available. Then, although he wasn't going anywhere, he brushed his suit and tried to sponge off the spots that had collected on it. Another minor ritual that it occurred to him to perform was to sort out his kit-bag. So he pulled out and laid on the bed everything that was in it, khaki shirts that he had inherited from soldiers who had been killed, woollen underwear that he wouldn't need until winter, a captured revolver he had kept as a souvenir, socks, handkerchiefs, scarves, sweaters. Among all this tangle he came on a thick envelope that he had forgotten and that he didn't trust himself to open; it contained snapshots taken years ago of himself as a boy and of his father and mother and sister. But when a small purple box tumbled out, he stopped and opened it. He took out the silver medal that was inside and turned it over in his hand and stared a long time at his name engraved on the back. He was thinking of the sun blazing down on the weapon-pit and of slapping one magazine after another into the breach of the automatic rifle he was firing and of the wisps of smoke curling out of the barrel at the end of each burst and of the smoke mingling with the heat-haze (that was almost as unnerving as darkness would have been, he was so uncertain about possible shapes moving through it) and then of waiting in a long line in the palace marshalled by a red silk cord while one after another of those in front of him walked up to the dais until finally he heard his own name called out and was going up to have the medal pinned to his tunic.

While he was looking at it, with all his few belongings spread out on the bed, there was a knock on the door and the grief-ravaged girl who had a room at the back of the second floor came in. It was clear that she wanted to stay and talk. But he didn't feel like talking to anyone and he didn't encourage her. He could hardly object, though, when she offered to wash out some of the dirty clothes that she saw on the bed. She insisted that it was something she wanted to do, he must let her; and finally she went away with a big bundle under her arm.

When she came back the next evening, she had not only washed them, she had ironed them as well. She came in and sat down on the one chair with its broken, half-exposed springs and he offered her some green grapes, the only thing he happened to have. She seemed calmer. She didn't talk about her drowned lover. She told him instead a little about her childhood. Her flaxen hair no longer hung unkempt over her shoulders, it had been washed and brushed until it shone. And her grey eyes, flecked with green, seemed to look out on a more serene landscape. He hadn't much to say, it didn't seem to be necessary. But their conversation flowed so easily and naturally that he wasn't prepared for it when a pause came which she allowed to grow longer and longer. Then she quietly switched off the light and came over and stood by him in the darkness and rested her fingers on his cheek and stroked it gently. He was so taken by surprise — and yet so affected — that he didn't know what to do in reply. He didn't want to hurt her. But he couldn't do what she was suggesting. At last he said in a low voice, "I couldn't. I would feel too responsible for you."

She took her hand away without a sound and went back and sat down and lit a cigarette. The room was still dark. Soon their embarrassment passed and in the stillness they were talking like old friends. She told him she had come to think that she must try to make something out of her grief; she had suffered, but there was suffering everywhere; she must try to use her own suffering to understand the suffering of others and to be of help; perhaps there was a warmth that could be made to glow from the midst of loss. "I wanted to do something generous and womanly," she explained simply, "and I thought you might need it." The room seemed to be richer, the squalor receded, the vines were no longer reaching out to strangle him. She asked him what he was searching for and he tried to answer; but what he said apparently made little sense to her, and he was not even fully persuaded himself. She didn't press him. But when she was about to go, she said softly, "You are searching for something. But remember that you are also being sought."

Now she was with her hand on the door. Before she opened it, he went to her and took her in his arms and kissed her.

After she had gone, he sat by himself for a long while. He didn't understand everything she had said. He was especially bewildered by what she had said about his being sought. He knew, although he seldom thought of it, that he was on the books of the police and the provosts. But clearly that wasn't what she meant. What did she mean, then? He went to the window and opened it and looked out. The particular aromatic savour of the quarter rose from the pavement, compounded of lust and loneliness and excess. He was dimly conscious of the labyrinth spreading on every side beneath him of mews and passageways and dives and brothels, all spiced and tinctured with unappeasable desire. But his gaze was ranging far beyond the confines of the quarter — to where trains were shunting or lengthening their stride as they began to move out to the far quarters of the realm; to the highways where produce was rolling in through the dark to be uncovered later in all its freshness at the market; to the ships hooting in the estuary or riding calmly at anchor. He was gazing out past the borders of the quarter along all the threads of the loose mesh that made this a capital. Out there the teletypes were clacking in the offices of the Ministry and in police-stations, where officers were scanning the latest reports and adding to the list of those who were wanted; the watchmen were doing their rounds of banks and warehouses; and clerks and merchants were turning in their sleep and, forgetful of ledgers and balance-sheets, were dreaming of some of the myriad abandoned pleasures that were here offered for sale. This quarter and the rest of the city, he had begun to surmise, were shameful accomplices. One could hardly live without the other. The city's wide catholicity needed this enclave as one of its indispensable elements, needed it if only as an object and pretext for the dreams of its sleeping citizens. The wide city was sleeping. But here the quarter was alive and awake, nourishing and sustaining it with dreams — blissful or pernicious they might be — with dreams of what it had lost and yet could never entirely give up, with dreams of agony and splendour. He must soon be moving on, he realized. But now he would never wonder why this quarter lay so close to the heart of the city, squalid, dilapidated, shunned, dishonoured, yet like the keep of a fortress.

The next evening he decided he would sally out to the Plaza to see if he could find Althea. It was the first time for weeks that he had been under the arcades. But it had occurred to him, however absurdly, that although he had never had a letter from her, although she had apparently never made any effort to get in touch with him, she might nevertheless be searching for him as he had been searching for her. The idea was absurd, but once it had entered his head he couldn't get rid of it. So again he stood in the shadows, still and stolid as a sentry, never moving his head but watching every face to see if it might be hers. For more than an hour he watched and waited, with the shadow coming down over his eyes like a visor or the fur of a bearskin, while the crowd flowed past his scrutiny, in a ragged, endless procession. But she wasn't among them; and finally he confessed to himself that he knew she wouldn't be; and he gave up and quitted his post and set off across the Plaza. As he was passing the base of the column, he saw that there were lights burning in the offices of the Ministry, and he was tempted to go in and present himself to the guard and ask for Mark. But before it had fully formed itself in his mind, he dismissed the notion, perhaps because of pride, perhaps because he was still ashamed of the curtness of his departure and didn't know how to make amends. He strode on anyway and soon was back in his room again alone.

As he looked over the city before going to bed, he noticed that a first few leaves had fallen and were lying in the street. It would soon be autumn, it would soon be time for him to be moving on. The leaves lay on the pavement and in the gutter like great gouts of blood that had dried and rusted. But as they were caught by the feeble light from the street-lamps that faltered down through the still almost fully foliaged trees, they moved and crinkled and glistened a little. Then they were like great petals that had fallen, the first-fruits of some glistening blood-red rose. Why did he see them that way? he wondered. Was it because of something mysterious his visitor of last evening had said, something about finding "splendour in the wound of suffering?" He didn't know. But at that moment a taste of blood came into his mouth. It was a taste that was salty along his tongue. And at the same time he was conscious of a sharp sea-breeze pricking his nostrils. Out there was the estuary, the tides, the sea, the salt from which he had been separated. And beside the sea was a weeping moonlit tree, with its leaves silvering, turning in the wind, silvering, turning as they fell. Yes, he murmured, yes, it would soon be time for him to be moving on.

But the time was to come sooner than he expected. In the morning when he woke there was a great commotion in the house. Doors were opening and shutting, belongings were being hurriedly collected and packed, news was being passed along breathlessly. He hadn't been reading the newspapers for some days and he hadn't learned that a large jeweller's had been robbed in broad daylight. The robbery had been in the very centre of the city and in the very middle of the day. A young man dressed in overalls had stepped out of the crowd and, with a few light taps of a hammer, had sent the whole wide plateglass shop-front toppling inwards. Then three masked men had scooped up handfuls of diamonds and watches and had driven off before the astonished salespeople could make a move or the police had the slightest idea of what was happening. Immediately the press was in an uproar. Something must be done; the police were becoming a laughing-stock; everyone knew that one quarter of the city was infested with deserters; it must be cleaned out. As the criticism mounted, the police authorities were forced to recognize that what was called for was something really spectacular.

So that morning shortly after dawn, hundreds of police, both civil and military, began deploying in a wide and well-planned operation. Road-blocks were set up on all of the main highways leading out of the capital; check-points were established; and, most important of all, an intricate police cordon was woven around and through the quarter, virtually sealing it off from the rest of the city. Now patrol-cars with two-way radios were prowling everywhere through the quarantined area, and the streets had the cowed look of a city that has just been occupied. Traffic was at a minimum. Doors and windows were sullen and shut. Outside there were hardly any signs of life to be seen at all.

But inside it was very different. There the agitation was like the fluttering in a hen-house. The young pickpocket kept racing up and down stairs, white-faced and squawking, ostensibly because he was trying to collect his belongings but really because he was torn between desire to be off and fear of setting foot in the naked street — and he couldn't make up his mind. Another of the lodgers was so frightened he shut himself up in one of the lavatories. The iron-grey major who had been retired with so little dignity from the service emerged as imperturbably from his room as usual and walked slowly downstairs; but when he came to the ground floor, instead of turning towards the umbrella-stand and the street, he made his way in the opposite direction and let himself out into the paved area-way at the rear. In not more than a few minutes the news came flying back that he had got into the cellar of a house a few doors along and had come out onto the deserted stage of one of the quarter's innumerable night-clubs only to walk straight into the arms of a waiting policeman.

Well, if he was going to be caught, he wasn't going to be caught like that. He wasn't going to be caught like a rat in a sewer. Before long Rusty had made up his mind: the best thing to do was to walk out confidently and trust to his spurious papers to get him through. His rent was paid in advance, his kit-bag was packed, he could leave whenever he pleased. He opened the front door as calmly as he could and crossed to the other side of the street and walked past a restaurant and two bars, that were all still shut, and the little shop at the corner where he had gone to buy newspapers and cigarettes. His heart was beating a little more loudly than usual, but not much; it was some advantage after all to have been under fire so often, he allowed himself to reflect fleetingly. Only once did he turn his head and look back to see if he was being watched or followed.

As he did, out of the corner of one eye he saw up on the roof the scared young punk who had been racing up and down stairs so cravenly. He must have found a skylight and pushed it open and clambered out, thinking in that way to make his escape. But he had been spotted and a policeman was following him from further back on the roof. Now he stood almost at the edge, terrified. His pasty face was white against the blue morning sky. He looked petrified, afraid either to go on or to go back. For a moment he stood as part of the skyline, a stone statue, almost a stone crenellation of a fortress that had been invested and was about to fall. Rusty seemed to be seeing it all through glass, through a thick glaze. He couldn't wipe away the youth's look of terror as he stood against the sky. But he couldn't let himself think about it, either. For now he had almost reached the police cordon.

He stopped and showed his papers and answered a few questions and in a moment was nodded on. It could hardly have been easier. He had himself under such strict control, though, that he didn't permit himself any thought or emotion, either about himself — about the risk he had run or what he had escaped — or about what he had just seen on the roof. Nor was he yet free to look back. He walked on numbly, even though there was some outraged sense within him that had heard, or had imagined, a cry and a thud behind him. It was only when he came to the next corner that he stopped as though to light a cigarette and turned and looked back. A body was sprawled awkwardly on the pavement just under the place on the roof where the youth had been standing. A patrol-car had driven up. And now two policemen were getting out with a piece of rough brown canvas in their hands to throw over it.

5

In the following few days there was an unfamiliar figure to be seen by people working or living around the docks. Sometimes he was wandering the streets, but more often he was loitering about while ships were being loaded or unloaded or moving through the deserted spaces which had once been occupied by warehouses but had been blitzed and flattened and now stretched raggedly, with broken bricks to stumble over and weeds waist-high, burdocks and fire-weed and meadowsweet and Queen Anne's lace. The area had been a vital target and had suffered severely, so severely that in spite of all the repairs that had been made since the heaviest raids, swathes of it still seemed marshy and lacking in definition. The lines of the principal streets and of the estuary itself were clear enough; but that was about all. The walls of some of the basins and connecting waterways had crumbled. The sides of warehouses slid off into rubble and rubbish. The signs for side-streets often pointed across empty cratered expanses that still looked like a battlefield. That was perhaps the reason why, for all the cargoes passing in and out of the port, for all the business being done, for all the bustle and confusion, the area seemed uncannily open, even empty, seemed uncannily dominated by the sky. It was a landscape against which anyone could be suddenly and unknowingly silhouetted; and moving among these open spaces, a stranger was particularly visible and vulnerable.

The unfamiliar figure with the collar of his trench-coat turned up against the September wind from the estuary was difficult to place. It was because of something free and purposeful in his stride and something passionate in his glance that he attracted the attention of a young housewife who had come to the window to see to the children playing on the tiny plot of grass in front of her doorway. But he was too smart and handsome for this part of the world. What could he be? A stoker leaning against the aft rail of a ship moored a little way from shore noticed him, too, and wondered about him. He didn't seem to have anything to do as he gazed into the chill bright light that swayed over the estuary; and yet he looked intent and absorbed. Perhaps he was some port official making a survey of what still needed to be done to bring the docks back into fully efficient operation. But a tramp cowering from a rain-storm in the lee of an almost demolished warehouse, who also noticed him, was completely baffled. What he saw was a figure of some strength and possibly even authority who kept walking slowly back and forth across a sodden tangled stretch of weeds and debris at the water's edge and wouldn't take shelter, although the rain kept lashing his shoulders and streaming down his cheeks.

To Rusty it seemed only natural that he should move down to the docks. For one thing, they were farther away — almost as far as he could get — from the centre of the capital and from the central bureaux with their detectives and card-indexes and machines that kept clacking and clacking as they punched and shuffled and sorted the cards and fingerprints and photographs. It was these machines, he imagined, that were pursuing him, and it was best for him to move as far away from them as he could. There were times when the idea of the city filled him with unreasoning resentment. He would forget the initial act of rejection on his part and would become incensed that it had rejected him and was casting him out and hunting him down. Was that view unfair? Then he would claim more precisely that the city, which had been glad in its extremity to call for succour on the very roots of his being, now had no use for him except in a way that would have him neglect everything that was deepest in him. In any case, the city was hunting him; he felt more and more convinced of that and convinced that he should try to move as far as possible out of the reach of its machinery of apprehension. And so he moved down to the harbour.

Living there had the advantage that at almost any time of the day or night he could look out on the estuary and see imaged everything he had been separated from. It was an image of everything he had been given and had lost, of everything he was trying to recapture. As he gazed out over the water, his eyes took in the sleek hulls and masts, the strings of barges, the mooring drums with the current swirling and sucking at one side of them or another as the tide rose or fell, the wind-veins, the light that drew so much of its quality from the water, so that it was enlarged and purified by moisture and swayed like a waterfall over the ripples and the shipping. But his eyes took in much more. As he grew more rapt, he saw in the bright swirling flood Althea restored to him, her thighs half emerging from the foam, and the heaven to which she had given him entrance; the rainbow covenant of adolescence, renewing old promises, diffusing many-coloured futures through his flesh, reuniting him with ancient springs; and still further back, the warm secret union before birth with the waters of oblivion, with the brines of nature. All these things were there for him to see. But they were distant from him, he couldn't approach them. Yet such perfections existed. In the bright watery air he saw shadows falling among the hulls of liners and the stacks of generating-plants and the derricks in front of warehouses, the shadows of blossoms falling, of blossoms shed one by one. This was what he was surveying as he gazed so intently over the estuary.

Often he hardly noticed where he was going or how unsure the footing was. As he walked along the foreshore, the pebbles would shift and give way under him, revealing a length of rusty chain or fragments of broken glass. Or he would slip on one of the slime-mottled steps of the narrow stone causeways that led down to the bed of the stream. Once as he was turning a corner and was coming out of a dark passageway to a tangle of masts and steeples and warehouses, he was startled to hear his name called, so he thought. It couldn't have been, for the syllables weren't repeated and there was no one anywhere to be seen. But as he turned his head to listen, he slid and almost fell; and in that instant he saw again the youth trembling on the roof and then heard him hit the pavement. It surprised him how often that scene returned to him. It had all happened, as it were, behind his back; he hadn't had the slightest whit of responsibility for it. And yet it wouldn't leave him alone. He hardly ever thought of any of the girls with whom he had slept, however casual or mercenary or anonymous their coming together had been — even when it had been anonymous almost to the point of brutality. They hadn't harmed him and he hadn't harmed them, he felt sure; and so they sank from his mind and his memory with hardly a ripple. But the youth who had fallen to his death obstinately refused to disappear. He returned so insistently that Rusty sometimes thought that he was being charged with contributing to the slipperiness of the world where the young man he had known so little had lost his footing.

There were twinges, moments when he thought not only of that death but of other incidents in the past few weeks that had shaken him subtly. The grinning mouths of deserters gloating over their kill returned sometimes to haunt him as he was about to fall asleep. And he shivered with distaste whenever he remembered that at least once he had been taken as someone who would be willing to serve as a common hit-and-run artist. But for the most part he was so preoccupied, his mind was so flooded and overwhelmed, that there was no room in it for regrets or questionings. The engorgement was so great in fact that it had modified the whole basis on which his sense of perception rested. He still had sensations that were sharp and clear, and he could still relate them to what it was in the world outside him that had caused them. But between the two, between his sensations and their causes, it was as though a medium had been interposed through which everything reaching his senses must now be filtered. It told no lies, but it heightened some truths while dulling others. Once in action, when he had been riding in a half-tracked scout-car, the vehicle had thrown a track and had floundered out of control down a steep bank. As they careened downward, from the bottom of the gully two huge splintered tree trunks on which they were clearly going to crash swam up through the windshield to meet them. But the inevitability of what was going to happen and their powerlessness to prevent it; and the absurdity of being killed in action in something not very different from a traffic accident; and, above all, the deafening crescendo of battle that was towering and boiling about them; all this made what they could see so clearly seem completely unreal. In the few instants before they crashed, the gross gnarled trees seen through the glass seemed insubstantial and to be swaying and floating freely, seemed to be as little rooted in the earth as thin green weeds waving lucidly at the bottom of a shallow stream. So now everything that he saw came to him, as it were, through glass. Its reality was shallowly rooted. It might be clear and bright, even hectically bright, like the geranium-red funnels of some of the vessels passing in the estuary. But if it was well nourished with pigment, it was starved of substance.

And the element through which his sensations were mediated to him was highly selective. It filtered out almost entirely the heavy bags of flour that were being swung up out of the hold of a freighter at the end of a long steel cable, and instead left weighing on his retina the great hook on which they were suspended. That stayed with him, like an enormous fish-hook, moving slowly up and down in the clear green watery light, and sometimes drawing him up with it, drawing him up to heights that made him giddy. Another freighter lying alongside had been completely unloaded and was now riding high out of the water: that said nothing to him, but he was fascinated by one of the propeller-blades that cut the oily surface like the fin of a shark or a barracuda. In a cargo-shed on the dockside, he hardly saw at all the merchandise that stood as though ready to be included in the trade and navigation returns (so many rolls of newsprint, so many hundredweight of flour, so many tons of aluminum ingot), but his eyes were sliced open by the sharp prongs of a fork-lift truck as they came sliding, sweeping, scraping, menacing, out of the door. Fangs, it seemed to him as they glittered there, seemingly unsupported — and he waited for some scaly animal body to follow.

But now he was little of an observer. He walked about endlessly, rain or shine, day or night. But he didn't take in much, he wasn't trying to. He was preoccupied — whether he always recognized it or not — with something that filled him with restlessness and drove him ceaselessly and aimlessly about the streets and the docks and the warehouses. But no longer could such things provide him with interest or excitement. What he was hunting for was not to be found by looking or wandering, he now knew more often than not, even though he must still look and wander, being driven to it irresistibly. Those pursuits were inescapable for anyone who was homeless, as he was. They could not lead him, though, to the object of his search, since it could not be surprised in the naked streets or be discovered, like pearls or ambergris, deposited in a secret corner of these vast warehouses with their more common riches brought from all over the world. It was more hidden even than that. It would be found, if at all, lurking inwardly, involved somehow with the viscous brightness with which his brains were swollen. His head was throbbing with the pressure from it, from a kind of hemorrhaging of light. Sometimes he longed to be rid of it. At least it might have been given to someone better able to deal with it, to someone with more intelligence, more education, more experience. For all his pride and vanity, he was humble enough to acknowledge that he was no match for it. He could lick his weight in wildcats, but this weight was too much for him; it would ruin him, ruin him. Then, growing quieter, he would admit that more intelligence, more education, more experience, might not have helped very much; the weight would still have been overpowering. And he would feel even a kind of pleasure that he had been matched with it, however unequally. And he wondered too whether others might not have been chosen to be hosts to this influx of impossible brightness; whether they might not even be legion, and many of them perhaps weaker and less able to stand it than he was. Now all that he looked to find in the streets and in his wanderings round the docks and up and down the estuary was a special kind of release, the kind of release that would come from companionship with someone who had been caught in the same way as he had, who had been similarly endowed and afflicted. Sometimes he even thought that the most he could ever hope for from the streets would be a sentence, a phrase, a word, from a fellow-sufferer; and that, though rolling in the gutter, would be of far greater price than any pearl.

But he met no one. He wasn't well acquainted with the dives and hideouts round the docks where he would have been likely to fall into some kind of acquaintance, and he made no effort to get to know them better. There was no one place he frequented. He slipped into a bar unobtrusively whenever he felt like having a drink and came out without having spoken to anyone. But for the most part he would spend his time in the open, walking and wandering by himself. Sometimes he would leave the room he had taken — it was over a small corner shop — almost immediately after breakfast and wouldn't return until late at night, dog-tired and ready to fall right into bed. Perhaps it was because he talked to so few people that the whole area around the harbour seemed to him conspicuously bare, in spite of all its activity and in spite of the large labour-force that ebbed and flowed through it each day. Or perhaps, more simply, that impression was due to the spaces cleared by the bombing and to the influence of the water that was never far away, opening and widening the prospect, leading the eye up to an outspread realm of clouds and sunlight and making the human figures seem few and far between. Whatever the reason, to his preoccupied gaze the whole area appeared singularly empty and unpeopled.

And yet occasionally he would notice someone. There was an elderly man who walked with a cane and always wore an overcoat with a black velvet collar, which had seen better days but was still stylish in an old-fashioned way. He would stand for as much as half an hour at a time leaning on his stick in the midst of a broken, barren patch looking down at the ground as though searching for something and then gazing out over the water. Then a look of pain might come over his face, and he would put his hand to his breast (was he suffering from heart-trouble?) and walk on brokenly. He was stiff as a scarecrow. But there was an air of absurd dignity about him, too. In the new position he had taken up, perhaps surrounded by clumps of purple loosetrife, he would stand stock-still for another fifteen or twenty minutes and then move on to a new station. Finally he would walk woodenly to the side of the road and wait there, absently picking burrs from the skirt of his dark grey overcoat, until in a few minutes a taxi would come up and he would climb in and be driven away. Rusty watched this same performance five or six times at different places around the docks before he found out the explanation. It came from one of the taximen. The old gentleman had lost his son in one of the air-battles over the estuary and couldn't be made to believe that he would never return. Some day the boy would reappear. He must have parachuted safely down and be somewhere among the docks. By this time his family had given up trying to dissuade their father from his folly. After all, it did no one any harm. And indulgent taximen were willing to humour him by agreeing to pick him up by appointment whenever and wherever he said. It was only now and then that they regretted their good nature when they drove up to the curb to find him sobbing like a child.

Then there was the girl whom he noticed one night after a liner had docked, standing alone in a pool of light and slowly walking round and round its green, reedy fringes, long after the foam of greetings and confusion had subsided and all the other passengers had left the landing-stage and were on their way. It was evident that she had expected to be met by someone and had been disappointed and was now uncertain what to do. Several times she went back to the information wicket to make sure that no message had been waiting for her and that none had come in since she last inquired. But no, none had, and she returned to her lonely circling vigil. She couldn't have been more than sixteen or seventeen, a little slip of a thing, hunching her shoulders against the deepening chill. It made him feel cold himself to see her so solitary and unfriended there, with the night wind nibbling her cheeks and minnowing about her ankles. Once or twice he was on the point of going up and speaking to her and asking whether he could be of any help. But he wasn't sure, it might seem impertinent, even silly. Anyway, he didn't. And she was still there when he finally left, long after midnight.

It was ordinarily only at night that figures would detach themselves from the large areas of vacancy left by his obliviousness and would swim into his vision. And almost always the figures were solitary; they would come trailing their isolation with them like stars. Out in the estuary flashing-buoys were making the dark more dense and perilous with their needling reminders every few seconds of hazards, of courses to be taken and courses to be avoided. The riding-lights of vessels lying at anchor were glimmering unsteadily white, red, green, over the choppy inshore waves, speckled with flotsam. On the wharfs and jetties, lamps scattered at wide intervals were netting the water around them and sprinkling the darkness with it. It was the scene for a ghostly ballet — but the parts were shifting and difficult to make out. At the very edge of the scene beside a black iron bollard lounged a young man in a blue jersey wearing a sheath-knife on his hip, who must have been a sailor. He seemed to be looking for someone. But he clearly had no interest in the only other person in sight, a short, stockily-built young Slav, one would have said, who was standing at the extreme opposite edge of the area that was visible. And he in his turn seemed to be looking for someone too. But for whom? Certainly not for the sailor, or at least not for that particular sailor. And then the darkness resumed, a darkness hardly distinguishable, Rusty recognized, from what was left waste by his own absorption.

Sometimes he knew the key to his obliviousness, knew why his brains were so gorged that he could take in nothing else. At other times the reason was withheld from him; and then he travelled on doggedly, as though the sealed orders that he carried in his breast had not yet been broken open. But when he was aware, it was different; then he knew that the orders he had been given *had* been opened — and had proved impossible. His brains were flooded with the madness of it. For what had he been bidden to do? To reach the headwaters of a perfection he had known once but had lost; to recapture that avalanche of light and bind himself to it indissolubly; to retake paradise by storm, to re-enter it triumphantly; to recover the absolute he had tasted once before birth and then again in early adolescence and still a third time when his limbs had been mated to Althea's in annihilating surprise, completeness, joy. It was madness. And yet now that he knew, it was a fatal knowledge from which he suspected he might never be able entirely to escape. A cleft had been made in him and ocean had rushed in. He could never rejoin it, and yet he could never escape from it. It flowed round and through him overwhelmingly, and yet he could never be part of it. When his eyes were open to what had happened, he was incensed by the unfairness of it. He had wanted to regain what he had lost, but he hadn't asked for this terrible, miraculous inflow. It had come unsought, and now he didn't know how to deal with it. Sometimes he was even angry with Althea for her part in his disablement and almost wished he had never met her. For it was she more than anyone else who had delivered him over to this crippling splendour. She had never come back, but the damage had been done. Now — at least whenever his servitude was most complete — there was a roar of ocean always in his head, of ocean rejecting him, buffeting him, taunting him, all at the same time. His ears now were sensitive to waves of all frequencies; they brought him word of stars forming and bursting, of catastrophes taking place in other galaxies; they oscillated with continued high-pitched tinglings and cracklings. And he had no defences. The flood was alien and engulfing, and at such times he was powerless against it.

Fortunately he wasn't always so vulnerable. One day he spent the whole morning playing with the children of the family from whom he rented a room, carving boats and then sailing them in a pool nearby that was really no more than a puddle. His moods were highly variable. Sometimes he seemed to be completely at the mercy of a ravaging perfection; it amazed him how little time it had taken for something he had longed for to become, without ceasing to be that, a thing of dread as well. It was as though the light over the estuary had swept him remorselessly to revelation. But luckily for him the revelation wasn't constant. Sometimes the reason eluded him why his brains were so swollen with brightness that there was no room for anything else. And sometimes the invading pressure itself relented, his preoccupation almost vanished, and he could look about him freely and take in everything he saw as easily as breathing. Those times certainly came as a relief. But they never lasted long; and he couldn't honestly swear that he wanted them to. What he had been given was dangerous and painful, but he couldn't surrender it without ceasing to be himself. Even at its faintest he was aware of it as an ineradicable tincture, a few precious drops, a vial that he wasn't permitted to lose or destroy; and he knew that he wouldn't have it otherwise.

He was angry sometimes with Althea; that was one of his moods. It was she who had opened the sluices and let in the torrent, and now nothing could ever be the same. And yet he admitted to himself that that was unfair. If it hadn't been Althea, it would have been someone else. He knew in his heart of hearts that he was a creature to whom this had been bound to happen. And as the impossible flood which she had loosed took more complete possession of him, Althea herself receded. Not that he was more consistent in his attitude towards her than in anything else. She was fading in his imagination, but he still sought her. He still returned occasionally to the Plaza and stood under the arches and silently ticked off the passers-by, "No … no … no … no." But his scrutiny was less intent and flagged more easily. He left off and wondered whether he would pick up a girl for the night. He half wanted to, but he realized, on the other hand, that what he would be attempting would be to scale some peak of absolute felicity by way of the treacherous iridescent slopes of animal excitement. Seen in that light, or half-light, he didn't have the stomach for anything so impossible. But he didn't fool himself that there wouldn't be times, other times, many times, when he would be willing to try it!

It was late. The last trains and buses that might have taken him down to the docks had all left. He looked at his watch and saw that he would have to walk. It was a fresh night with no moon or clouds, and he strode along briskly. His head was clearer than it had been for days. His eyes looked out confidently and were stayed wherever they turned by the certitude of familiar stars. It was only as he was crossing the bridge that he felt a tremor, almost as though the stonework had trembled under him or the temperature had suddenly dropped by ten degrees. What was it? All he had done had been to look down momentarily into the water and see the stars reflected there, with their colour "running" a little in the outgoing tide. But all at once he had felt giddy, seeing the stars beneath as well as above him and knowing that he was everywhere surrounded by darkness. He had always been frightened of heights, and now he seemed to be drawn up to a great height and to be looking down on the star-splashed water under his feet. The stars were moving outward on the tide. The darkness everywhere about him was expanding. And in such a universe what foothold could he have? What place could there be for his glimmering consciousness, his ambiguous cravings?

It would have been easier to deal with his ruinous appetites, he knew, if there had been something in the universe to hold on to. But there wasn't. If he was to be steadied, he must somehow find support in himself. Reassuringly he felt his fingers closing over the medal that he now always carried in one of his pockets, as though it contained some irreducible, inalienable essence of himself, his final virtue. But in the same instant a second tremor shook him as he remembered that the name on it was different from the name on the identity card in his wallet. His inner world was as slippery as the spreading outer darkness. One was the reciprocal of the other.

When he came to the end of the bridge, he was still a little giddy. He was swaying, he almost staggered. And then as his animal spirits got the upper hand, he broke into a lope through the empty streets, he did a kind of hop, step, and jump. And then he was stamping out a chorus, "Through streets broad and narrow," that he finished with a great leaping, exultant shout, "Alive ... alive-o!"

The next morning, though, when he woke, the eaves in the small attic room he had rented seemed to be pressing down and almost smothering him. What he needed, he realized with the clearness of morning, was work and exercise. His big body was thirsty for it, as at other times it was thirsty for drink or sex. But how should he go about it? He hadn't had a job since years ago he had been a delivery boy. He knew that he would need an insurance card, forged in either his own name or someone else's, and then a union-card and that there would be some risk in trying to get them, especially in this part of the city where he still didn't know the ropes very well. Would it be possible to do without them and to trust to luck or pull to get him a job for at least a few days? He doubted it; in spite of the shortage of manpower, dock-labour was still tightly organized and highly resentful of outsiders. But it might be worth a try. The owner of the house where he was living had friends all over the docks because of a little betting business that he ran on the side and that probably brought him in more money than the shop he owned. Perhaps he might be willing to help.

His landlord was a weedy, wheezy, tubercular type, who had had one lung removed or collapsed. When Rusty broached the possibility to him, he was very wary.

"I know quite a few people about the docks, that's right. But what do I know about you?" he asked.

"I have a room in your house. You know me that well, anyway," Rusty replied, trying not to take offence.

"Beggars can't be choosers. Do you think I would rent you the room if I didn't need the money? A fellow like you who comes from nowhere and for all I know may be up to his neck in all kinds of rackets?" His tone was pointed, almost belligerent. Then he went on more philosophically, "But you can't afford to be particular if you have a wife and three children to support and only one lung to do it on."

Rusty took the hint that his landlord probably knew he was on the loose. But he also took the hint that in his complaining, one-lunged way he might be willing to help if it were made worth his while. And so it proved. When he had pocketed the money that Rusty offered, he wrote out a chit to the man who did all the hiring at one of the largest docks.

The work was tiring and refreshing both. A freighter bringing a shipment of lumber was being unloaded by four towering cranes on the dockside, and he was set to work stacking and sorting the planks and boards after they had been swung up out of the hold and deposited on the dock. Over the side of the ship came the loads one after another, secured by heavy chains and swaying at the cable's end, sometimes a flutter of unruly scantlings that the chain could hardly hold together and sometimes only a few huge saffron timbers that swung down as stately and rigid as the corpse of a king. With the other members of the gang, he was kept busy scrambling over the shifting, uncertain lumber to release the loads from the chains and then, with short steel hooks, rather like meat-hooks, to straighten out the criss-cross, slithery, growing piles on the dock.

There were five other men in the gang. But the only one who had any word for Rusty or even took any notice of him was a curly, fair-haired joker, who seemed to be an interloper, too. He looked out on the world with wide-eyed blue-eyed enjoyment (which might have come either from innocence or from the coiled strength of a masterful physique), shaking his tight curls at it playfully, daring it to try and put the gloves on him. The others were older and seemed withdrawn, even sullen, forming a little cabal of their own, and resentful of their powerful young mate's high spirits. Unobtrusively he took Rusty under his wing. There was very little said — there was not much chance for it with the crane depositing a new load every few minutes. But an alliance was sealed all the same. It took only a few sentences.

As a heavy plank almost clipped him in its descent, Rusty heard a voice at his elbow saying, "It's desperate, eh?" He turned and grinned back, knowing that all that was meant was that the loads were coming so thick and fast it was hard to keep up with them. And he answered gaily, "You can say that again."

Then the other added, "Sing out if you need any help. Everyone seems to call me Dragon. But don't ask me why."

A little later in the morning when a break came and he moved back and lounged on the grass and lit a cigarette, forgetful of all the "No Smoking" signs there were about, his new ally took the trouble to come over and say, "I'd put that out if I were you. There's plenty of law around here."

He was pinching out the end of his cigarette and about to put what was left of it behind his ear when Dragon added, "You seem to be about as popular in these parts as I am."

But he had no chance of following up that remark. Another dock-worker came within earshot. Dragon sidled off, and he was left by himself until the cranes started up again a few minutes later. That day and the next he worked hard and felt the better for it. He went back to his room at night with the smell of fresh lumber in his nostrils and dreamed of pine forests and of logs being floated down northern rivers. But yet there was an insidious hostility where he worked that he couldn't altogether fail to notice, in spite of the way the air was purged by salt from the estuary and by the more subtle resins from the piles of lumber that were neatly sorted and stacked in the long sheds just a little way behind the docks. As often as not the hostility was unexpressed. It came in glances and silences. Sometimes, though, he overheard mutterings about "taking the bread out of other people's mouths" and "generations of effort and sacrifice." And there was a shadowy figure who came and went in the background and to whom complaints seemed to be made from time to time.

On the afternoon of the third day, the outcome of these discussions became clear. Dragon was leaning over to free the end of a plank when he was caught by a swinging blow on the back of the neck from a large steel buckle. At the same moment Rusty was felled from behind by a scantling. But neither of them were stunned as they ought to have been. Dragon was the first to get back on his feet and stood guard over his mate until he could recover himself. The others were so enraged to see their intended victims still in one piece and on their feet again that one of them rushed in with his fists flying to try to finish off Dragon before he had properly got his wind back. But with one swing he was stretched flat on his back. Then there was a pause. And then one of the other dockworkers pulled a hook from his belt and swung it in a wide, glittering swathe in front of him. Almost as though that had been a signal, men from other gangs broke off what they were doing and started to come running over. It was a signal as well to the two men who had been attacked. There was no time to lose if they were not to be surrounded and cut up. They both turned and started to run, not too fast, not too slow, with Dragon towering in the rear. And they were still running when they came to the dock-gates and wheeled out into the street — and then on past warehouses and blitzed stretches and other dock-gates to make sure they had shaken off anyone who might have been following them.

It was raining a little when they finally pulled up. And all the time they had been travelling away from the house where Rusty was rooming. So he was glad to be invited up for a drink to Dragon's hideout. You approached it by going down a narrow passageway, then crossing a deserted open stretch (being careful not to trip on the barbed wire or stumble over the rubble) and then climbing up a set of rickety wooden steps to the second floor of an abandoned, half-ruined warehouse. Looking at the coarse grey facade in the louring evening twilight, with one great corner of it sliced away and the empty windows clumsily boarded up, Rusty couldn't help remarking as they stood there before going in, swaying a little on the wooden landing, that it was certainly very out of the way. To which all his companion replied was, "If you're someone like me, you can do without too conspicuous an address. Might attract crowds, you know? Even the police." The idea of his having a conspicuous address seemed to tickle him.

There wasn't much inside except a camp-cot set up in one corner and some stools made from timber picked up on the shore and a hand-made stove with a pile of fire-wood beside it. But the concrete floors were cleanly swept, the doorway had been carefully repaired, and a black tarpaulin was slung over the gap at one corner of the ceiling. And the tenant was as pleased with his apartment and his few possessions as a new bride.

"I see you admiring my tarpaulin," he called over his shoulder as he was fishing out a bottle of whisky he had cached in the empty stove. "Got it for a song. Well, not even a song, to be exact. Just picked it up in the market one night when no one seemed to be looking. And I'm sure I'm making better use of it than they would. It gives the place quite an air, don't you think?"

Rusty agreed that it did, but he couldn't help wondering whether in a really heavy storm it didn't let in quite a lot of water.

"A little," his host admitted. "But it takes more than a little water to get me down. I've seen me wet for three weeks on end, three weeks non-stop, not a stitch of dry clothes on me anywhere, and my feet squelching like a bog. But did it do me any harm? Not a bit. I was as fit as a fiddle. Had to be. Why even in peace time, doing guard, I've seen the rain come right through my tunic, my shirt, everything. My rifle-barrel was full of water. When I came off duty and turned it upside down, it ran like a river. What can you do, though? If you grease your rifle, it stains your tunic. If you don't, it rusts."

He was taking the bottle back from Rusty and leaning back to take a long swig. When he finished he slapped the cot where he was half stretched out and asked, "What do you think of that? Isn't it a dandy? And folds up as neat as could be, too. Lucky, because I don't know how I could ever have got away with it, set up like this. It was much easier, rolled up under my arm."

By this time Rusty was breathing more easily. He didn't feel free to ask many questions, but he couldn't suppress his curiosity any longer about his host's extraordinary name. "Where did you get it?" he enquired. "Is it a nickname or a Christian name or what?"

"It's the name I was born with, same as anyone else's," Dragon replied. "Though with a mother like mine, you can never be sure," he added in a rueful effort at honesty.

"But I have hundreds of names," he went on. "Do you want to see?" Out from his pockets tumbled one letter after another addressed to Frederick, Anthony, Roger, William, James. There was a whole cascade of different envelopes and names and addresses.

As Rusty looked at them with bewilderment, the other eyed him almost suspiciously. "You must be very new to this life?" he speculated at last. "These are my real names. Ask for me in the records and that's what you'll find — Anthony … Frederick … Roger … James. Oh, I know I'm Dragon all right. But that's just for sentiment's sake. I ought to drop it — if only people would let me. But these others are the names that really count, the names that officials write down in their books. You know how it works, don't you? Whenever I need a new identity, I sit down and write myself a letter, with a new name and a new address. Then I go to the employment office and get myself a new card. I tell them that I've lost my wallet with all my papers. Of course they don't believe it. And of course it doesn't take them very long to find out — not necessarily to find out who I am but at least to find out that I'm not who I say I am. And then I have to move on and start all over again. But in the meantime I have a week or two's work if I want it."

It didn't seem to worry him at all, this ceaseless change of identity; but it made Rusty feel tired just to think about it, picking a new name for himself and then exhausting it before long, and then picking another, and another, and another — in a series that stretched away out into the darkness. After the little episode at the docks that afternoon, Dragon said he thought it might be best for him to disappear for a few weeks. He was running low in funds, and it mightn't be easy to find any work for a while without giving himself away. Perhaps he might set out for the north that very night, he remarked lightly and as casually as though the idea had just occurred to him. Rusty took that as his cue to be off.

It was teeming as he stood on the shaky wooden landing saying goodbye and then began to grope his way out to the street. Teeming and almost pitchdark: he wouldn't have been able to find his way at all if it hadn't been for a little light (probably it came from a searchlight on one of the docks) that reverberated faintly back from masonry on the other side of the low, blitzed area. He would sleep like a log, he thought with anticipation, as he slouched along the sopping streets and then as he had something to eat at a cheap little restaurant and, now soaked to the skin, walked the last mile or so back to his room.

But he didn't sleep like a log. He had difficulty getting to sleep. And shortly after he did, he was awake again. He knew he had been dreaming, but he couldn't recollect what it was. Then it returned to him, his dream, unfolding slowly, diffidently, unmistakably. It was coloured with washes as delicate as those showing the tissues laid bare in an operation. There was pale pink, and veining and marblings of cream and crimson and blue, and green the colour of light under sea-water; and these shades were combined into tissues that seemed highly vulnerable and yet firm and smooth as a cylinder. At first he thought it *was* some kind of cylinder, with something in it moving slowly up and down and almost brushing the curving, delicate sides. And then he knew it was a tube, a throat, yes! his own throat, with a fish-hook in it that might at any moment catch in the membranes and tear them to shreds. He should have been terrified, he should have wanted to cry out. But he was calm, completely calm. He lay on his back in the dark and watched the slow-moving, fatal hook with the detachment of a seer. And then he fell asleep again and slept soundly until morning.

The next morning he knew as well as Dragon that it wouldn't be worthwhile for him to try to seek another job around the docks. He would be too marked a man. Fortunately he still had some money. He didn't need a job. Not yet. He would resume his calling as a wanderer; threading his way from one street to another; circling a basin that was choked with freighters, tugs, barges, and going on to one that was almost empty, with a few boards floating on the slight oily swell; picking up the estuary at one point, losing it, and then coming on it again.

The air was growing grey and cold and lonely. He returned to the closed world of his own pursuits, his own whisperings and stupefactions, to the world of perfection and loss and estrangement. One morning while he was watching a freighter prepare to slip its moorings and put out to sea, it occurred to him why those whose blood kept bringing into their mouths the salt taste of some vanished perfection must always be lonely. They were lonely because of what they had lost. But that wasn't all. There was another reason why they couldn't be at ease with their fellows, even with those who also knew themselves to be exiles. For him it had been like a play that began with the one word "Banished!" So it had been for others. But each of them had been banished in different ways, at different times, they associated their estrangement with different faces and gestures and voices. The circumstances of their banishment were special, and isolating. All they had in common was their exile and the loneliness that flowed from it. And how could a community be built out of that?

It was a night or two afterwards that he first met Steve. Only, to be accurate, that wasn't his real name, it was Stefan; and he was the first person he had met for a long time of whose real name Rusty felt certain. There was a light mist that night. And in the halo it had formed round one of the lamps on the wharf, a figure was to be seen, with soft, cloudy waves of green, gold, and white light lapping about his blue serge suit. Rusty wasn't sure whether he had seen him before or not. But he thought he had. There was something familiar about his squat, sturdy shoulders and, when he turned his head, about his rather full lips, snub nose, and thick wavy hair. Turning this way and that, he seemed to be looking for someone through the mist. But no one came. Finally, he left his place under the lamp, which he had obviously chosen so that he would be sure to be seen by whoever it was he was expecting, and carried his search a little way into the shadows. Then after venturing a few paces in one direction and being disappointed, he returned to his place within the lamp's nimbus and kept watch again. A minute or two later he was penetrating the mist in another direction. It was on one of these sallies that he almost bumped into Rusty, who was standing merged in shadow and stock-still.

His words in apology were polite, almost too polite, but spoken in a marked foreign accent.

"Don't mind about that," replied Rusty, cutting short his apologies. "If I choose to stand in the dark, I can't object if people almost run into me."

There was no reply. The other seemed to have been unnerved, almost dazed for a moment, by this encounter with someone he hadn't expected.

To help ease the silence, Rusty added, "It's getting chill, isn't it?" And the stranger agreed.

They had moved back now a little toward the lamp, where Rusty could see him more clearly. He was wearing a scarf knotted in front of his throat but seemed to be shivering in spite of it. His eyes were anxious and tremulous. Probably the two of them were much of an age, but the other seemed much younger and in need of protection. The mist was flowing milkily around them, and in the privacy it created Rusty wanted to tell him that he should be wearing a coat; but he couldn't, he didn't know why, and the silence lengthened.

Then out of the mist the stranger said tonelessly, "In the country where I come from it will be snowing soon."

Rusty had guessed that he was as homeless as he was himself. But now he knew. The mist rippled and folded around them and stretched far out, into snowflakes.

Then without a warning the other looked up wide-eyed at Rusty and asked, "Why do you think there are so many people homeless nowadays?"

In reply all he could think of was to put his arm around Steve's shoulder and say, "Don't you think we should go in out of the cold?"

In the bar that they finally found, after hunting a little, some mist had seeped in from outside. There were dusty paper flowers decorating it, and flies, and few customers. But it would do. It had whisky and even a few dilapidated sandwiches under a glass cover.

When they got their drinks and took them over and sat down, the young refugee eyed his glass with the delight of a child; it might have been lemonade or ginger-beer or sarsparilla. Indeed, there was often something particularly childlike about his manner. After his first swallow his eyes widened as though he had been tasting barley-sugar for the first time. But he could be as moody as a child, too. All at once the glitter in his eyes was not laughing but sullen and angry; they darkened and smouldered without contracting in the slightest.

"Yes. So many people homeless?" he repeated. And he looked up at Rusty again with an air of wide enquiry.

But there was no answer. It wasn't a subject that Rusty wanted to explore. He just wanted to sit quietly and have his drink. He knew that it wasn't good for him to be so much by himself as he had been recently, but there were so few people he could talk to and even fewer he could trust. He was glad of this chance encounter and glad to be sitting with the young foreigner. He needed someone to talk to. It lessened the bright viscous pressures in his brains. But he didn't want to become too deeply involved. Or he might merely be exchanging his own problems and pressures for another's.

Still, he must try to say something. That was another thing about the stranger that was like a child. If you had any heart at all, you couldn't leave him for long aggrieved and disappointed, as he was now, staring down into his glass. Fortunately Rusty noticed a divisional badge screwed into his lapel and asked about it. He brightened at once.

He had been in one of the same campaigns as Rusty and in no time at all they were chattering about the dust and the heat and the flies and the best specifics against dysentery and the biggest barrage they had ever seen and the bad staff-work at one of the river-crossings and the wonderful skill which the enemy had shown in retreat, hardly ever losing a gun. Steve had been a dispatch-rider and had ridden about not only within his own division but to the headquarters of other divisions as well. It was even possible that they might have met before. And all of a sudden it seemed of importance to decide whether they had or not. Was it possible that hot afternoon when the whole corps had started streaming in pursuit and the corps commander had stood on a low bank watching one unit after another come splashing through a shallow ford? Or at the pink house on the crest of feature 59 which had been won and lost so many times? They applied themselves to the problem with the simple-minded concentration of collectors comparing two specimens to decide whether they were identical. But in the end they couldn't be sure. All Rusty ultimately knew for certain was that, however strange it might seem, it comforted him to think of those days of his honour and extremity, each one of which was incised with minute particularity on his memory. For Steve it was different. He couldn't find refuge for very long in these recollections of campaigning. They tired him. And they were beginning to seem increasingly irrelevant.

"How far away it all seems!" he said at last, almost with the weariness of a child who needs to be put to bed.

"I don't know," said Rusty rather shortly. "I don't think that there's any of it that I'll ever forget." He didn't feel that he could tell anyone who seemed as young as Steve about the avalanche of light and the roaring in his ears or try to explain why he needed to think of something else; and it irritated him that he couldn't be honest.

"I don't mean that," replied Steve. "There's none of it that I'll ever forget either. But I have to try to go on living somehow. And what has it to do with the big tailor-shop where I work? I sit over a heavy sewing-machine all day long. Does it matter there which of the river-crossings I was at or whether I was a despatch-rider or a gun-layer or a cook or a general? Who knows? Who cares? Who cares? Who wants me?"

His eyes again were smouldering with excitement. Rusty could see that he was circling back in a dangerous direction but didn't know how to stop him.

"And the trains! the trains!"

Now Rusty was utterly lost.

"I can't get them out of my head. The doors slam to. And they lock us in with a heavy iron bar. Fifty or sixty of us. Like beasts. Not a drop of water. The bar clanging. Moans. Children screaming. And the dark, so dark you can't see your hand in front of your face. And cold, your feet cold from standing in the snow outside. Nowhere to sit or lie down. Nothing to eat for days on end. And then only two or three loaves of bread and soup with fish-heads in it. Passing other trains. Standing in sidings. Locked in the same car for weeks. Where are we going? I didn't know, no one knew. But there were thousands of us. Trainload after trainload after trainload. And the stench. And the lice. At least I thought we were all going in the same direction. But we weren't. Now I know there were other trainloads travelling the opposite way. Thousands of cars rolling east, thousands of cars rolling west. What can it mean? What can it mean? The world so full of homeless people. Can God have forsaken us? I lie down to sleep and the trains start rolling out in all directions, they cover the world, I hear the wheels clattering over the rails, the people rolled together in filth and moaning, screaming ..."

Rusty sat there, impassive, while the other's eyes burned over him. It wasn't that he was unfeeling. But what could he say? He didn't know what was being talked about, he hadn't a clue. The trains? That didn't mean a thing to him. It was not until later, until he had seen more of Steve and had pieced together something of his story, that he began to understand.

He had been only sixteen, Steve, when his country was first attacked and its army almost crumpled by powerful armoured columns driving across the plains. But in spite of his youth and his parents' objections — "my mother would never give her consent, I left early one morning without saying good-bye" — he thought he should try to join the army. He got about halfway there when another attack was launched from the opposite frontier. With thousands of others he was picked up and imprisoned and a few weeks later deported to the east. Then after two years in a labour camp in the far north he was released by a kind of miracle and set out on his wanderings again. And so he joined his country's army at last and served in the campaign that Rusty remembered so well. But if his homeland was at peace now, it still wasn't free. He had heard that his father and mother were still alive, but they weren't free either to write him or receive letters with a foreign postmark. And that was why he was at the docks. He was looking for a sailor who was sometimes willing to carry messages back and forth.

"I don't know how far I should trust him," he said later that evening after he had quieted himself by telling Rusty a little of his story. "But he's already brought me two letters in my mother's handwriting and one in my father's."

As he spoke, his eyes were brimming with questions. But he must have learned something about Rusty in a very short while, because he didn't ask any of them, although Rusty sensed that he would have liked particularly to know what *he* was doing around the docks — and, to do him justice, not because he was curious but because, if he knew, the slight fragile bond between them might grow. Well, could he tell someone he knew so little that he was a deserter? There was something within him that cautioned against it. He had become very wary of admitting that to anyone. It was one thing for people to suspect it, if they wanted to; it was quite another for them to be sure. He gazed around the almost empty bar as though for advice. But the dusty pink and yellow paper flowers had no help to offer and he couldn't decipher anything in the curls of mist that were still seeping in from outside.

He didn't want to brush off this invitation to share confidences. But he didn't want to shock the young foreigner either.

Steve was still looking up at him expectantly. Then as the silence lasted, he finally dropped his eyes and said, "Anyway, I hope I can see you again sometime."

That got in behind his guard. He felt himself rocked back by it a little. How niggardly of himself he must have been if this young exile had to feel so diffident about merely asking to see him again! And he hurried to assure him that, of course, they could meet again and to set a place and time a few days ahead. And then Steve spoke all in a rush of how lonely he had been: there were plenty of his countrymen in the capital; but they lived to themselves and were full of cliques and factions, half-crazed most of them with anxieties, suspicions, defeated pride. They were his people. But could he spend his whole life fighting old battles over again? In gossip and intrigue and in trying unsuccessfully to keep alive the old customs? Somehow he must try to make a new life for himself, either here or at home.

As he walked back slowly to his room, Rusty felt his isolation washing and trailing about him. The mist had suddenly cleared away like the sliding panel in an observatory, and he could look away up into the heavens and feel the unsheathed, icy starlight slicing down his sides and leaving him not a stitch to stand up in till his own glimmering glow worm light was all he had for protection. If he lived under any particular star, it was a star of nakedness and necessity. But there wasn't any star in all that vast indifference that was twinkling for him or for anyone else. He lowered his head and turned up the collar of his coat and stopped for a moment or two in the doorway of a shipchandler's shop while he lit a cigarette. On the other side of the glass was a limbo of cook's hats and steward's coats and lamps and life-jackets and nautical tables, a limbo that made him think of tides and departures. At this very instant there might be a ship leaving the estuary or an old man drawing his last breath or a train moving off with its freight of refugees. His thoughts returned to Steve. He was embarrassed by what the stranger had said about being so lonely. He wasn't accustomed to a man speaking of his emotions so openly, and he didn't find it easy to make allowances for him, even if he was a foreigner. But his own loneliness was just as extreme, he knew, and his own need of some kind of society. And he remembered how in the regiment, when you were getting into your full kit, you always needed someone to help you into your webbing and to settle your pack on your shoulders. Perhaps that was a law in the dark hemisphere as well.

During the next few days, as he wandered about, he wondered if he shouldn't try to get in touch with Mark. He didn't know exactly what he would say, but that could be left to look after itself. The great thing was to see him again and then let the conversation flow as it would until he could ask the questions he wanted to. Mark wasn't the man to stand on his dignity; he could be trusted to let bygones be bygones. And he wasn't easily shocked. He felt in himself enough of the tension between light and dark so that he wouldn't be uncomprehending, Rusty knew, about the gap between the name on his identity card and the name on his medal. It was Mark who had spoken of the two hemispheres and who had admitted that he had a taste for the dark, "perhaps as brutal a taste as you have," Rusty remembered him saying. He would telephone him. But there was no reply from the flat when he rang. He tried several times; and when the next day he travelled up to the Plaza and enquired for him at the Ministry, he was told that he was abroad for a few weeks attending a conference.

It was Sunday afternoon when he next met Steve. There was a Sunday calm even over the harbour. The cranes hung motionless. The warehouses were shut; there was no traffic in front of them or in or out of the docks. What drifted occasionally through the spars and tackle of such shipping as could be glimpsed over the rooftops was the sound of church-bells, fading seaward, rather than the clank and whine of winches. The weather was superb and still, as though the sun had stopped in a premature solstice. So fine was it and so unseasonably warm that they decided to stay outside, lounging first in a little park where mothers brought their children to play and then moving downstream and sitting in the sun on a stretch of warm seawall.

"I used to love Sunday," Steve said as he sat there in his shirt-sleeves, his blue serge jacket over his arm. "It was like a festival all day long. After mass in the morning, I had nothing to do but bring in wood for the big stove in the kitchen. But I used to like to stay and see the pies going into the oven. Always we had a pie for Sunday dinner, a big pie, with meat in it and rice or cabbage and onions. And before that, soup, beet soup with sour cream. And then for dessert perhaps fruit soup and a cake with cherries in it. Then my father would have a glass of vodka and go into the parlour and play the cello. And I would go out to sport in the oak forest at the edge of town, chasing rabbits or gathering chestnuts."

He was summoning these memories back from over the water. Then he turned, and said artlessly, "But tell me about your home, Rusty. Where was it? What was it like?"

He hadn't been listening very closely. He had been content to let his senses sink in on themselves in the warm sunlight while the words fell on him soothingly. The question took him by surprise. So much so that he almost blurted out, "My home? It's in that avalanche of light that you see swaying over the estuary. That's where I come from. That's where I used to live. It haunts me. It pursues me. But I can't go back to it. I can never reach it again."

Instead, though, he roused and mastered himself enough to say, "I used to go hunting chestnuts at this time of year, too. It was fun."

Disappointed with what he had been given in return but noticing the perplexity at the back of his friend's eyes and how he seemed to be looking out on a scene quite different from a forest of autumn trees, with boys scampering beneath them and throwing up sticks into the branches, Steve had to leave it at that and be content.

But he went on talking about his own boyhood. Now he was telling of the crossing-sweepers with their long twig brooms, who used to sweep up the fallen leaves at this time of year. Now of the statue of the famous astronomer in the town-square that he used to pass every day on his way to school and of the snowball-fights that used to swirl around it in the winter. Now of his mother in the kitchen with her sleeves rolled up, flouring pastry and cutting it out or preserving cherries in wine. As Rusty half-listened in the warm sunlight, there was forming in his mind a picture of Stefan's life as a boy, a picture which rested him and kept him from thinking of anything else.

Then he heard him say, "I loved my home … but I can't go back to it." The sentence that he himself had left unsaid was now out in the open and floating between them.

The young refugee turned on Rusty almost accusingly. "Well, can I? Can I go back to my home?"

"I would hardly know enough about it to say," Rusty floundered.

"Oh, I wish I knew what to do, I wish I knew what was right. My parents tell me I ought to come home. But how can I go home with those murderers ruling the country?"

"Are you sure they're really so bad as all that?" As he heard hysteria approaching, he couldn't think of anything to do but to temporize.

"You don't know them as I do," Steve replied. His voice rasped on the gold of the bland afternoon sun like the edge of a file. "It was they who packed us into cattle-cars. And it was they who made us freeze and die in the north. I've seen us stand for an hour and a half at roll-call in the early morning with the temperature down to fifty degrees below freezing. Old men, young men, the sick, everybody. Some were so sick they could hardly stand up, and when they fell there was nothing we could do to help them. The guards wouldn't let us. So they froze, froze to the earth like turnips. What could we do? We were half-dead ourselves.

Nothing on our feet but old scraps of felt tied on with twine. We were so hungry we were ready to drop before we began. And they expected us to work in that condition! Drove us out to cut trees through the drifted snow. They treated us like beasts, like beasts! Have you ever wanted to die? I did then. I stared and stared at the dark green of the fir trees, and I wanted to crawl under them and die. I was like that a long time."

"But you survived."

"Yes … At last my spirits came back to me. Like an army marching over the snow in greatcoats and bearskins and beautiful leather boots. And I didn't want to die any more. I wanted to live. And I did." He was quieter, the excitement was passing. "But those are the people who are ruling my country."

Yes, he was quieter. He didn't seem any longer to be expecting an answer. Then after a moment he looked up and said, "Do you believe in heaven, Rusty?"

No, not in the sense you mean, Rusty thought. But in another sense … While he was silently trying to discriminate, Steve went on, "There is a heaven … but we are shut out of it."

And his words chimed and drifted like churchbells through the golden Sunday afternoon, drifted and faded over the salt of the estuary.

After Steve had gone — there was a meeting of a patriotic society that evening — he thought about him a long while. He wondered whether by letting him talk so freely he was becoming too responsible for him. But, more, he wondered why, in spite of the way their ideas and sometimes even their words chimed and locked together, they were yet so different — Steve thinking all the time of his home and parents and longing to go back, and he knowing that he could never be at ease where he had been brought up.

For he didn't fool himself. Something had happened to him during the war which had so deeply affected his sense of reality that he couldn't stand a closed domestic life — or even believe in its existence. He hadn't been wounded, he hadn't suffered a scratch. Yet it was as though his skull had been trepanned by what he had seen and his brains left exposed. After seeing so many roofs off, how could you believe in the possibility of having a roof over your head, where you could provide shelter for a whole family year after year after year? The world was naked, roofless, homeless. That was the only certainty; anything else was evasion. And then through that opening left by the war had poured his experience of Althea. It was an experience that would have come to him anyway in some form or another, he acknowledged. But it had been more devastating, more overwhelming, perhaps, because he had been left so exposed. And that influx of ocean had set him even more irrevocably adrift.

But for Steve it was different. He had seen what Rusty had seen, and more. He had seen more, suffered more. But he had never ceased to believe in the sufficiency of the life under his father's roof, with his mother flouring the pastry and cutting it out and then putting her pie in the oven. And that Rusty couldn't understand. He couldn't see why the boy's sense of reality hadn't been so radically affected by the war as his own had been. And he was mystified by someone his own age whose principal image of perfection was still the dark, glowing interior of his mother's kitchen. The truth was, he knew that, in spite of his outbursts of feeling, Steve was a much more domestic creature than he was, the blood coursed much more mildly in his veins. But why was that? Why was he so much gentler and tamer? Was it something due to his nature at birth, his cells obedient to another edict? Or to the way he had been brought up? Or to some effect of his faith, the catechism colouring, as it were, his very veins and arteries?

What did it matter, though? He might want to return to his home as though that were paradise enough; except for that longing, he might have no sense of having been separated from some perfection that was overmastering, sovereign, unattainable; the only exile he might recognize might be from his parents' hearth.

What did it matter? The world was dealing as brutally with the milk in his veins as though it were envenomed with insatiable cravings. He had been torn off from the parent stalk and flung to the winds and scattered far and wide. In his case the world seemed bent on denying every article of the mild faith that kept coursing through his heart.

The next time he met Steve, the sailor he had mentioned was with him. They were sitting together in a corner of the bar when Rusty came in at the appointed time, and Steve was reading a letter. The letter was long, and Steve was preoccupied by it, only glancing up for a moment to say hello when Rusty came in and then returning to it, absorbed, so that Rusty was left to make conversation with the sailor. He was a taciturn type who was either unable or unwilling to say very much. But Rusty distrusted him almost at once, he didn't know why — there was something, for a sailor, too smooth and white about his hands as he rolled himself a cigarette and something too complacent about the way he spoke of the service he said he was doing in taking letters back and forth between refugees and their families. Rusty didn't attend to him much, though. His eyes were on Steve, who was racing through crinkled page after page of violet ink and frowning and shaking his head.

At last when he came to the end he kissed the letter and looked up at Rusty. "It's from my mother," he said. "She says that she'll die if I don't come home. What does she mean, what does she mean?"

And he put his head down in his hands and burst into tears.

6

An avalanche of light. An avalanche of tears. Didn't they come to much the same thing in the end? To exile and homelessness. And to ocean flooding the brains. When he had first known Steve, talking to him had been a relief; it had kept the roaring and crackling in his own ears a little at bay. But now the turbulence he was subject to was reinforced by the sound of what had been done to Steve, of what he had been made to suffer, the sound of doors clanging shut on the trains and of the heavy wheels creaking as they began to move in the bitter cold. The two torments merged in his mind. And the light that swayed over the estuary, scintillant already with separation, was now barbed with the far-below-zero cold of arctic winter. The brightness was made still more poignant by it, lancing, needling his eyeballs. Sometimes he put off going to bed almost endlessly, with one excuse to himself after another for fear of what might assail him in the dark after his head was on the pillow.

He would almost have prayed if there had been anyone to pray to. Prayed for sound, dreamless sleep. Or for calm dreams, if there must be dreams. And sometimes his prayers were answered.

It seemed to be a large sphere turning slowly in the dark and with light glimmering faintly round its shoulders. As his closed dreaming eyes enfolded it, it was a sphere of crystal, and scooped and hollowed out till all that was left was a thin transparency just substantial enough to let the half-lights echo and re-echo from the inner surface of one hemisphere to the other. It turned. It glimmered. It grew, it grew until it had engrossed the whole prospect. Then it was gone, dissolving with soap-bubble swiftness. But now it had turned into a number of spheres, falling like tears, like globes, like the globes clustered about a decorative wrought-iron street lamp, five or six globes arranged now in a spherical, now in a pyramidal, order (grape-like or like an orrery), at one moment so dim they could hardly be seen, like lamps through fog, but then growing in brightness till they were almost intolerably incandescent, globes that trapped the sun, and precise as a dial. And then the intensity became more moderate, and what shone out from his dream was a great single crystal sphere, ennobled by a belt flung round it like the riband of an order or the zone of the ecliptic. This path wavered with starry insignia — a water-carrier, an archer, a fish, a lion, a bull — that glazed and clouded the crystal. And then still another change. The one great sphere faded, and its place was taken by what seemed to be a whole system of spheres, as far as could be judged from a patch of green curving iridescence here or from faint silvery movement somewhere else like the shimmer of propeller-blades. But this time, instead of hanging in a cluster, the spheres were all centred on one point and seemed to turn and move together, rippling out in perfect stillness. Although so tranquil and filmy and seemingly evanescent, the dream weighed on him, weighed on him with such heavy authority that he struggled to awake. But no, he couldn't: his lids were sealed, his limbs without response. And now the slowly turning concords and concavities had slowed and settled into a heavy marble urn into which tears were falling drop after drop. And he knew whose tears they were, as he had known who had lain together at the point of perfect stillness round which the circling spheres had been so mercilessly, so magically, re-formed.

When he finally shook himself free and awoke, the dream was still with him, he could remember it with perfect clearness, he was haunted by it, it hung over the docks and the ships and the warehouses with the persistence of illusion. He knew that it was Althea whom he had sensed at its core; and he knew that the spheres he had glimpsed were the world as it had re-formed itself about him that night after he had slept with her, out further and further, from the mice skittering behind the walls to the bells and the ships calling in the estuary, the same world (with its spires and teletypes and brines and handcuffs) but now turning on a different centre and tinged everywhere, tinged and tainted by her fragrance. But he recognized, too, that his dream owed something to what he had heard about the sun-dial which was being set up again in the privy garden of the palace, with its complicated system of crystal globes clustering upward in a kind of pyramid. It was a long time since he had read anything about it. He wished he could see it or at least learn more about it. And the urn? He recognized that, too; it was being slowly filled with the tears of exile, with Steve's tears over his mother's letter.

The next time he saw Steve … But his thoughts were broken off by his landlord calling up from downstairs. It was about the rent. He knew he had been a little slow with it. But it was only an oversight. He still had money in his wallet. And he detested having his name called repeatedly through an early morning miasma of fog and baby's diapers steaming over the stove and then hearing his landlord's querulous voice continue, "It's overdue, you know. And we can't live on air." You almost could, on the air in this house, Rusty thought of replying. He could have drifted him one, in spite of his collapsed lung, he felt so irritated by the tone of flannelly accusation. But he didn't. He got up and put on some clothes and went down and paid the landlord the rent without saying anything. Then he went back upstairs to his own room and counted out his money on to the bed. There wasn't so much left as all that. How long would it last? Two weeks? Three weeks? He would have to start watching it carefully anyway. And when it was finished? He didn't know; but he wasn't going to worry.

He had thought about it a good deal and had come to the conclusion that he should take the next opportunity of telling Steve that in spite of all the risks and uncertainties he should go back to his home and his parents. That was where his heart lay and he could never be happy anywhere else. But when it came to the point he found it wasn't so easy. The next time they met, Steve was so agitated that he hadn't the heart to cut in with the advice he had intended. His friend had had further news and was full of it, so full of it there was nothing Rusty could do but listen, while the young refugee poured out his problem, refusing to be deflected or even to be persuaded to go in anywhere out of the cold. They walked on and on past rows and rows of warehouses closed and locked (it was already dusk) with great dangling dog-berry padlocks and faint chalk tallies at the side of the doors. Then when they came unexpectedly to a dead end, they turned to one side through a break in the wall and came out on an open stretch of weeds and rubble, where they paced back and forth, back and forth, occasionally almost stumbling over bricks or a coil of rusted wire, but hardly noticing, as Steve went over and over what he had heard.

"So soon though! They were just my age, and they hadn't been back more than two weeks when they disappeared. Disappeared without a trace. All that anyone knew was that the two of them were asked to call at the police station one afternoon — and then they vanished. Their parents were frantic, but what could they do? Nothing, nothing." And his voice for a moment trailed off and was lost among the withered fire weed.

"Can you be sure, though?" Rusty put in half-heartedly.

"It was a judge who told me, a judge from my own hometown."

But then he swung back to his mother; he had had another letter from her.

"She says that my father looks twenty years older. He never plays any more. He just sits and stares at my picture. I've told you that, though, haven't I? He never plays a note. My mother says she thinks his mind may be going. And she says if I weren't so stubborn I could be home within a week and he would begin to live again. So stubborn! I'm longing to be home. But whenever I suggest that I might want to be repatriated, do you know what my friends here tell me? They tell me I'd be a traitor to my fatherland. A traitor! And they warn me, too, I'd probably be shipped off to the labour camps before my parents had finished feasting me and making merry. I don't know. I'm torn in two, Rusty. I still hear the trains, I hear them now. But my mother says she prays every day for me to come back; and I believe her, I know she does, I can see her kneeling in her shawl before the altar and praying with all her heart. She can't live without me, she writes. She'll die if I don't come back."

In the twilight, suffering stood out on his face like a kind of sweat. There was no advice Rusty could trust himself to give to that ravaged, upturned pleading. He didn't know enough. He remembered that Mark had said his work involved him in problems like this. But he didn't have Mark's knowledge of the issues or the circumstances. He didn't dare say a word that might tip the balance one way or the other. Yet he felt that he couldn't remain silent. He must try to give something in return for all the confidence that Steve had placed in him.

"How could I advise you?" he said at last awkwardly. "I have a home, but I don't want to go back to it."

"I don't understand," Steve said in a tone of bewilderment.

"I am a deserter." The word came out nakedly. It loomed between them like a butcher-knife, hacking the darkening air and making Steve cringe back a little involuntarily, till what Rusty had intended as a rare attempt at baring his breast in sympathy was in danger of turning into a cause of offence. If only the other standing with him in this desolation could realize what it had cost him to say that! He had told Mark; but that was weeks and weeks ago — and since then not a soul. Once or twice when it was still early days and he hardly knew what he was up to himself, he had confessed jocularly that he was on the loose; and in the weeks since he had not been able to prevent some people from guessing that he was a deserter. But that was very different from admitting to the word himself. Recently he had become wary of using it about himself even in his own mind. It had such a ring of finality. It clanged the doors to. Now that he had brought it so painfully out, he felt it burning him like the great D that used to be branded under a deserter's arm after he had been caught and convicted. But how could Steve be expected to know how he felt?

Only a moment or two before it was too late he had the instinct, as he stood there disconsolate, to add hoarsely, "It's because I trust you that I tell you."

And with that Steve took his hand and held it in a grip of iron.

Then they walked back together to Rusty's room. They talked a blue streak, and now Rusty had as much to say as Steve. Sitting on the edge of the bed and talking about his boyhood, he seemed years younger: his eyes sparkled with mischief beneath the deep creases in his forehead as he spoke about the tricks he had played at school, and his brief wanderings the once he had run away from home, and his stratagems to earn enough money to buy a bicycle. For a few minutes it was as though the war had never been. Then he told about enlisting and how miserable he had been at first before he got used to it and began to make some friends. He even spoke about Althea, whom he had never mentioned before to anyone. And when Steve asked him why he had deserted, he tried to explain. From the puzzled look on the other's face, he could see that he wasn't succeeding. But it was equally clear that Steve wasn't troubled by this failure: here was a mystery, but not more of a mystery than so many other things in the world that had to be taken on trust. It was to be accepted as something within the providence that had brought him so far safely and had given him someone he could talk to at just the moment he needed him most. So that when Rusty paused to gauge more fully what effect he was producing, his friend looked at him evenly and said in so many words, "I don't understand, but I can believe even where I don't understand."

There was only one thing that did trouble him, and that was that Rusty had been so long out of touch with his family. He could hardly get the idea through his head, and even when he did, he still couldn't accept it.

"Don't you realize how they'll be worrying about you, how they'll be longing to hear from you?" he asked.

Rusty hung his head.

"At least you ought to try to write to them," he urged.

Rusty promised that he would, that he would try; and they said no more about it. It was clear that neither of them wanted to pursue a subject that they differed over, for fear their differences might so intrude into the refuge they had created for themselves out of what they had in common, the tent they had pitched on an icy windswept slope, that it might collapse and leave them again completely exposed and alone.

It was a moment of calm, where even the problem that was tearing Steve apart seemed capable of being treated dispassionately. Instead of offering any advice, Rusty wondered whether there wasn't someone who could give an impartial judgment. It was only natural for Steve's father and mother to implore him to come home. And the members of the refugee community might easily be prejudiced in the opposite direction. Wasn't there anyone who could see both sides of the story?

The notion appealed to Steve, and after a few minutes he came up with the suggestion, "The sailor … I never thought of asking him. But he goes back and forth between the two countries. He sees both sides."

They canvassed that idea a little, but before long Steve himself was backing away from it. "I don't know," he said. "I'm not sure I could trust him. He carries letters back and forth safely. But he doesn't seem to care much one way or the other. Once when I was thanking him for a letter he had brought me, he said, 'Don't bother thanking me. I don't seem to care any longer what I do. Is it something good? That's fine. Is it something evil? That's fine, too. It's all one to me.' He was only joking, I know. But I didn't like it."

Rusty didn't like it either. And he liked it even less when he learned that recently the sailor hadn't been willing to accept payment but instead had been asking for information about the various refugee organizations, and that Steve had been collecting letterheads and leaflets and membership-lists from a number of club-rooms and had been handing them over in exchange for the letters he had been receiving from his parents. He knew that anything Steve was doing, he was doing in complete innocence. But he was vaguely worried by it just the same and wondered whether he should warn him against it. But he didn't: the moment was too good to spoil. And they turned back to talk about themselves as boys again until it was time for Steve to go.

The next day he sat down to try to write a letter home, as he had promised he would. But he didn't get very far. First he tried writing to his father. He ruminated for a long time without finding even a first sentence. It was only gradually as he sat chewing the end of his pencil that he began to realize what the trouble was. He couldn't write his father without telling him he was on the loose and trying to explain why he had deserted. But he knew his father couldn't be made to understand or be relied on to trust him without understanding. His sense of respectability would be offended, and he might even try to hand his son over to the police. Rusty tore up the sheet and threw it in the wastepaper-basket and tried again. This time he addressed the letter to his sister and began, "I hope this finds you as it leaves me." Then he apologized for not having written for so long, explaining that he had made a great many moves recently. But he couldn't go any further. He knew that what he should tell her next was when he would be coming home and that he could hardly wait; and to write that was impossible. He didn't know when he would be coming home again and, if he were frank with himself, he didn't ever want to. No, it was impossible. The gap was too great. It was folly to try to bridge it with hypocrisy.

He sat back. What would he be doing now if he had been properly discharged from the army and were back home as a civilian? Serving as a salesman probably in the establishment where his father was the head book-keeper. Or filling some other job that he would have got through his father's influence. Working as a clerk in the city hall, perhaps, or as a driver on one of the municipal buses, where his medal ribbon would have been an advantage. Was it any wonder he didn't want to go home? But what did he expect, then? That the heavens should open and he be drawn up again into that perfection he had known with Althea? No. He knew (at least when he was as sober as he was now) how rare and elusive that experience had been and how fatal it could be to try to recapture it. Yes, he knew that, he knew that, he almost shouted out at himself. But even if he weren't to travel so far toward the headwaters of perfection as that, surely he had been born for something better than to answer politely, "It's out of stock, I'm afraid, ma'am, but we'll be glad to order it for you," or to inquire with deference, "Would you care to charge it?" Surely the stripped wand-like strength and suppleness of his body had been intended for something other than that. Couldn't he at least go back to some woods with his stag-like strength, where each year he could grow great royal antlers for the glories of rivalry and rutting? Or be a bear to hibernate all winter long before stretching himself in the spring sunshine and loping out to look for honey?

Impatiently he tore up the one sheet he had written and put the pad back in his kit-bag and went out and wandered the streets, smoking one cigarette after another. The sky was clear except for some vapour-trails, immensely high up, ruffling towards the zenith. But to Rusty it seemed to be arched everywhere with colourless, or almost colourless, rainbows. To his eyes they were given away by faint tell-tale prismatic streaks, which suggested the sweep of vast arcs staining the crystalline purity. In the play of these almost invisible manoeuvres the integrity of what he saw — ships shining in the morning sunlight, cranes stilted forward like enormous herons, the stacks of electric generating plants — were subtly undermined and dislocated. These inklings came in at the corners of his eyes, where crow's feet had been etched prematurely. But he hardly noticed them. He was thinking of something else, of how long ago it seemed since he lit out from the depot and of what a long way he had come. Or so it seemed to him at least. He seemed to have been on the run for years.

It was at that moment, as he was thinking back over the way he had come and was passing a small shop that sold surgical bandages and artificial limbs, that he was stopped by the police. They couldn't have been more correct or polite. They asked for his identification and carefully examined the papers that he took out to show them. But after handing them back, they smiled genially and apologized for bothering him. "We're just checking," one of them explained, "because there's been a troublesome number of thefts from vans around the docks. I suppose with everything still in such short supply, the temptation is just too great for some people."

Rusty smiled and agreed and put his papers back in his wallet. It was only when he was past them that he became aware of how fast his heart was beating. That was something new!

And yet as he thought about it, he had to admit that lately he had been more and more conscious of the police, of all the various kinds there were (civilian, military, provost marshals, plainclothesmen, detectives, constables, sergeants, inspectors), of how he was surrounded by them, of how they had their hooks out for him. Fantasies were sometimes woven in his head of police streaming after him in pursuit, with his name on all their lips and his particulars in all their notebooks — fantasies light as cobwebs and as easily brushed away when he came to himself. But as they dissolved, a drop of something was left in his mind to colour his outlook for hours. It wasn't that he was growing afraid of the police, that he was sure of. Rather the reverse. He wanted to tangle with them. He hated them as much as ever, because they had sold out to the cause of law and order, lock, stock, and barrel, and in its interest were willing to hunt down their fellows and turn them in. But he was becoming dimly aware, too, that there was something he had in common at least with the best of them, a kind of animal vigour that wanted to assert itself, to impose itself, to be exercised and extended — and hardly knew how to go about it. So that when he thought of his pursuers he thought of them as sharing some of the same baffled appetites that he recognized in himself. If he were not to be permitted to recapture what he had lost, then he almost wanted, however perverse it might be, to be brought to the test with them, to lock horns with them, making the air ring with the clash of antlers. Or so at least he was half-inclined to explain it to himself, whenever he realized that the police were much more in his thoughts than they had been before.

As he walked on, he wondered where he would go. Not back to his room. But he didn't want to stay out in the streets much either. He thought he might look in at Dragon's if he could find it again. Perhaps he might be back from the north, you never could tell. He didn't know much about him but he liked his style. There was someone, you could see, who didn't let the world push him around. He might be beaten into a corner, but he would come dancing out for more. He had pride in himself, a kind of animal pride and exuberance.

He *was* back, too. When Rusty knocked at the weathered, ill-fitting door (with pieces of crating nailed across where panes of glass had once been), it was opened almost immediately. Dragon had evidently been seeing someone out, a heavy-set bruiser with large pock-marks round his neck, which were only partly covered by a frayed white scarf, who passed Rusty silently on the landing. Then Rusty was welcomed warmly and taken inside.

The hideout was very much as he remembered it, but there were two other guests beside himself. One, whom Rusty could hardly see, was kneeling down by the stove with his back to the door, trying to caulk the seams in the crude metal-work with some kind of damp clay. The other was sprawled on a chair beneath the tarpaulin. He was young and swarthy, with a scar down one cheek, and Dragon introduced him as Walter. Then with a glance over his shoulder towards the stove, he added, "And that's Tim. But you needn't mind him. He isn't all there."

Dragon didn't say how he had fared in the north, and he didn't seem to invite questions about it. No doubt he had run through a few more identities while he had been away. But that wouldn't worry him. His sense of himself rested so largely on the vigour in his limbs and so little on his relations with other people or on anything he had thought or done that a few new identities, more or less, hardly counted at all. He had no need to ask, "Who am I?" The patent to his being was firmly displayed in his own good-humoured, careless flesh in which he lived perennially at ease. It was there that his selfhood was constantly attested and renewed, whoever he might be nominally from time to time. So long as that strength and lustre lasted, he didn't need to worry about his identity. A flutter of aliases about his head affected him as little as the dusty sunlight now falling across his throat from the one window, incredibly filthy, that had somehow escaped being blown in.

Rusty had time only to take the first swallow of his drink and to find out that the quiet, swarthy type was a driver who did long hauls from the capital to the north when there was another knock on the door and it blew open and a great bear of a man came in, with shaggy black hair, wearing a thick, dirty sweater rolled up to the elbows and torn khaki trousers.

"Come on in, Brandy," the host called out. But there was no need. He was in already and was standing with one hand on the door-knob, huffing and puffing and almost convulsed with a mixture of laughter and indignation and breathlessness and high spirits.

"They thought they had me that time," he bawled. "But I fooled them. I fixed them. They thought they had me in a corner, the flatfeet, those stupid bastards. I almost thought so myself for a minute. I was running hell-for-leather, with them pelting after me, up one row of stacked lumber and down another, a whole forest sawed up into planks, scantlings, God knows what all. The only kinds of wood missing from that shed were toothpicks and Christmas trees. I was going strong, they weren't gaining on me, but they were getting me into a corner. I knew it. But I didn't know what to do about it. And blowing their whistles all the time. Any minute they might be joined by the whole bleeding force. Calling in the pack because they thought they had me. Then I doubled around a pile of lumber, nice clean sticks stacked about fifteen feet high. And they were on the other side. And then I thought that those sticks were just about right, not too heavy, not too light, two-by-fours I think they were, or perhaps two-by-sixes. Anyway I thought I'd have a go. I jumped up as high as I could and pushed the pile from the top as hard as I could. And down it came. So help me, I haven't had so much fun since I used to kick down my brother's building-blocks. Down it came, all that wood, on top of the two flatfeet. I roared. Even though I had to keep moving, I couldn't resist going round to have a look at them on my way out. As I looked back, there they were, the two of them, capsized on the floor, struggling in a sea of scantlings and cursing and trying to get free."

"You must be dry after such a good day's work," laughed Dragon. "Will you have a bash?"

"I don't mind if I do," said Brandy.

As Dragon stood up to hand him the bottle, they seemed, standing there together, immensely animal and primitive, one with as sleek a coat as a stag or a roebuck and the other bear-like in his black, thick-set shagginess.

Dragon sat down on the floor with the bottle between his knees. But Brandy was still too wound up to sit down.

"So help me God," he went on, "when I saw them tangled up in the scantlings I was reminded of the first time I ever did guard at the palace. To do it properly the first time, you're supposed to finish up when you come off duty by having a woman on top of the colours. Isn't that right, guardsman?"

"Gospel truth," replied Dragon.

"Well, I was very proper in those days. If that's what the tradition said, then that's how it had to be. Really regimental, I was. So they got me a woman and got me the colours. But the battle didn't go according to plan. Not by a long shot. I was still almost lily white and she didn't help very much. We thrashed and wrestled till I didn't know whose limbs were which or whether I was coming or going. Then the colours got into the act. First they got tangled up between my legs and then they worked up between her thighs, too. At one point it looked as though stuffing her full of the colours would be part of the drill. I remember looking down at all that fucking crimson and thinking she must be bleeding to death. Or me. One of us anyway. Then I must have passed out or died of laughing, I can't remember which. I was half cut, of course. Oh, that was quite a party all right."

"But you're always having yourself a party," said Dragon. "Do you remember the time we were out cruising around, smart as paint, in new uniforms, and we picked up those two girls and when we got back to their flat we tossed to see which should have the blonde and which the red-head? You won the toss. But a few days later it was you who had clap, while I was scot-free. And when you got the news, you lay back on your cot and laughed yourself silly."

"Yes, I was really tickled by that," admitted Brandy.

"By the clap or by the luck of the toss?" asked Tim, who had finished what he was doing with the stove and was now lounging in the background.

Everyone guffawed. But Tim hung his head sheepishly. Sometimes it was difficult to tell whether he knew himself what he had said, he seemed so simple and foolish.

"By both, I suppose," Brandy answered indulgently and let the conversation simmer a little.

In the lull Walter ventured to ask what it was like, doing guard at the palace. He seemed ill at ease and uncertain how to establish himself in company like this.

"Same as anywhere else, sonny," replied Brandy, unconscious of how unwelcome the epithet was. "Two hours on, four hours off. Two hours on, four hours off. Till you're fit to be tied. You have to look smart of course. But there's not much difference beyond that. Except for more people staring at you; you might as well be in a zoo. But the time goes just as slowly if you're guarding a palace or guarding a coal-dump."

"Did you ever see the crystal sun-dial?" Rusty inquired unexpectedly.

"How could I miss it?" Brandy replied, turning and noting his new questioner for the first time. "Coming off guard, you go right past it. A great big nonsense of a thing. Balls floating in the air as though they'd been put there by a magician. I've seen me so mean when I was coming off guard in the middle of the night that I could have taken my rifle and busted it to pieces. Balls! balls! balls!" His great voice rippled through a whole gamut of tones and emotions and meanings. "But it looks pretty in the moonlight," he added.

"Why is guard's drill so different from any other?" the young driver asked, returning to the attack as though anxious to recover himself.

"Is it different? I hadn't noticed."

"Well, it looks different," Walter replied, trying not to show how deflated he felt.

"Oh, you mean all that stamping, and a hundred and sixteen paces to the minute, and so on and so forth? I don't know. I've never thought about it. Do you know, Dragon? You're more of a scholar."

"It's just to be different," he hazarded not very illuminatingly. "To set the guards off. Because of bringing the king back and all that crap we were told when *we* enlisted. The guards can't be the same as the rest of the army because they guard the palace. And they're thrown in when the day's almost lost. They're there to protect the court and the country; but they're outside. So they're different, they have to be."

"You may have something there," Brandy admitted. "The only other place I know where they do the same drill is in the glass-house. Right turn, left turn, about turn, stamping it out hour after hour. And they're outsiders, too, in spite of being inside, if you know what I mean; that's for sure." He grinned as he thought of guardsmen and prisoners in detention having one thing in common, that they were both outside society. Then he chuckled grimly and looked straight at Walter as he said, "Well, don't let's despair: we may all get a chance to brush up on our drill if we're lucky!"

As Rusty came away, he was still relishing some of Brandy's exploits, rolling them over on his tongue and savouring them. He had supper by himself in a restaurant in a back street; but what he was feeding on was not so much the gristly liver that had been set in front of him as the rich juices of what he had been listening to. He liked a fellow like that, with great animal spirits, who didn't let anything get him down. And Dragon, too. They were both obviously deserters, but that didn't necessarily mean they were cowards or criminals. Hell, he had seen too much to be cock-sure. He supposed it was true that most men on the run had deserted before the war ended in order to avoid going into action, and that some of them had then turned to crime to keep body and soul together. But you couldn't be sure. All you could say about Brandy and Dragon was that they didn't fit in anywhere now. They were misfits. He remembered enough, though, about men in extremity to know how thin the line was between the misfit and the hero. How could you judge? Anyway they weren't like those brutes whom he had seen drooling over the woman they'd slugged. They would be hard men in a fight, all right, but you'd expect them only to pick on their equals. In a lot of ways they were like him, in fact. He could remember when he had been as sleek and innocent and instinctive, when there had been as beautiful a fit between what he was and the flesh that clothed him, when there was never any possibility of his spirit either sulking in its tent or ranging so far abroad that the containing fabric seemed left far behind. He regretted those days. Why couldn't they have lasted? Nowadays he and his hard, tanned body were sometimes so estranged as hardly to be on speaking terms. The stitching that held them together was loosening. There was a process of unravelling. And in that incertitude he was left to struggle with the sticky brightness by which he had been invaded. It was his body which had betrayed him originally and given it entry, and now his body was deserting him and leaving him to flounder alone with his adversary so that sometimes he seemed locked in mortal combat in the inmost recesses of his being and at other times ranging out over abysses, but always alone, alone with it, and exposed. Exposed to the shapelessness of ocean beating on his ears, the ocean of his own loss and ruin. And exposed to the roar that was claiming others for destruction, the roar that was tearing Steve apart, a roar flooding everywhere. By going to Dragon's he had hoped that it could be mastered and muffled for a while. And it had been. He had sat revelling in their innocence and gusto, only pricked every now and then by envy of how perfectly congruent they were with what fleshed them and by regret for the time when he had been like that, too. But now it was beginning to return, the old turbulence, and almost as powerfully as ever.

To hell with it! He slapped the table so hard with the palm of his hand the waitress came hurrying up to know what he wanted. He didn't even see her. He must break out of this servitude. It was no good going on like this. He went out and walked through the damp chill streets and when a girl smiled at him wanly beneath a street-lamp he turned and followed her like a man blindfolded, down a dark street, through a doorway into a dark hall, and up three flights of stairs. There was still one thing that could seal his ears and stitch body and soul together again and make him at least for a few moments less alone and exposed. When they reached her room, he wanted to turn on the light and see what she looked like; but she didn't want him to, and he let her have her way. Then he did what he had to do, but he was surprised by how detached he was. His soul melted into his flesh as little as his flesh melted into hers, deeply though he was penetrating her. He was aloof and blind or gazing into a face which he couldn't see and had never known. It was like a ghostly parody of something else, or so it seemed to him, a parody tinged by the faint baffling colours of great whirling arcs of illusion.

That impression was renewed when after a while he shifted and, supporting himself on one elbow and one out-stretched arm, gazed down at her. In the virtual dark he could see little beyond the outlines of her face and that she was smiling and content. But gradually under his heavy-lidded gaze the contours of her head and cheeks and throat stood out more clearly, becoming almost as legible as silver-point, and then bewildering him with echoes, with similarities — but to what? Her face reminded him eerily of others, although there were none he could think of that it much resembled. What he read there was a mixture of delight and suffering. Her lips were now curled into a light smile. But the lines beneath the closed eyes were still heavy with pain. And the whole composition, spoiled as it was even in this lenient light by the grossness of fatigue, was spread on bones as delicate as Althea's. Yes, that was it, that was the echo he had been trying to identify, he concluded sadly. And that was the source of the patches of iridescence that in the darkness were circling and confusing him.

He got up wearily and dressed. She was still lying back with her eyes closed, gratified, smiling a little. Now he was ready to leave. But before going, he touched her on the shoulder and told her where she would find the money he was leaving.

At that she opened her eyes very wide. "What makes you think I wanted any money?" she asked, coming up with astonishment from the depth almost of sleep. "I'd be more than repaid if you'd just promise to come back again sometime."

Rusty hardly knew what to say. But at last he promised he would. Then she turned on the light at the side of the bed, looking among the books and trinkets and medicine-bottles for a pencil, so that she could give him her name and address.

She put the tip of the pencil to her lips and licked it. But before she wrote anything, she lifted her head and stared at him wonderingly. For the first time he saw her fully. She looked as he had half-seen, half-imagined her in the dark, only more worn and rather more divided. Around her eyes suffering had sunk deeper than he had realized. Her skin was blotched and sallow. And about her lips there was a conflict between desire and something that was more than modesty, almost primness. They looked at each other for a few seconds without speaking. Then she wrote down her name and address on a slip of paper and gave it to him.

He was about to leave when she said, "You will come back, won't you?"

He leaned down and kissed her on the forehead. And again he gave his word.

It was only the following evening when he was sitting waiting for Steve in the bar they had found when they first met that he idly took out the slip of paper and read, "Anne, 17 Acacia Road, No. 3." And then in the corner she had added, "Don't forget." He was irked by the tightness of her grasp on him and especially by that added injunction. There was something almost desperate about it. But he wouldn't forget. She seemed not a bad sort. And, anyway, he had promised, hadn't he? Irritably he put the slip back in his pocket.

Steve was late. Rusty wondered what could be keeping him as he picked up the evening paper and glanced at the headlines. On the front page was a picture of a wreck that was at last being cleared from one of the harbours. The trial of war criminals was still going on. A conference on the payment of reparations was about to open. The government was worried over slowly rising output, and in a number of industries was moving to establish productivity councils — whatever they might be. Talk like that about the country's economic future always left him cold. It just didn't interest him, he didn't know why, even when it was linked (as it was in a letter to the editor tonight) with suggestions of an amnesty for deserters. "Put these men to work," the writer argued, "and a big new push will be given to economic recovery." Rusty smiled to himself; he liked the idea of Brandy and Dragon being harnessed to the wheels of industry and clocking in from eight to five. He turned to the back page and read the football news and then a police report about large persistent thefts around the docks that were believed to be due to deserters.

There was Steve at last. As he came through the door he looked pale and shaken. He brightened a little when he saw Rusty, but the smile he managed to muster up flickered out very quickly.

"I'm sorry I'm late," he said. "But I couldn't help myself."

"Don't worry about that," Rusty replied. "Sit down and I'll get you a drink."

When he came back with another whisky, Steve told him the story. It had begun that morning with the sailor coming to see him. After reminding him of all the letters he had delivered, the go-between asked him whether he would be a good fellow and distribute some copies of the *Voice of the Fatherland* to refugees who were still undecided whether to return home or not. The embassy had the addresses of most of them and could reach those through the mail; but it wasn't sure of the whereabouts of others and yet didn't want to overlook any of them. As a personal favour to him, would Steve be willing to take around a few copies by hand?

Where was the story heading? Rusty wondered. He couldn't guess, but it seemed of such importance to Steve that he did his best to follow. Perhaps some questions would make it come clearer. At least they would prove he was listening and wasn't indifferent.

"What sort of sheet is it, this *Voice of the Fatherland*?" he asked.

His voice sounded like a kindly doctor's, asking questions about a disease he had never heard of and half-expected would turn out to be imaginary.

"It's propaganda. It's trying to persuade people to go home. The embassy puts it out. But I expect everything in it comes from the new government at home."

"Then you wouldn't have anything to do with it, I suppose?"

Steve hung his head before answering. "I didn't want to," he said. "But the sailor told me he couldn't promise to bring me any more letters if I didn't agree."

His voice was very low. He didn't say that he had agreed, but his eyes told Rusty that he had, ultimately. He had even accepted a little money for what he had undertaken to do, and had given the sailor a receipt. Then he had gone off with a bundle of copies. But almost at once his conscience began to revolt. After walking only a little way, he took out the money and threw it in the gutter. Then he turned down a side street and, passing a ruined house, tossed the bundle in through an empty window. He walked on, breathing more easily, as though he had rid himself of a heavy weight. It was only when he got back to where he roomed that he realized how mistaken he had been. He must have been trailed every step of the way. For the bundle had been recovered and was waiting to greet him on the landing just outside his own door.

Then he was beside himself. He knew now that they would find ways to make him do as he had promised. But the more he thought of it, the more he loathed it. He was frantic. At one moment, he would decide that he had no alternative but to deliver the papers; and then he would realize that what he would be doing would be trying to persuade others to a course he was still unwilling to follow himself. At another moment, he would decide that he would have nothing to do with the whole filthy business; and then he would hear their feet coming after him. And always he saw his father staring at him reproachfully and heard his mother quietly weeping.

"Finally I got down on my knees, Rusty, and prayed," he said. "Then I untied the string around the bundle and threw my raincoat over it and went out with the copies under my arm and started to put them in the letter-boxes and under the doors where I'd been told to. But I had delivered only two or three when I had … a mishap. I was still stooping down from slipping one under a door when it opened and one of my old officers came out. I don't know whether he recognized me, but I recognized him. As soon as he saw what the paper was, he shouted after me down the stairs — I was away like a shot — that if he ever got his hands on me, he would cut my heart out with a whip."

"And that's why I'm late, Rusty," he pleaded. "What am I to do? I'm at my wit's end. What am I to do?"

There was only one thing Rusty was sure of. The time had come when he must take some responsibility for Steve or see him go under. He wasn't made to take pressures like these and survive. Rusty couldn't make much out of the drift or meaning of what was happening. But it was obvious that his friend was being darkly attacked and felt helpless. At the very least a night-light must be lit to guard him in the dark, and he must be given instructions as simple as you would give to a sick child. Gently but firmly Rusty told him that he wasn't to take any more money from the sailor; he wasn't to undertake any more commissions for him; he was to put off deciding whether he would stay or be repatriated; he was to get in touch with Rusty at once if either the sailor or the embassy tried to put any more pressure on him. The boy was as much quieted by these instructions as if he had been given a prescription and told to stay in bed for the next few days and to call the doctor again if there were any further complications. Rusty hadn't so much confidence in his own advice but he was glad that already it seemed to be doing the patient some good. It seemed best not to pursue the matter further and to assume, hopefully, that the dark powers had now been allayed. Resolutely he steered the conversation away from any further speculation about what had happened and insisted that Steve join him in another drink. Yes, there were two nondescript sandwiches beneath the clouded glass cover on the counter and they must have those, too, and settle down to easy reminiscence about battles that they both remembered and that seemed simple and sunlit by comparison.

They said good-night cheerfully. But after they had separated and Rusty was walking back to his room alone, there was one image that he couldn't get out of his head. It was of a worm being threaded on a fish-hook, a worm being shoved this way and that by a strong thumb until, still wriggling, it was everywhere caught securely and nothing was left that could be nibbled away.

His fears must have been exaggerated, though. For the days passed uneventfully. It grew colder. One day there was even a little snow, although it didn't last more than an hour or two. He walked about and watched the shipping and the gulls wheeling and the sooty swans paddling through the shallow water by the foreshore. But his wanderings had become, if possible, more aimless than before. For the time being at least, the pressure of brightness seemed to have receded. But it had left him dazed and groggy. He had become like so many of those around the docks who spent their lives, it seemed to him, in waiting — for a message, a letter, a lover, a new ship or a ship's returning. He, too, was waiting now. He was waiting, although he didn't know for what. He waited, gazing out over the estuary. There was no news from Steve — and that was good news. He hadn't yet seen Anne again. He was waiting. And while he waited he watched the water of the outgoing tide sluice back through the heavy corroded chains that were slung along the wharfside by his feet.

One night, not many days later, as he was wandering sluggishly down an almost deserted and silent street, he heard behind him the sound of running and then a long low whistle. He turned into a doorway in order to avoid being seen or being involved even as a witness in any incident. He couldn't afford to be mixed up however innocently in any imbroglio for fear that the police might pick him up and then discover that he was a deserter. He listened. There wasn't a sound. Opposite, the crumbling front of a partially blitzed warehouse loomed chalk-white and still as a tomb. On both sides of the street the limestone masonry rose like cliffs. There wasn't a soul. A cat crossed the street. But the sound of running feet had vanished so completely that he thought for a moment he must have been imagining things. But then he heard the same long low whistle, with this time a little trill at the end of it. Still once again, with the same trill. And then he made out a figure standing directly beneath what seemed to be a disused hoist in an upper storey of the warehouse. The next thing he knew the door beneath the hoist opened and a lantern shone out, showing how splotched the stonework was with ochre and red oxide. Where the lamplight fell through the darkness might have been the inside of a cave. Then a rope with a great hook attached to it was quickly let down through the block hung on an iron stanchion; the bulky figure standing on the street grasped it in both hands, and in a matter of seconds he was swung up to the narrow platform and was disappearing inside in the wake of the lantern.

Rusty was still wondering what had happened when a patrol-car glided up and a policeman sitting beside the driver flashed a wide beam along the side of the street where he was standing. When he was caught in it, the car stopped and the policeman got out. Had he seen a fugitive running this way? No. Had he seen anyone at all on the street in the last five minutes? Not a soul. Had there been any strange lights or noises? No, nothing. The policeman, standing with his notebook open in his hand and staring at him piercingly, was becoming irritated. What identification had he with him? Rusty took out his papers and handed them over. The officer examined them and handed them back. But still he wasn't satisfied. What was he doing here at this time of night? Now Rusty felt the muscles of his diaphragm contract involuntarily. Was he about to be booked for vagrancy ("wandering abroad and lodging in the open and failing to give a good account of himself," or something like that, the charge ran)? But luckily he remembered that the proof the magistrates, the dirty sods, ordinarily required was that the suspect didn't have any money. So he smiled and said, "Look, you're wasting your time, mate. I haven't seen anything, I'd tell you if I had. And I'm not a vagrant, I've got plenty of money in my pocket. Would you and your partner care to join me for a drink?"

The policeman still looked sceptical. But he shut his notebook muttering, "No, not while we're on duty," and then he got back into the car and it drove away.

He was still sweating all over with apprehension, he had to admit, as the patrol-car turned the corner and disappeared. But at the same time gross bubbles of amusement were seething and plumping up inside him. For while he was being questioned, it had come to him that the doorway from which the lantern had emerged was almost certainly one end of Dragon's hideout and that the bulky figure who had been hoisted up was almost certainly Brandy. He must go around to the more usual entrance and see what was going on.

There was some haze, and it was slippery underfoot from a slight frost. But he found his way around safely enough, although he had to watch himself going up the stairs that led to the rickety wooden platform. When he was almost at the top he became aware of a suppressed din on the other side of the door. Then it was opened in answer to his knock, and he could see that there was a real celebration going on. The big bare room was almost full, he thought, although it was too shadowy and confused to be sure. A few lanterns had been spotted here and there, but there was no place to put them except on the floor, so that their light was muffled and twisted upwards above people's heads, where it went pluming and feathering out this way and that. But he could make out Dragon and Brandy and Walter and a few others among the shadows. And it was Tim who was guarding the door and who let him in.

"A lot of shooting stars tonight," the slow-witted boy observed, with his hand on the door-knob, looking out.

Rusty hadn't noticed that there were particularly, but he didn't dispute it.

"I guess all those guns firing these past six years must have shaken them loose," the boy added wonderingly.

Then he was inside and Dragon came bounding up to welcome him, explaining that, surprisingly, he hardly knew how, a vat of beer had come into his hands and he thought that such a miracle deserved a celebration; and then Brandy had dropped in unexpectedly; and now here he was to make the party complete. He led him towards the keg and told him to drink up.

It stood ceremoniously in the middle of the room and centred what otherwise might have been in danger of reeling and falling apart. It wasn't an overly large keg but it was magnified by shadows until, resting on its wooden trestle, it seemed to lie at the heart of the celebration as though it were an animal — a young kid, perhaps — steaming on an altar, or a bear to be disembowelled and eaten, every last scrap.

Rusty turned the spigot and filled up a glass for himself. Then he stood back and looked about him. Through the fumes and shadows the walls glimmered and broke into irregular passages and recesses. The damp peeling whitewash and the patches of naked stonework vibrated in and out a little with the din. Faces were slashed and scarified by black lines and chalk-white reflections, while above their heads stalked larger forms, shadows larger than life, furry or horned or antlered, crowning them, cresting them, almost brushing the ceiling. It might all have been a cave where primitive men had returned in triumph from the hunt and were now feasting in secure glee and defiance.

Most of the others at the party were away ahead of him, so he was content to stand and listen and try to catch up, drinking one glass after another. In the far corner beneath the tarpaulin a game of crown-and-anchor was in progress, illuminated by a lantern on the floor alongside; and every few minutes the man who was running it would call out dogmatically, "You have to speculate if you want to accumulate." Presently two burly figures whom he hadn't met before drifted up and were introduced, one as Boozer and the other as Bruiser — or so it seemed to him, although he couldn't be sure or even remember which was which. But they soon drifted off, one saying to the other, "I have contacts in the west end who can dispose of any haul we want to send them," before they passed out of earshot. Then for a while he found himself alone at one side with Tim. The boy was as vacant and taciturn as ever. But Rusty thought he should make some effort to talk to him even though he couldn't think of anything to say. Finally he turned and asked him what part of the country he came from. He was prepared for almost anything from such an innocent, but hardly for the answer that actually came. "Nowhere," he answered. And Rusty repeated the word stupidly, "Nowhere?" wondering if he hadn't heard properly. The party was getting noisier: someone had just fallen with a loud crash on the other side of the room, splashing most of his drink against the wall. "Yes," Tim explained, "I was a gypsy. But now I don't know what I'll do. Where we used to camp has been taken for an aerodrome." Strange, he never would have thought of this boy as a gypsy. But as he looked at him more closely, he could see there was something there that could only be at home in woods and hedges. For all its openness and simplicity, that face with its occasional twitch and its blunt nose (which was more of a snout than a nose) reminded him of some animal, perhaps some inoffensive burrowing animal, a badger, say, or an amiable fox. But his wondering was interrupted by the swirl of the party eddying round them. "That's tough," was all he had time to comment before they were joined by Walter and someone whom he had in tow. At the other end of the room Brandy could be heard exploding, "But I was drunker than a fiddler's bitch ..." And then in a moment came Dragon's laughing addition, "Oh, it was desperate ..." The party was beginning to heave and break and explode like surf over rocks. It was becoming laced with foam and laughter. The gusts that blew up and down the room hilariously were filling even Walter with confidence. "I see the law-makers have been talking about us again," he began almost gaily; and his mate, who was a little well-knit, wiry fellow, grinned and said, "Smiling! smirking!" Rusty didn't know what that was supposed to mean. On the other hand, he knew only too well what was meant by Walter's reference to "us" and didn't want to encourage him. So he said nothing and waited. "Yes," Walter went on, "they say there are twenty thousand of us." "Twenty thousand," echoed his mate. "Mad Christ!" Rusty was half listening to the whole wash and swirl and eddy of the party and half to what Walter had to say about the most recent debate on deserters and to the exclamations interjected by his spruce little companion. An absurd zany — his name was Bud — with his fair hair slicked back and his complete vocabulary apparently confined to the two phrases, "Mad Christ!" and "Smiling, smirking!" Yet there was something engaging about him, too, Rusty thought. Far too good to be true, he suspected, and hiding something like everyone else — perhaps hiding even more than almost everyone else. "How do they know there are twenty thousand deserters?" Tim questioned mildly, picking up Walter's piece of intelligence. "For all they know, I might be dead, killed by a stray bomb. I'm sure my family don't know whether I'm dead or a deserter. Sometimes when I wake up in the middle of the night I almost wonder myself." But no one was listening and his voice trailed to a stop. Now the din was foaming higher. The walls no longer seemed to be vibrating only a little, they were moving in and out like a concertina. The vat was doing its festive work, it was serving its purpose to an admiration and repletion, its virtue was being widely diffused into the bowels and veins of all the revellers. As Rusty looked around, they all seemed to be well away, at least as well away as he was now, and some of them a good deal more so. One who seemed especially above himself was Walter. He had outsoared all his embarrassments and timidities. His swarthy face was flushed and belligerent. "I feel loaded for bear," he confided. And that was the moment that Brandy came up.

"How's big mouth tonight?" was Walter's truculent welcome.

"What's wrong with you, sonny," Brandy boomed affably. "Do you want your ring punched, or what? So help me God, you wouldn't have lasted half an hour in the outfit I was with, you long-haired, hollow-chested, two-faced, puking, diaper-wetting son of a whore. We wouldn't have had a runt like you even as a drummer-boy."

"The outfit you were with!" the other mocked, "The outfit you were with! The blessed guards! All spit and polish and nothing else. Strictly the parade-square soldiers."

"God Al-fucking-mighty! Yes, I was a parade-square soldier, which is more than you'd have the guts to be — or the back, or the legs, or the balls. But I've seen more action in the two minutes of silence than you'll ever see in your whole life. I've manhandled more mortars into position than you could shake a stick at. I've laid more line, I've fired more rounds, I've dug more slit-trenches. I've stopped in the middle of shit and corruption to turn a gun-carrier right side up by brute force. I can carry a machine-gun farther and faster than any other man in the whole army."

"Than any other deserter," banteringly corrected Dragon, who had sidled up to keep the peace and to enjoy himself, too. But Brandy wouldn't let a little thing like that put him off his stride.

"What difference does that make? I'm the same man I always was. Same as when I was doing guard in a scarlet tunic or charging machine-gun posts with only a bayonet. I can rim as fast, hit as hard, fight as long. I could knock any of you right out of the ring with one hand, and you'd be falling for a week."

As proof, he held out his right arm, tensing his muscles and clenching his fist. In the lamplight could be seen, rippling round the muscles just above his wrist, a broad snake that had been tattooed there with bright diamond markings and with both the head and the tail flickering out to the side in lascivious suppleness.

"I can still fight, fuck, or hold the light." Now he had picked up the lantern and was swinging it around dangerously. "So where's the difference? Besides, I might decide to go back one day. You never know. I wouldn't like the tradition to die out."

"The tradition?" Dragon asked laughingly, taking the lantern from him. "I never knew you to care much about tradition. You mean all that about the guards restoring the king and ever after guarding the throne?"

"Hell, no!" He glared and spat disgustedly. "What do I know or care about all that bull-shit! I mean the real tradition, the tradition that runs all the way back, the tradition you carry in your guts. What did we care whether we supported one king or another or none? It didn't matter to us so long as we got paid and fed, so long as we were kept kennelled and ready for danger wherever it came from, ready to wrestle down catastrophe. That's our tradition, to stave off judgment day."

"Even Jesus Christ himself couldn't do that," objected Walter, who was beginning to look very green.

"We were here before Christ!" Brandy thundered. "We were guarding the tomb when he rose from the dead and rolled away the stone."

"And as usual you were so thick-headed you couldn't see what was happening," Walter said, and then made for the door.

"Smiling, smirking!" put in Bud in an effort at truce-making while his mate was otherwise engaged. It sounded, though, like the crisp barks of a terrier darting around the legs of a bull or baiting a bear. And Brandy wouldn't be mollified.

"Listen, youngster, there was something in the slime that made even your bird brain, and it wouldn't give up. And even if you give up, it won't. It will be in there fighting at the last day. That's what the tradition is, too."

But now Walter was back in action, sourer, but more sober, more deadly. Brandy looked soaked in beer but solid as a rock. If he were ever to succumb, he would go down like a column, Rusty thought.

"The trouble with you," Walter insisted, half afraid of his own daring, "is you're obsolete. There may have been a time when there was a use for big black bastards like you; but there isn't any longer. You're obsolete. You think you had something to do with winning the war. What a laugh! Some chemist sitting in a lab with asthma and fallen arches had more to do with it than you did. Or some numbers artist who found a cheaper way of shipping dehydrated mutton. Get wise to yourself, you're finished."

"Why do we have to listen to junior when he can't even hold his liquor?" taunted a hard beery voice from the back of the circle.

But Brandy didn't seem to mind. These insults were hardly more to him than a few mosquitoes buzzing around his head. "Let the boy finish," he boomed grandly.

To Rusty standing in shadow, the cave seemed to be heaving with smoke and flames and vatic giddiness and the thud of drumheads being slapped, slapped. At some moments Brandy was standing there for court-martial in a blood-red tunic, at others he was all shagginess and glistening darkness. Was he as good as he boasted? Or a bladder of piss and wind? He didn't know. But he stood firm among the shadows, the braggart, while most of the other figures blurred and slipped out of focus except as they were brought near him, or opposite him, or somehow into relation with him.

"Ah, what's the use?" Walter broke off. "What's the use whether you realize you're done for or not? You'll be vaporized with all the rest of us. If you haven't been exterminated before then, exterminated with nothing left of you but a thick skull and two outsized testicles in a jar in some museum, a bounty put on your heads and exterminated, all you wild men, just like the wolves or the bears."

"Don't worry about me, sonny. I'll make out all right. Bears? But who's talking about bears? You don't need to worry about bears when I'm around. I could go bear-hunting with a switch! They're my meat. So help me God, I'm stronger than a bear, I can sniff farther, hear farther, I could track a grizzly downwind and kill him with my bare hands. Bears?" Now he was bellowing and holding out his hands like claws. "I know all their tricks. God Al-fucking-mighty! I've worn a bearskin on my head so long I've sucked in all their cunning, I know their wisdom, how they think, it's flowed into me, their strength, their cunning, what they can do, tear off your scalp or wrench you to pieces, I even have a pelt like a bear." And he tore open his shirt and stood revealed with a great glory of thick black hair running clear down to his navel.

Tim moved closer to examine this marvel. When he had done admiring, he said, "Brandy may say he isn't bear, but he certainly looks like one." Then he turned to his own particular hero and asked, "And what are you, then, Dragon?"

"Oh, I must be a buck or a stag, I guess," Dragon laughed. "I wore those buckskin breeches long enough, anyway, when I was part of the guard; they must have had some effect. They may have sunken in and given me a sleek new hide."

"Is that why you're so swift and agile?" Tim asked.

"Am I? I hadn't noticed," he answered, shaking his tight blond curls and chuckling. As Rusty looked up through clouds of vertigo (which were made to tremble by someone collapsing in a heap in one corner of the room) he seemed to be watching the lantern-light twisting and glancing up through Dragon's hair and pointing, spreading out on the ceiling into great antlers, and blazing there, blazing black and gold, blazing and spiked and brilliant as unquenchable candelebra.

"I never think of myself as an athlete," Dragon was saying. "I'd prefer to stand in foliage up to my rump, with meadowsweet and Queen Anne's lace foaming about my balls and a few saplings nearby with fresh twigs to nibble. That would be the life for me."

"Have you ever thought of the winter," Walter questioned, "with no twigs to browse on and soft snow to sink in up to your belly?"

"Have you ever thought of going home if you have to be so miserable?" retorted Dragon; and even his speech was getting very husky. But by now many of the party were slumped on the floor by the wall, their heads fallen on their chests, snoring. Some were still on their feet, but Rusty couldn't be sure which. He felt very heavy. He could hardly keep his eyes open. He slid down and stretched out with his back to the wall and closed his eyes and let the few stray sounds that were still floating about drift in and be trapped in the passages of his ears.

"… didn't know whether I was dead or alive," someone was saying.

"Smiling, smirking."

"… Al-fucking-mighty." (But the boom was now very faint.)

"… speculate if you want to accumulate."

"It's desperate … desperate …"

Then he must have fallen asleep. When he woke or half woke, all but one of the lanterns had gone out and the other levellers either had left or were lying dead to the world. The walls were splashed in places, and there were thin pools here and there on the floor. It looked like a command-post after an attack has gone in and a few hours later has fizzled to a stop. The only figure in charge seemed to be a tilted, empty chair with straw coming out of the seat.

Was he awake? Hardly. Or asleep? Not quite. Or dreaming? Perhaps. Perhaps a little of all three. He was lying at ease with one hand still round an empty glass. His eyes had fallen shut again. But he was listening and was picking up from the heavy sleepers bands of sound that hadn't been able to reach him before. Now they were speaking with the candour of the grave.

"I deserted," said Tim, "because I have a roaming mind. I don't like clocks or bugles, so I listened to a little bird and flew away."

"I deserted," said Bud, "because of crimson foam on my face. Always in action I was frightened — of being hurt or of seeing others hurt. The first time I saw a man lying dead I fainted. But I made a friend; and when I was with him, I went proud and happy. We even slept together once, but only once — that was all there was time for. Then one day he was caught by shrapnel and he broke all over me in a red froth that splattered my eyes and streamed down my cheeks. I screamed and ran and hid under a vehicle. I wouldn't come out. My whole body was stiff, I couldn't move it. And the first chance that I got after that I lit out.

"Now I say as little as possible for fear I may scream."

Yes, said Rusty, I knew a case like that. Only he was court-martialled. The last I saw of him he was under escort. He was sitting at the tail-gate of a fifteen-hundredweight, with his head shaved, about to be driven off to two-years' detention.

"I don't know why I deserted," said Walter. "There were so many reasons. My nerves first. I was always nervous, even as a boy. There was always something like cheap woollen underwear prickling me. I itched with whatever it was that ran from my brain through the rest of my body, and yet there seemed nowhere to scratch. I wasn't cut out for war. But who is? The more action I saw, the more it came to me that the world had gone mad. Not only the gun-numbers and sergeants and padres and generals and politicians, but the factory-workers turning out guns and aircraft, and the businessmen, and the debutantes entertaining the troops, even the dear old things sitting at home and knitting comforters and writing letters to their nephews at sea. Mad, the whole issue."

One night at eleven o'clock exactly, remembered Rusty, I watched our cause sum itself up in the throats of a thousand guns all firing at once. And the birds started to sing, thinking it was day.

"It was a revelation to me," continued Walter, "and a kind of sickness as well, that the whole world was mad. Then once when I was on leave I took up with a girl, as you will, not thinking about it much. In her thighs, though, I rode at ease. I had peace for a while. And when she suggested that I should stay, I stayed, I didn't go back, I deserted.

"I think I know why most people dislike me. It isn't only my swarthy face and the scar all down one side. The reason is that I'm neither one thing nor the other. I am bright enough to be exasperated but not bright enough to understand. How could I be? My trouble is I know enough to irk people but not enough to help them. But in a mad world what more can you do?"

"I never deserted," said Brandy, "because I never joined. Early I learned that I was stronger than most men and braver, and that the cowards and weaklings were out to trap me. So I took evasive action: I relied on myself, I lived by my wits, I blustered. I sometimes ran with this pack and sometimes with that, but I never joined. I drifted, but I never drifted into the pack of milksops who are everywhere and who think they are all there is. I sometimes think I come from another age. I should have been one of the praetorian guard who set up Caesars and pulled them down, just as they fancied, and who didn't give a shit so long as they got their pay and had an emperor who could keep law and order."

"A stiff prick knows no law," put in Dragon.

"When I joined the guards," went on Brandy, "I was a bear tethered by a chain that I knew I could break whenever I chose. I joined because strength and courage are honoured there and because I would have plenty of freedom for chasing tail. And I chased it, too. There has to be law and order, and there has to be strength to support it. But the strength can stand to one side and not be committed. That's how I stood. I joined, but it was on my own terms; and as soon as the war was over, I had had it, I deserted."

"I deserted," said Dragon, "because I'm a stag and I run as I will."

I am the same and not the same, said Rusty. I wish I could be so simple. Are these men? Or animals? Or men masquerading as animals? For me it would be a masquerade. I remember too much, I desire too much, I know too much, to be merely an antlered stag. I would have to toss and balance a whole world of perfection on my horns. It was to hunt for Althea that I lit out. But I was carried along by my runaway muscles, too. They were my accomplices. We set out exultant together. But now I knew that I was exiled from the animal kingdom by coupling with another animal; and to try to return would be to become less than myself. I must grow new antlers for a new world. But can I?

But now the voices were beginning again.

"It was perfect," said Tim, "when I was in the tent, sucking from my mother's breast. The tent was dirty, but I was warm there. I was warm there even when it was cold outside and there was little to eat and the police were chivvying us. So long as I could stay in the tent, I was at home, I felt safe. But ever since I was forced to leave, I have been a bird piping in bare branches."

"It was perfect," said Bud, "when my mother used to read to me. Tales and fairy-stories. She had a lovely voice, I wish you could have heard her!"

"No, it was never perfect," said Walter. "Even when I was riding with that marvellous girl. There was always some flaw, an odour of cooking that came in through the window, or the way that she looked at me or something she said. I could never forget — was it my scar or my face or myself? Perhaps what I could never forget was that I was going to die."

"There is nothing perfect," said Brandy. "Why should there be? I've been around, and I've seen plenty in the world that is hard or hopeless or ugly, but nothing that's perfect. I've been around a long time and I know. I was there the night they say the stone was rolled away. Well, it wasn't. It was all a put-up job. And there was no ascent. No one ascended into heaven, because there isn't any heaven to ascend to. Some people say you can climb into it by climbing between a woman's legs. So help me, you can't. I've had them under bushes, I've had them in canoes, I've had them in caves, I've had them on billiard-tables. You can't get into heaven that way, because I tell you there is no heaven, there's nothing perfect, paradise doesn't exist."

"Why make such a fuss about perfection?" said Dragon, "I never ask whether something is perfect or not. I just get on with it. I enjoy myself. I take life as it comes and enjoy it. I put up my dukes and tell it to do its worst, and still I seem usually to be able to hold my own. When I clap my hands for the dancing girls, as likely as not they appear; and then I take my pick and it's not often that I'm disappointed. I just take everything as it comes and never bother to ask if it's perfect."

But paradise exists, said Rusty, it must. Once you have known it, you can never deny it. That stillness I still remember. Limbs glistening like petals in the moonlight. Light spiralling outward. A fragrance of hay and honeysuckle. A perfection tangled — that's strange! — in flesh, in lips and brows, caught there, a bird caught in the rigging. When you are least expecting it, to come on it by surprise like wild honey hidden in a tree. In a tree that will rot. Althea! I knew heaven with you once and can never forget it. It exists. It exists. Freshened by dews … but then clouds over … disappears … a garden (you can build nothing there) and not a city … a garden that fades … fades; but leaves resplendent behind it unfading peacock dreams that, feathering and fanning out on the roof of the cave, re-echoing greens and purples, have eyes to watch whether we will betray them. I am pierced. I dream of my dreams, watching the eyes that watch.

And then the other voices resuming.

"It's the eye of the policeman," said Tim, "that most makes me feel guilty — even when I've been good. Sometimes I almost hated them when they would come questioning and badgering and moving us on."

"Guilt," said Bud, "is what you feel when everyone turns against you. I got to know that when I screamed and ran and afterwards nobody would have anything to do with me. Their eyes made the air so black and cold I wondered if I could ever stand to live with myself again."

"I have been made to feel guilty, too," said Walter, "by what other people thought of me. But why care so much for what people think? It's silly. There isn't any kind of behaviour that some society somewhere hasn't permitted, even honoured. What every society does, I've read, is to pick out only a few from the thousands of possibilities there are and then wrap them around an axe and call that the law, and then anyone who doesn't confirm *is* liable to lose his head. I try not to feel guilty for anything."

Rusty was conscious of a movement of prisoners, of an effort to slip out of manacles. It seemed to him, too, that he was being appealed to. For himself, he had the illusion of perfect freedom. He seemed to stretch up to his full height, lithe as a sword, and to be twirling this way and that. As he twirled one way, every shadow fell from him, he was naked, guiltless, he had been purged of every shadow cast on him by the fear or envy of others. But then as he twirled in the other direction, the shadows were rewound about him. The sword of himself shone through, it was hardly tarnished. But the shadows clouded it. And now they seemed to be part of its trappings, to be associated with its splendour. Were they caused by the sword's brightness faltering, failing, falling short of itself? Tirelessly he spun this way and that, this way and that, but could reach no conclusion.

Guilt is, he said … But he couldn't go on. He collapsed again in a heavy heap on the floor.

"Guilt," said Brandy, "is a conspiracy of the clergy to get you down. Guilt is one of the methods of the weak."

"I have never known what guilt is," said Dragon, "because I have never felt it. An animal is no more innocent than I am. I feel as guiltless as a great sleek caribou with balls as hard as chestnuts."

Guilt is, said Rusty, trying again … But he could go no further. He couldn't finish. He had fallen asleep. This time there could be no doubt about it.

When he woke up a few hours later, everyone had left except Dragon, who was asleep on the cot, and Tim, who was swabbing the floor. As Tim let him out, the stars were almost gone. It was nearly morning. But the streets were still empty as he walked home through the grey vaporous dawn that knew itself so little it could hardly tell yet whether it was making toward light or darkness. It had not yet declared itself. The only heat it knew came from the lonely sparks that Rusty struck out now and again on the pavement as firmly, vaporously, he strode back toward his room — with the world in his mouth like a bullet.

7

The festival was over.

As he looked back, he could hardly believe there had ever been such a party, it had all foamed up so unexpectedly. Foamed up, and dissolved just as quickly. The ricocheting, opalescent froth, the revealing swirl and eddy of intoxication, its jet and spray and sheen and spread, had all been reduced in no time to the suds covering the children's wash and to water in which cabbage was boiling. He didn't go back to Dragon's for a few days. He hardly went anywhere, in fact. He felt a deep lassitude, almost as though he were coming down with flu. One morning he slept in till noon. Another morning he spent in endless, unrealistic calculations about how much longer his money should hold out on the basis of a number of possible hypotheses. He couldn't rouse himself. Steve sought him out, and he spent a long time listening to the worried boy's misgivings about his relations with the refugee community. Did they know about his dealings with the sailor? Had he been recognized by the officer when he was delivering the paper? These possibilities were canvassed over and over again. But nothing new had happened since their last meeting, so Rusty couldn't get too excited about dangers he couldn't apprehend or too involved in the complexities of a society he could hardly imagine. It even seemed to him, as he listened, that Steve himself, obsessed though he still was, was nevertheless almost a little bored with his own obsessions at times and longed to be rid of them. Or was it rather that his problems and Steve's had by now flowed so completely together that the lassitude of one was bound to be communicated to the other? In any case, he listened and was glad that Steve was doing as he had suggested and for the time being, at least, was not being drawn further into danger. Another afternoon he thought of visiting Anne again, as he had promised; and he checked to see that he still had the address. But that could wait, he told himself. Instead, he found himself making his way back to Dragon's. The weather was cold and raw, and earlier in the day there had been a few snowflakes. He walked along dully, hardly wondering whom he would find or whether he would find anyone. But when he had circled in behind the warehouse and was standing at the foot of the shaky wooden stairs, he noticed that the door at the top was swinging open. As soon as he got to the top, he could see that the hideout was deserted. The few possessions were gone, the tarpaulin had been taken down, the wind blew through it. There was nothing to suggest it had ever been inhabited.

The party had been a chance gathering of fugitives, and now they were all once again scattered and wandering.

In his own wanderings he noticed increasingly now how a strip would sometimes peel off from the surface of things and impose itself on his perceptions and remain there — but completely without meaning. This would happen with street names, for example: he would look up and see the name "Trincomalee Avenue" and it would detach itself and become fixed in his retina, but without any meaning as a pointer to a place where people lived or worked or where cargoes were stored and sorted. It had become merely a design in black and white that was as unintelligible to him as if the characters had been in Arabic. Or a sign that read, "Artificial legs, arms, and eyes." Or a sign saying, "The end is at hand!" Or even such a practical warning as "Danger. Cranes working." Any of these might suddenly and unaccountably turn into a meaningless scribble that nevertheless stayed on his eyeballs teasingly. Or he would find himself ticking off with his eyes the posts in a railing like a child trailing a stick along it or else weaving endless patterns in a plain brick wall until what had once had purpose — and in some lights might have even flamed into radiance — was drained of all structure and reduced to unrelated surfaces and designs, with arbitrary shapes, dimensions, textures.

Although he was wandering farther and farther, his mood was still one of lassitude. He must try to rouse himself, he knew. He made various efforts to create routines for himself, but none of them came to much. He blamed himself for his lack of will power; but he was less aware of another possible reason for his failure. Any routine would mean that every day he would appear at the same place at about the same time, and that might make it easier for anyone who was looking for him to find him. If his movements were random, if he came and went more unpredictably, he would be more elusive, he would be more able to throw off his pursuers, who remained mostly invisible but who were working with growing power in his imagination.

So he was driven to longer and longer marches. From his base in the docks he made long forays to the zoo, to the palace, to the market, to the Plaza. Usually he went on foot because he liked the sense of exhaustion that was given him by walking mile after mile after mile. But sometimes, when he was in a different mood, he would go underground and take one of the trains that spread out beneath the city. It reinforced his sense of the light and dark in himself to sink underground and sit withdrawn and musing and then to emerge into a completely different environment, stirred and quickened, it might be, by lights and signs and traffic. And he was tantalized by another effect. Sometimes as the train pulled away from a station and the tunnel-wall slipped itself ironically behind the window opposite like the silvering behind a mirror, he would catch a glimpse of his own face. His reflection always seemed to be smiling. And that was strange. Why did the darkness persist in returning to him such an ironical likeness of himself? Why was it always smiling at him? He was baffled, because as he sat in his skin and watched his image opposite, he was not conscious of any signs of a smile on his face. What he felt, on the contrary, had more the feeling of pain.

Of course the city, too, had changed with the season. Early winter had emptied the parks. The guards at the palace were muffled in greatcoats. The trees were bare and melancholy and dripping. A few street-artists were still sticking grimly to their trade, but they looked miserable. The streets were no longer for loitering or lounging. Even in the old foreign quarter where he had roomed at first and where there were usually more people loitering or standing at corners than anywhere else, the streets were appreciably emptier. On the other hand, the bars were fuller, as he soon found out; you could hardly press your way through from the door to order a drink. In the Plaza, decorum had come further into its own. The grey facades were enhanced by grey skies and touches of frost; the column in the centre seemed more gaunt and martial; the offices of the Ministry more synoptic and severe. Under the arcades there was still a ragged procession flowing, but it had thinned and congealed with the onset of winter and moved less fluently. As Rusty watched, he was no longer looking particularly for Althea. And it no longer seemed like a flood being borne to judgment. It was under judgment already. It was a line-up of suspects being scrutinized by wakeful, baleful eyes. No one could escape from the rigour of his examination, he felt sure, so sharp an edge had been given to his glance by the whetting within his own person of blade on steel, back and forth, back and forth, in one of the oldest of all complicities — a complicity he had long felt, but more diffusely, never so keenly, so extremely — the magic complicity between hunter and hunted.

These were salt-licks, the Plaza and the old foreign quarter. From one season to another they were frequented less or more. But they never ceased to draw those who craved what they had to offer, and not only citizens but migrants and wanderers as well, animals who came out of the woods to savour with parched tongues what had been missing in their diet.

One evening when he was in one of the bars of the quarter he came across the sailor whom he had met with Steve. There was no mistaking him in his oddly cut reefer-jacket, pinched in at the waist and then flaring out, and his limp, white-topped peak cap. Yet Rusty was surprised to see him. Somehow he had imagined him, when he wasn't at sea, as staying close to his ship and never moving far away from the docks except to carry out some special errand or commission. Not, anyway, as he was here, leaning back amiably against the bar, with his cap pushed back from his forehead (to show that, although still a young man, he was already almost bald, with his crown covered by only a little blond fuzz) and welcoming him jovially and calling for another round of drinks. This was a new aspect that was hard to fit to the others he had been shown. The once Rusty had met him before, the sailor had prided himself complacently on the service he was doing by bringing families into touch again. But what was it he had told Steve? That he no longer seemed to care about anything? And clearly he had been trying to manipulate the boy for some malign purpose. Yet here he was behaving like a good fellow at the bar, slack and affable and perhaps a little drunk. What did all that add up to? The triangulation didn't seem to yield a possible character. The pieces didn't fit together. He had been given back and front and sides but he couldn't use them to construct a person.

A few evenings later he had an encounter that was much more disturbing. He was sitting by himself in a bar when a total stranger came up and spoke to him as though he were an old acquaintance. He was bull-necked; and Rusty didn't know him from Adam. But he called him by name and seemed to know a lot about him. He knew the unit he had served with and the medal he had won. Rusty was completely at sea. It was only when the stranger mentioned Dragon that he began to see some possible light. Was this someone he had met at the party at Dragon's? Possibly, he supposed. But he doubted it. Certainly he had no recollection of ever having seen him before in his life. He still didn't have a clue. And the conversation was turning in a disconcerting direction.

"We were hoping that you could come in with us," the stranger was saying confidentially.

When Rusty didn't respond (he couldn't, he didn't have the faintest idea what it was all about), the stranger didn't press him. "We'll keep track of you anyway," he said, "because you're just the sort of fellow we're looking for."

Then with a cheery farewell, he was off.

When Rusty left the bar a little later, there was a high wind that was reaching down gustily between the dark glimmering facades and blowing the light from the street-lamps helter-skelter. He was anxious. He couldn't imagine who it was that knew so much about him or how he had been set on the trail. He was anxious: the number of his pursuers seemed to be growing. He almost wanted to break into a run. He still had sense enough not to, but he quickened his pace. The black wind clutched at his collar, muttering "… but you are outside it." He was anxious because so much of himself seemed to be lost; layer after layer of tissue spread almost lifeless around the tiny all-important vial that he was guarding. It was as sovereign and essential as ever. But it was covered by so much apathy! He couldn't understand it. Now he was coming to an area that was more brightly lit. As the restrictions had been relaxed, advertisers had taken advantage of the opportunity to promote their wares again with coloured lights. But the more strokes of colour that had been added to the enclosing skyline, the more void it had become. As though a man were to say of an experience, "This once can't matter," and let himself be scored by it, and so on, again and again and again, until his whole flesh was a livid mass of stripes, a carnival of brutal colour that ran together and ultimately went reeling away, grey and dull and lifeless.

The lights ran together in Rusty's head. He hurried on and clattered down a flight of stairs and caught the last train back to the docks. But when he got out, he didn't go back to his room. He found the slip of paper with the address on it and then made his way to 17 Acacia Road. As he walked up to the third floor, he wondered whether he would find her in. He should have telephoned, he supposed. But that wasn't the way he did things. Anyway he needn't have troubled: when he knocked, she opened the door for him. Her hair was carefully done, she was wearing a brown and white print dress, her shoes were an expensive-looking pair of trim brown pumps. The room was as dismal as it could be, but she hadn't succumbed to it. She stood out so unexpectedly against it that he couldn't resist telling her how smart she looked.

She turned her head away and smiled a little before saying, "I thought you wouldn't care for a girl who didn't look smart."

Then she came up to him and put her arms around his neck and said, "Oh, I so wanted you to come back!"

He stroked the back of her neck but said nothing, and she released him and went to a cupboard and got cigarettes and a drink. She even had some cocktail biscuits, too, and brought them out. Rusty was so impressed by the style and quality of everything he was offered that he asked good-humouredly, "Do you treat all your visitors as well as this?"

"I don't usually have visitors," she answered. "I haven't had anyone in the room since the last time you were here."

Rusty hadn't intended to spend the evening in conversation but he hardly knew how to come to the point, the atmosphere Anne created was so proper and domestic. Finally he went over and clumsily began to undo her dress. She didn't resist but as his hands were busy about her throat and bodice she asked hesitantly, "You wouldn't like to talk a little longer first?" He didn't answer but turned off the light and got undressed and led her over to the bed.

All his anxiety left him. He was no longer haunted by the thought of who might be pursuing him. But his apathy hadn't disappeared. He felt remarkably little. He was aware of her drawing away from him at first and then of compelling her until she was more than acquiescent. But in spite of his ardour and mastery, he experienced little feeling; he might almost have been anaesthetized. At the height of his passion he noticed with a shudder of surprise that he was left quite cold. As he filled her with himself, he might almost have been a salmon spawning in cold fury along a river-bed.

Then they lay back. She curled her hand in his. In a few moments he asked, "I didn't hurt you, did I?"

"A little," she answered. "But I like pain when you give it."

How much did she mean by that? he wondered dreamily. Then he fell asleep for a while. When he woke up, he found that she was sitting at the foot of the bed. She was still naked except for a coverlet that she had pulled around her thighs, and was sitting there watching him. But calm as her gaze was, there was still something unnerving about it. He loomed too large in it, he felt. He had been given a place in her eyes that he was afraid he could never fill.

Rusty pulled the covers up to his waist and asked her if she would get him a cigarette. "And please don't stare at me," he added.

"Was I? I didn't realize," she said.

She lit him a cigarette and smoothed his hair and then lay down beside him. "I could trust you," she said, "trust you with any of my secrets."

He slipped his arm under her head and around her shoulder and held it in a strong grasp. But he didn't say anything. He knew that she wanted to talk, but he wasn't willing — not yet, at least — to become so involved with her. They lay quietly a little longer. Then he leaned over and kissed her and was surprised to find that her eyes were moist. They agreed they would meet the following week-end and settled on a time and place. And then she lay back on the bed watching him as he put on his clothes and got ready to leave. After he had said good-bye and was standing with his hand on the door, she held him only a moment longer in order to go over the arrangements they had made for another meeting and to make sure that they both understood them.

Then he was going down the dark stairs and was thinking to himself, Perhaps by then I will have started to feel again.

But it was Steve who first broke through his apathy. He appeared very early one morning before Rusty was up. His eyes were glazed and unfocused and his lips were trembling. He looked as though he had seen a ghost. But he had seen something worse, Rusty had to admit after he had heard the story. They went over it so many times — and there had been such a confluence of Steve's problems with his — that he came to feel before long that everything that had happened to the boy in the last twelve hours had happened to him as well. In a while he could almost recite the story by heart.

At about eight o'clock the previous evening the sailor had called at the house where Steve had a room. At first he was easy and genial. He was sorry he hadn't seen Steve for so long and that he didn't bring any word of his parents. He made no reference to the *Voice of the Fatherland*. But Steve was on edge because he couldn't believe that the sailor had come only to indulge in pleasantries. For his own part, he managed to put in a remark now and then, but he knew that his voice sounded strained and nervous. The sailor, though, seemed not to mind, or even hardly to notice, as he laughed and joked about his life at sea and his adventures ashore.

Then he went over to the window and pulled down the blind, shutting out the black world outside with its trickle of light from other windows. When he turned around, facing his victim, his face was completely different. It seemed to have been frozen. His eyes had taken on a stupid, fishy stare that was not mitigated by any signs of expression either beneath his bald brows or around his mouth.

He stood impassively, twirling the blind-cord in his hand as he said, "The people I work for want something from you."

When Steve didn't say anything, he repeated flatly, "They want something from you."

Finally the boy managed to not much more than whisper, "What is there they could want from me?"

Satisfying himself with that meagre response, the sailor then proceeded to outline tonelessly what it was they wanted. There was a group of former officers who were believed to be meeting every week and planning something, perhaps in co-operation with the leaders of one of the political parties in the homeland that had now been proscribed and driven underground. Two of the officers were known to Steve. What he was to do was to find out what they were planning.

At once the boy flashed white with anger. "You mean you want me to spy on my own friends?'

"No. Just to get information from them," the sailor corrected.

"That's spying!" the boy insisted.

"I wouldn't say so," the sailor maintained stolidly. "But call it what you like. I don't care. That's what you're going to do anyway."

"I won't, I won't," he protested, his voice getting shriller with each repetition.

"Even if you don't care what happens to you, you might think about your parents," the sailor suggested. "They're both still alive, you know, and things might happen to them if you don't agree to co-operate."

At that Steve almost broke down. He looked helplessly at the smooth null figure facing him. There was nothing that he could appeal to, nothing even that he could latch on to. He felt as though he were dealing with a fissure rather than a personality. He was inside the open gullet of a shark — and he sensed that his tormentor might be inside the gullet of another larger shark, and so on and on, until the whole world was swallowed up in a ravening leviathan. But the shadow of that apparition somehow strengthened him. He wouldn't cry.

"Have you no pity?" he asked. "There was a time when you used to bring me letters from my parents. You said you were glad to, that you were glad to help people. What has come over you?"

"I've done many things in my time. I've had to. I've had to live, like other people. Now I don't much care what I do. But all that's beside the point." His voice, which before had been firm but dull, now took on a new edge. "I'm here to tell you what you're to do. I've told you, and I now want to know whether you're going to do it."

Steve's momentary strength had all vanished. He shrivelled. He could only fight back like a child. "I won't do it, I won't, I won't," he almost screamed.

"You will, you know. If not for me, then for someone else." The sailor spoke in the tone of someone trying to deal with a tantrum. "I've gone as far as I can go," he added ominously.

Then he said that he would be off. But he told Steve to think it over; and if he knew what was good for him — and for his father and mother — he would meet him in an hour's time at a rendezvous only three streets away.

By this time Steve was exhausted with worry. He tried to get in touch with Rusty, but couldn't. He was left to decide by himself whether he would keep the rendezvous or not. If he did, he was afraid of what might happen to him; if he didn't, he was afraid of what might happen to his parents.

When he reached the address he had been given, he was afraid to go in. Sheltering under the shallow portico a few steps up from the street, he still couldn't bring himself to ring the bell. But as he stood there hesitating, the door was opened from the inside and he was ushered by the sailor into a nondescript hall. It looked to Steve like any hall in a thousand other boarding-houses, with an old-fashioned marble-topped hall-table, and a mirror above it, and a green notice-board beside the mirror, and a rubber-plant beneath the notice-board — everything you would anticipate, except for a photograph hanging at the foot of the stairs of the new political leader in his homeland, a photograph enlarged to heroic size and supported on both sides by coloured graphs of rising industrial production. But he had only a moment to notice his surroundings before he was led into what seemed to be a long dining-room on the ground floor. It had two more rubber plants and a player-piano … Then the door at the back of the room swung open and a short, powerful man came in. He must have been watching, Steve suspected, through a small pane of glass in the baize-covered door. He had gnarled shoulders and was filling his pipe with square, pudgy fingers. The sailor introduced him and said he was the chauffeur in the embassy. At that Steve relaxed a little: there couldn't be much harm in a chauffeur. But this was a different kind of chauffeur, it was soon clear. He took charge of the situation at once, and the sailor was obviously afraid of him. He motioned the other two to pull out chairs from the dining-room table while he stood beside the piano. Then he went over again what it was the embassy wanted. When the boy still refused, he put his hand into the breast pocket of his jacket and pulled out a white cardboard folder. What he leafed out first and passed over to Steve was a photostat of a receipt that he had signed for money received in return for membership lists. Then another photostat. Then a photograph of Steve delivering copies of the *Voice of the Fatherland.* Then another photograph, this time showing the name of the paper more clearly and giving a very good likeness of him in sharp profile. As he stood up to examine them, the boy's knees were so weak he was afraid he might fall. He felt so giddy that it was only as though from a distance that he heard the chauffeur say, "I don't imagine you'd like these to come into the hands of some of your friends here?"

He didn't say anything in reply. He couldn't. Then he heard the voice continuing, "If you don't want them to, you'd better agree to do as we say. Within twenty-four hours."

It was only then that he managed to find his own voice again, pleading for more time to make up his mind — a week, say, or at least three or four days.

The chauffeur at first was adamant. But finally he said, "Forty-eight hours." With that he turned and walked chunkily to the door at the back of the room and disappeared. And then Steve was ushered out by the sailor.

It was now after midnight. He went back to his room and paced up and down, his mind whirling with his mother's tears and the notes of his father's cello and the curves of his own signature and then, increasingly, the flailing arms of a discharged refugee soldier who a few days earlier, according to the newspapers, had flung himself off one of the bridges. Had he been pursued and caught like this and taken what he thought to be the only way out? And staring down, Steve saw the midnight water rising to meet him. He knew he should try to sleep. But when he lay down, he found himself in even greater jeopardy; he was being swirled around in a black abyss. He got up and started pacing again; and it was only toward five o'clock that he fell into a sleep of utter exhaustion. As soon as he awoke, an hour or two later, he set out to find Rusty.

Now Rusty knew the story almost by heart. And he knew what he must do about it: he must put Steve in touch with Mark. But that was easier said than done. When he telephoned the flat, there was no reply. He assumed that Mark must be either at the Ministry or else on his way there. So he waited half an hour and then called his office. Yes, his friend had arrived, he was told, but was already in a meeting. Would the caller care to leave his name or try again in perhaps an hour? But when he called back, Mark was still engaged — and an hour later — and an hour later still. It was almost one o'clock when Rusty finally reached him. His voice showed neither surprise nor irritation; but he explained that he would be busy almost all day long with something that had flared up unexpectedly. However, he would have to come back to the office after dinner and would be there until at least nine. Could they both come in to see him then?

Steve had been fractious enough all morning, but this further delay made him so nervous and anxious as to be almost unmanageable. They played patience for a while with the greasy cards spread out on the bed. They talked. They went out and wandered morosely under the chill leaden sky. They came back and played more patience.

By the time their appointment was almost due and they were crossing the Plaza towards the Ministry, Rusty had thoroughly caught the contagion of the boy's nervousness. Although the sky was heavily overcast, he was reminded by the column in the middle of the Plaza and by the steep roofs all the way round it of how tranced and frightened he had been so many weeks back, looking up into the straggling routed heavens and then noticing the police patrol across the Plaza and taking to his heels. He wondered how the interview with Mark would go. He had often longed to talk with him, but now that the opportunity was so close he would have avoided it if he could. If it hadn't been for Steve, he would have been tempted to take to his heels again. Because in talking with Mark he knew he would be confronting part of himself, and he didn't know what the judgment would be. The architrave was black and heavy as they passed beneath it into the portico of the Ministry. The only time he had ever been here before it had been summer and he had been a soldier in uniform, proud of how spruce he was and enjoying his freedom as though he had come to town for a fortnight's leave. Now he wasn't even sure of his own name. If he was asked for it at the door, should he use the name on his forged papers or the name on the back of his medal?

They were going through the swinging glass doors before he decided that he would merely ask for Mark at the desk and then wait and see what the security guard said. Mark would have left word about the visitors he expected. Whatever name the guard used, Rusty would follow suit. His heart was racing; but he soon learned that here, at least in the capital, he was the same man he had always been. He glanced at Steve, but the boy was too excited to notice that his companion had changed identities. He filled in the pass, a messenger was called, and they were on their way upstairs.

They were led up a broad marble stairway and down a wide hall, where the frequent failures of diplomacy were lavishly commemorated by paintings of naval and military engagements, and where its less numerous successes had been composed into busts of proconsuls and envoys and plenipotentiaries. Rusty fancied that some of these figures were eyeing him and knew all about him and were discussing him between themselves. But he resolutely thrust the fancies from him, bracing himself for when they should be delivered at Mark's office. Behind a closed door a typewriter was still clattering. And, a few paces farther on, piles of locked leather-covered boxes were being drawn up on a trolley by another frock-coated messenger. The next moment they had arrived.

It was a different office from the one he vaguely remembered. Larger and more elegant, with a fine mahogany bookcase rising almost to the ceiling and on the walls a few small but choice water-colours borrowed from the national collections. But it was still unmistakably Mark's; each of the three easy chairs in the office was littered to overflowing with newspaper clippings and statistical abstracts and transcripts of debates, so there was no place for anyone to sit down. After greeting them, their host apologized for the disorder and then made room for them by drastically sweeping everything from two of the leather chairs onto the floor.

It was odd and inhibiting to see Mark in these circumstances and in the presence of someone else. But Rusty was pleased to find that he could explain readily and comprehensibly enough the problem that had brought them there. Although Mark listened carefully, it was not until a stenographer had brought in a telegram for his approval and he had read it through and initialled it that his brow cleared and he seemed to be giving the story his undivided attention. He asked a few shrewd questions, bit his lip, and then suggested that he should talk to Steve by himself for a while — but the minister's office next door was empty and Rusty could wait in there.

That mystified him. To Mark these high-ceilinged stately rooms might be commonplace. To him they held all the mystery of the interior of a doge's palace, suggesting dungeons, galleries, audience-chambers, embassies from far places — and the crooked passages connecting dungeons and audience-chambers. He was reassured by his friend's whispering in his ear as he took him by the arm and guided him toward the adjoining office, "It may take a little while, but afterward we'll have time to talk by ourselves." But it was only reluctantly that he allowed himself to be finessed through the door.

On the other side stretched a sea of glass. What it would be in daylight, Rusty would never know. But now it shimmered with dark mirrors and prisms. It was a darkness that ramified evasively into the distance, flecked here and there in its sinister branching by tiny unstable trills and notes of colour. Then his friend turned on the light in a floor-lamp that stood beside a low table and a few easy chairs. A pool of light spread over one corner of the expanse of red carpet; and it was only then that, standing at its edges, he could see how deep the darkness was. It seemed to stretch illlimitably. Over the mantel-piece at the far end was a mirror that reflected what was in the mirror behind him, creating an ambiguous crystal dialogue, in which was involved a huge chandelier that hung over the centre of the room like a catafalque. Beneath it lay in state an empty, leather-covered conference-table, enlivened by nothing more than the thin spectral rays that came and went as the prisms in the chandelier shivered and broke up the pale white glow that entered through the windows or by the faint Christmas-tree reds or greens that were caught distantly by the surrounding mirrors from the Plaza's changing traffic lights. At first that was all the foam or life that he could see moving on this sea of glass.

His friend now had closed the door behind him; and he was alone. As Mark had suggested, he tried to divert himself with one or other of the political or economic journals that lay on the table. His interest soon flagged, though, as he struggled with an article on India's long-term balance-of-payments problems; and he fared little better with a discussion of the pattern of world trade in specialty steels.

He was wondering how Steve was getting along. He put down the periodical and lit a cigarette and gazed into the distance. Now in the darkness, with its undercoating of deep red, he began to be aware of gold, of gold picking out the cornices and the panels on the walls and gilding the mirror-frames and many of the chairs. And now he could discern obscurely in the far corner a huge battle-piece. He went closer and could make out hints of bearskins and busbies and tri-corns, of raised sabres and chargers being reined in, of crimson jackets and gold gorget-patches and black cartouche-boxes, of plumes and ribands and cockades. This was a room in which the past had silted up, in which the present was emaciated by being rebuffed from mirror to mirror. But the picture held him. He missed his own uniform. Anxiously he wondered how far he had cast off his honour, too.

He went back to the pool of light in the corner and sat down and tried to read a little more. He wished that Mark would hurry.

He was so restless that he couldn't sit down for long. This time when he got up, he turned off the light in the lamp above his chair. Now the room and the Plaza flowed more fully into each other through the windows that reached from the floor almost to the ceiling. He went over and looked out. It was strange to be looking down on the Plaza, to be seeing the top of the bronze cannon around the foot of the column and to have beneath him the arcades where he and Althea had met, where such countless other encounters had occurred — lyrical, lustful, conspiratorial, violent — where he had returned so often either avidly or with dull, but still not entirely extinguished, hope. Did such encounters find their way into this great room of mirrors? It seemed labyrinthine and unearthly. But perhaps it might be humanized by accumulating on its polished surfaces these stains and tarnishes from life in the nether world. Gazing down, he could imagine it just conceivably becoming a pure reflector where human hazards and miseries would be deposited like gold foil.

He went back and sat in the rich dark, leaning back and letting the cigarette-smoke curl up above his head. He wondered again how Steve was getting on. He hoped that his friend was dealing gently with the boy. But of course he was; there was no need to worry about that. Perhaps he should worry more about himself. He didn't know what to say to Mark or even how to begin. So much depended on how his friend saw him; and that he couldn't gauge or guess at. A few minutes ago he had thought that the mirrors were gazing at him and sizing him up; but he hadn't been allowed to hear their judgment. Would he be found diminished, tarnished? Or would he be still as he had always been? His hair was as glossy a chestnut as ever, his eye as clear, his arm as strong. And yet he was anxious about the impression he would make.

Perhaps he might fill in time by trying to guess what was being said next door. Obviously Mark would want to know in more detail about the boy's encounters with the sailor and the chauffeur. He probably would want to trace back step by step the way Steve had been hunted down in order to judge more accurately what his pursuers were ultimately after. But the trails in a big city were so hard to follow. The scents criss-crossed so. There were so many of them. Its pursuits were so confused, so endlessly tangled. Would even Mark be able to unravel the noose around the boy's neck? There were networks … networks. His mind was scored by dark possibilities. He saw above the city innumerable tight-ropes, and acrobats walking on them blindfolded, teetering with long poles; the sky full of wires tingling and singing and vibrating; and here and there white riders on them, riders as white as paper, who stepped cautiously or glided or were made to dance in time with the vibrations or were thrown entirely off and fell past him headlong; riders or acrobats with clown-white faces as the darkness swallowed them.

Networks … misadventures. His mind was fretted by them. He stood up to try to shake them off. But now something was beginning to happen to him in this room where he was quite alone. In the wateriness of the mirrored dark he was being stripped naked. He was being subdued by stillness. He stood there like a swimmer. There was no one else in the room, not a soul. Yet he was aware of a dark presence before which all the cords scoring his brain, all the nets, all his anxieties, were falling away. He was perfectly calm. He was naked, and was being clustered with gold. Slowly he moved to the window, and what he saw now was not the Plaza but something much wider and more outspread, something that curved gently far beneath him, the city and the estuary and the sea, the salt sea leading home. Home … even though he might never return to it. His left hand floated and rested on the surface of the large globe that stood in front of one of the windows. He felt the world curving away beneath him like the side of someone dear, or someone sleeping. It was sleeping in exhaustion after a spasm that had affected city after city, country after country, desolating and ravaging and laying waste, had involved earth's farthest extremities, guano-islands lying far out to sea and veins of pitchblende deep in the Arctic. It was sleeping, resting. But even in its sleep he could hear it heaving with undischarged torments, unsatisfied cravings. With dilated attention he was listening to the murmuring of millions of creatures who remembered being separated from the bough, who remembered falling like blossoms and then, it might be, being reunited to it in transient perfections. There were some whose memories and perceptions were too dull to have recollections or regrets. Perhaps there were some who had passed beyond regret. Certainly there were others whose instincts were so luckily modulated that they could live almost entirely for the moment. But there were millions more who remembered, at least at intervals, what had happened to them or, if they could not remember, still cherished their disappointment inwardly, like a wound, grieving over it in secret. It was their grief he was listening to as they turned in sleep. Longings unsatisfied even after such a brutal consummation! And he wondered what new spasms might be brewing. It was their murmuring that came up to him in the darkness. It was they that he was looking down on from above, and pitying. He was above himself and could see immeasurably far. He had been made other than himself by the ambiguous presence he sensed with him in the room … other than himself. Yet it was his own honour, he knew, that was being restored to him in the stillness. He had cast his uniform away. He was naked, homeless, wandering. He could be the prey of anyone, anything. Here on this promontory, though, as he stood for a while and stared out and felt the gold falling on his flesh in dark prodigality, he knew he was being clothed again in his own riches.

But now he must begin the descent. He was surrendering province after province of vision; and what still spread beneath him was being drained of life. With his left hand, which was still resting on the globe, he began to tap blindly. The sound that came back was hollow. He rotated the world this way and that, and it responded smoothly but brought him no intelligence. He was descending. The pressure on his ears was increasing. With his finger-tip he was tracing the paths of meaningless migrations and dispersions. The sense of meaninglessness had returned, had perhaps even increased. If there was a whirling world and millions of creatures whom it had spawned and then thrown off without help or hope or purpose or relation …? But he couldn't pursue it further. He was tired. Under the overcast sky the salt flood spread endlessly. And now the tree standing beside it was utterly leafless. If there was still sap in it, there could be no more than a trickle, no more than the tincture in the vial that he was still clasping to his heart.

He was in poorer shape now to face Mark than he had been when he first arrived. His nervousness had gone, but he had travelled so far afield he felt exhausted. Yet when the door opened and light streamed in and Mark called to him, he managed to put on a set smile. Clearly the interview had gone well. The boy looked as though he had just had a tooth out — spent and pleased and relieved. And his friend assured him that there was no need to worry, everything would be taken care of.

"I've been in touch with our security people," Mark explained, "and given them the whole story and they have it under control. If Steve here will just sit tight, he probably won't even hear from the sailor again or from his boss in the embassy. Anyway, nothing will come of it."

"You mean that not even my friends here in exile will know of it?" Steve asked, round-eyed. He had been told so before, but he could hardly believe it — or hear it too often.

"That's right," Mark said. "Don't ask me how we're going to manage it, because I can't tell you. But we will: we have ways and means."

"And nothing will happen to my parents?" Steve persisted.

"I don't want to promise more than we can deliver," Mark replied. "But I think we may have enough influence, particularly with your friend the sailor, to manage even that."

As the boy (who was almost tearfully grateful) began to thank him again, Mark broke in and suggested, with a kindly nod toward the hall, that perhaps he wouldn't mind going out and waiting in the messenger's office, since he hadn't seen his friend for some months and wanted to have a chat with him. And when the messenger came to the door, he added, "Perhaps you could find a cup of tea or coffee for our visitor, or whatever it is that you're brewing tonight?"

They were alone together now, Mark and Rusty. But neither spoke.

At last Rusty said, "Well, how does the world look to you?"

"About the same as usual, I guess," Mark replied flatly. "It's always had its bowels in an uproar." Here in the Ministry it sounded even more incongruous than usual to hear Mark shift into the army vernacular from his own more polished style.

"I was thinking of the crisis in the Middle East," Rusty countered. He couldn't tell yet what mood his friend was in and he didn't want to make a mistake.

"Oh, that. That will blow over. It's almost over already. No, what has been worrying me and keeping me busy all day is something that hasn't got into the newspapers yet. I can't tell you about it; but if it were to materialize, it might cripple us for years. What people seldom seem to realize," he added wearily, "is that our triumphs are to be found more often in the things that don't happen than in the things that do."

Rusty felt himself floundering and out of his depth. Until he felt surer what Mark was feeling and thinking, he couldn't tell him how he had seen the world only a few minutes ago from the adjoining office; and he couldn't talk about it intelligibly in any other way without having read all the telegrams and dispatches and newspaper comments that his friend had read. So he said nothing.

This time it was Mark who broke the silence. "What do *you* make of the world?" he asked fixedly.

Still Rusty was silent.

"Perhaps I should put my question a little differently. How are you and the world getting along together these days?"

What answer could there be to a question like that?

"Are you still on the loose?" his friend continued.

"Yes," answered Rusty in a low voice and looked down at his hands, which were spread out on his knees. He hoped his friend hadn't treated Steve like this. Never before with Mark had he been conscious of the dirt in his finger-nails or of how frayed his cuffs were.

"I thought you must be, because I had the police in to see me about you a few weeks ago."

"What did you tell them?"

"That you had stayed with me for a few days early in the summer when you were on leave and that I hadn't heard from you since."

He was grateful that his friend hadn't given him away, but he was so crushed by his coldness that he couldn't bring himself to say so.

"Have you been in touch with your family at all?" the interrogation went on. Mark was now playing with a silver paper-knife as he put his questions, flexing it, running his thumb delicately along the edge, as though he might use it the next moment to peel a pear or to slit open secrets. "Your father and sister, I mean."

He confessed that he hadn't, and then listened while his friend took him to task. "What you're trying to do, you know, is to contract out of the world. You want to escape from necessity. And that's something that no one can do. Not even you."

"I wouldn't argue with you," said Rusty. He wanted to say that that was surely what everyone would like to do, to escape necessity, to triumph over it, if only once, if only for an hour. But he was too depressed by the way the talk was going to try to argue. He let Mark suggest that it was only because he still had some money that he thought he could escape and that things would look differently when his money ran out. He didn't object when he was told that he couldn't do without a society of some sort, and that if he forfeited the society he had been born into he would probably find himself surrounded by something worse. It was only when Mark spoke of the "riff-raff" he would find clinging to him that Rusty was stung to reply; and even then his outburst wasn't a rejoinder to what had just been said but to something much earlier.

"You say I want to escape from necessity and that I'm a fool for trying to. But what are you doing?" Rusty flared up. "Do you have to bow down to necessity? Do you have to sell out completely? And are you sure that you haven't?"

His friend had been so lulled by Rusty's listlessness that the retort took him by surprise. The paper-knife slipped from his hand. His face looked grey. It was clear that he *wasn't* sure, that this was a question he had often put to himself and couldn't answer with confidence.

"I'm sorry," Rusty said at last. "Do we have to go on like this … savaging each other? I'm grateful to you for what you've done for Steve. But I need your help, too. Often in the last few months I've wanted to talk to you. I've needed you."

Mark went to a cupboard in the corner and opened it and busied himself finding a bottle of whisky and glasses on the bottom shelf. When he turned and set the bottle and glasses down on the desk and poured out some water from the carafe, his face had almost regained its composure. He handed Rusty a drink and then sat down again and leaned back and ran his fingers through his thin receding hair and asked to be excused for being so tired and preoccupied. But he didn't leave it at that.

"Now tell me about yourself," he apologized. "How have you been? Because I've been worried about you. I still am."

Rusty was so conquered by his friend's gentleness that he could hardly begin. But after a while he was telling him about Althea and about entering a world that he had always dimly apprehended but had never known before; and about losing it, being exiled from it; and about setting out to look for it again; and about not knowing what it was he was seeking and then simultaneously discovering and being inundated, engulfed, stupefied by the discovery until he could hardly support it, knowing he was irrevocably separated from what he had lost; and about the pressure gradually relaxing but leaving him listless and groggy and surrounded by more and more patches that seemed entirely without meaning. Why was there so much that was meaningless? And why had he been so overwhelmed?

"You *have* been wandering far and wide!" he could hear his friend responding. And Rusty nodded enigmatically, conscious that he hadn't told him the half of it, that he couldn't tell him.

"I don't know whether I can say much that will be of any help, but I'll try," Mark said. "Have you ever thought of something so simple as this, that man was made for activity and that he can't live without it? You can't expect to deny something so fundamental as that and get away with it. There's bound to be a backlash. If for no other reason than that for millions of years our ancestors had to be active merely in order to survive, to get food and shelter. That's bred into us. We can't escape it."

Rusty found himself wondering whether his friend really believed that he knew what man was made for. And surely the principal purpose of activity now was to conceal from a man what an odd thing he was and how uneasily he fitted into the universe?

When he picked up the thread again, he heard his friend saying, "And you're too much alone. I suspect you're not living in the real world at all but in a kind of bubble that you've blown for yourself. And you test everything against some private criterion of your own that may not be applicable outside the greenhouse where you've watered it till it towers like a bean-stalk."

"I haven't had to water it," said Rusty ruefully. "It's grown that way by itself. Anyway, what can I do but put what's of most value to me at the centre of my universe and let everything else find a place around it?"

"Exactly! That's just what I mean," continued Mark, who had picked up the paper-knife again and was flourishing it modestly as he made his points. "You set yourself at the centre of the world, and whatever you value most becomes the touchstone by which everything is judged. You're the judge and the jury for everything. You view everything from your own standpoint. But there are more people than you in the world. Who do you think you are?"

"The same as you, I imagine," Rusty answered almost sullenly. "An animal … an animal crazed by something it's tasted."

His friend was now less assured. "I remember your saying months ago," he mused, "something about feeling like one of the supporters to a coat of arms and wanting to wander off and live like a stag or a bear. Have you found any woods where you could do that?"

"No … no, I haven't," he answered slowly. "Perhaps I haven't learned much in my wandering, but I've learned that. Some men can live happily as animals. I can't. I wish I could. Don't ask me why," he went on moodily, "but I still envy the types who can roam without a mist coming into their mouths of what they've tasted, who don't go clouded by memories and can travel light, as free as the animals. I know I'm not like that, though. I have to find another way through the woods. Sometimes when I would think of how I had been enchanted and driven wild — I know it sounds silly — I wouldn't be conscious of another living thing, except perhaps a stray unicorn over there in the corner. But now the scene doesn't seem so special. I may not see many of them at any one time, but I know the woods are full of them, other creatures driven into the wilderness and yet unable to live like beasts. There are thousands of them, millions driven out by one thing or another, and crazed and wandering."

"I know there are," Mark sympathized. "But how can you do anything about it if you stay within your own sphere of infatuation, if you won't see anything except from that point of view?"

"How *should* I see things then … from the standpoint of statistics?" Rusty asked contemptuously, glancing at the statistical abstracts that were open on the floor. "Or from the order of two or three hundred years ago?" he added truculently, nodding towards the next room.

Now Mark was on his mettle. "You needn't be so superior even about statistics," he replied. "If we manage to avoid massive post-war unemployment, it will be chiefly because we've become familiar with large statistical aggregates and learned how to apply them. And what was so disgraceful about the eighteenth century? At least it didn't produce catastrophic wars every twenty-five years. But the point is that you can't do without some kind of order … and you can't base it on outcasts and wanderers … you can't base it on anarchy. And that's what there'd be if everyone were to follow your example. I know it sounds stuffy to say so, but the truth *is* that there have to be people who will take some responsibility for holding society together."

"With the help of the police," added Rusty.

"Yes, with the help of the police," conceded Mark, "whom I've asked to provide some protection for your young friend down the hall. What you don't seem to realize is that even for you to indulge yourself as a wanderer, there must be some kind of order and people who are willing to work to maintain it. Otherwise you'd starve or freeze to death or be clubbed senseless by hoodlums. You couldn't even be a deserter if there were nothing to desert from."

"I don't know," said Rusty after a while. "But let's agree for the sake of argument that there must be some kind of order. Does it have to be based on so few possibilities? There ought to be room for everyone. Not only for the few types who are Grade A, government-tested and approved, certified free from wanderlust and worms in the gut. Not only for the few specimens of that kind and for the millions more who try to imitate them. For everyone." He leaned back and covered his eyes with his hands to keep out the light. "The city I dream of," he said hesitantly, wary of exposing even to Mark what it was he was seeing, "is spanned by a sky so wide it can include — I don't know how to put it — can include millions of parabolas, one for each person, coloured differently, on a different trajectory, till the whole sky is blazing with millions of paths rippling across it. Do you remember how packed the crowds were on victory night, gazing up at the fireworks? Room for everyone there to blaze in his own way."

Mark's face was kindling with shadowy, flickering enthusiasm.

"You can have my vote for that program anytime," he said. "That's the only political objective I care much about. But have you thought how much planning and effort are going to be needed if we are to move even a little closer to that ideal? It's staggering. You know what Steve has been through and what he's run up against these last few weeks. That's only a tiny illustration. There's more than enough violence and malice still floating about to blow the world to bits; and the only way it can be curbed is by power. You can't have a society without power. But to use power so as to curb power and to widen opportunity — that's the problem, that's the difficulty, that's a task that everyone has a duty to share in as far as he can. These things don't just happen, civilizations that are freer than others and come closer to leaving room for everyone. They have to be made. There is something arbitrary, chosen, willed, about it. And worked for. If you want a city like the one you describe, haven't you a duty to help build it?"

Rusty had been listening intently, but his very intentness had served to carry him on to a different destination. With the word "duty," he found himself looking, not at a city, but at a blank barrelled wall from which the eyes of his dreams looked down at him. They were watching, watching, to see whether he would betray them. He looked up, with his hands still covering his eyes, and knew what he must do, whether right or wrong. I am a soldier, I will be true to the death, he answered them.

Then he unshielded his eyes and said abstractedly to Mark, "I know there's logic in what you say. My duty may be different, though. I don't see it clearly … it beckons me this way and then that. It may lie on the margin of things … with people you would consider lepers and outcasts."

Now Mark was frightened. But he answered bravely. "We are all outcasts, but we still have to help guard the city. Don't desert us."

"I may not be deserting you," Rusty replied. "I may still be on the establishment, I may be part of the guard, but my duty may be to wander. Perhaps what I am is a roving picket."

Mark smiled, thinking of all the nights they had done guard together, in leather jerkins to keep out the cold, tired, heartsick, in one position after another, roving about the command-post in the middle of the night to guard against infiltration or a surprise attack.

But his face returned to full seriousness as he asked, "Have you ever thought of what happens to those who never come in out of the rain?"

When Rusty didn't answer, he added, "Have you ever thought of what's happening to you already?"

Yes, Rusty had thought of that, often. But he still didn't answer.

"Have you looked at yourself in a mirror recently?" Mark persisted. "When I knew you first, you were as smart a soldier as there was in the regiment. And you were just as smart when you came to see me last summer. Now your shoes need shining, your suit needs pressing, you could do with a haircut. In my case, that might not matter, I always was sloppy. But it does matter in yours, it means that you're changing."

If Rusty looked far-away and unconcerned, it was because he was remembering how he had felt in the great room of mirrors next door, with its rich undercoating of red and its surface foam of prisms and cockades; of how he had been stripped naked in the darkness there, as he looked out over the city; and of how his own honour had come to clothe him. There was nothing to fear. That was how it would be in his wanderings, as he went down alleys and byways and among the homeless of all kinds, who might be mad or maimed or deformed but who were more indicative merely because they were homeless. There was some virtue in the very vial he was carrying that would protect him, he explained. "So don't worry about me," he said.

Mark now could see that his friend had almost certainly escaped him. But he would make one last attempt.

"You don't know what you're doing," he charged passionately. "You don't see that what you're doing springs from despair. And that isn't like you. You've given up hope. You've surrendered. Because of some scruple of perfection, you've bound yourself over to darkness. That's why you find the world more and more meaningless."

But his attack didn't make even so much as a dent. "No," said Rusty unperturbed, "that isn't true. At the very worst I'm no worse than you — a double agent for light and darkness. But really it's the other way round. It's you whose life rests on despair. Since you haven't any hope of changing people, the best you can do is to spend your life in making thousands of small adjustments and compromises that perhaps may improve things a little. If I go down into the dark, it's to find out where we are and what has gone wrong."

He didn't know how far he meant that, what he had just said. But he knew — they both knew — that they had come to an impasse. There was nothing for them to do but disengage and go their separate ways. As Rusty got up to put on his coat and say good-bye, his exhaustion had returned; and now it was total.

In a moment, the messenger appeared in response to Mark's summons; and he had Steve with him. "He's a hard man, your friend," Mark told the boy, regaining his equanimity and his most engaging manner, detached and friendly at the same time, "a hard man to argue with. Look after him for me, will you?"

He went with them to the head of the staircase and shook hands and seemed about to say something further. But he didn't. It was only when they were at the bottom that he called out, "Good luck!" And Rusty turned and called back, "Don't work too late. Remember there's a reconnaissance at first light." His friend's laughter came rippling down the marble staircase and followed them out to the door.

As they went out into the Plaza, Steve was still in the seventh heaven. He couldn't stop talking about how kindly Mark was, and how courteous; of how powerful he must be to be able to take care of such a problem so quickly; of how spacious and splendid it was inside the Ministry. Rusty didn't demur, but the colour of what he was thinking was very different. He felt depressed, there was a leaden weight on his mind. While the boy had been helped (and he was grateful for that), now he knew there was no one from whom he could expect help for himself.

Before separating, they stopped for a cup of coffee at a little restaurant, dismal and not too clean, that they happened to find still open. By now the predictable reaction was beginning to set in. The fear and tension that Steve had felt in his interviews with the sailor and the chauffeur, and his long sleepless night, and the day spent anxiously waiting, were all beginning to tell. The assurances he had been given by Mark were wearing off, and now he wanted to hear all over again that he had nothing to worry about.

"I'll not see them any more?" he asked. "Was that what your friend said?"

"Not exactly," Rusty amended patiently. "You probably won't. But whether you do or not, you have nothing to fear any longer."

Then he had to listen once again to the boy's gratitude. "I'll never forget what you've done for me today," he said, "never, never, never."

Rusty was touched and embarrassed, both. But more than either just tired, tired to the bone. It was a relief when he could finally say good-night and set out for the docks.

As soon as he got back to his room, he fell straight into bed and didn't wake up until almost noon the following day. When he was dressed, he counted out the money in his wallet. It wouldn't last for more than a week. Then he did a little washing and spread out the few pieces, shirts, socks, and underwear, to dry at the foot of the bed. After a while he went out and walked around the basin that was closest to where he lived. It was empty, and he stopped to skip a few stones across its gun-metal smoothness. Grey ripples mottled the surface, and then the skin of oil closed over again. In its own way, too, the sky held as dull and uneventful a pallor. He walked back through the light slush without meeting a soul. But on entering the door, he was surprised to find that while he had been out he had taken a decision: when he came to the end of his money, he would try to find work in the market.

It was that night that he had arranged to meet Anne again. She wanted to go to the pictures, it turned out; and so that was what they did. Then they went to have something to eat. To him, as they sat there among hundreds of other couples and had coffee and sandwiches (the bread still just as grey as in the worst days of the war), both of them feeling awkward and diffident, he hardly saying anything and she trying to keep the conversation alive and almost failing, but not giving up, almost desperate in her flowered hat and frayed suit but with a white blouse crisp around her neck — to him it seemed like a parody of a young man keeping company with a girl. He was impatient to be off. After paying the bill and helping her on with her coat, he suggested that they go back to his room. That made her more nervous than ever.

"Isn't it too late?" she asked. "What will your landlord think?"

"Whatever he likes," he replied irritably. "What did *your* landlord think?"

"But that isn't the same. What I have is a small flat," she tried to explain. "At least that's the theory."

He didn't answer. Instead he put his arm around her waist so that she followed along after him, at first grudgingly but then looking up at him and smiling. They reached his room without being questioned, and a few minutes later they were undressed and in each other's arms. His hands were under her buttocks: they were rich clusters of grapes that he was pressing, they were great sun-flowers, they were baskets of currants. Under the chill eaves it grew warm as summer. In the warmth his head drooped down to hers, their lips melted together, his drowsy wits descended.

But then his hazy relish was penetrated and knifed open by her withdrawing her lips from around his tongue and whispering, "I'm frightened, Rusty."

"Not of me?" he whispered gently in return.

"No."

"You're not still worrying about the landlord?"

"No."

"What are you frightened of, then?" It was so quiet he could hear her breathing. "I don't know … I don't know," she said. "Of myself, I think."

While she held him round the neck, he lifted her and laid her on the bed. He felt as little as before, his fury was as passionless. Startled from its deep nest, and now flying and fluttering aloof, his consciousness glimpsed that coldness momentarily like a patch of glacier or like ice floes (white against blue sea) seen through cloud. But that was not what it was fastened on. Rather he was wondering about her, about what she was feeling, as she lay beneath him. Vaguely at first but then with deeper and deeper bite, he realized that what he had entered was a region of pain. A region of freezing metal. Of metal plates held rigidly together. Plates that had suffered some agony of hammering and riveting and had then been cooled lower and lower. A region of almost absolute cold where the tongue is frozen to anything it touches, where the membrane clings to metal.

When they had done, they lay hand in hand, comforting each other, for now they were both frightened.

After a little while she asked him, "Why are you so withdrawn tonight?"

For a moment he believed he might tell her about himself. But he didn't. Instead he leaned toward her on his side and put his arm under her head and told her Steve's story and how he had become involved in it and how it had affected him. "If I seem withdrawn, that's probably the reason," he ended. "It may seem strange, since I've been around a lot myself, but the world's seemed different ever since I heard of it."

Again they were silent for a little, and then she asked him, "Why are so many people homeless nowadays, do you think?" He didn't answer. That was the same question that Steve had asked him, he remembered. And again he felt tempted to tell her about himself. But whom could you trust? He turned the temptation aside by asking her about her own home and family.

A shiver seemed to pass through the whole organism, the metal leaves cringed rigidly and painfully. But she told him that she was an only child and that her father had died when she was small and that she had been brought up by her mother. "But she was killed in an air-raid," she explained. And the tremor spent itself.

In a few minutes he pulled the blankets up about them. It was as though he was covering them both with leaves …

They must have slept long and soundly, because the figure at the foot of the bed, blocking out part of the grey light from the dormer window, had to raise his voice and repeat himself before they were fully awake. "I said that this isn't a whorehouse," the landlord wheezed stagily. "There are children living here. We're respectable people. This is a respectable home. And that's the way I intend to keep it. I'll give you just half an hour to get packed up and clear out."

As soon as he realized what was happening, Rusty wanted to leap out in his bare pelt and paste the snivelling little hypocrite until there was nothing left of his hollow chest but the wishbone. But Anne held him back: "It isn't worth it," she said. And his impulse was sapped, too, by realizing that if he tangled with the miserable one-lunged wonder, the police might be called; and then his goose would probably be cooked. So he sat bolt-upright in bed, shamefaced, furious, speechless, his spirit oozing away and his anger mounting till he almost choked, while the landlord repeated, "Half an hour!" and then shuffled back to the door muttering, "Disgraceful! Disgraceful!"

When he had dressed and packed and they were safely outside, Anne invited him to come and stay with her, at least for a few days. But he wouldn't hear of it. Yes, he would be sure to look her up in a day or two, but he wouldn't move in. He would fend for himself. So he saw her to the bus and waved her good-bye.

Only when her bus had turned the corner did he realize how much he wanted to be by himself. He felt humiliated. To have been unable to beat the intruder into a pulp! And no one to blame but himself! He didn't care about being caught with a girl in his room. Who would? But it cut him to the quick that by being on the loose he had been prevented from teaching the little sneak to mind his own business. His muscles ached with frustration. He could feel the acid eating into them. His pride was hurt, and he wanted to be by himself until he knew how deep the damage went and could let it heal. He stood with his kit-bag over his shoulder and gazed blankly ahead of him. He didn't know which way to go. In the light fog he vacantly watched a dog go scavenging up an alley. Always before when he had felt his honour stained he had had someplace where he could go and be by himself and lick his wounds. He followed the dog up the alley. Now he had no place to go and he couldn't rouse himself to find one. The thought even crossed his mind of not bothering to look for a room and sleeping in the open. His money wouldn't last for many days anyway; and he was just as strong now as when he had been a soldier and had slept out night after night. He didn't seem to mind how far down he went. These ruined buildings would provide just as good shelter as a slit-trench or a straw-stack. But when the alley came to a dead end and the dog turned, he turned, too, and began to walk in the opposite direction. The fog was thinning a little. It seemed ages since he had stood in the Ministry and looked out and seen the world curving away beneath him and had felt himself both naked and clothed with honour, joined to everything that was human and foiled and suffering. He wanted to be alone. And yet he was worried by how much more alone he had become since he had seen and parted from Mark in the Ministry. So long as he could feel that his friend was there to help him, he was not entirely alone, however solitary he might seem; there was still some refuge, some recourse. He had at least one friend at court. But now that recourse was gone. He had met a part of himself and had been rebuffed, shut out. The ties between his two identities had loosened still further. In the fog the name he had been born to seemed to flutter and waver and almost to disappear. He drifted down to one of the docks, where spars broken by the thick mist hung leadenly over the sheds. He picked his way through a wilderness of metal drums and came out to the leaden water that was heaving lumpily under an oily scum. It was like looking down at a dirty mirror. There was nothing to see, nothing lurking in the depths and nothing reflected. Still he gazed down in fascination. He was alone at last. And not without a remedy.

He gazed down until he felt almost dizzy. He needed something to hold on to. He gripped the medal in his pocket as though it had been a stanchion, gripped it until his fingers hurt. Then he picked up his kit-bag from where he had left it standing by a bollard and sauntered with it back out to the street.

He had decided he would start to hunt for a room by going to a little tobacco-shop he knew which had cards in the window of accommodation to rent. As he stood in front of the glass and was reading the dingy notices ("Single Room: Elderly Gentleman Preferred," "Competent Masseuse: All Types of Treatment Undertaken," "Will Share Expenses"), a stranger drifted to a stop only a foot or two away from him. At first he seemed to be studying the advertisements, too. But then he said unexpectedly, "You don't happen to want a room, do you?"

Rusty didn't answer or even turn his head. That didn't deter the interloper, though.

"Because I know a place," he went on, "that I think might just suit you. It isn't expensive. And there are others there of your sort. You'd soon find yourself worked into things."

Rusty wasn't pleased by anyone presuming to know what he was like and what would suit him. But he was paying too little attention to be really offended. He hadn't the slightest intention of making use of the address that was mentioned.

Yet it was hardly more than half an hour later that he found himself heading for it. What did it matter after all? If he wasn't going to sleep out of doors (and he hadn't taken leave of his senses to that extent), he needed a room. And one room was never very different from another.

When he got there, he didn't much like the look of the place. It wasn't that the stucco was peeling and the curtains on the ground-floor windows were torn and dirty; that was true of most of the houses with rooms to rent. He didn't know the reason. But why was it that, when moving into a new position, a soldier sometimes had the feeling that one house had been left mined, and another not, with booby-traps fastened round the top of doors and trip-wires lurking on cellar-stairs? or that one particular turn in the road had been registered in by artillery-fire so that unless you passed it at a terrific clip you would be caught there by guns waiting patiently for you five miles away? or, for no apparent reason at all, that a harmless-enough-looking wood, drowsing in the sun or nondescript under a grey sky, was full of the enemy and murderous with weapon-pits? He didn't like the look of the place, that was all. But he went in just the same. He hardly noticed that what had stood just beyond it had been blitzed and that one whole side of the house had to be supported by great timbers that were anchored, at one end, in the ruined foundations of the house that had stood next and fastened, at the other, into the rough exposed masonry high up on the house that was still standing.

It was inexpensive, anyway, as he had been promised. The proprietor occupied large gloomy quarters in the basement, and it was just outside his half-opened door that they stood to discuss what rooms were available and what they rented for. He didn't even insist on payment in advance.

"I size up my guests," he explained in an indeterminate guttural accent. "Some have money. Some have not. What does that matter? They will have it later." He laughed with a flightiness that seemed to be belied by his heavy jowls and by the hairs on the back of his bald head that stood up as stiff as boar's bristles.

"I prefer to trust my clientele," he added. And he called over his shoulder for confirmation, "Isn't that true, Rudy?"

From the steamy dimness on the other side of the door a thin young man appeared, who had nothing on above his waist and whose chest was lurid with a great sickle-shaped scar curving down from one shoulder almost to the bottom of his ribs on the other side.

"My nephew," the proprietor said by way of introduction. "He'll look after you whenever I'm out."

It wasn't until well on in the evening that the key to his room (he had been given one at the back, on the third floor), which the proprietor said must have somehow been mislaid, turned up and was delivered to him. The young nephew brought it. Now he was wearing a shirt, but it was unbuttoned down to his waist and a large slice of the dark, angry scar still glared out — plaintively, was it? or accusingly? or beseechingly?

After handing over the key, the young man sat down and lit a cigarette.

"It's not often that we see someone like you in these parts," he said with only too undisguised admiration.

"No?" replied Rusty.

"I suppose you were in the forces?"

Rusty said that he had been.

"Wish I had been, too," the other regretted. "No chance though. They wouldn't take me."

But Rusty didn't ask why. The young man was disappointed. The cigarette drooped so low out of the corner of his mouth it seemed about to fall.

After a few more puffs, he had summoned up enough weak resolution to go on without encouragement. "See this scar?" he said. And with both hands he opened his shirt wider till the curved wound was revealed in its full length, gleaming like a scimitar.

He had seen it. He didn't want to see it again. He didn't want to be shown what this stranger had suffered. Leave it, leave it, he wanted to cry out. But he didn't have the heart to. He would listen — but with as little of himself as possible — while the proprietor's nephew told of having had rheumatic fever as a boy and of his heart being affected by it and of the doctors at last deciding that they had to operate.

"It was touch-and-go," he explained. "Doctors didn't think much of my chances. Nor did I. I was frightened. My parents were both dead. There was no one to visit me."

He would listen. But he wouldn't look him in the eye. Why did he have to go on, this youth whose nickname was so like his own? He refused to lift his eyes above the scar, where they hung fixed. Scar or sickle or scimitar — but now it was more like a moon, a sickle moon, a deep red harvest moon.

"After that I couldn't get a job. And the services wouldn't have me. I didn't know where to turn. That was when my uncle took me in."

One moment he was listening. The next he had managed to stop his ears and the harvest of suffering washed past him. He resented being told all this, he resented this young man's name, he resented the misery he brought into the room. He felt pity for him; yet he couldn't stand him either, the waxy whiff of defeat, of weakness, that he gave off. With one breath, as he listened, he was humbling himself, asking, "In what way am I *so* different from him?" But with the next breath he was telling himself royally, "I wasn't born to lick the sores of lepers." So his breath came and went, came and went, now deflating him, now puffing him up, as the story went on — it seemed interminably. No, he would listen no longer.

"I'm sorry, but I have to go out," at last he cut in firmly.

"I haven't been boring you, I hope?" the young man apologized, getting to his feet, abashed now, almost servile.

"Not at all," Rusty replied. "But I have an appointment to keep."

He hadn't any appointment, of course. So what to do? He stood on the pavement in front of the shadowy house and leaped up in a kind of fragmentary sword-dance, so exhilarated was he to be outside. What the hell! He still had a little money left, he might as well use it for a few drinks.

He found a bar soon enough and stood by himself at the counter and laid out his money lavishly on double whiskys, one after another, until he was feeling much better, almost light-headed, and it was only a few minutes to closing-time. One more glass, and then he was passing effortlessly through the door, to be hit by the cold night air. He laughed out loud … he was drunk! The top of his head was sliced off obliquely and went skimming up among the wintry stars. But before it did, it hinted to him that he hadn't had anything to eat all day; he had been drinking on an empty stomach. Now as he careened along, he was seeing double-street-lamps, shop-fronts, signs, wires, even himself. The one eye that was floating up in the heavens and the eye that was still fixed in his head were having difficulty in getting him in focus. There he was striding along, a young man in a trench-coat, not too steady on his feet, perhaps, but still with something of a swagger, sure of himself fundamentally, he would make it all right. But the picture was troubled by other images that he was seeing or remembering: a soldier clear-hearted and serene in danger; a straggler who had lost his place and his honour; a searcher; a paraclete going among the lost and the wounded; a young man whom he had seen by accident very early in the war, unmanned, with the snot running down from his nose, as he stood weeping, disconsolate, in the blackout. With an effort he gathered all the shifting images together and halted in the angle of a building and pissed into the light covering of dirty white snow. Ah, that was better. But he wasn't done yet. Before he knew it, he was doubled up with cramps and was vomiting his guts out, and again, and again. At last he could straighten up. He took out a handkerchief to wipe his mouth, and with it came the last money he had in the world. He knew there was nothing left in his wallet. And he didn't think there were any other coins in his pockets. He searched with methodical thoroughness. No, that was the last. Now he was really flat.

What was the coin? He wasn't focusing well enough to know. But he could feel its heaviness and could see the head stamped on it. Slowly he brought it up to his eye until he was staring straight at the sovereign and the world was covered with majesty. And then wryly, gaily, emptily, he threw it away in the snow.

8

The next morning he went to the market looking for work. He had often heard that if you were on the loose and played your cards skillfully and were lucky, you could get a job in the market and no questions asked. Now he was out of money and needed a job; but he was nervous about speaking to any of the foremen. He walked up and down the covered passageways, which in some reaches were thickly silted with sacks of potatoes and in others were banked high with crates of cauliflowers or cabbages. Once or twice, as he wandered back and forth, he was mistaken for a buyer and was invited to admire boxes of apples that had been opened and tilted up for inspection or to finger mushrooms that glimmered fresh and pink as rabbit's ears in the weak winter sun. Embarrassed, he moved out from under the glass-and-iron roof and sifted down one of the side-streets. It was almost choked with goods that wholesalers had on display in front of their premises and with porters trucking loads of fruit and vegetables while a heavy transport tried to edge its way through the traffic. He watched irresolutely. Then at last he plucked up courage and approached a foreman in a leather apron, who was standing with a tally-book in his hand, and asked if there was any work for someone "with a strong back."

"And a weak head?" the foreman responded good-humouredly. But he didn't ask any more searching questions. And in a few minutes Rusty found himself taken on and set to work helping to unload crates of cabbages up from the country. Then it was crates of oranges up from the docks, then crates of lemons, then boxes of apples. Then there was a lull and he had time to go with three or four of the other porters to a coffee-stall at the edge of the market and have a sandwich and a cup of coffee. And then he was back at work again loading up a van from one of the big hotels with all the purchases that had been made for it that morning. An hour later and the market was almost over. Some of the dealers had already closed, and cleaners were sweeping up the litter from the passageways — straw and greasy cabbage-leaves and soiled tissue-paper and crushed onions and broken crating. Rusty was paid off with the others and was told there would be work for him if he showed up again at six o'clock the next morning.

When he got back to his room near the docks, he was so tired that he went straight to bed, even though it was still only mid-afternoon. As he was falling asleep, he heard a light knock on the door and supposed it was the landlord's nephew. But he didn't answer and before long the knocking stopped. And then he was fast sleep and dreaming of a garden, a kind of market-garden, where he was spading up new potatoes (they were honey-coloured in the clear sunlight, a pale delicate mulatto) … and then he was picking strawberries from beneath dewy leaves … and then he was in an orchard where cherries were ripe … for this was a garden of unending summer, where everything seemed to ripen together, without difference of season, and seemed to go on being harvested, perpetually, profusely.

The next morning it was pitch-black as he set out. The whole world might well have been another tunnel as deep and black as the one through which his train was running. When he got to the market, it had started to rain; and the pavement, slippery enough at the best of times, had become doubly treacherous. He had difficulty in controlling the light hand-truck he was using to unload crates of cauliflowers. Especially as he was going down-hill on slight slopes, it had a tendency to run away with him, and he was afraid of losing his footing. But he was given a few pointers by the middle-aged man with whom he was working, and steadied into the job. Not everyone was so lucky that morning, though. The sun had just risen (making hardly any difference at all) and he was sheltering deep under the eaves taking a breather when a young soldier came pelting into the market pursued by two military police. He was going at a terrific clip and seemed to be pulling away from them when one of his boots caught on a piece of sacking, his other foot slid on a greasy leaf, he skidded helplessly and came down hard in the gutter. He lay there on his back, incredulous, frightened, his legs splayed out, one arm on the roadway, the other on the curb, his eyeballs staring. He was young and slight. He looked to Rusty like a deer brought down by hunters. But his pursuers weren't taking any chances on how vicious their quarry might be. Avoiding his boots, they ran and grabbed him by his sodden shoulders and tried to pull him to his feet, and when he resisted, dragged him along the paving-stones, his legs thrashing, his shoulders writhing, his finger-tips scraping on the pavement for something to hold on to, his head bumping now and then in the gutter, as they wrestled him forward. In a few minutes a police van drove up, and with the aid of two other policemen they bundled him in. By this time blood was streaming from his nostrils and he looked as white as the underside of a young fawn. But all he seemed to care about was his cap, which had been knocked off as he fell and was lying on the sidewalk. One of the policemen went over and picked it up and gave it to him. And then they slammed the door to and drove off. But now the foreman was calling Rusty to get back to his cauliflowers.

That evening, after he had had a sleep, he telephoned to Anne and Steve to let them know where he was living and what he was doing.

"Thank God!" the boy said as soon as he heard Rusty's voice. "I feared for you when I found you were gone and they didn't know your whereabouts, or wouldn't tell me. And I feared for myself."

He had relapsed into a state of ceaseless anxiety. He worried about Rusty, he worried about his parents, he worried about himself. Was it possible that anyone in the Ministry could be so powerful as to protect him from the sailor, and to prevent his friends in the refugee community from learning what he had done, and even to ward off reprisals from his parents far away in his homeland? He couldn't believe it. His store of trust seemed to have been exhausted by what he had been through. Now he had none left. He who had always had so much faith now seemed hardly able to believe in anything. He believed in Rusty, but only when he could see him or hear his voice. Without that focus to hold on to, his mind spun round and round in endless questioning.

Rusty listened patiently and tried to give what reassurances he could and promised to keep in touch and agreed they would meet very soon. "God keep you," Steve said not once but over and over before he would ring off.

With Anne it was very different. "I wasn't worrying," she said. "I knew you would get in touch with me as soon as you could."

Then they talked about his new room and where he was working. They joked a little about how they had parted. She was trying to salve his wounded vanity and put him at ease. He recognized that and was grateful. "Well, we'll have to be more careful in future" she said.

"Yes, I guess so," he admitted. "If you can't be good, be careful."

He heard her laughter sparkling at the other end of the line. "But when are we going to get together? I've missed you, you know," she said. And they agreed to meet at her place in an hour.

She poured him a drink as soon as he arrived and they sat talking and joking about the last time they had been together and about what had happened to them both since. She was wearing a grey skirt and white blouse buttoned crisply about the neck, and seemed in especially high spirits.

"I have a job now, too, did you know? And not the kind you're thinking of," she said teasingly, almost brazenly.

He blushed, remembering the first time they had met. But she put out her hand and laid it softly on his sleeve and said, "No, I'm your girl now, never fear, you can't escape from me." And he covered her hand with his without saying anything.

"I've got a job as a stenographer, but only mornings," she went on. Rusty had wondered how she kept herself but hadn't wanted to ask.

"I didn't particularly want to work, but the payments were slow in coming in," she explained. Now that she had brought the subject up, he could confess his curiosity.

"The payments?" he asked.

"Yes. Haven't I ever mentioned them? The payments from my husband."

She smiled at how startled he was. "What will he say about *us*?" he finally blurted out.

"Oh, nothing," she replied airily. "Not a thing. We're separated, you know. He goes his way and I go mine. But he still sends me money and it's only when it doesn't arrive that I take a job for a while." It all sounded rather sad and feckless beneath the high spirits. But he took another swallow of his drink and didn't think about it.

In a few minutes she asked him if he would care for some supper. He hardly knew what to say: all he had had — and that some hours ago — was two or three sandwiches; but he couldn't believe that she could have much ready. He needn't have worried, though. She went to the end of the room and drew two chintz curtains, and there was a kind of tiny kitchen with a hotplate holding a casserole on one burner and a saucepan on the other.

"I thought you might be hungry," she called over her shoulder gaily, "so I whipped something together while you were on your way over."

It was good, too. She must have been saving her meat ration for weeks to have so many pieces of meat of one kind or another to go in the casserole. While they were eating, she asked him one question after another about the market. She was like a young wife who must know every last detail about her husband's first job, so interested was she in everything that concerns the flesh that sleeps beside her night after night.

After they were finished and the dishes had been put away and the curtains drawn again, he stretched out at one side of the large bed. Then when he had smoked down his cigarette, he called to her to come over. She turned out the light and came to the bed and was leaning above him while he was exciting himself with thoughts of what he would do as he was undressing her, when she said, very low, in the darkness, "Have you ever felt guilty, Rusty?"

"Not that I can think of," he answered non-committally. He didn't want to talk. He had had a good dinner; and now he looked forward eagerly to what was to follow.

"Not ever?" she insisted.

"I suppose so," he conceded with only the faintest edge of irritation.

"What were the times that made you feel guilty?" she continued probing. Now she was sitting on the edge of the bed.

"I do my best not to have to feel guilty," he evaded her.

"But you must have, sometimes."

"Oh, I suppose I felt guilty once when I ran away from home as a boy," he contributed indulgently. "It's so long ago, though, I hardly remember. And another time I felt guilty was when an order got twisted and I was late at a crossroad and two men were cut off and killed." But what was she getting at?

"Never anything more than that?"

"What are you trying to do? Make me admit that I'm a deserter?" at last he broke out angrily, completely losing his patience.

As he got up on one elbow and glared at her in the darkness, her tone dropped lower. "I knew that," she said. "I knew that all along. You didn't need to tell me."

There was a hush between them. Then she said, "Do you ever think of your mother, Rusty?"

He dreamt of her sometimes; but, no, he didn't think of her. "Why do you ask?" he replied gently, surprised at how quickly his anger had gone.

"No reason," she said wanly. Her faced glimmered like a water-lily in the darkness.

"But there must be a reason. Tell me." He put out his arm and took her by the hand.

"Oh, I've been so longing to tell you," she brought out at last. And then what she told him was about her mother, about their difficulties in living together, about how much was expected of her as an only child, especially after her father died, about their constant quarrels; and then when the war came how she thought she could escape by taking a job away from the village where they lived, but how her mother wouldn't hear of it, the merest suggestion of it seemed to drive her almost frantic; and then how she finally just left ("It was very, very wicked of me, my mother kept saying") and took a job as a typist in an aircraft factory and in a few months got married; and how one night not much later an enemy plane after missing its target was unloading its bombs before heading for home, and her mother's house was destroyed by a direct hit. "It was dreadful, dreadful," she said colourlessly. "I still often wake up dreaming about it." He tried to interrupt only long enough to suggest that although some might think she had been at fault in leaving her mother, no one in their senses could possibly hold her responsible for her mother's death. But she was so carried away by remorse that she hardly heard him. "I don't know that I can ever forgive myself," she said from a region beyond tears.

There was nothing he could do but listen. It was no use — not now at any rate — trying to interrupt and stem the flood of memory and pain and remorse. He lay back against the pillow and let it flow over him. And then he even stopped listening. Now she was one of the crowd flowing under the arches, faceless, voiceless, innumerable. He thought of those he had seen there, of a girl with a great tear in her skirt and with jet-black pain in her eyes. And of another girl, whom he hadn't thought of for almost as long, shorter, slighter, her hair lifted a little by the summer breeze, fluttering against the columns, Althea it was certainly. What had become of her, he wondered, that delicate-veined apparition of flesh and blood who had transfigured him and ruined him so that now whenever he thought of perfection he thought of judgment; whenever he thought of pursuit he also thought of being pursued; whenever he saw the face of ecstasy he saw also the hollow cheeks of pain, metallic, featureless? Had she gone on to some equable destiny? Or had she been driven as wild as he had? The vaulting barrelled into the distance without offering any answers. But then he became aware of something in the dim ceiling directly above him, watching him. Two eyes with peacock greens and purples. The eyes of his dreams impaling him.

When he came to himself she was still talking, but more incoherently. "It's all very well to say these things are relative, but the theory of relativity is in the heavens, it doesn't take you from here to there. If snakes leave trails, we leave trails, too, but some people leave different trails from others, and all sorts of things are like that."

It was as though the script of her thought had been replaced by a blot that was completely indecipherable. He stiffened. And his shudder, transmitted to her, was enough to return her to herself.

"I'm sorry, Rusty, if I've been wandering," she said. "It's because I'm so distraught tonight."

He asked if she would like something hot to drink and when she said she would, he went over and warmed up the coffee they had had earlier. They sat and talked quietly for a while together, and then he thought it was time for him to go.

It was only when he was back in the black frosty street that he realized that for once he had spent an evening with her without making love. Again he shivered. And however obscurely, he sensed that there was some reason for his shivering beside the cold.

He was kept on at the market and found that he liked it more and more. It was healthy, it gave him something to do, it kept him from thinking too much. During the past six years he had come to associate the earth only with shell-fragments and weapon-pits; now it grew less arid, its reviving moisture and pungency began again to suggest things growing. He liked talking to the market-gardeners who brought their produce directly to the market and who sometimes were accompanied by their young sons, boys often of not more than ten or twelve, who helped unload what their fathers were offering for sale and then curled up exhausted until it was time for the journey home. He liked it, too, when there was time for a break and some of the younger porters organized a game of football with a derelict cabbage or cauliflower. Others of those he worked with were middle-aged or even elderly, but he seemed to be able to get on with them all. There was one old man with white hair who suffered from heart trouble and had to be careful about the size of the loads he trundled on his hand-truck. But when Rusty sympathized with him one morning when the going was rough, the old man shrugged philosophically and said, "He bends the back to the burden."

This was only a pause, he supposed, in wherever it was he was going. But he enjoyed it. For the time being he had no desire to go lower. His vehemence seemed to have almost completely left him. And as the small metal wheels of the truck clanked across the paving-stones and in the side-streets the light portable conveyers trickled with their loads of boxes, he could hardly hear the city asking him where he was going, where he was going?

The provost marshal's headquarters was only a few streets away from the market; but his mood was so placid that that didn't worry him much and he saw the patrols of military police going out on their rounds and coming back without feeling anything more than a slight tremor. For all he knew, provost headquarters might be plotting a campaign to bring him in as though he were the most wanted man in the kingdom. Or they might be preoccupied with trying to solve the two or three sordid murders for which deserters were thought to be responsible. Or they might be spending all their time filling in routine forms and returns. He hardly cared. His temper had become as smooth as the water above a falls. He found, for example, that he could chat quite easily and mildly with the other civilian police who wandered through the market and kept it constantly but unobtrusively under surveillance.

Each afternoon he went back to sleep in the room he had by the docks. Sometimes he passed shadowy unpleasant-looking figures on the stairs, but he was usually so tired that he hardly noticed them. Whenever Rudy tried to engage him in conversation, he managed to put him off with some excuse or other, although he pitied his look of hang-dog disappointment. Some other time, he would say to himself, as he closed the door behind him. In fact he kept so much to himself that the proprietor remarked on it, cackling out one afternoon, "Don't you like us any more? I thought you would feel at home here." But Rusty silenced him with a glance. The truth was that not only where he lived but even the whole estuary was bulking smaller and smaller in his life so that days went by without his being conscious of the spars piercing the sky above the rooftops.

When the weekend came he was in such good humour that he couldn't resist the young nephew's invitation to come in and have a few drinks. The uncle was out, but on the unmade double bed in their basement room another young man was sprawled who was a good deal larger and stronger than Rudy. He was holding forth on how easy it was to make a good living without working if you kept your wits about you, and Rudy was drinking it all in. Obviously he had struck up some kind of admiring alliance with this tough self-confident schemer. Rusty couldn't fathom what kind of spell it was he cast, but he didn't care so long as he was relieved of the nephew's constant importunate gaze. He concentrated on his drink, glad that the great scimitar-shaped scar was hungering now in another direction. Gradually three or four other characters drifted in, till it was quite a party. He wasn't sure which of them lived in the house and which came from outside. They all looked both familiar and unfamiliar. He didn't know any of them, but they all seemed at home here, bearing as protective markings either the defeated greyness of the house's peeling wallpaper or the varnished effrontery of its cockroaches. Most of the talk seemed to be about what you could work if you had good contacts in the west end. The young man with his feet up on the bed was now talking about the outlets for stolen cloth and the profits to be made if you could establish reliable connections. But the details drifted past Rusty in the liquored haze. He let his glass be filled up again by his pale young host and drank on doggedly. He couldn't conquer his distaste for him, but there was still something in him that he pitied and something that he felt they had in common. If he couldn't join in the conversation, at least he could show his appreciation by doing his full share — and perhaps a little more — of the drinking. So one glass followed another. When the time came for the party to break up, he didn't exactly have to be put to bed, but he did have to be helped upstairs. He resented the unknown arm around his shoulder: he had been listening to things he didn't like, he didn't relish the company he had been in, now he felt clammy as though with spider-webs, beetle-trails — and suddenly as he undressed he was offended by the hue and shudder of his own flesh. Before he fell into a heavy sleep, the thought crossed his mind for the first time, Why shouldn't I turn myself in?

Later that week-end he went as usual to see Anne. It was beginning to be almost like being married, he told himself as he set out. He was coming to feel responsibility for the girl and to worry about her. He didn't like her obsession with her mother's death, or her sense of guilt about it, or something else — what was it? — that he couldn't quite define. If there was a chance, he would try to talk her into a different view of herself.

But when he got there, she wasn't in a mood to be serious. She was full of some absurd letter she had had from her husband in which he asked for the return of a trifling family heirloom that he claimed she had taken away. "He's the kind of man who would want to divide the jars of jam in the kitchen cupboard," she mocked and gave an imitation of her estranged spouse, filling his arms with jars of marmalade and preserves and walking off huffily and then dropping them all on the floor. Then she described a little incident that had happened that week at the shipping agency where she worked: her boss had got tangled up in what he was dictating and she hadn't been able to help smiling a little and he had lost his temper and stormed up and down, telling her she would never be a success that way — and she mimicked his petty fury. "You'd imagine he thought I wanted to have a big career in business," she went on ridiculing him.

"What is it you *do* want then?" Rusty put in quietly.

She was startled. "Why do you ask?"

As he tried to make out what her glance meant, he could see her throat mottling faintly, carnation and white.

"Because I care for you and am worried about you," he replied.

"But we met on the street. Remember?"

"Yes, I remember," he agreed gravely, "I know we did. When we first met, I thought I would sleep with you once and that would be that. I didn't want to get too involved because I didn't want to become responsible for you. But now — I don't know why — it's different."

She seemed almost irritated. "I'm not worth worrying about," she said. "I drift in and out of people's lives. I will drift out of yours."

"No." But he didn't know how to give his voice conviction. After a moment he repeated, "I'm worried about you and I'd like to help you if I could."

"A lot of people have tried that. It's too much for them," she replied. At some moments she seemed to want to deny that she had any problems; at others she was almost claiming that they were insoluble; and whatever the implication, her tone remained jauntily evasive, even though she sometimes seemed on the verge of tears.

"Well, what do I want?" she mocked, returning to his question. "Security, children, money, a man? What does any woman want?"

"I'm worried about how guilty you feel. You're letting yourself be carried away by it."

"Yes, that's what the doctors say," she laughed. But she wouldn't talk about it, although it was she who had first spoken of it, almost in rapture, in agony. He felt she would do anything tonight rather than engage with him seriously. She kept him at arm's length, fending him off with quips and sullenness and rallies of laughter. Then thinking of another means of evasion, she turned his question back at him. "For that matter," she said, "what is it that *you* want?"

He had been prepared to tell her about himself and his wandering and the reasons for them, so far as he understood them, if she seemed to be interested. But her manner was so baffling and so different from what he had expected that he sat silent. He couldn't say a word.

"There, you see!" she exclaimed. "You know as well as I do that it's a mistake for us to try to talk to each other. You can't reach me: I can't reach you. I'm just a girl you picked up. And a pick-up shouldn't have a soul."

And then she sank down on the bed and burst into tears. He went over and tried to comfort her. But instead of being soothed by his hand stroking her forehead, she clutched grotesquely at his crotch and opened her legs convulsively. It was eerie. It was as though she were under a bell-jar and at his touch her limbs were moved automatically, like sheets of metal foil. He didn't know whether to laugh or cry. He was empty of desire. But sadly, awkwardly, heavily, he knelt down and gave her what she wanted.

He lay back. He felt exhausted. He felt as though he had been gored and his guts were dribbling out on the sand. The unshaded light hurt his eyes, but he was too tired, or too indifferent, to get up and turn it off. He thought of Althea but he couldn't call up anything more about her than a trace of perfume, and then even that disappeared and was replaced by a faint sour, waxy smell. The sky was empty. There was no sky. There was nothing spiralling out in the darkness. The room was closed inviolably about him. It was hermetic and yet filled with a desolation of rubble — craters, weeds, ruined windows, aimless roads, rusty bed-springs. He tried to rise and reach the night sky, embracing its pure distances in his arms. But he was pulled back like a tired swimmer. He felt himself being drawn down by an undertow that weighted his heels, and he gave way to defeat. When he felt her finger-tips on his temples, he was impatient. All he wanted now was to be by himself, to drown and not be troubled. But he concealed his impatience as well as he could, and she said in a low voice, "I wanted to show you where they put the electrodes." And her wandering fingers paused and pressed lightly. She said that, no, she hadn't minded the treatments. At first she had been frightened, but the doctors and nurses had been very kind and the therapy had done her good, she had felt the better for it, she said wanly. Perhaps. Perhaps. But the light touch of her finger-tips now screamed through his flesh. It was a scream of anguish they transmitted, so shrill it couldn't be tolerated. It had to be quenched, he supposed, however brutally; there was no use blaming the doctors who had fastened the electrodes and put in the gag and made her limbs stiffen convulsively. He remembered once under a heavy bombardment how the whole platoon had been ordered to file down into an underground shelter that the enemy had built (and no doubt had occupied before them), deep, beautifully constructed, the roof made of logs covered by two feet of earth. The shelter was vibrating from heavy shells falling very close, but they were safe there against anything except a direct hit. Although the place reeked with fear, there was not a word said. Then a young soldier began to scream, his hysteria splintering the logs and bringing down thin trickles of earth. It was unbearable. But there was an officer standing beside him and he slapped him with a leather glove, hard, across the open mouth. Now there was only sobbing. And the soldier was still sobbing when the shelling slackened off and they could file back into the ruined air. At the next opportunity, of course, he was shipped back to a neurological hospital for treatment.

As he was straightening his clothes and combing his hair, she said dreamily behind his back, "I can just remember a heaven when I was a little girl. That's what I really want, I suppose. But how can I ever get back there when I'm so guilty?"

He turned and sat on the edge of the bed, and they talked for a little while. Then he said, "You go to sleep now," and covered her up warmly and told her he must leave if he wasn't to be late for his job at the market.

He was on the night shift now and he liked it even better than working during the day. From midnight until he knocked off at six o'clock was when the market was most itself. He liked to see the transports rolling in not long after midnight, like ships to a jetty, with their loads battened down under tarpaulins and lashed tight; and then the ropes being untied and tossed back and forth by the driver and his helper in smart matelot fashion; and then hundreds of crates of green beans or tomatoes being unloaded. There was a rhythm and vivacity that lasted all night and that he was now a part of. But the thought of her didn't leave him. As he was prising open the tops of boxes of apples and tilting them up for display, he heard echoing in his mind some words she had murmured before he left, "What I want is something impossible, too — not to feel guilty." He went on arranging the boxes of apples and then turned to deal with crates of melons and then with cartons of cucumbers. But their freshness was now contaminated for him, however slightly, by the strange waxy odour he had smelled as he lay beside her, as though there were a trace of some foreign colouring in her blood or her urine. He finished what he was doing and walked back to find out what he was to do next. There was thin fog drifting through the passageways of the market, and it was out of that that he heard the voice saying, "I can't believe in anything now unless I can feel it as pain." He passed displays of artichokes and then of oranges and then of pears. Still she pursued him. It was as he was passing a window of expensive grapes, plump, with a midnight-blue blush about them, that he heard her repeat, "I might be cured if only I could have your soul, too."

Six o'clock came. He knocked off. He walked out into the early morning darkness, a broad-brimmed felt hat pulled down over his ears, the collar of his trench-coat turned up, to take a train back to his room by the docks. The glass roof of the market was hardly behind him when a young man came up and called him by name. He didn't recognize him at first, but then he saw that it was the character whom he had heard holding forth a few days before, with his feet up on the soiled unmade bed. Why should he stop? But Rudy's ne'er-do-well hero insisted that it was something urgent and suggested that they drop into one of the neighbouring bars which were permitted to open early for the convenience of night-workers at the market.

The fog was thickening, he thought, as they crossed the street together. He couldn't see more than a few yards in front of him.

"I was to let you know that the operation is on for a week from Thursday," the young man said as soon as they were established at a table in the corner.

Rusty didn't flicker an eyelid. He was waiting.

"The plan is for us all to meet at the Bunch of Grapes at zero minus two. We've cased the warehouse and found where the most valuable bolts of cloth are stowed and that the door from the fire-escape can be easily forced. That's your job, to force the door and then to stand watch. I'm driving the car. We picked it up last night and put on new licence plates; it should carry fifty bolts easily ..."

He spelled it all out minutely as though he thought of himself as a junior officer explaining the plans of a commando-raid. But Rusty wasn't listening to the details. His brain was working with great rapidity on its own problems, its shutters opening on one question and then clicking shut and focusing on another. Had he ever heard of these plans before? He couldn't be absolutely sure; he didn't think so. Had he ever talked to this young punk? No. Was it possible that he had been told by someone else that night in the proprietor's basement-room? Yes, it was possible, he supposed; he might have been drinking too much to remember. Was that probable, though? He couldn't believe it, he would have remembered a thing like that. What was the reason, then, for his being told now? That was more difficult … But was it conceivable that the plan of the burglary was being confided to him now so that he would be implicated, so that he couldn't escape, so that he could refuse to participate only at the risk of being marked down by this and every other gang in the underworld? Yes. Yes. That was it. The suspicion had grown in his mind to a certainty.

He would have to move skillfully and warily.

"I've never heard a word of all this before in my life," he said evenly when the man on the other side of the table finished.

"But it was only Saturday night that you said you'd come in with us, and you were given the whole story then!" the emissary expostulated, affecting to be incredulous.

"I can tell you all this is news to me, I've never heard a word of it."

"Well, you can't welsh on us now."

"I've never welshed on anyone in my life."

"Then we can count on you … a week from Thursday at the Bunch of Grapes?"

"I don't know."

"What do you mean, you don't know?" But behind the truculence Rusty detected a glimmer of fear — probably not of him, but of what might be in store for an envoy who came back empty handed. He would press his advantage.

"I'll have to speak to my own mob first before I can let you know," he replied coolly. "I don't want to get any lines crossed if I can help it."

That caught the other off balance. Clearly he hadn't reckoned with the possibility of his belonging to some other mob. But would he believe it? Rusty eyed him closely. He hesitated just long enough to show that he didn't know what to believe.

"When can we expect to hear from you, then?" the other asked weakly.

"I don't know," he repeated. "That's all I can tell you for now." And he got up curtly and left the young punk staring into his nearly empty glass.

His mob? He smiled a little to himself. It consisted now only of a girl friend and Steve, that was all. The bluff had worked, though. Yet as he made his way through the grey streets where more and more people were eddying to work, he felt depressed thinking how alone he was. He could remember when the mob he belonged to had included Spike and Mark and Slim and Bob and Sailor, and a dozen others — and each of them a host in himself. Well, it was different now.... He tried to console himself by recalling that among these growing early morning crowds he surely had millions of secret confederates. Straggling into office-buildings in clammy raincoats or being carried along in buses and munching over headlines of the city's and the world's distempers were millions of others who were victims like himself; who had been flushed with paradise, had been fulfilled, had been made perfect; and who still had that and the taste of rejection, the taste of death, in their mouth. But there was some reason, which he had known once but now couldn't remember, why that common lot couldn't produce community. He frowned, trying to shake off his depression; and his thought vapoured away over his head.

He told himself that he wouldn't worry about the trap that had been set for him. But when he got back to his room, he spent more time than usual in locking and bolting the door. And it took him longer to get to sleep. He lay awake, listening, for more than an hour, and only then, when there hadn't been any knock, did he manage to drop off.

The following night at the market he was preoccupied as he went about his work. He was waiting for something. They wouldn't leave it at that, they would make another approach.

But when would it come? He was working in the lofty glass-covered shed that was set aside for flowers. Usually he liked working there, unloading cartons of cut flowers and trays of potted plants — azaleas, cyclamens, lilies. The loads were lighter, and the swirling scent of the flowers brought sun into fog, and spring into winter, and country into town, even more poignantly and exuberantly than in other parts of the market. Tonight, though, he was far more conscious of plants for sick-rooms and lilies for the dead than he was of violets to be pinned at a girl's throat or of orchids to be made up into corsages or of flagrant stocks and dahlias and chrysanthemums to be arranged in great festal hot-house pomps. His apprehension seemed almost to infect the flowers with malice. Their throats were not innocent but fanged. Their roots had been corroded by the gardener's hand, he mused, as he worked and waited. He was so expecting something that when a young lad came up and told him that he was wanted on the telephone, he felt a kind of relief. Walking towards the office, he meditated who it would be and what he would reply. It might be the same young punk again; but it was likely to be somebody more formidable, he thought, someone with greater weight and authority in the gang. The young know-it-all had been given one assignment and had failed; it wasn't likely that he would be entrusted so soon with another of the same kind. With lightning speed, he prepared his answers, bracing himself for whatever might be attempted, practising his footwork. But when he got to the telephone the caller had rung off.

Now the market was full of voices. Of an angry scar calling for redress and satisfaction. Of a girl being held down while a gag was forced in her mouth. Of guards shouting, "Get cracking" to frightened deportees being prodded with bayonets up out of deep snow and past iron doors. Of a young soldier screaming. Of strangers who said, "We'll keep track of you." Of distracted mothers. Of policemen calling for reinforcements as they had almost cornered their prey. Of lips smarting from being struck. Of Spike's blood blessing, blaspheming him as he carried the world on his back. Of sailors and chauffeurs and police and provosts pursuing, pursuing, and being pursued. Of a boy falling from a rooftop without a sound. Of someone saying over and over, "What's to become of me?" The voices fell like soot on the throats of the lilies, the cyclamen were spotted with them, the tongues of the flowers' blessing were torn out, their bells were tolled backwards. They were fanged, fanged. There was no trickle of fragrance even from the violets.

He leaned back against one of the wooden stands and felt almost as though he might faint. He had never felt like this before. He looked up, and through the glass roof a full moon was shining. Whether because of the way the large panes were glazed or because of this momentary faintness, it seemed to be shining and dripping in great white blossoms that fell and floated above the dimly lit counters, twining up and down luxuriantly, reigning over the bare boards and the slowly spreading beds of pale spotted flowers ranged out for sale. This was the full moon of women in hysteria. This was what drove adolescents wild on summer nights until they hardly knew themselves. The swaying stalk that was rooted both in heaven and earth, branching into the night sky and pulsing with blood sucked from the earth, was here almost warm and tropical, heavy with blossoms deep as pools, with magnolia blossoms. It made him think of Althea's open thighs glimmering moonily in the dark. But now he was utterly cut off. He felt so little that he hardly knew whether he regretted his separation, his exile. It wearied him, wearied him to the bone. And his weariness had created a kind of calm in which he couldn't tell whether what he had lost was illusion or the only meaning there was. He gazed down brooding, uncertain, anxious to decide but unable to, too tired to, with half a mind to use the dagger on his arm to cut this brightness from before his eyes, but without the will to disfigure himself so. He leaned back again and looked up and let his eyes be drenched by this showering incandescence. What would become of him? He didn't know. It would reappear, this splendour. But for tonight he must ruthlessly cut it down like a bean-stalk. He turned back to his work and began trundling his hand-truck back and forth over the white glistening petals that lay scattered on the floor.

It was only half an hour later that another telephone call came for him. This time he didn't try to prepare what he would say. He would let nature take its course. But when he picked up the telephone, it wasn't a strange voice at all; it was Steve's, and he was pleading for help. He had been in bed for forty-eight hours with a high fever and hadn't anyone to look after him and was afraid of what he saw in his delirium. "I need you, Rusty," he said, calling out of the dark like a child calling for a glass of water. Rusty said he would be there as soon as he could; it wouldn't be more than a few hours. He waited until it was time for the night shift to knock off, and then he spoke to the foreman in charge and told him that an emergency had cropped up and he mightn't be able to work the following night but he hoped there would still be a job for him.

"Don't worry," the foreman said. "So long as I'm here, there'll be work for you."

When he got to Steve's he found that his temperature, which had gone down during the night, had shot up again. He made him as comfortable as he could and made him drink plenty of water. But he couldn't persuade him to have a doctor. There was no one he would trust in the room except Rusty. He was being hunted. He wouldn't feel safe with anyone else. In his fever the embassy chauffeur had become a hunter with a pack of hounds, and the sailor a merman who could assume a thousand disguises, who could even turn himself into a detective, a convict, a jackal, a turnkey, a lamprey — even into a doctor poring over him with a stethoscope. And sometimes above the barking of the hounds and the white shifting and ravening of the waves he could hear his mother's voice. "She says she'll die if I don't come home," he repeated to Rusty out of his delirium. "What does she mean? What does she mean?" It was only after he had been with him for more than an hour and had talked to him soothingly and had given him more sedatives that Rusty managed to get him to sleep.

He stretched out in a chair by the bed. He had promised the boy he wouldn't leave until he was better, and he couldn't desert him. He was being hunted, too, and he wondered whether his pursuers could track him down here. He doubted it, but he didn't feel sure. In time, though, he, too, fell asleep with the morning sunlight streaming in over his face. He was disturbed by Steve's moaning and tossing, but it didn't wake him, his limbs were so heavy from the night's work in the market that he slept on tranquilly, almost dreamlessly, except for voices calling him, calm voices though these were, women's voices calling him in sleep, softly, without reproach, perhaps Althea's voice or perhaps it was his mother's.

When he awoke at last and rubbed his eyes, Steve seemed a little better. He thought that he could manage something to eat and he was willing to let Rusty leave him for a while to go out and get it. They ate what he brought in, and then they played cards on the bed for almost an hour, and then Steve talked on and on about his home. His eyes were still glittering with fever and his cheeks were flushed; but his mind seemed clear enough, and now Rusty didn't see any need to prevent him. And that was how they passed the time, hour after hour, sleeping and having light snacks and playing cards and talking about where Steve had lived as a boy. In the end Rusty came to feel that he knew the town square as well as anywhere in the world, although he had never seen it and never would. There was the church with its twin slate-covered spires and its clock where two mechanical men came out with gilt hammers to strike the hours; and there were the flower-sellers beside the church; and in the centre of the square was the statue of the astronomer, a little bent with thought, cradling in one arm some kind of instrument with a complicated system of circles; and behind him stretched a row of old gabled houses that had not been much changed since the middle ages. He could place it all securely from what Steve had told him.

By the following night Steve was much better and Rusty had come to think that neither of them had anything to fear, that they both would be safe. The boy had been telling him of the music his father loved most, and then they had gone back to playing cards, and Rusty was putting down a red Jack when there was a knock at the door. Before the boy could stop him, he went over and unlocked and opened it. It was the sailor. Clenching his fists, Rusty had almost drifted him one in the mouth when he noticed that he was wet to the skin and pale and shivering.

Weakly, womanishly, the sailor put up one hand to cover his face. But Rusty unclenched his fists and drove the question at him instead, "What the hell are you doing here?"

"I'm … I'm looking for shelter," he faltered.

It was such a surprising answer that Rusty was taken aback.

And the sailor went on in a low voice he could hardly catch, "Your friends have no mercy."

"What mercy had you?"

"I've been on the run for days."

"Go back to your friends in the embassy, or die in the streets, that's your business."

"If you could only take me in for a few hours and ask your friends to have mercy …"

"Look, there's someone sick here," Rusty delivered his ultimatum. "If you don't be off and never come back, I'll call the police. Off with you!"

He waited until the sailor had turned and was going down the stairs, supporting himself with one hand on the banister; and then he slammed the door to.

He didn't know what was happening. He supposed that the sailor had been playing both sides of the street, that the embassy had their hooks into him and the Ministry, and that now he was being torn to pieces. He had heard of such things. But that wasn't his business. He had enough on his hands with Steve.

It was lucky he had been there, he thought, as he turned back to the boy sitting up in bed with the cards sliding down over the coverlet. He had his work cut out for him to convince him that he was still safe, without exposing him too much to the swirling limbo that he had glimpsed on the other side of the door. Gradually, with evasions and some grains of the truth, he succeeded in convincing him that the danger had passed, if there had been any, and that now he was safer than ever before. In the morning Steve was well enough so that he could leave him and head out again for the market.

After a night of sleet and rain, it had cleared, and he was glad to be out and about. He felt stronger in the winter sunlight. Somehow he found himself remembering and relishing Dragon's nimble defiance of the world and Brandy's great shaggy animal boisterousness. Where were they now, he wondered, those deserters, conquerors, supporters — unflawed and untroubled — of a primitive order? After his vigil with Steve, it cheered him to think of them feasting and moving on, knowing the world was desperate but not caring, baiting it, challenging it with its own heat, guardians and wastrels of its most essential carnal warmth. They would create festivals in the cold, he was sure, wherever they were. He was glad they existed, although he was shut out of their perfection, too. At the market he was relieved to be welcomed back and told he could work the rest of the day shift, they were so short-handed. It was good to be at work again, hauling crates of grapefruit and stalks of bananas and sacks of potatoes. The pale blue sky was whisked with white wintry mares' tails, and his muscles were combed by exercise into the same wiry rejoicing, so that he went back and forth lightheartedly, not thinking of what he knew or of what might be lying in wait. When the break came, two young porters were clowning to a jeering, admiring audience and pelting each other with plums; and as one of them was hit squarely and the plum trickled down his trouser-leg, he skipped a little and looked down ruefully and threw away the line, "I thought that one of them had dropped"; and lounging on sacks of potatoes, the audience showed its appreciation by dashing out what was left of their coffee in applause on the paving-stones; and for a moment the world seemed candid and young. He went back to work with enthusiasm, trundling the sunlight stored in cucumbers and tomatoes and lettuce on its way to be parcelled out by careful grocers to housewives all over the city. There were the seeds of life and health in what he was doing. The virtue locked in the crates he was moving broke open and burst through the slats, running down juicily, the warmth of summer in the thin winter light, frosted but as luscious as pomegranates broken open and their seeds burst on the tongue. He was so lighthearted that he stopped for a minute or two to have a word with a policeman who was standing circumspectly by the railings at the edge of the market. That afternoon he even found that he was whistling, and not a bar or two but complete tunes, one verse after another. When the time came for the market to close for the day, he felt disappointed, cheated almost. He hadn't tired himself out yet, and he would have liked to go on much longer working and whistling and stretching his muscles. He felt a sense of letdown. Most of the other porters were making for home, and for a moment he almost envied them, thinking, "Why shouldn't I go home, too?" And as the answer came flashing back, "But you haven't got a home," he thought for the first time in months of his father and mother, his mother in the kitchen cutting tomato sandwiches for him after school as she had done so often, and his father, his father … how hurt he would have been by not having heard from his son, by not knowing whether he had a son or not, by having lost him! What would he have said to his cronies? How would he have answered the police when they came around with their notebooks open, questioning?

As he sat in the train travelling back to his room by the docks, encased in light and advertising and outer darkness, he saw himself once more in the glass. But he wasn't smiling, he was frowning, he didn't know why. There was a look almost of disapproval in the face that he faced in the dark mirror opposite. And again with surprise he asked himself why he shouldn't turn himself in. Then he saw the face of a soldier he had known who had gone crazy in the glass-house, laughing hysterically into the mirrored surface of the washbasin he had to polish until it shone. But he wasn't afraid of the glass-house. He could take it. That wasn't the trouble. He had gone through far worse than that. But there was something that he had promised, that he felt committed to. It was his vanity — no, more than that — his pride that was at stake.

He wasn't tired when he got back to his room, but sleeping was all he could think of to do. He locked and bolted the door and put the back of a chair under the knob and lay down. At first he couldn't fall asleep, he was listening too intently. But at last he dozed off. Although he had drawn the curtains, the room still murmured with sunlight. And what he saw in his dream was sunlit enough. In the square (it might have been in the town Steve had been describing) a scaffold had been set up. The scene rippled. He could make out the scaffold … the crowd … the rope. It wasn't the rope, though, he was frightened of. It was the two figures below the scaffold who were standing ready to clutch at his feet and weight him down and see that he didn't dangle too long. He tried to scream. His throat was too dry. Then with exquisite relief he struggled awake. He lay back sweating in the cool fading light. He thought of his mother and of how much he wished she were still alive, of how she had nursed him whenever he was sick, of how she had protected him. And then he thought of how he had loved to swim, of how good he had been at swimming underwater, escaping like a sleek scaled fish along the bottom of the pool. He was almost dozing off again when at last the knock came.

He got up and put on his coat and went to the mirror and combed his hair. The knocking grew louder. He tossed his head as though to shake the sleep out of his eyes and walked over to the door deliberately and took away the chair and drew back the bolt and turned the key. What he saw when he opened the door was much what he expected.

"I've brought some of my friends to see you," Rudy was saying. He was in bedroom slippers and his shirt was unbuttoned as usual to show his livid grievance against the world. Behind him in the dimly lit hall were two other figures. One Rusty recognized as the young tough who had approached him in the market. The other was shorter, slighter, better dressed, almost as spruce as a business man with ten or twelve directorships. There was even a clean white handkerchief in his breast pocket.

After his initial act of betrayal, the landlord's nephew had no more part to play and drifted into a corner. It was the business type who came forward and took charge of the interview, swinging around a light chair by the table and sitting down astride it in the centre of the room.

"We've come to see you because I don't think you realize how serious this is," he began.

"Oh?" was the extent of Rusty's reply.

"Yes," he went on, taking a cigarette from a silver case and puffing out smoke through his nostrils. "Although we've never met, I know enough about you to know that you don't like a sloppy operation any more than I do. Now here's the situation. We have a neat tidy operation planned. It's promising and nicely timed. It can hardly miss. You heard all the details from Jackie here, so I needn't go over them. But this is the point. It's set for Thursday night, just six days from now, and we still don't know whether we can count on you, although you gave us your word more than a week ago. You know as well as I do that that's not a situation that can be allowed to continue."

"I suppose not," Rusty said innocently. "If I were you, I wouldn't lose any time in signing up someone else."

"It isn't that easy."

"Why?"

"Because you know our whole plan. We can't leave you out now."

"I don't see why not."

"Look. I don't need to tell you how important security is in an operation of this kind. If there's someone on the outside who knows what's in the wind, there's always the risk of a leak; and we can't afford that."

"I don't care what you're going to do. It's nothing to me. I didn't ask to know about it, and I don't want to know about it now. If there's a leak, it won't come from me."

"But in your own interest just remember that if there *is* a leak, you'll be the first to be suspected."

"Why shilly-shally about like this?" objected the young bruiser at last. He was lounging up against the door and scowled disgustedly. "Tell him straight out that if he doesn't come in with us, he's had it, he's finished, kaput."

"You'd better tell your Jackie, or jackal, or whatever it is you call him, to mind his manners," Rusty said quietly. "I don't like to be threatened."

"Leave this to me," the man at the table laced back at his subordinate. "You'd better go out and wait downstairs — and take the kid with you."

After they had filed out reluctantly, the director of operations seemed to relax and confided apologetically, "I don't like that kind of talk any more than you do. But I think you and I can come to an understanding. I've been glad to give you a good deal of rope, because I know how special you are, but I don't want you to hang yourself. You see through society as clearly as I do, you see what a fraud it is. If a big company wants something, what does it do? It just takes it, or gets around the government or manipulates people in power. And if the worst comes to the worst and the big interests are put in a corner and a war comes, they shove people like you and me out in front to take the racket. I've been through your record and I admire it. I know the sterling sort you are, reliable, the sort you can depend on. But you've had the good sense to contract out before it was too late. You don't want any more than I do to end up peddling matches in the streets. Now, what I'm offering you is a chance to get your own back."

"I don't want any part of it."

"Don't answer too quickly. I don't think you know yourself yet. Not fully anyway. You've left society, you've deserted. And you don't owe it anything. But don't think you can stay in a kind of no man's land. That's a sure way of getting shot down. If you come in with us, you'll have protection — and a good deal more. I can tell you, you won't suffer by it."

"I don't want any part of it."

"Or you might think of it this way. You've left society, you've deserted. Well, where are you now? In another world, in the underworld. You may not have made up your mind to it yet, but that's where you are, whether you like it or not. Right? But the underworld has its laws, too, and they can't be broken. One of them is that if you've been cut into a deal, you go through with it."

"I still don't want any part of it."

"I'm beginning to be disappointed in you. I thought I could help you see where you stand. You want to live in the underworld and not share in its obligations. You want to be in it and not of it. And that you can't do, not even you."

Rusty didn't answer.

After a pause the other went on, "What do you suggest I do then?"

"Whatever you like."

"You know how vulnerable you are?"

Again there was no answer. And the interrogator repeated his question.

"You mean you can turn me in anytime?" Rusty said at length.

"Not only that. I have to answer for you to my partners."

So that's what all his slick talk came down to! In that case, the mastermind might as well have left it to his young jackal. But there wasn't much room for manoeuvre. "I said that I didn't like to be threatened," he repeated. "Remember?"

"I'm not threatening. I'm just giving you a little friendly advice."

They stared at each other steadily. Then after a few seconds the other glanced aside and said with finality, "Well, I've warned you. You can still come in with us. But if you don't and anything goes wrong, you know now what to expect." And he got up briskly and went to the door. He had half opened it before he turned and spat back viciously, "We've got our hooks into you now, and we're not going to take them out."

Was it a victory of sorts? Rusty didn't know. He knew he was frightened. And he was glad to see the back of him. He went over and locked and bolted the door and then came back and lay down on the bed. The light was almost gone. He glanced at his watch, but even its familiar face failed to reassure him what time it was. After sleeping in the afternoon and then waking to find so much malice in the room, he could hardly distinguish between light and dark, between day and night. They flowed into each other and were almost obliterated. Such light as there was was being diffused in the darkness and lost. As it faded, he lay wondering what would become of him. He must try to concentrate. But he felt too exposed to think calmly. Stretched out on the bed beside the wall, he thought he could hear the timbers cracking that supported the side of the house and the masonry starting to shift and give way. It was time, high time, he left. They might try to shadow him wherever he went. But if he stayed here, they would be able to keep watch over him virtually hour by hour and keep track of every move he made. Where should he go, though? He felt something close to panic when he thought of how little refuge he had. The only thing he could think of was to ask Anne to take him in for a few days. He debated then on how he could get to her. They might be waiting still on one of the landings or in the hall downstairs. Even if they weren't, he didn't want to have to pass the damp treacherous nephew or the gross cackling uncle, who would notice anyway that he had his kit-bag with him and was checking out and might try to stop and question him or at least pass along an alert.

Finally he got up. He stuffed his few belongings back in his kit-bag and left on the mantel what he owed for the rent. Then he put up the window and let himself down to his full length, still clinging with his hands to the sill. And then he dropped as quietly as he could to the roof of a sloping slate-covered shed. And from there he leaped down much farther into the rubble-strewn cellar where the house next-door had once stood. One of his ankles was twisted a little, but not much. Cautiously he picked his way through the debris until he came to the street. Twice he tried to pull himself up, and failed. The only thing for it was to try one of the supporting timbers. It sloped up steeply. But slinging his kit-bag around his neck, he cat-walked halfway up, and then, before he could think how wide the gap was, leaped out and landed on the pavement.

He waited there for a full minute, getting his breath and trying to quiet his pulse and looking about to see if anyone was watching. The light was piss-poor, but there didn't seem to be anything stirring in the shadowy house beside him or anyone lurking in nearby doorways. Then he crossed lightly to the other side of the street and, sheltering beneath a crumbling portico, looked back. No, there wasn't anyone watching from the house he had just left. Swinging his kit-bag over his shoulder and lengthening his stride, he set out, turning into alleys every now and then and waiting to detect, if he could, whether he was being followed and then, reassured, going on. Several times he doubled back on himself. But in spite of all his ruses and hesitations, it wasn't long before he was knocking at the door of Anne's flat.

She might almost have been expecting him. He told her quickly what had happened; and, without his having to ask, she assumed that he would be staying with her for a while. By now his ankle was swollen and painful, and she got him a basin of hot water to bathe it in and then poured out a drink and set it beside him. He might have been a workman coming home after a hard day.

It was the week-end, and they both stayed in and grew accustomed to living together. She shifted her clothes to leave some hooks free for him; and she cleared out two drawers for his other belongings, although he objected that he didn't own nearly enough to fill them. In the small cupboard above the wash-basin (which was hidden by a screen) she re-arranged the many bottles of medicine and shampoo and lotion that she kept so that there would be room for his shaving equipment. There was no problem about a place to sleep, since the bed was just large enough for them both to sleep in comfortably. The cooking she did in the little recessed kitchenette — she said it was fun to be cooking for a man again and she wouldn't let him help, claiming there wasn't room for two. When supper was ready, they sat like man and wife at either end of a small table which she had cleared off and covered with a striped cloth.

They didn't talk much. She told him a little about where she had gone to school, and he thought of a few army stories to tell her, to make her laugh. But they didn't discuss her problems any further or the complications he had got into. They were content to sit quietly most of the time, listening to whatever was being broadcast or leafing over magazines and only occasionally looking up to make a remark or two. He felt such relief and relaxation after what he had been exposed to that his senses were drowsy, so perhaps there were some other things she said that should have disturbed him; but in fact it was only once or twice that she made him feel at all uneasy. He had been following her idly as she sat talking and knitting when he heard, or thought he heard, her say, "I like cats and then again I don't, not anyway when they leap over things like chairs or tables or the moon or balls of wool and get in your hair and tangle it. But when they're lapping up milk at midnight, aren't they adorable? My mother always kept cats." He didn't know what to make of it, but perhaps he had been listening too inattentively to catch what she said. A little later there was an even more noticeable strangeness. She was talking of her time at school and she said (he was in no doubt this time), "I used to play noughts and crosses with the marks I got and write them on my hands with indelible pencil, on the palms of my hands so that I could look at them whenever I liked and not let my mother see them." Her mother, her mother — she was never very far away; and that worried him. But he didn't say anything. He leaned back and drew more deeply on his cigarette. In a few minutes the news came on, and he reached over and turned up the volume.

A large new plane had exploded in mid-air, and sabotage was suspected. There had been a severe snow-storm in the north. The reparations conference was deadlocked over the issue of deliveries from current production. The new world organization was wrestling with the problems of colonialism and trusteeship.

"It's all pretty meaningless," said Rusty as he turned it off, not intending much more than that he had been hoping for the football scores and had been disappointed.

But she must have understood him differently, because she said eagerly, "Do you know that sometimes it seems to me to be full of meaning? It was only last week that the manager used a phrase as he was dictating that I didn't know and I asked him about it and he told me. 'Found on board,' he said it was, f.o.b. And suddenly I saw us all 'found on board,' you and me and my mother and thousands of others, all in a kind of ark, with the waves curling away on both sides, like lions' manes, as they do sometimes in the pictures the old monks used to draw. I could see it clear as day. The ark had a kind of halo around it, and it went billowing on safely over the waves. And all that because of f.o.b. Isn't it strange?"

Rusty asked her if she often saw things illuminated like that.

"I didn't use to," she said. "But now I do more and more."

"And do you know something else?" she added after a pause, holding up her knitting to examine it. "Whenever I do, it's always associated with the smell of butterscotch."

Rusty didn't say anything, but now it all really *did* seem meaningless to him.

He went to bed early, explaining that he felt worn out; and he slept soundly, although he hadn't expected to. It was only once or twice that he was dimly aware of her lying beside him as she turned in sleep and their cold extremities came momentarily into touch and then as involuntarily parted again.

They didn't go out much. Before he was awake, Anne had been to church and had brought back a few groceries on the way home. After he got up — late, because he was to work that night in the market — he went down to the landing and telephoned Steve to let him know where he was. And a little afterward he walked to the corner to buy the Sunday papers. But that was as far as he ventured. He didn't know why, whether it was because he was still tired or because the weather was raw and drizzly, he didn't know. But he was quite content to stay indoors.

When the time came to go to the market, he had to force himself to. He knew now that he was afraid. They had tracked him down in the market once before and might easily again; and this time, if they wanted him, their purpose would be more brutal and determined, they would be less easily turned aside. He must assume that they would be on the watch for him there; and in spite of the silting of its passageways with piles of fruit and vegetables and empty crates, it would offer little protection. As he approached it through a maze of narrow streets and, still some distance off, caught the first whiff of its pungency — the bitter tang of citrus-rind coming to him through the drizzle — it seemed to have shifted into another quarter of his mind. No longer was it redolent of moist earth, of sweat, of straining muscles, of health, of honest work. It had lost those moorings and had floated adrift until it was now a brutal, tantalizing spice-island, where the senses could be crazed and betrayed by longing, and where a stranger might well be annihilated as soon as he set foot on shore. For an instant he blazed with unappeasable cravings. But they were soon quenched by the dark drizzle over the greasy paving-stones and by the fear that went with it. Because of the rain (which strengthened during the night and by early morning was pelting down) most of the porters were disguised in one way or another, some with parkas pulled over their heads, others with black sou'westers, others with sacks folded into rough hoods to keep off the rain and with more sacking corded around their waists and shoulders. Under one of these sodden head-dresses was probably recessed a pair of eyes that had been charged to keep track of him, and more often than he would have liked he found himself staring narrowly under the disguise to see whether it sheltered eyes that he knew. He couldn't keep his attention on what he was doing. His glance wandered over one shoulder and then over the other. He had trouble controlling his hand-truck, which was in danger of running away with him and almost upset a dozen times. He cursed the slipperiness of the pavement and passages and roadway, which glimmered with a dull sheen under the sopping street-lamps; and he was cursed in return by other porters for not minding where he was going. Only the policemen sheltering in doorways in black glossy rain-capes seemed superior to the misery and confusion. For the rest, as they struggled with their loads of fruit and vegetables, they made him think, not of gardens and cultivation and plenty, but of desperate men trying to rescue what little they could from a wreck at sea.

When the night ended, he was soaked to the skin — and so miserable that all he wanted to do was to get home and get dry. He hardly cared whether he was being shadowed or not.

And so one day followed another, distinguished by little more than variations in the weather. His worries didn't disappear, but they were domesticated by routine. He worked in the market; he stayed with Anne, sleeping with her sometimes, giving her money each pay-day; he kept in touch with Steve. He was wanted as a deserter, and there were others who had their hooks into him; and that worried him. But he managed to live with it, partly because he couldn't think of anything else to do and partly because Anne was filling more and more of his mind.

He worried still less about himself after he heard over the air one night that there had been a large theft from a warehouse of bolts of cloth, which the police were afraid would find their way on to the black market. Apparently the operation had gone according to plan, although the nightwatchman had put up some resistance and had had to be knocked unconscious. He could just hear the spruce mastermind congratulating himself on having achieved "complete tactical surprise." Anyway, there had been no leaks: that rather took him off the hook.

It was Anne who now seemed to be the more seriously menaced. Something inward was tracking her down. He didn't know what it was, whether the dregs of some perfection contaminating her clearness as his had been contaminated, or something even more insidious advancing along her bloodstream. As he lay beside her, he found himself wondering about what she wanted, about her dreams, her secrecies. They were sealed, impervious, to him. He could embrace the flesh from which they sprung, but her dreams themselves eluded him. They even seemed to be becoming more impenetrable as the days went by. He lay back silent and defeated, wondering — he was surprised how passionately — whether his dreams and hers might flow together, anxious with the simplicity of a word or a touch to make those fastnesses tremble and dissolve, to turn them (without surrendering their own colour or uniqueness) simply and miraculously into a stream that would flow with his, distinguishable but together, two streams of variously watered, variously purpled, hues. He tried to coax her to talk in the hope that, as she did, he might find some phrase that would rescue her from what was haunting her. But with little success. She seemed to be growing more and more reticent, more and more remote. She seemed to be withdrawing from him into a world of glass. And he fell asleep with a heavy heart.

When the break came, it was over something quite ridiculous. One afternoon when he came home from the market (he was working days now) he happened to mention that he thought one of the policemen in the market had been paying special attention to him that day.

"Paying special attention to you!" she laughed. "I like that." Her tone had a hard, unfamiliar edge.

"Well, what's so strange about that?" he replied, perplexed. They had often spoken matter-of-factly about his problems in keeping out of the hands of the police.

"I like that," she repeated, baiting him.

"What do you mean?" he shot back. He was beginning to be really irritated.

"If you can't see it yourself, I know I can't explain it to you," she taunted.

"Why not?" he complained, trying to control his temper.

"Why should the police be so concerned with you?" she burst out at last, glaring at him with full-faced anger. "You'd think that you were the centre of the world, that everything revolved around you."

"Oh?" he mocked. "I suppose it still revolves around that no-good husband of yours?"

"I'm not so sure he isn't a better man than you are for all his faults."

His hands tensed. They were almost around her throat before he was overcome by remembering the nights he had lain with her, excluded, uneasy, wondering about her and what it was that was troubling her.

"Do we have to behave like this, savaging each other like animals?" he asked as humbly as he could.

Her face had become secretive and enigmatic. "I want to be rid of you," she said dully.

When he said nothing, she repeated, "I want to be rid of you." Her look was both cunning and stupid.

His anger had quite evaporated. "I'll go if you want me to," he said. "But I don't know that I should. You need someone to look after you. I'm not sure that you're well."

"So you're in on the plot, too!" she seethed. "I suspected it all along. You talk about the police! They've been watching me all afternoon, circling the apartment hour after hour, three policemen on motorcycles about twenty yards apart, circling, circling, never giving me a moment's peace. I can't stand it! They take down everything I say to myself. They even take down everything I think. They have machines that can do that, you know, little machines no bigger than your fingertip. They have instruments that can look right up you. And they report it all to my mother! And you! You're helping them! I can't stand it! Get out! I can't stand it!"

She was almost screaming. She was quite unrecognizable. Several times he tried to speak. She wouldn't let him. He put out his hand and tried to touch her. She shrank back in fury. At last, resignedly, he got out his kit-bag and began to fill it while she stood dull and rigid in the opposite corner of the room.

When he was ready to go, he didn't know what to say. It was no use trying to comfort her in this state or hardly even to say good-bye. The only thing he could think of that might be of any use was to leave her some money. So in the darkening twilight, as he stood with his trench-coat on and the cord of his kit-bag loose in his left hand, he turned to where she loomed grey and motionless as metal. "Bless you," he said, but so low you could scarcely hear it; and then he furtively put some money on the table, and said, "I'm leaving that in case you might need it."

That brought her back for a moment to life, and fury.

"I'd rather die than take anything from you," she screamed. "You think you can pay for having slept with me, for what you've done to me. I'll see you in hell before I take a penny of your money. In hell, with my breasts cut off and bleeding. In hell, with your penis cut off and hung up to dry."

When he was out on the street, he felt old and dazed. He wanted to howl like a dog. Stupefied, he walked on and on, not knowing where to turn. At last he noticed in the dim light from a street-lamp a dingy card in a window that read "Room for rent." He went in and took it. He thought that he might be moving from one room to another till the end of time.

In the morning he just managed to pull himself together enough to go to work. It was a crisp, frosty morning, and before many hours had passed there was a great gauzy sun rising, whose glory was refracted through ice-crystals and through the glazed roof of the market. But he hardly saw it. His pupils had contracted until they hardly took in any light at all; and anything that found entrance burnt his eyes like freezing needles. It was only that afternoon as the market was closing (although it seemed centuries later), that he was told he was wanted at the office. When he got there, he was given a letter. No one seemed to know who had delivered it; but whoever it was hadn't been willing to wait.

He couldn't bear to open it. Yet he knew that if he put it in his pocket, he might never have the courage to face it. So there in the office, with the foreman making up his books for the day and a light metal conveyor trickling back boxes of unsold apples to wait in the cellar for other opportunities, he slit it open. Deliberately he willed his pupils wider apart to read it.

"This is to say good-bye," she began. "I told you once, I think, that I drift in and out of people's lives and that I would drift out of yours. That was true. By the time you are reading this, I will be on my way to the north. I know I am getting worse, and when I am that way I want to be by myself. But don't worry about me, I am going someplace where I will be close to the hospital that cared for me before.

"I am sorry that I have given you so much trouble and perhaps hurt you, too. But I couldn't help it. I needed you, and I like to think there were times when you needed me, too. Good-bye, darling, and bless you.

"You told me that I was too much troubled by guilt, that everyone bruised everyone else, husbands and wives, parents and children, and friends, and lovers, and that there was no avoiding it. That may be so. But I couldn't live with myself if I knew I was dragging you down — as I would, I know I would. That's why I'm leaving. But you go back. Go back, Rusty. I am slipping over the edge, I think. You needn't. Go back, into the light. You are strong, and so much gentler than you think."

Then there was a sentence he couldn't read, his eyes were so blurred with tears.

"I don't know what I said when we parted," she went on. "If it was hateful, forgive me, as I try to forgive myself."

Then after "Love" and her name and a row of kisses she had added a postscript.

"Never despair," she said. "You have a heart big enough for anguish."

He brushed his eyes. Already his pupils were contracting again. Light hardly entered. He carefully folded the letter and put it in his inside breast-pocket and then went over and drew the pay that was coming to him.

9

The ground had shaken under his feet. But he still tried to go on. He kept on working at the market, although his life had lost all sense of rhythm and routine. Instead of going home as soon as he finished work, he would sit drinking hour after hour or would walk endlessly trying to tire himself out. He called unexpectedly on Steve a couple of times at the tailoring establishment where he worked. He dropped in at the pictures or at one or other of the clubs in the old foreign quarter, but he never stayed long. Gradually the shutters in his eyeballs were widening and were letting in images to torment him. His horizon would tilt disconcertingly and could threaten in broad daylight to pitch him down head over heels. All he could think of to do to steady himself and make his vision contract was to sit drinking and to exhaust himself with walking. Once he was so tired that he stretched out on a park bench and slept there for two or three hours, although the winter was not yet over and there was still frost in the air. But his physique was unconquerable. He got up and went straight to the market and worked from midnight through till morning.

It was only with the destruction of the sun-dial that the ground beneath him began to shiver and crack in all directions. No one knew who was responsible for it. But one morning the crystal spheres that had been put up again so few months before were found shattered and lying in great jagged flakes almost within the shadow of the palace. At the court of inquiry that was convened that same day, the guard who had been on duty said that in the early hours of the morning he had heard the sound of running feet, that was all, but no sound of anything being struck or fractured — and he had taken no action because his orders, sir, were to stay at his post whatever happened until he was relieved. None of the other witnesses who were called could add anything. When Rusty read about it in the newspapers, it crossed his mind for an instant that it might have been Brandy or Dragon who had done it; it was just the kind of witless, arrogant outrage that would have pleased them. But how could they ever have got past the guard and over the wall and into the privy garden? He gave it hardly more than a moment's thought before he put down the paper and ordered himself another drink.

But the papers themselves wouldn't let go of the sensation. They knew it would interest their readers more than details about rationing (the meat ration had been reduced again after a temporary increase) or about the continuing coal-shortage. And it gave them another stick to beat the government with. It was scandalous, almost sacrilege, that such a crime could be committed so close to the palace; there must be slackness — or worse — in high places. Of course this wanton destruction was the work of deserters. If the government had shown more vigour in dealing with the problem, the outrage would never have occurred. And the long-standing public debate boiled up again, some arguing that what was needed was a much stronger policy to see that the deserters harassing the capital were brought to book, while others contended that considerations of expediency and humanity alike showed the wisdom of granting a general amnesty.

As the controversy mounted, the government was forced to reformulate its position: a general amnesty would be unfair to those who had completed their military service and had been discharged, to those who were still being called up because of the country's continuing military commitments, and to the deserters who had already surrendered or been apprehended and were under sentence in the various detention-barracks; but the public could rest assured that the case of each deserter who was brought to trial would be considered fairly, with full weight being given to any extenuating circumstances; in the meantime measures to round up absentees were being intensified and the co-operation of everyone was requested; in particular, the relatives, friends, and employers of the men concerned were reminded of the penalties provided by law for those convicted of sheltering a deserter, and were called on to do everything possible to see that deserters either surrendered voluntarily or were discovered and arrested.

It was a good statement, carefully drafted, balanced, judicious. But it failed of its principal purpose. In spite of it, the controversy continued unabated, bringing fresh shoals of letters to the editor. The causes of desertion were canvassed as well as possible remedies; and a wide range of explanations were advanced by earnest correspondents. It seemed strange that no one even hinted that when a society had revealed so brutally its ultimate thrust and meaning it was only natural that some should decide to desert it; or that in the uncompromising glare of battle other deserters should have been unknowingly prepared for the moment when they would recognize themselves for what they were. But beyond that, Rusty took little interest in the controversy, one way or another.

It was the breaking of the sun-dial itself that affected him. That night it came to him again — crystal orbs slowly turning and weeping, moonily brightened and then darkened by passing clouds and then brightened again, a standard round which globes were clustered, and then one great globe into which all the others had dissolved, revolving above him, around him, within him, a whole system of globes as clear and watery as tear-drops but heavy as the world. If it should break? A shiver ran through his dream. He was so involved in these spheres that the tell-tale iridescences that were reflected back and forth from their inner surfaces shimmered with the pale hues of his own flesh. He was incorporated in their perfection. Any shiver through them threatened him, too. Himself, his tissues tinting them. But the light that made it possible to see the tints of these slowly turning circles in the dark came from another source. He thought he knew who gave them light. There was a freshness scenting the darkness, and quivering — but it filled him with unease. Whose tears were they? Who animated the darkness? Who? He was oppressed by the heaviness of uncertainty, where everything should be clear. The fresh, grassy honeysuckle savour was disappearing, was being replaced by a scent that rose from other limbs, the strange waxy smell of limbs deranged, fatally tinctured with some discolouration, powdered with glass, abandoned, dedicated to death. Althea! Anne! He tried to call. But which should he call? At the bottom of his dream lay a sediment of anguish. The spheres were fracturing. They were breaking open. They were breaking, they were tearing him apart. To awake! He must waken or be lost. He was staked down with grief.

When he finally awoke, bathed in sweat, he was lying spread-eagled on the bed, his arms and legs flung out like those of a man being broken on the wheel. At first he was so panic-stricken of the dark he didn't dare open his eyes; he was sure a masked torturer was standing over him. There was someone certainly in the room. Only with a struggle did he manage to bring his right arm up to his eyes and look askance at his watch as though to find out how long it was till his execution. Willfully he accustomed his eyeballs to the dark and then moved them slowly round the room. He made the circuit again. There was no one. He was alone. Now he noticed how violently he was shivering. He concentrated all his power on trying to calm himself, breathing deeply, trying to control his pulse, exercising his will on the twitching nerves in each part of his body, one after another. At last he was able to move and put down his feet. He sat on the edge of the bed with his head in his hands. There were three hours to put in before he was due at the market. But he couldn't go back to bed. Slowly he got up and began to dress. He would go out and walk the streets till it was time to go to work.

He was seeing very little. A pool of dirty yellow light blotched the stone wall of a warehouse. A grey cat crossed his path, meowing. A policeman on the other side of the street looked as though he might cross and stop and question him — and then thought better of it. He didn't care whether he did or not.... She was stretched out under a tight rubber sheet, they were adjusting electrodes to her forehead; he heard her scream through the deserted streets. Could he have done anything to save her? There was no one who would answer. But he knew that he wouldn't have had even a chance of doing her good without rejoining the world where there were hospitals, doctors, nurses — and the money to pay for them — and order, continuity, identity. Perhaps even then he could have done nothing. But without that, there wasn't a chance; he couldn't even have begun. He would have had to turn himself in, in order to try. To surrender, surrender, surrender. He might have helped to keep a roof over her head. If things had been different, if he had surrendered. Yes, for that he would need to have his name back again. And to have it back, he would have to surrender.

He was going toward the centre of the city, toward the market. But where was the argument leading him? One dark street flowed into another. Then they opened on the river, and he was crossing the bridge. It was a clear, starry night, but he didn't look up. On the smooth, outward-moving tide he saw the stars weeping, bleeding. There was no one to answer. As usual when his brains were so flayed and naked, he gripped the sharp edges of the medal in his pocket as though to ask it for counsel. Now it would tell him nothing, however hard he grasped it, grasped it until he cut his fingers. He couldn't believe in the palace where he had been invested or in the heat around the weapon-pit or in himself slapping in one clip of cartridges after another — in himself least of all. There was only a haze where the enemy might be moving, and spent smoke curling out of the end of the barrel. He gripped the medal even tighter, the medal that was the only thing about him that still knew his name. Then he drew his brown blood-stained fist out of his pocket and threw the medal into the dark, another star shining for a moment over the river, then bleeding, sinking in the outward-flowing tide. He hardly waited to see it disappear. Striding along, he put his hand to his mouth and licked off the few drops, taking the salt taste of his own blood down the back of his throat.

How could he surrender? he asked of the shrewd salty air. There were other things he had to be true to … hours plucked from the tree of time and made immortal … didn't those miracles deserve devotion? Without them there was only waste, tundra, dying stars, apathy, meaninglessness spreading everywhere. Or was it they that made everything else seem meaningless? He moved through a great room of mirrors. Were those hours delusion, or the only truth there was? If he should let them go … but that was impossible: they would never let go of him. He was held by them as by the claws of a bird, he lived under their eyes, under their glistening feathers. His world was coloured by them, he couldn't escape from their dark greens and purples, their dark fading radiance. Theirs in the ranks of death, he thought, theirs — though striped, scored, torn. His duty … but, as he turned to it, he heard her whisper, "I might be cured if I could have you body and soul." In the watery darkness she had called to him, had needed him; she had needed in the dark to hold something as hard as a watery emerald. She had needed him and he had failed and now she was slipping over the horizon. His eyes opened to admit her wholly and the deep draught of his own failure. It burned him as he drained it. He felt it burning, corroding round his heart, prisoning still deeper the few drops of heaven that he could never surrender.

His eyeballs closed again. He walked on blindly. When he reached the centre of the city, there was still time to kill before he was due at the market. He roamed this way and that. He went in one direction down a street where every second window seemed to be a gunsmith's. Then he turned and went in the opposite direction down a street full of shipping-offices. He came out on the empty Plaza and crossed and stood by one of the cannon at the base of the column. There were no lights on even in the Ministry. There was hardly a soul to be seen. But his nerves told him that it was still a battlefield. He remembered huddling one night in a slit-trench when the guns had fallen preternaturally quiet and in the silence hearing (with the sharpened senses of an animal crouching in a hole), hearing or imagining the sound of footsteps through the dark — reinforcements coming up on both sides, patrols going out, units moving into new positions, partisans crossing the lines, escaped prisoners-of-war groping their way back, deserters trying to evade detection, refugees travelling with what little they could carry — till the whole darkness seemed to be scored with footsteps, seemed to foam into a crescendo of running feet. He felt the city trembling with it. It was a battlefield, and the lines ran through his heart....

In another corner of the battlefield a council of war was still going on. The provost marshal was there and the chief of police and a dozen other officials. They were putting the finishing touches on a plan of attack that was to be presented to the government in the morning. During the next week all police leaves were to be cancelled, police reinforcements were to be drawn from the provinces, the army was to contribute additional provost staff and signals and vehicles. It was to be a real blitz. This time nothing was to be left to chance, cordons were to be woven through the whole city, a centralized command-post was to be established and all the detachments, all the foot and vehicle patrols, were to be tied back to it by a special signals net. Everything was to be ready for a seven-day round-the-clock operation. It was at about the moment when Rusty was reporting in at the market that the chief of police, who was presiding, looked up and glanced around the table. "Well, I think we've done a good night's work, gentlemen. You all understand what your role is to be?" They all nodded. "Then I'll issue the code-word to you as soon as I get the green light from the government." As they filed out, the secretary went round the table gathering up secret waste for disposal in accordance with the security regulations.

That day there was little effect of the plan to be seen in the capital. Rusty worked steadily at the market and in the afternoon went back to his room. But the following day the atmosphere in the market was transformed. The number of police had been tripled and the air was blue with rumour. Late in the morning all the porters were called up individually to be interviewed in the main office by two police officers. One young fellow tried to make a bolt for it but was tripped up and taken off to the police-station with a fractured wrist. When Rusty was ushered in and asked for his papers, he tried to hand them over without concern; he had been through all this so often before. The sergeant lingered over his identity-card, though, turning it over several times, running his finger over it, holding it up to the light. For a moment Rusty thought that this was it. But then his patron, the foreman, who was standing by, said confidently, "You needn't worry about this man, officer; I can vouch for him." And the sergeant returned the card and cleared him and let him go. He went back to wheeling crates of cauliflowers, but he couldn't help wondering whether he mightn't be called again, the sergeant had been so suspicious. Time passed. The scrutiny continued. It was mid afternoon. It was only as the market was almost closing for the day that he was asked to call at the office again. But this time the policemen were gone. The foreman was there by himself.

"I don't want to ask any questions," he said. "That's not my business. But I can't keep you on here any longer. You saw yourself what a narrow escape you had this morning. Next time you may not be so lucky. And then I'd be in for it as well as you. I hate to let you go, but I haven't any alternative. The fact is I can't shield you any longer."

He held out his hand, and Rusty took it and mumbled his thanks. The doors were closing. Living with Anne hadn't been like really having a home; but it had been a kind of a home. Working at the market hadn't been quite real, either. He always knew it couldn't last. But it had earned him some money and given him something to do. And sometimes — perhaps only for a moment or two at a time — he had had hints of spring and sun and freshness and had felt his feet planted in the earth. Now he was being shut out of that, too.

There were 63 deserters arrested during the first full day of the campaign, so the newspapers reported. One of them had been hiding in an attic for four years and hadn't seen the light of day in all that time. Another confessed to more than a score of burglaries while he had been on the loose. The next day the total of arrests rose to 87. The papers reported the totals each day with a combination of moral righteousness and sporting enthusiasm. And they were provided by the campaign by some stories that they wouldn't have had otherwise and that served to import some liveliness into the languors of post-war reconstruction. One unlucky young suspect running from a patrol slipped on the edge of a station platform and shot out over the live rail and was electrocuted; and it was more than an hour before the line could be cleared and brought back into service.

After losing his job at the market, Rusty's mood unaccountably veered and he found himself sharing, however grimly, in the excitement. Now he went out courting danger. For the first time in weeks he visited some of the haunts he had known in the old foreign quarter. His former acquaintances — bar-tenders, runners, door-men, tobacconists — hardly knew whether to recognize him or not, their world had been so riddled by arrests and by a withering fire of suspicion, with talk going around about the unexpected agents the police might be using and about the penalties for those failing to divulge information which might assist in the apprehension of deserters. Even the huge, jovial, beer-bellied barman at the bar he had principally frequented only permitted himself to remark, "Well, you're a cool customer, if I ever saw one," as he served him. Then he turned his back and hurried to the other end of the bar, leaving Rusty straight and soldierly, sipping his drink, but with one eye watching the door.

With nothing to do, he walked in the parks and noticed how much more nervous and fleeting the chance encounters there had become. After dark the shadows under the great elms (which were now beginning to bud again) were arabesqued by tentative circling movements of pursuit; but whether these shifting and broken manoeuvres always involved the police or were sometimes caused only by one fugitive forlornly hunting another, he couldn't be sure. Once he was stopped by a plainclothesman, but all that happened was that he was told he wouldn't wander in the parks after dark if he knew what was good for him. Sometimes he felt almost disappointed to look back and find that he *wasn't* being followed.

It was Steve who worried about him much more than he did himself. As often as not when he got back to his room there would be a message that the boy had been trying to reach him; and when they got in touch on the telephone, his friend's first question was always the same: Was he safe? He tried to shrug it off reassuringly, but Steve would repeat, "I'm worried about you, Rusty, I'm worried." It was chiefly over the telephone that they talked these days. He didn't tell Steve the reason; but he felt dumbly that his luck had turned against him and he didn't want the boy to be involved in anything that might happen to him. But if they hadn't met at least occasionally Steve would have been heartbroken. As it was, he felt their meetings came all too seldom.

The first time they met after the beginning of the big police round-up was for dinner in a restaurant in a back street that was run by one of Steve's compatriots. Rusty was there first and took a place where he could watch the door. The newspapers reported that that day no fewer than 126 deserters had been picked up.

When Steve came in, he didn't see Rusty at first. The winter had told on him. His face brightened as soon as he caught sight of his friend, but there was a lethargy, almost a dead-ness, about him that Rusty didn't remember. He hadn't heard from his parents for months. He had almost given up any thought of ever going back, he said. With that decision his mind had grown calmer. But it was as though the torsion which had been wringing his brains had now worked lower and was twisting and skewering his guts.

He didn't want to talk about himself much. All his interest was in his friend. Was the danger very great? Was he taking good care? What was the chance of a general amnesty?

"Not a hope in the world, I imagine," Rusty said.

"That's what I'm praying for," the boy confessed, undeterred. "That one morning I'll wake up to find that all the deserters have been pardoned, even the cowards and the criminals, and that the prisons have been opened and that you are standing there again in the sunlight."

"It won't happen," Rusty insisted, refusing to lift his head.

"For my sake, you mustn't say so," the boy went on with wan eagerness. "Often when I was in the camps I feared I would never be released. But the day came when I was. I have had my miracles — even if it didn't turn out to be what I hoped. Now I pray for one for you."

I have had my miracle, too, thought Rusty. But all he said was, "I'm not important enough for that."

"You are to me. You came when I needed you most. I think … I sometimes think that you must have been sent to me."

"I was cruising around the docks, that was all."

"You can't hurt me by speaking that way, I know you too well. Whatever you say, you know you were a saviour to me."

Rusty still hung his head, afraid or ashamed (he didn't know which) to look up. Then he said evasively but with a flicker of interest. "Even if there were a general amnesty, what if there were things that I couldn't forgive myself?"

"How are you different from anyone in that? I know you don't understand yourself. Don't be angry, but I asked a young priest, a priest of my own country, about you. I said that I couldn't see why anyone like you should want to leave his home and abandon everything and sink lower and lower. He told me that there were people who have to go down into the dark, we don't know why, it may be the will of God."

"I don't know," said Rusty heavily, for once meaning every word. But he lifted his head and smiled, accepting at last the boy's bewildered and bewildering gratitude and admiration.

"I will pray for you anyway," Steve said.

The next day more than 150 deserters were brought in. The papers were jubilant. Rusty found that he couldn't stay in his room for long. He was too restless, too nervous. He had to be out and about even at the risk of making it more likely that he would be picked up. More and more he felt that he was being followed. As he wandered at night through the streets in the centre of the city, a face would disengage itself from the crowd, with eyes that pierced through his, and would ride along abreast of him for a while in the slowly moving stream, glancing across at him and then looking away, or moving a little ahead of him but glancing back to see that he was still there, or falling sometimes a little behind but eyeing him still, he felt certain. Always it was a face that he felt he should remember, although he couldn't place it. Was it someone he had seen round the docks, or at the market, or at Dragon's, or in the house where the mastermind had come to corner him, or in the house before that, or before that, or where? He didn't know. There had been so many faces, so many encounters. Sometimes he was convinced it was the face of the young pickpocket who had ... but the strange thing was that now he couldn't remember the poor young punk's pasty face. He could still see him racing up and down stairs on the morning of the raid and then standing there on the roof silhouetted against the pale blue sky. But his face had completely vanished. He might have been beheaded. Whose face was it, then? Or was it only an imagined complicity, a face that had been formed to fit the image of his pursuer?

The crowd was slow and sluggish. But the chase was quickening. Faster! Faster! The crowd barely moved. Yet he felt it being given the velocity of the whole world whirling through the dark. He heard the sound of running feet. That was what came to him above the idling engines of clogged traffic, the clank of bus-drivers changing gears, the cries of "Taxi, taxi," the dim shuffle of crowds oozing from the theatres. The sound of running feet. He could hear them rustling through the grasses in the parks, slithering through the rubble, pelting down alleys, sliding into one futile refuge after another. The city was rushing on through the darkness, the neon signs spinning like Catherine-wheels, the edges of the buildings streaming with comets' tails, and the almost motionless crowd racing and whirling and streaming, too, a city of pursuers and pursued. The face of the suffering city that he had once gazed down on swam up to him. And with it came the face of the city in pursuit, blank, blindfold, running in its sleep. What was it running from? What was *he*? From something that had happened to him? from estrangement? from himself? Why was the city so full of running? Because, as the trees began to swell with new blossom, it was so full of creatures who had been broken from the bough? because it was running from its suffering? And the two faces of the city coalesced. But he could hardly bear that single twofold image, congruent, incongruous, two faces superimposed and inseparable. He walked as a link in this slow, chained crowd — convicts in lock-step, citizens with sad routines, wild hunters, wild animals being hunted — each one of them, it might be, in his own person convict, citizen, hunter, hunted. But he couldn't stand the sluggish pace. It galled his ankles. Everywhere he heard the sound of running feet. He wanted to run, to run for his life, to run till the blood was so pounding in his ears that he could hear nothing else, no other footsteps, no voices, nothing, till his eyes were bloodshot and heavy and closed against all knowledge of the city's two blanched faces in the darkness.

In a few minutes the sluggish street delivered him to the edge of one of the parks. He crossed and penetrated it deliberately a little way. Then he took to his heels.

It was as though that were the signal for which the shadows had been waiting. Immediately a tremor spread through the park, it was full of running. Shadows detached themselves from trees and were off like a shot. Gravel was stirred up into a dull spray that subsided when the racing footsteps had passed. He could see two, three, half a dozen figures startled from their hiding by his flight; but he knew who none of them were as they blundered and zig-zagged around him. A shadow crossed his path some twenty feet in front of him but didn't look aside. There was another shadow off to his left. And another behind him. Now he was running like the wind. It didn't enter his head that some of these deluded creatures might think he was chasing them. All he knew now was that he was being followed, he didn't know by whom, but he *knew.* They were after him. Conviction had settled irresistibly to the back of his neck, to his spine, down the ultimate cord and fluid holding him together. His consciousness had retreated, gathering thickly, till it was little more than an inescapable conviction of pursuit that drove him on and gave clumsy, heavy wings to his feet. He flew on, splashing through the loose sand where the guardsmen exercised their horses. He raced past empty benches, abandoned huts, an ornamental pool. He wouldn't look back, but he knew they were gaining. He raced on till he came to a summer-house, whose fragile, filagreed roof had collapsed and slipped sideways. There he drew up, sheltering beside it.

Now he could see them. The branches were still almost bare and afforded little cover. There they were, two figures in the broken moonlight, running towards him. They were not in uniform. Probably detectives. He sidled under the wide crazy eaves, keeping his back to the wall, watching them. Then he turned the corner and swung round the floppy, shadowy structure. He was doubling back now at an angle, crouching down, running from the shadow of one tree to another, hoping they wouldn't spot him, making (it was all he could think of) for the abandoned huts. They were almost at the summerhouse before they realized he had doubled back and wheeled after him. The huts loomed up grey and deserted, closer and closer. But they were hedged by high barbed wire that hadn't been carted away and that he hadn't expected. He didn't stop. He leapt flat on the coils with arms and legs outspread, bearing them down, as he had been taught, not minding how much his hands and clothes were torn, and then somersaulted to the other side. He crawled to a tree and then on, in deeper shadow, to another tree. And then a little farther still, into a crumbling trench.

He had just fallen into it, panting, when a bullet 'tsinged over his head. His eyeballs started. That wasn't the police! They wouldn't shoot just to bring in a deserter. Then there was another shot, a little wide this time, splintering the trunk of a tree. The trench was shallow, but he sucked himself down as close to the earth as he could and waited, breathless. From the far side of the park a police-whistle sounded. On the other side of the barbed wire a hoarse voice he didn't know said, "We'd better be going." And another voice answered grudgingly, "I guess so. But we'll get the dirty squealer yet." He waited. He waited. He looked at his watch. He would wait five minutes more. Then he raised his head a little above the top of the trench. A car was starting up some distance down the roadway. He raised his head higher and looked around. There was no one now. The park might have been deserted.

He was so exhausted that he slumped back into the trench and slept a little.

It was well after midnight when he awoke, cramped and stiff. It was too late to go back to his room by the docks: the last trains had left and he was too tired to walk. He looked at his hands. Then he took out a handkerchief and tied it around the one that had bled the most. Slowly he got up and made a wide slow circle out of the park.

He walked on stolidly. He wouldn't think about what had happened. He wanted something to eat. But there was no place open. Absently he reached down and brushed off some of the dirt that was clinging to his clothes. His bandaged hand was too conspicuous; he put it in his pocket. All he could think of was of damp earth, crawling and wormy, like a battlefield crawling with wounded.

After walking for half an hour (or an hour, he didn't know) he came to one of the main railway-stations serving the city. The station buffet might be open for him to get something to eat. He went through to the wide, empty, glass-covered platform, where the only people he could see were a sailor sleeping on a bench and a porter dozing over some trunks. But the buffet was open and he stood at the bar and bought sandwiches and coffee from a heavy-lidded waitress. There was a torn paper lying on the counter and he glanced at it idly. The day's total of deserters arrested had been 131. The reparations conference was still deadlocked. Two suspects accused of a large theft of cloth from a warehouse had been arraigned. According to the summary of evidence given by the police, the intended receiver of the stolen goods had become alarmed by intensified police activity in the capital and had led them to the rendezvous that had been arranged. There they had been able to pick up the suspects red-handed.... So, the young jackal's contacts in the west end hadn't been so reliable after all!

He didn't care. He wasn't going any farther tonight. And tomorrow would have to look after itself. He walked back to the empty platform and stretched out on one of the benches. This was the station where he had arrived in the capital so innocently months before, he remembered drowsily, as he turned from one side of the hard bench to the other, trying to sleep.

The arched glass roof swayed over him, its large frosted panes held by iron girders. The glass dripped moonily over him, twining tantalizingly down to him, reminding him of something that was so far back he couldn't remember it, curling its tendrils round his heart, a glass heart stained by only a few drops. The glass dome was rooted and nourished there. If one should crack, so would the other. But there was more iron than glass in what he saw as he dozed. Iron crowbars threatening his outstretched limbs. If the trance were broken, they would truncheon him, he would be broken on the wheel. Iron spikes, iron crow-bars, blue-black, pistol-barrel black. A region of rigid metal. Of cold creeping up his limbs. Had he been infected with cold by limbs moving convulsively, opening like freezing petals? He shivered. A fatal illness was infiltrating him, bent on capturing something he had vowed he would never surrender. Vainly he tried to beat it back. His courage was fatally divided. He was torn, being torn apart. He didn't know which way to turn.... The horizon spread dull and misted, shivered by ice-cold green. There was nothing living in it. Then a pale twittering was lifted, voices twittering. One, a sweet voice, but so far off he could scarcely hear it; while accusingly out of the cold another voice called, "Rusty, Rusty," the voice of someone he had known, of someone he was parted from. When he didn't answer, the horizon was tranced again with frost, subsiding, sealed. Mist. But through it was scrawled — a message? a sentence? a line? something in a letter that he hadn't been able to read, his eyes were so blurred? He knew he wouldn't remember it when he awoke, but now he could read it clearly "... but your heart would have to break before you could give it to me." He read it again, as intently as a child, "Your heart would have to break ..." He shivered with distress. Jagged flakes lying on the grass. Snow blown over tundra. Barrens. Waste. Then he slept more deeply, calmly, the glass roof floating over him.

He wakened to a hand grasping his shoulder and to a voice saying — what was it? — he couldn't hear. He opened his eyes. Lying on his back, all he could see was steam from the early morning trains swirling up and spreading out under the roof.

Then the voice repeated, "What's wrong with your hand, there?" There was nothing wrong with his hand! And, anyway, whose business was it if there were? He sat up and turned his head. At the end of the bench stood two provost corporals, smart, beautifully turned out, with their greatcoats beautifully pressed and their heavy boots beautifully polished and their revolver lanyards falling neatly from their collars down to their holsters, as smart-looking soldiers as he had once been himself. He resented their smartness when his own clothes were crumpled, stained, slept-in; and he was irritated by being wakened. He stood up, knowing that, the next thing, he would be asked for his identification. But he didn't wait. Only glancing aside for a second to see where the way to the street was and that the route to it was reasonably clear, he tautened every muscle and swayed back a little and then drove the nearest provost full in the face with his clenched fist. He sent him down like a wall. Then before he could topple over after him, he swung round and raced for the street. The thin early morning crowds flew past him, wide-eyed, horror-struck, as though he were falling past them to God knows where. He had a little headstart, the other corporal would have to pause a minute or two to look to his mate, but now he would be after him, he couldn't be far behind. He raced on. The shop-fronts swam together into the race above a falls — groceries, hardware, flowers, fruit, old clothes, drugs, drink — a mirror racing to the lip of the falls. He wouldn't look back. Beneath his sleek, sure speed his blood was boiling. There were shouts; he didn't hear them. He veered out into the road and back again, breaking this way and that to avoid obstruction, streaming past. Speed frothed and foamed in him to a thick angry passion. He wouldn't be caught. He would think of something yet. He had passed two turnings blindly, but now at the next intersection he changed direction and went on gathering speed. Another hundred yards, and he thought he would burst; this passion would have to discharge itself or he would fly to pieces. He slowed, he slowed to a halt and grimly took cover in a doorway. He would wait for the other provost to come up and then deal with him, too. He stood beside himself, waiting. Why didn't he come, the dirty flatfoot? He was so debauched by speed and anger, he could have killed him, beaten him into a pulp. Still he waited. This couldn't last. Boldly he stepped out onto the pavement and looked back. A cleaning woman was limping into a block of flats. A child was starting off to school. There was no one else.

He couldn't believe it. He slunk back into the doorway, humiliated, bruised, cheated. The dirty yellow bastard, he kept muttering over and over. Then he spat out a volley of curses into the empty street. But he was slowly coming to himself. Where should he go? He couldn't calculate, he couldn't think. There was no place but back to his room. His sigh was almost a groan. He walked slowly on into busier streets, where there were more people going to work or to do their shopping. After a night of running he limped back into lock-step with them. His eyes were almost half closed, but once or twice he looked up: the sky was glistening with mackerel clouds that were thinning out in the pure, clear blue. It was going to be a beautiful day.

He turned in out of the sunlight and went down and caught a train back to the docks. His fury was passing, he was cooling off. His eyes widened a little. In the window opposite, what he saw being drawn remorselessly down the black tunnel was someone he could hardly recognize. The face seemed flushed, the eyes puffy, although he couldn't be sure, the reflection was so elusive and sketchy and fugitive. He was glazed and flattened by the glass, which skinned the dark like talc covering a map-sheet. You could write on it with chinagraph pencils, he imagined, to indicate what was happening on the battlefield, arrowing in the axis of advance in red, circling pockets of resistance in blue, making a rough stab at where the front might run, and then adding yellow dotted-lines and question-marks for the direction of possible counter-attacks. When he had finished marking it up, he saw that his own face still wavered uncertainly behind the battle-map. For a moment he felt that all of it — all the pursuits and conspiracies and shocks, all the captures and evasions, all the shifting entanglements, what was happening to Anne and Steve and thousands of others, even to the sailor and Rudy and his criminal friends — that it was all taking place within his own darkness, that he was the battlefield for it all. And then the battle-map that he had sketched rippled and thickened and grew more filaments, spreading nervously, till there was mirrored beneath his face layer after layer of thin transparent sheets — the battlefield, his heart, his guts, his muscles, his brains and nerves like a downward-branching tree, his bleached bare bones.

It was risky to go back to his room. He knew that now. But he wouldn't dwell on it. He would hardly face it. And, besides, where else could he go? When he reached it safely and slipped inside, he locked the door; but he wouldn't even bother to barricade it with a chest or a chair. Nature would have to take its course.

What was to become of him? He wouldn't, he couldn't, think. He took off his clothes and got into bed. The lines ran through his heart, but all day he lay dead to the world.

★ ★ ★

While he slept, in another sector … the chief of police was presiding over a meeting to appraise the results of the campaign to date, to consider any problems that might require attention, and to coordinate plans for what still remained to be done.

"I think, gentlemen," he was saying, "that we can all take solid satisfaction from what has been accomplished so far. Everyone deserves congratulation. There has been a fine spirit of energy and co-operation, and I am indebted to you for it. I hope that you will pass along my thanks to every member of your staffs.

Now, with your permission, I think we might best begin by hearing a brief, factual report from our secretary."

The secretary reported that since the start of the round-up the number of deserters apprehended had totalled 783. Of these, 33 percent had been absent for a year or less, 25 percent for periods of between one and two years, 27 percent for periods of between two and three years, 12 percent for periods of between three and four years, and 3 percent for periods of four years or more.

("The real veterans, eh?" someone remarked at the foot of the table to smothered laughter.)

In addition to the charges they faced under military law, the secretary went on, 330 of the suspects who had been arrested were being charged with criminal offences as well. It was estimated that as many as 500 unsolved crimes might ultimately be cleared from the books as a result of the roundup.

When the time came for questions, the official handling public relations wanted further guidance on what line he should take with the press. Then the representative of the palace (a weathered fashion-plate whom no one seemed to have much use for) asked whether any progress had been made toward the arrest of those who had broken the sundial in the privy garden.

"No, I'm afraid not," the chairman admitted with both deference and condescension.

"Or towards discovering how the crime was committed?" he persisted in isolation.

"That's still a mystery, too, I'm afraid."

"Then I must observe that those to whom I am responsible continue to take a very serious view of the outrage."

"I can well understand," the chairman commented drily. "But I'm sure we can all depend on you to see that they appreciate that the campaign, with all respect, has wider public objectives than the solution of one particular crime."

"Have the security services any questions?" he asked, passing on briskly.

"No, not at the moment, Mister Chairman," their representative replied. "But perhaps I might have a word with you when the meeting's over?"

"Well, I have a question," bluntly put in the provost marshal. "How long is this campaign to last? It's all very well to bring in deserters. I'm delighted with the success we've had so far. But we can't go on indefinitely working our staffs around the clock. Already a number of my men, I won't say how many, have gone absent themselves. It mightn't be much of a gain to have all the deserters under lock and key and all the military police on the loose."

After discussion, it was agreed that the campaign would be pursued with full vigour for another four days and that to ensure the maximum success additional reinforcements would be secured from the services and from provincial areas so that surveillance could be still further tightened around the railway stations, the docks, clubs, dance-halls, hotels, lodging-houses, and other places where deserters were most likely to be apprehended.

* * *

In another sector … the ambassador (who looked very much like the chief of police and who, in fact, had had a good deal of police experience) was seated at his wide polished desk initialling an aide-memoire to the Ministry about the control commissions in occupied territories. He didn't know that only down the hall in his embassy, near the communication centre, the assistant military attaché and the chauffeur were meeting to consider a problem of their own. Under the tension created by the police campaign they wondered whether the sailor mightn't lose his nerve and do something that would compromise them. The military attaché was inclined to let matters rest, but the chauffeur thought that the risk was too great and was convinced that they should act at once.

"He hasn't brought in anything of value for weeks," the chauffeur was urging methodically. "It isn't worth the risk to leave him where he is."

"There are risks both ways, you know," the attaché reminded him.

"I know. But if you entrust me with it, the risks will be kept to a minimum. He's so demoralized now that you can't tell what he might do. As I say, best to get rid of him."

The attaché pondered. "Well, you take care of him, then," he granted at last. "But make sure you don't bungle things."

"Have you ever known me to?"

"See that you don't this time, then."

⋆ ⋆ ⋆

In another sector … Mark was ushering in a member of the security services to see the minister. Crossing this expanse of red carpet, the young official never knew when to say good-morning; if you said it too soon, the greeting was lost in the room's mirrored spaces; if you waited too long, it seemed impolite.

"I'm sorry to bother you, sir," he apologized. "But there's a memorandum for you I have to deliver by hand."

The minister took it and read it through, underlining passages with his pencil. Then he read it through again more slowly, frowning.

When he was finished, he put it down and said with a trace of irritation, "I don't want to do anything, if I can help it, that might disturb relations with our allies. God knows they're delicate enough as it is. Are you sure this is necessary?"

The official assured him that it was. "As you know, he's been working for the other side as well as for us. I don't know whether they're as disappointed with the returns as we are; but lately we've been getting virtually nothing. The likelihood is, we're convinced, that the balance of advantage is now running strongly in their favour."

"I can see that isn't something you can allow to continue," the minister conceded. "But I'm still worried about the possible consequences."

"You really needn't worry, sir. As you know, we have ways and means for handling these problems very quietly. In this particular case, I'm not sure that the other side may not have much the same idea as we have. At any rate, we can arrange it so that no one will know the difference."

The minister sighed. "Take care of him, then, in your own way," he agreed reluctantly, putting his initials on the memorandum. "But see that you do it discreetly."

* * *

In still another sector … the mastermind was pouring out drinks for his guests from an elaborately equipped bar that stood at one end of the living-room in his flat. For once Rudy was wearing a coat and tie, but he still looked damp and pale, like a plant that has sprouted in a cellar. To fill up his badly depleted ranks, the director of operations had called in reinforcements; and they were scattered in ungainly comfort here and there through the low-ceilinged room on low chairs and sofas that were heavily upholstered in lush brothel red.

In spite of some natural discouragement and impatience, the conference had gone well. Rudy (with the belligerence of someone who was to play very little part in the show) had wanted to know why there had been so much delay.

"After all," he complained, "Jackie is in jail, and two others; and we know who really gave the game away. So what have we been waiting for?"

"We've been tiring him out and driving him wild," the mastermind explained tolerantly. "Now we're ready to go in for the kill. According to the weather-reports, there's likely to be a thick fog tonight, so the conditions should be as favourable as possible. That may make tracking him a little more difficult, but you all know where his haunts are and what directions he's likely to take. I don't see how he can escape, with so many on his trail. And the weather should give us invaluable cover."

Then he went over the method and timing of the operation, how the available personnel should be paired off, how they should communicate with one another, what they should do in case of emergency or in case the scent was unexpectedly lost — but it wouldn't be.

Rudy had no more questions. He knew that the mastermind wouldn't be so indulgent with him again. It was the other operatives that the brains at the centre of the plan was more concerned with; he wanted to know if there were any snags that they could foresee, and he polled them one by one. But for the most part they were sublimely indifferent. They had a job to do, and they had been given a large slice of their pay in advance. What more was there to say? It was only the last of the reinforcements to be polled, a thick-necked type, still wearing a cap and dirty white scarf — Bruiser, was it, or Boozer? — who came up sluggishly with one question.

"What happens if we come across another of his mob?" he wanted to know.

"Look after him, too," the mastermind replied decisively.

Since there were no more questions, the host poured out another round of drinks, using Rudy's services as a waiter. When everyone's glass was full again, he toasted them from behind the bar with a sporting, confident smile.

"Good luck and good hunting!"

* * *

When Rusty finally awoke, the room was filled with the pearly muted light of an early spring evening. He lay still for a while, both wondering what was to happen to him and certain that he knew it already. The lines that criss-crossed through the city ran intersecting through his ribs to find there a kind of dead centre. Out past the slums and the suburbs and the farthest reaches of the estuary the city spread fracturing in all directions. He had only to move and the cracks would become dazzlingly, shatteringly apparent. He lay still for a little longer.

Then he slowly got up and looked around. A folded sheet of paper had been slipped in under the door. Well, it could wait. It was only after he had washed and shaved and dressed as smartly as he could and carefully combed his hair that he went over and picked it up and opened it. All there was in the message from one of the two elderly sisters who kept the house was that someone had telephoned who hadn't been willing to leave his name. "But he was sure you would know who it was," the note concluded, "if I mentioned that you had arranged to meet him at the Bunch of Grapes."

Rusty sat down and lit a cigarette and waited. He felt a sense of absolute vacancy and immobility. He was falling as insensibly as a paratrooper after the chute has opened above him.

He waited. It was almost dark.

But when the knock came it wasn't what he had expected. It was Steve whom he opened the door to, and the boy was wide-eyed with fear.

He had just come home from work, he explained breathlessly, when there was a knock on the door and when he opened it the sailor glided in without saying a word. He was being hunted and had to find refuge somewhere.

"I didn't know what to do," the boy said thickly. "I remembered everything you'd told me, I didn't want to have anything to do with him. But I couldn't turn him out on the street, I didn't have the heart to." Rusty could see the scene with clairvoyant certainty — the sailor slunk into one corner of the room, grey, deflated, struggling for breath, his gills working convulsively as he brought out one gasp of his plight after another, pleading incoherently; and Steve, panic-stricken but struck with pity as well, wanting to be rid of him, to be rid of him forever, and yet unwilling to deny shelter to anything so pitiful, and yet wondering, too, whether all his power to hurt had finally been extracted, a prey still to old terrors, still mesmerized by this deflated carcass of what had once held so much malice.

"Where is he now?" Rusty asked at length.

"In the street outside, just outside the door. He followed me every step of the way."

The momentary calm he had felt only a few minutes before had vanished completely. He was in unknown territory and jarred and helpless. As they sat in the gloom, he felt as though any knock on the door anywhere might come homing in on his heart at once. What could he do? He couldn't tell Steve about what he knew was tightening around his own neck: that would only drive the boy even more distracted. But neither could he let him stay and share in whatever it was that was going to happen. Whichever way he turned, he was baffled; and as his frustration mounted, it twitched into restlessness. He got up and pulled the curtains and switched on the light. He would have to be off, and take the boy with him. It would be more difficult with him, but he couldn't leave him here in the room alone. Not with what he knew to be threatening. They would have to be off, to be off. He cast about in his mind for what he could say. His restlessness was becoming intolerable. And all the time Steve's face was shining more and more with the innocent cheer of someone who has escaped from danger into the hands of a protector he knows he can trust.

It might seem brutal, but there was no time to lose. If he waited too long, it might be too late.

"The best thing, then," he brought out huskily, "is to go out and shake him off and prove that there's nothing to fear."

Steve looked as though he couldn't believe his ears. "But I've only just come," he exclaimed incredulously. "And I'm afraid of what's out there!"

"That's what I mean. If you're afraid of something, it's better to face it."

"No!" It was almost a cry of terror. His eyes were staring. "I can't do it. You mustn't try to make me. I've wandered too far, Rusty. I can't go any farther. I've wandered thousands of miles, east and west, in the trains, in the trains …" He was crying unshamedly. His voice was breaking into hysteria.

Rusty wanted to stop his ears. He couldn't stand it. He couldn't look Steve in the face. He got up heavily and took a few steps to where the boy was sitting on the bed crying hysterically, and with his strong wide palm slapped him once across the cheek. He turned away as the crying subsided. When he looked back, Steve was lying on the bed sobbing, with his hands covering his eyes.

Rusty waited a minute or two. Then he went over to the washstand and folded back his sleeves and took a towel and dipped it in the basin. Gently he drew the shielding, imploring hands away and then washed the tears from his face. While he was doing this office, the boy never opened his eyes or spoke to him. But there was a murmur fluttering between his lips like a spray of strange leaves or blossoms or berries. With a pang of surprise, Rusty realized that he was speaking in his native tongue. That was something he had never heard him do before! And from the way he moved his hands, he thought he was praying.

At last he opened his eyes. They held no resentment. Far down in them there was a glimmer of light, almost of a smile, that was welling to the surface; and he was actually smiling as he thanked him and said, "I'll do whatever you say." In reply, Rusty ran his fingers through the boy's thick, wiry, blond hair as though that were the only way that he could ask for what he had done to be forgiven. Then he added, "If I can't always explain everything, try to take it on trust."

"I will," Steve promised. "I only wish I weren't such a weight on you."

Rusty didn't reply. He was already preoccupied with what gear he should take with him (his kit-bag? no, that would be only a nuisance … his revolver? he wasn't sure.) But he caught his mind acknowledging darkly that it *was* a weight, yet perhaps … (as an afterthought, a silvering to the cloud) perhaps it was the kind of weight that helped to make the clock go round.

A few minutes later they stood outside the front door, alert, ready for flight, their coat-collars turned up against the fog that was beginning to roll in from the estuary, peering down the few steps into the almost empty street. The sailor could hardly have moved. He was clinging to the railings only a few yards away, ringed by the faint urinous lamplight. He had lost his cap, and the fuzz on top of his head seemed manged and sickly. His mouth hung open. His loose lower lip might have had a hook in it. Rusty was about to shout at him to be off when he swayed and stared around blankly and then saw that Steve was no longer alone. Unsteadily he released himself from the railings and, gathering himself together, turned and wavered away down the centre of the road till he was lost in still darker clefts and channels. "A poor fish," Rusty muttered under his breath. Already he could see him floating belly-up in the oily swell somewhere in the harbour.

Then he stepped down into the street, with Steve only a pace behind, to reconnoitre. It wasn't for him to wonder too long about what claws might be lying in wait for the pitiable figure he had just disposed of so easily. There were other problems more pressing. There would be other eyes, more piercing, to reckon with. He strode off in the opposite direction, hoping to lure them out and to free himself once and for all from the uncertainty that he felt throbbing at the back of his neck and constricting his chest and his breathing. He couldn't tell the boy what was on his mind. But already his companion seemed to have recovered assurance and even some measure of buoyancy. Perhaps it was merely because with every stride they took they were widening the distance between him and the sailor. But he had the appearance rather of having entered unquestioningly into whatever his hero was up to, as though it were some new game, mysterious and exciting, whose rules and meaning he would learn only later. They spoke very little. All Rusty's senses were alert, all his instinctive fieldcraft: he was watching, trying to penetrate the fog, listening intently, snuffing every scent; so he could spare little attention for Steve except to glance down at him every now and again reassuringly. And the boy would always smile back, his fear conquered, at ease now with someone he trusted.

After they had gone a little way, Rusty stopped and looked about. The fog was drifting in more thickly, trailing long sleeves and streamers. It wasn't possible to see farther than back to the last corner or on to the next. The dim street-lamps were being muffled more closely. He couldn't see anything moving. He couldn't hear anything, although he knew the air was dense with pursuit, the salt wind hankering for prey. The police stood watching at all the sluices, trailing wide nets as well. The sailor was being trailed back to where he came from. And he was being trailed, too, although he still hadn't been able to pick up his pursuers. Then on the far side of the street a heavy figure came breasting, dispersing the fog. Standing in shadow, Rusty waited a moment or two longer (noticing out of the corner of his eye that the advancing figure was wearing a white scarf and a cap) until the fog was broken on the same side of the street as he was by a figure who kept glancing across at his partner and moved at the same pace, only always a little behind. Rusty took that as a sign, and, touching Steve on the arm, turned smartly and moved off, neither fast nor slow, as though accommodating his speed to the rest of the convoy. At the next corner he turned to the right. Then when they had gone twenty yards or so on this new course, he looked over his shoulder without stopping. As he expected, the two shadows were still in his wake; but now the white scarf was directly behind him while the other, slighter figure had moved to the other side of the street and was following closer. Rusty couldn't see him well, but he could make out a newspaper under his arm. They followed, neither closing nor widening the distance. And each time that Rusty turned (touching Steve's arm each time) they were still there, still following, the only difference being that white scarf and newspaper had shifted places, first on one side and then on the other, back and forth, back and forth, but still following.

Rusty didn't know how it would end, how it *could* end, how it could *ever* end, this nightmare pursuit where intervals were kept so invariably. He had no plan, and he couldn't tell what plan his pursuers might have. Clearly they were unwilling to face him and have it out — not yet anyway. And he was as unwilling to turn and have it out with them. In his feverish restlessness, he had intended to lure them into the open and identify them if he could; beyond that he hadn't thought. But now with the night air sobering his cheeks, he realized, realized with leaden finality, that he couldn't risk tangling with them, not with Steve by his side; that it was folly ever to have admitted even the possibility of it. And so he had lapsed into nightmare.

On and on they went, while Rusty wondered how the unvarying thread between them could ever be broken. They were tracing out a labyrinth that seemed to serpentine endlessly. It would never come to a conclusion, there would never be any remission. But then suddenly their path was cut by another pursuit that came plunging in from the yawning street to the left — a young man flying past in front of Steve and Rusty, and then, a few seconds later, two military police who streaked across between them and their pursuers. When the turbulence had been reabsorbed into the grey, featureless drift, Rusty noticed that their two constant shadows had wavered and fallen back a little. A minute or two more and they were no longer visible. Then two motorcycle police came splintering through the fog, riding in the opposite direction to which they were going — and with that their pursuers must have taken flight. For although Rusty stopped and lit a cigarette and gave one to Steve, stopped and waited for a full three or four minutes, they didn't reappear. Steve's eyes were brimming with excitement and relief, but Rusty didn't seem to invite comment or questions. They moved on more slowly to where a house was being repaired and where a brazier had been left glowing; and only then did they make a halt and rest.

The brazier was set to one side of the street in a little clearing of rubble. Bravely it sustained a frail perimeter of light round new bricks neatly stacked, a mound of fine sand, sections of ladders, rebuffing the swirling formlessness, hollowing out a beginning of warmth and order, under its dark heavy coals thrusting out homely prophetic tongues against unravelling and collapse. Rusty sat down beside it, his knees hunched up under his coat. And Steve squatted down on the other side, warming his hands. He had some chocolate with him (it was still virtually impossible to get) and they sat munching it silently until they had finished the whole bar. In the brazier's glow, the boy's face seemed ruddy, playful, almost mischievous. His eyes were dancing. He puckered up the tip of his snub nose.

"What did all that mean, Rusty?" he said at last, not being able to contain his curiosity any longer.

Although he didn't want to be, Rusty felt irritated. How should he know what it meant? He was being hunted, his pursuers had trailed him and then had been frightened and had broken off the chase, that was all. What explanation could he possibly give to the boy? He didn't even know who was following him. Oh, he was sure enough that it was the mastermind who was sicking them on. But he still hadn't been able to identify his pursuers. They were utterly faceless to him. And it would only throw Steve into panic again to be told about Rudy and Jackie and the theft from the warehouse and being confronted by the slick business type and the shots in the park.

It would frighten him out of his wits, and (Rusty half-knew) he was also a little ashamed to admit to the boy how all this was still clinging to him.

So all he said, with a twisted grin, was, "I guess someone wants to keep track of me."

The face on the other side of the brazier waited eagerly for him to go on. When he didn't, there was a long pause while the sparkle of expectancy drained out of Steve's eyes. He wasn't going to learn the meaning of the game after all.

At last he said, "I know some people have to go down into the dark, but you weren't made for this sort of life, Rusty."

He thought bitterly. Does he think he knows what I, or anyone else, was made for? But he answered mildly enough, "What was I made for, then?"

"I don't know … but I think to be a hero." Steve brought out the word as simply as though it were something in a legend. And for a moment Rusty saw what he had once been, what he had been at least in his own eyes, flashing off the shield that the boy's eyes held up to him. But his pupils weren't open wide enough to admit much of that gleam. He didn't say anything. He merely scuffed the sand back and forth with his heel.

"Like the heroes who rid the land of monsters," the boy added, enlarging the legend unflinchingly.

"And what did they do when all that was over?" he asked wryly. How could he deal with the boy? He could hardly bear being responsible for someone so innocent and not being able to tell him anything. He wasn't afraid for himself any longer. He had passed beyond that. But his bones were aching and cracking with restlessness and with the weight he was carrying.

"They went home and built something." His faith was unshakable. He had an answer for everything.

"And what if they didn't have a home to go back to?"

"Then they began by building one. That often happened. A hero would come back from the forest, the great forest in the centre of my country, full of bears and wolves, or from fighting on the border, to find that his home was destroyed, burned to the foundations. So he started all over again, right from the ground."

But what if he didn't have the heart or the strength? Or if somehow he had been driven wild so that all he wanted was to go back to the woods, seeking some one bough (a bough of hawthorn or plum or cherry), some one blossom, or else, failing that, to relapse into savagery in the brutal marches? That wasn't what Rusty said, but that was what he was thinking. He was chewing a bitter root that was driving him wild, chewing it right to the end. His restlessness was becoming intolerable. It was so far back that he couldn't follow the process, but somehow everything he had known — horror and perfection and loss and exile — had all been distilled into the pure instinct for flight, which was now diffused through all his nerves, through all his muscles, enflaming them, crisping them so that he couldn't think, he could only flee, anywhere, anywhere, without purpose, measure, reason.

They sat silent. The brazier was as constant as ever. They were in the open, but it spread a kind of refuge about them.

Then Rusty got up, muttering, "Well, I guess we'd better get moving."

The boy's face clouded, but not this time with revolt, only with incomprehension and sympathy. The friend who had done so much for him was homeless and hunted, he didn't know how or why; he couldn't fail him, wherever he was going.

Afterward Rusty could hardly remember where it was they went or how often they were followed, by the police hunting down deserters or by his own particular pursuers. The fog had thickened, and his eyes were hooded. The city was so criss-crossed by pursuits that he couldn't be sure when they were following and when they were being followed. But it seemed to him that they looped in great circles like infatuated animals, like migrant bison or reindeer. Now the masts and cranes of the docks were hulks looming above them, and they were tracing precarious paths through indistinct shimmering basins, careful of their footing for fear they should slip and be lost in those sullen mirrors. Now they were in the centre of the capital, and he was gazing dazedly at some lights that drizzled through the fog, high up, wondering whether they were the windows of the Ministry or the windows of Mark's flat or the windows of the lookout he imagined the mastermind would keep. Now they were crossing the river (but in which direction he didn't know) and he was looking down aimlessly to see if his medal was still there. Now they were trudging through crescents grey as a labyrinth where the fog mingled with peeling stucco. Once in a still street an old man passed them, urinating vociferously. Once they were joined for a few yards by a young man with long hair down to his shoulders, who said he had been in the Air Force and who gave them each a pamphlet headed, "The end is at hand," before taking his leave. A bus slowly blundered towards them, being led like a circus animal by a man walking backwards. Then there was a man with a bandaged head who seemed to keep them company for a while. Now he was gone, and they were in one of the passageways of the market, peering enviously at hoards of apples and oranges and lemons, that were locked in (was it Saturday? Sunday?) behind strong iron netting. Drunk with fatigue, they circled almost obliviously, often in streets that were shuttered and deserted but sometimes where the fog was still mottled with spilt, uncertain crowds. They even went down into one of the dives in the old foreign quarter — that was madness, he knew; it was sure to be alive with police and informers — and he found that the blond young tenor in corduroys and a turtleneck sweater was still singing, "Last night I got a letter … telling me to come home." They went out without even ordering a drink. The tower of a ruined church was hovering vaguely above them, and they sat down on one of the tombstones. But hardly more than a minute later Rusty thought he heard the sound of running feet, and they must get up and be off again.

Always Steve was beside him. Several times he suggested that he leave and go back to his room, that it would be perfectly safe now. But always the answer came back, "I'd rather stay with you, Rusty"; and he gave up trying. He was almost unconscious of him for long stretches, although occasionally he would put out his hand and ask if he were cold. There wasn't a whimper out of the boy as they circled on and on, wandering now through the fog in the centre of the city that tasted of scorched linen. It would be easy on a night like this, he ruminated, for a man to be killed and no one to be any the wiser, so long as there weren't any ties that could be traced between killer and victim (shot and tipped over into rubble, or stunned and dropped into the river); and he shuddered a little, remembering how faint were the ties between him and his pursuers, that, so far as he knew, he had never even seen them. Odd! … But this random reflection, that hardly worried him, that hardly even got through to him, was interrupted by the boy tugging gently but insistently at his sleeve. What he wanted him to look at was in a basement window they were passing where a mother had got up in the middle of the night to look after an infant and had turned on the light without drawing the curtains, and there they were, mother, father, and a child in a crib; and as the sleep-walkers looked in through the glass, Steve said, "It's just like Christmas. It's just like …" While he struggled for a word, Rusty realized that he was thinking of a crèche, a crèche set up in a church at Christmas. They walked on, and Steve began to talk (Rusty not answering, hardly listening) about his home — the white picket fence, the porch at the side with a hammock, the lilacs, the goat tethered behind the house, the birch-wood piled in the shed. "It was always my job to bring in the wood," he was saying.

But Rusty wasn't listening. His closed, infatuated senses had opened a little, and he was hearing other voices. As the grey shapeless continents of fog swirled and eddied and drifted, broken only infrequently by headlights or a window or by the street-lamps that now seemed almost submerged, he heard a voice saying, "But your heart would have to break ..." It came back and back to him, like surf breaking on a beach. A surf full of exhausted swimmers. A girl was washed past him in the fog and was gone before he could save her. How many were drowning! The stitching was coming out, his fibres were unravelling. And the city, too, was unravelling; in this inundating lymph, its tissues were separating, dissolving. What was left was a cloudy gall, as though one bite of the apple had spiralled out as far as the nebulae in a bitterness that was as much insipid as nauseous and that still must be mouthed, a venom dripping from the dugs of the whole, wide, poisoned world. It was like metal on his tongue; there were whiffs of burning; and his ears vibrated with that one insistent voice. "If I could only have you body and soul ..." In the damp air she was sucking him dry, he was aching to be released from her. Would she ever let him go? Now hers, entirely hers, he heard the motorcycle police circling, circling, feeding his flight with their interminable pursuit.

Once, twice, he didn't know how often, they had passed safely through the police cordon. Each time as they approached a check-point, where the police were standing with lanterns, he wanted to run, to run in any direction, it didn't matter. But each time he managed to collect and control himself just in time to put on a good face for the inquisitors and to submit his papers calmly, even to venture a quip or two, before he was cleared through by the flatfeet, the stupid bastards. It was only afterward that his wild instinct revealed itself as he lengthened his stride more and more until Steve could hardly keep up with him and had to ask at last if he wouldn't go a little slower. And he did — impatiently, seething with frustration. But by the change of pace his sodden, sunken wits had been jostled a little and freed just long enough to dart down the question, Why didn't he turn himself in? He would be safe then, and Steve, too, and the long night would be over. But he wouldn't listen, he hardly heard. He was a man under orders, he replied stubbornly; there was something he must witness to. He couldn't recollect what it was he was to witness to, he couldn't remember the orders. But they were there. He went on, pillared by fog. A witness. A man under orders. In some recess those words kept echoing. He heard the sound of running feet and the teletypes clattering out the messages that must ultimately bring him in, if others didn't track him down first. Yet deeper than any tread or any clatter was the thud of those words in his bloodstream. The fog was a long tunnel arcading him in on every side. He couldn't penetrate it, it was wound around his brains. He was moving down a colonnade that stretched endlessly, that he could never escape from. He couldn't remember, although to remember was vital. Was he dead already? Or only about to die, when a man should remember everything with peculiar clarity?

Then suddenly his eyes were purged, and the fog presented to him untormented arches, cool, breathing with honeysuckle, where a light breeze dallied with a scarf, and hair, where the vaulted distances swam in amethyst twilight. He was treading down carnage and triumph and defeat, he was going through a heavy door, he was climbing to pure starry quiet, the sky was embracing gleaming petals, there was nothing but stillness, stillness folded about white limbs. A point of perfect stillness. Still spheres revolved around him slowly. A perfection he could never re-enter. But that, he was sure, that irresistibly, was what he had been born to witness to. Those were his orders, to witness to a paradise he had known once and could never recapture, to bring that freshness into the city (without it there could be nothing but broken branches, bleached bones littering the plain); from the nether world to offer remembered freshness that might even sweeten the great room of mirrors. Already the savour was fainter, but calmly he let it go, for over him arched the splendour of his commission, the irised majesty and misery of memory that only a strong man under orders could support, the vault of a faith old as birth and the night-sky, empurpled, gilded, damascened, gleaming with emerald and sapphire and watery with unquenchable fiery eyes, a whole realm that he was bearing on his shoulders. Without those dreams, the city would wither; its people become cattle or numbers, unless that inheritance were carried on some soldier's back. He strode on in a blaze of glory that was secret, yet for everyone to share; outcast, yet guarding the city. That was his only honour. And now as even the radiance of witness and memory, that had arched down to him in renewal of the treaty between them, was disappearing, all that was left was a few drops, a few precious drops, lodged in the intricacies of his heart.

The fog was as thick as ever. His senses had closed again, and the shutters in his brain. He didn't know where they were going, although he thought they were circling back towards the estuary. Steve was now so tired that he would often fall behind, and Rusty would have to stop and wait for him to catch up. He didn't feel tired himself, only lightheaded with wandering and lack of sleep. Sometimes he seemed to be walking in the clouds, drifting through fog that had enveloped a lost order far below. At other times he was walking on the sea-floor, where ships had foundered, and wharves, perhaps a whole city; and he was looking up at drowned masts and roofs but could see little through the murk (peering cautiously as a diver) except chasms and great looming shadows that might be collapsing walls or sunken bell-buoys or monstrous rudders or propellers, fouled and bent. A drowned city, where cries were muffled, where at any moment a diver's supply of oxygen could suddenly be cut off, where sharks cruised unmolested. There were anchor-chains at his feet, the flukes were dragging in gravel. He looked up: there was a black hook that swam down into his half-closed eyes. And again a voice coiled round him accusingly, "But your heart would have to break …"

How could he escape? There were hooks out for him everywhere. He was being torn to shreds.

At the next check-point he was again submissive. But as soon as it had drifted back into the fog, he told Steve that he was sure the police were following him, and he broke into a run. The sound of running feet was on all sides of him as he raced on, with the boy at his heels, and then turned sharply, never slackening, and then turned again, making the street-lamps spurt and race beside him in thin streaks of light through the fog. It was only when he heard his name called faintly, piteously, "Rusty, Rusty," that he pulled up and waited for Steve. The boy was spent. "I knew I shouldn't have called," he apologized as he came up, panting, on the verge of tears, "but I was afraid of being separated from you." His eyes were swollen, his cheeks stained; his hand trembled as he took the cigarette he was offered. Rusty realized with a pang that he hadn't said a word to the boy for hours. At the next air-raid shelter they came to, they would go in and rest for a while.

The confined darkness was bare and rectangular, but Steve slumped down gratefully on the hard concrete floor. The only light in the elongated narrow cell came from the tips of their cigarettes; but when Rusty shut his eyes he could still see thin threads of light struggling to shine through the fog behind his lids. What if he were to stop running? Could the sense of perfection and loss that was pursuing him be used, not for appetite and pursuit, but for something else, for sympathy … and wisdom? And community be built, after all, out of loneliness? He put his hand out and asked the boy if he were cold. It was time he was going home if he weren't to come down with pneumonia. The early morning trains and buses would soon be running. He would insist on it this time. And at last the boy yielded sleepily.

Rusty went out to check his bearings. After walking up and down a little, he thought he knew where they were and where the nearest bus-line ran. He came back into the shelter and lit one match after another and, as they burnt down to his fingers, sketched on the dusty floor for Steve where he was to go. He didn't say so, but he was relieved to be getting the boy off his hands. They had circled back closer than he had realized to the house where he roomed, and he didn't want the boy to still be with him when he returned, for fear of what might be lying in wait.

Steve got up drowsily, and for a moment they stood together at the door of the shelter. The fog was still thick, but somewhere the faintest possible source of light was welling up dimly and giving a different tone to the darkness.

"It's been a long night," said Rusty.

Steve seemed to hesitate. Then he half-turned and put his arms around his friend and Rusty heard him murmur, "Take care of yourself — for my sake."

"I will," he promised. "And I'll be with you all the way."

And then the boy was vanishing, walking slowly and heavily away. As Rusty watched, he felt relieved to no longer be so encumbered. But part of his heart went with him just the same.

His wits were clearing. They were taking on the unnatural sharpness of prolonged sleeplessness and very early morning. Well, he would need all of them if there was waiting for him what he imagined. As he drew closer, he even felt a kind of exhilaration. He was glad he had decided not to bring his revolver. They wouldn't be likely to risk many shots, if any. And it was harder to hit a moving target than people often supposed. He wasn't the least afraid. In spite of having been up all night and on the prowl, there was still plenty of spring and strength in his muscles. And now he was completely on his own. That was a situation he could deal with; that, and the scent of danger, could always lighten his spirits and make his blood foam with airy bubbles of excitement.

He sauntered down the middle of the street with all the bravado he had often shown in action, when he would go up openly to a cross-road or a farm-house to see whether the enemy were still holding it. He had taken off his hat. It was the same gesture of respect he used to make to his own fearlessness by taking off his steel helmet and letting it dangle in his hand.

There they were! His alerted senses signalled back smartly to him. The heavy bruiser, with a white scarf, propped sleepily against the house opposite; and his slighter partner on the other side of the street leaning against the railings. He was close enough to see the pockmarks on the thick bull-neck of the one and that the other had had his nose badly broken.

He didn't know what their instructions were or what tactics they were likely to follow. Better not take any chances with anything fancy. Filling his lungs, he sprinted right between them and was well beyond them before they could rouse themselves and realize what was happening. Then they swung in, on the run, behind him.

At the next corner he turned and drew them behind him like cheated bulls. Then, before they could be barely sure they were still on his trail, he turned again, his coat flying loose and his hat swinging in his hand. He was playing with them. He was enjoying himself as he swung them this way and that behind him, racing through the cool fog that was now beginning to silver with the light of early morning. What should he do next? He arrowed through a low tunnelled passage that led to the estuary and then down a flight of stone steps to the foreshore. They were slewing about in loose gravel behind him as he jumped up on a beached lighter and then from it to another, and another, and another, and up again over a low stretch of sea-wall and out into the street. He was their master all right, but he wasn't shaking them off. He raced on through the empty spectral streets past locked warehouses and stretches of rubble. He had gone a mile or more from where they had been waiting, and they weren't much farther behind than they had been at first. Well, he would try something different. At the next turning, during the few seconds he was out of their sight, he plunged through the door of a gutted house. He was counting on them losing some ground when they found he was missing and had to stop to consider which way he had gone. What he hadn't counted on was how tangled he would find it inside the house. A litter of broken furniture, charred laths, empty picture-frames clogged the way as he lurched through to the back over the sagging floor and then out to an area of puddles and broken bricks. He ran on for fifty yards or so, and then charged out through an alley to the street again. He had gained a little — but not much. They were still following, only now a little farther behind. There was nothing else for it but to try a burst of speed and draw them as swiftly as he could to one of the main arteries serving the docks, where their fury would be made helpless by traffic and police.

He streaked down the centre of the street, not looking back, his blood pounding, his lungs ready to burst. He couldn't be sure of anything, but he thought the fog was lifting a little over the estuary, and a streak of sky and masts and spars was racing along beside him in a viscous slick of speed as great as his own. The ships were racing so fast there was bound to be a collision.

Then a bullet tore past him, a little to the left, rippling his coatsleeve. He veered sharply to the right. But then something as heavy as a crow-bar ploughed into his leg somewhere between his ankle and his knee. He toppled over and fell heavily on his shoulder, his head flopping against the pavement. He was almost stunned. He had just enough sense and strength left to drag himself up and over the low retaining-wall and then to drop down into the debris of a blitzed cellar. He didn't feel anything in his leg. He was more worried by the brambles that were scratching his hands. He waited, panting, trying to get his breath. There were heavy foot-steps racing towards him. Sheltered a little in brambles and barbed wire, hiding like a stag in bracken, he peered up at the top of the wall. His sight was blurred and he couldn't see them clearly, but there were two faces there looking for him, anxious to spot where he was before dropping over to finish him off. As he crouched down, making himself as small as he could, the only thought that crossed his mind was relief that, anyway, Steve would be safe. With his hands over his eyes, he cringed and waited, waited, it seemed, for an eternity.

But nothing happened. When he took his hands away and peered up again at the top of the wall, the faces were gone. He couldn't understand it. But then out of the fog (in the street or his head, he couldn't be sure) he heard the siren of a police-cruiser; and he knew that now the hunters were being hunted.

He couldn't move. He wouldn't even try to move. All he wanted to do was to fall asleep. Steve was safe, and in time he would be safe and well, too. And yet as he drifted into unconsciousness, he felt a deep ache as though something were missing, as though something were being lost to him forever.

He didn't hear Steve call. He couldn't have, even if he hadn't been stunned; he was too far away from the boy, who had lost his bearings and had wandered back into the area of danger instead of away from it, circling back almost to the rooming-house without knowing it. The first turning or two he managed all right, but then his sense of direction and his memory of Rusty's sketch began to falter. Should he turn to the left or the right? He wasn't sure. He was too stupefied with fatigue. But he was worried that the landmarks Rusty had mentioned weren't showing up as they should. He didn't know which way to turn. Rather than circle round and round in the silvering fog, he had better retrace his steps. And then after he had walked a little way, he heard footsteps behind him. He must have lost the turning. Now there was nowhere to turn from the footsteps that were still following. He was at a dead end. The nimbus of a solitary street-lamp washed over broken glass on the top of a high wall.

Slowly he faced about. If he was the one they wanted, he would soon know: they would speak in his own tongue, whether they had come for him from the Embassy or from the refugee community, and what they would have to say in either case would be about his loyalty to the fatherland. But whose eyes were these? And what were they saying? Something about "being part of the same mob" and "squawkers and squealers" and "the only good rat …"? The words he couldn't understand, but he knew what the eyes meant.

He looked up into the light and cried, "Rusty! Rusty!" The cry rose on eagle's wings, bright, soaring, burnished.

Then a fist smashed into his teeth.

When they were finished with him, a hoarse voice said, "Well, that's one of them, anyway."

"Not the most important one, though," another voice answered. "I wonder what happened to his mate?"

"He's likely got his by now. Our first string wouldn't miss."

As they moved off, the boy was lying under the lamplight, blood trickling from his mouth, his nose broken and his cheek-bone and his ribs, his lungs punctured; and now as the air was leaving the blood-stream, his face was turning a deep dusky purple.

10

Now he was utterly lost.

When he came to, the sun was high, the air was flawless, there was not a trace of fog. It was a perfect spring day. From the shallow depression below the wall where he was lying coiled up, he could see pennants fluttering and masts glittering in the sunlight and, high above him, gulls wheeling and crying and banking. On the other side of the wall was a steady rumble of transports rolling past and, farther off, the calls and shouts of men working at one of the warehouses. All around him the world was going about its business. But he was as outcast as if he had been lying in swamp far up the Amazon.

Slowly he uncoiled and turned over painfully to free himself from the barbed wire where he had fallen. Here and there his coat had been tufted by the barbs, and he had to tear one of the sleeves in order to release it. Then he edged himself a foot or two over the rubble until he was lying on ground that was a little more comfortable. His leg was throbbing and he sat up to examine it. Moving his toes didn't seem to make the pain worse: perhaps that meant that nothing was broken. He pulled up his trouser leg and looked with dazed intentness up and down his calf, first on one side and then on the other, to see what the damage was. At first he couldn't see anything remarkable at all among so many tears and scratches; and he gave away momentarily to a sickish feeling that it had all been hallucination. But the throbbing was real enough — unless possibly it was only an echo of the throbbing in his head. He pored again over his curiously alien flesh, taking the back of his calf in his hand and moving it about and gazing at it like a blind man, until he found two marks not much larger than would be made by a blunt pencil (although one a little larger than the other), where the bullet must have gone through. He lay back exhausted. He didn't know what had been torn or what the risks of infection might be. But he had been lucky; with a little more luck the wound would probably heal of itself. His head was another matter; it felt thick and throbbing; there had probably been some mild concussion. Obscurely he knew, though, that what he was suffering from was more than barbs or a bullet wound or concussion; it couldn't be localized; it was a diffused sense which he couldn't account for of something missing, of some-thing — what was it? — that was lost. Without knowing it, without even admitting it to himself, he was suffering from what in his marrow he knew had happened to Steve.

Sometimes his head seemed full to bursting, at other times as empty as a blown bird's egg. Perhaps he slipped into unconsciousness again for short intervals, perhaps he fell asleep, he didn't know. But he knew that he couldn't think of anything. When he was conscious, he was aware of a few children playing raggedly towards the water's edge, and the notion came to him vacantly of calling to them and asking them to get him something to eat. He did nothing, though, because he couldn't plan, he couldn't think. He turned over on his side and through a haze of children's games saw a large freighter moving slowly out to sea with a smooth silky wake widening behind it. But there was a sharp stone pinching his ribs. He turned over on his other side.

A little distance above him, toward the street, one corner was still standing of the warehouse that had been blitzed to make this desolation; it was only a small part of one storey, but it formed a kind of primitive open gallery, and his instinct told him that it held shelter and that he should try to make for it if he could. He began to crawl up the gentle slope towards it, slipping back on loose bricks, scraping his hands, but moving closer all the time. After a few yards, he tried to stand up. The idea hadn't occurred to him before. He was so dazed and astray that he had assumed he was incapable of doing anything normally. He managed to get to his feet, though, and found that his bad leg would support him all right. But he was so dizzy! He sank back down to his hands and knees and, after resting for a few minutes, started crawling forward again through dead brambles that reached wickedly up and plucked almost at his eyeballs.

The last step or two of the way he got to his feet again and walked. But he had to cling to a charred wooden beam before he could swing himself in and slump down in the middle of his empty refuge.

It has been used before for shelter, he could see. Someone had had a fire, there were still cinders and clinkers on the rough cement floor. And broken glass, the jagged necks of bottles, and a little sand blown in by the wind, and crumbled plaster, and a few blackened turds. Perhaps it had been used by some tramp or perhaps by boys watching the ships and dreaming of adventure.

Whoever had used it before had skirted part of the shelter with sheets of corrugated iron tacked to the charred beams. They would provide a little protection against rain and wind; but they were as uncouth as the twisted stumps of metal that still stained the rough walls of the adjoining buildings, where the great steel joists had been torn from their sockets the night the warehouse had been bombed and had come blazing down to the ground. He stared at them as though they were eyes put out. Then, taking full possession of his new quarters, he slid down flat on his back and lost consciousness again.

It was dark when his lids next fell open. A bell-buoy was tolling far down the estuary. After a while he sat up and looked out. There were markers blinking in the channel, and a faint glow above the roof-tops, and then tangled stars. They prickled his eyeballs like tattooists' needles. But there was no design anywhere among them. No bear, or eagle, or belt, or sword, or serpent. No design you could look to or could wear on your wrist, embellished with flowers, or a wreath, or a cross, or a date, or letters that spelled out "Mother" — or any other name. Nothing but impinging darkness. Out there was nothing, whatever might be reported by those who were wiser perhaps or perhaps only more deluded or more frightened. His leg throbbed. He felt a great ache of desolation. Something had happened to someone who trusted him, but he didn't know what it was. His hair grizzled by the sand and ashes where he had been lying, his cheeks drawn and white, he sat there hour after hour, tattered, vacant, staring, in a kind of vigil (which was also a kind of stupor) for what he didn't know. The night wind wavered past him, smelling of brine and fish and sea-weed, but not bringing any annunciation of birth and beginning, only hints of the salt water that a castaway knows must sooner or later drive him mad. Madness, meaninglessness, indifference, darkness, death pressed against his eyeballs; he seemed to be buried in graphite. He didn't stir. He couldn't stir. He felt not the slightest prompting of any impulse, of any desire. There was nothing within him and nothing outside. He was so little alive that he could hardly distinguish between when he was conscious and when he was not, between when he was awake and when he was sleeping. At times perhaps he slept, with his head fallen on his knees. But he heard the bell still tolling in the distance whether he slept or not, the salt wind still knifed around him. He knew he was alone. He knew isolation, grief, loss. But beyond that nothing, nothing. Only occasionally the faintest possible glimmer, a light over marshes, moved across nothingness. He felt old, immeasurably old, without having gained any wisdom. It was almost morning before he lay back among the ashes and fell asleep again. His head was so empty he felt that, if he should wake, he might find he had blown his brains out.

With the variability of early spring, the morning when it came was cold and drizzly. But the children appeared just the same. They had a rather furtive and fearful air as they materialized skittishly out of nowhere, and he wondered whether they had caught a glimpse of him and were frightened of what they had seen, of his matted hair and the sharp red stubble on his chin. Or perhaps they were only frightened of their mothers, who might have warned them against playing among these craters and hummocks. But in a few minutes any diffidence they might have felt was forgotten and they were absorbed in playing king-of-the-castle on a mound of slithery rubble, pulling, shoving, punching, their cries as thick and hoarse as the gulls', while the smallest one (who couldn't be shaken off but who was too young for such frolics) sat to one side, pattering happily on a toy drum.

It came to him all of a sudden that he was dying of hunger; he would call out and ask one of them to go and buy him something to eat. He got up shakily and tried to call. But no sound came out of his throat. He might have been locked up by himself so long that he had lost the use of his voice. He tried again, and this time what he produced was hardly more than a leather bat-wing of a whisper that zig-zagged crazily before falling to the ground only a few yards away from his feet. Fighting down his panic, he braced himself with his two hands on top of the corrugated iron and leaned out and shouted, shouted as loud as he could. It was as though he had blown the stopper out of his throat: the children stood transfixed and then came running towards him. Singling out the eldest, he sent the others back to their play; and then he asked the boy (he was no more than seven or eight) to run to the nearest shop and get him some bread and cheese and some milk, too, if he could. And he gave him money and a ration-book. Before long the boy was back holding in one hand a parcel wrapped in newspaper and in the other a pint of milk. "They didn't have any at the shop," he explained, "so I picked up a bottle from a doorway."

Inside the newspaper was some processed cheese and half a loaf of bread and two apples, which the youngster had thought he should have as well. Ordinarily he didn't like milk; but he felt the need of it now, he was so weak, and he drank it down as though it were beer. When he had finished, he spread the newspaper under his head and lay back, drawing his coat closer about him to keep out the damp. He felt feverish. But the food would do him good. He dozed off, and in a while half-opened his eyes, and then dozed off again; and that was how he spent most of the day.

When he next came fully awake, the children had gone, the drizzle had stopped; but it was still grey, and darkening towards evening. He sat up and looked out. In the failing light the ruin where he was sheltering, between high walls on either side, seemed like a foundered hulk. There was nothing left to eat. But brushing away the crumbs, he spread the paper out between his feet and looked absently at the sporting news. Then he turned the pages slowly until his eyes lit on the heading "Cul-de-sac Murder." He had known all along that there was to be a final encounter.

He couldn't read it through, but fragments from it lodged in his dazed brain like shrapnel. "Young refugee … not believed to have any enemies … perhaps a victim of gang warfare … identified as Stefan … ribs fractured … body purple … jaws also fractured … mucous membrane of the mouth torn, and ragged fragments of bone showing through … found early yesterday morning near the docks."

He got to his feet and teetered to the edge of the narrow lean-to and was sick down the side of the twisted jagged metal. How had the boy lost his way? He would never know now … and it didn't matter, he was dead, he was dead. He had known it without knowing it, but now he could see it all as though he had been there himself. And suddenly he was staring into the very face of death itself. He might have been reading of his own death, of any man's death. And what it called out in him was deeper than grief; that would come later. It was sheer animal instinct, sheer animal recoil. He must be off, he must rouse himself and be off.

He stood up and brushed off his clothes a little with the back of his hand. He got out his comb and combed out some of the ashes from his matted hair. He was worried because he couldn't see his hat, and he peered about for it in the livid gunmetal twilight. Finally he saw it still caught in the barbed wire where he had fallen, and he limped over and recovered it with a stick and then made his way to the far corner of the blitzed area where the debris rose to the level of the street and where he had seen children going in and out. His leg was troubling him — it was stiff and throbbing — but he thought it would get him back to his room. He climbed over the low wall and stood in the street for a minute or two to get his breath and to accustom himself to the lights and the dizzying speed of the traffic. Then he turned and started painfully on his way. His fever had mounted and he was more conscious of it now that he was on his feet and taxing himself with exertion. After he had gone a few hundred yards he felt as though he could hardly go any farther. He stopped and supported himself against a lamp-post. His best chance would be to try to get a lift with a driver travelling in the same direction. In a minute or two a heavy transport pulled up at the traffic lights and he hobbled out and asked for a lift. The driver looked suspicious but he swung open the cab door, and Rusty clambered in, and almost before he knew it, he was approaching the corner where he should turn up to his room and was asking to be put down and was back in the street again. Another short painful stretch and he was swaying past the railings where the sailor had been hanging so cadaverously and was going up the steps from which Steve and he had set out.

One of the two sisters who kept the house was in the front hall and she followed him upstairs to his room solicitously, giving him her arm whenever he seemed too tired to go on. She didn't ask him anything about where he had been or what had happened to him; but as soon as he was back in his room and had collapsed on the bed, she said firmly, "You ought to have a doctor." When he shook his head vigorously, she didn't say any more but busied herself trying to make him comfortable, taking off his shoes, loosening his coat, unbuttoning his shirt-collar. He wouldn't let her do anything else and she went out. But in a few minutes she was back, anxious as a mother.

"I could get you a doctor, dearie, who wouldn't ask any questions. Would that make any difference?"

This time he nodded, and she hurried back down to the telephone.

When the doctor came, Rusty showed him his leg; and he examined and probed it. Then he cleaned and dressed the wound and gave him an injection with a hypodermic needle and left him some tablets to take every three hours and told him that with complete rest he should be all right in three or four days.

The next few days were dropped out of his life. He slept most of the time; he drank the liquids that the landlady kept bringing to the side of his bed; he slept again. He hardly thought at all. The doctor came in once or twice again to change the dressing on his leg and to tell him that the wound was healing nicely and that he would soon be as good as ever. And Rusty knew himself that he was getting better; the fever was going and his head was a great deal clearer. But he didn't care. He was surprised at how often, when he woke, his lips seemed listlessly to be forming the words, I want to die.

I want to die. His lips kept forming the words over and over. Yet in spite of his withdrawal and absence from himself, he knew there was something he still had to face. When he was well enough to get out of bed and move about the room, the form his grief took first was complete vacancy. Fever had scoured his skull white as a cenotaph. Occasionally when the good soul came in with soup or a custard, she found him staring at the ceiling and was alarmed because of what she thought those haggard eyes might be seeing, swarming from the cracks in the plaster or swirling round the shadowy cornice. But she needn't have worried; he was seeing nothing. His skull might have been drilled open and his brains sucked out. His head was as hollow as a drum. He sat that way hour after hour, conscious of nothing but loss.

The next day he felt stronger, and he drew up a chair to the table to open an inquisition into how far he had been responsible for Steve's death. He felt as though he were up for office in the orderly room — but there was no one but himself to represent authority and sit in judgment on the other side of the table. It was himself that he was facing; and before the charge could be read out, he was anxious to put in such defence as he could. It had all been an accident, as much of an accident as the once he had been late at a cross-road and two men had been cut off and killed. The boy must somehow have lost his way and wandered back into danger and … but hadn't he done everything he possibly could to set him straight and see that he got safely home? He had drawn off the only pursuers he had seen and couldn't have known there were others lying in wait. Even his first meeting with Steve had been completely accidental; the boy had almost bumped into him that misty night on the wharf. He hadn't asked for his confidence or to become in any way responsible for him. Anyhow, could he be held responsible for the great whirlwind around the world that had uprooted him and swept him from his home and driven him thousands of miles, this way and that, across the face of the globe? It had all been an accident, a terrible accident, part of an almost universal accident that no one could be expected to shoulder or understand.

While he was making his case, his double was waiting on the other side of the table, silent, absorbed, as though intent over some card-game or over the black and red entries in a ledger. But then the charge came blistering out.

Hadn't Steve trusted him? Hadn't he died because he had trusted him? The boy had needed him, true. But, for his part, hadn't he taken up with him because he was wandering and lonely and needed Steve's company and comfort almost as much as Steve had needed his? Perhaps as a refugee he might never have regained his home. Would he have died, though, except for falling in with a deserter, with someone who had wanted to go down into the dark and whose finger-prints connected him, however lightly, with the brutal world where the boy had been kicked to death? He was dead, his lungs punctured, his blood breathless, his body livid, the bones showing through the roof of his mouth. And why? Because of the friend he had trusted. It was a drumhead court-martial; and as Rusty listened he had no doubt what the verdict would be, or the sentence. Already he felt the lashes beginning to rain down on his naked back. He was bowed over the triangle, bound tight at the knees and the ankles and the wrists; the cords steeped in brine were tearing the flesh from his shoulders; the drums were ruffling to mark the strokes and to cover his cries. And it went on and on.

When it was too much to bear, Rusty got up and stood looking out of the window. He felt naked, the blood ran glistening down his back. In the littered yard behind the house a stunted tree (it looked a little like a fig tree) was gleaming in the spring sunlight with new leaves and smooth, sleek bark. Appealingly he gazed up into the clear sky; but with its merciless toccata of accident, design, and destiny, it only rubbed more salt into his wounds. He squared and straightened his shoulders, and for a moment knew himself for what he was, an animal crazed and driven wild, driven avidly and irresistibly to experience and explore — but with no hope, no right, to be let off any of the consequences. Uncertain how to plead, but no longer innocent, knowing that no act is innocent, he stared at the flawless sky unflinchingly. Having tasted perfection would excuse him from nothing. He was both a wild stag, he knew now, and a beast of burden.

He sat down again, heavily, alone; and now the arguments, both black and red, were shuffled together. They had met by accident.... But he had become responsible for the boy.... It wasn't his fault that the war had swept away old landmarks and uprooted millions of people and left them homeless.... No, but if he had been a different type from what he was, Steve would still be alive today. (A rope was being tightened at the back of his neck and lead being poured in between his skull and his brains.) ... He could face it, but he couldn't piece it out, he couldn't solve it. He had thought so little, it was hard for him to follow it very far. The farthest he could see was that Steve had died because of his desertion; and desertion was something he had been born to; he had been born to wander and to explore the wound left by his dropping from the bough. And the argument trailed away in low tidal flats like the currents of a river losing itself in salt creeks and marshes and lagoons.

As he sat back, he felt very tired. Again he was nothing. For a long time he stared up in complete vacancy. Then, at last, an inkling trickled through to him of how he might give his own sense of nothingness its only proper consummation.

He went over and got out his kit-bag and dumped the few things that were still in it out on the bed. Then he went back and, without taking it out of its canvas holster, laid his revolver beside him on the table. When the landlady next came in to see how he was, she found him sitting in his shirt-sleeves in the silvery speckled evening light, playing solitaire, with the cards trailing red and black across the table like a poisonous creeper and with something rough and clumsy lying at his elbow in a dark grey cover. He said that he was feeling better, and she went out again. He had told himself that if he could play all the cards and finish the game he would put the muzzle to his forehead and press the trigger.

He kept putting red cards on black and black cards on red till the end was almost in sight. Then there came a check. He shuffled the cards and tried again. This time he didn't get so far. He swirled the cards together in a heap in the middle of the table and took the revolver out of its holster. A few minutes later when the landlady came back (there was something about him that worried her, she didn't know why), she didn't disturb him but went out softly because he seemed to be praying. His head was bent and his hands were clasped in front of him. What she couldn't see was that he was holding the revolver in his hands and that the muzzle was against his forehead.

At moments he was glad that he could put an end to everything so easily. Gratefully he pillowed his head on the steel of the muzzle, taking comfort in the pressure of the slightly raised inner rim of the barrel. But at other moments he was worried, worried that he might press the trigger out of sheer absence of mind. And he couldn't decide. He swayed gently back and forth, teetering on the brink.

Although he couldn't be sure, he thought that the first thing that called him back was something Anne had said, something she had said about his heart, about his heart being big enough for anguish. With that, there was a faint glimmer moving over the face of nothingness. He felt his heart clenching and unclenching like a fist, the blood still coursing through it with animal heat and trapped rainbow radiance. And then he saw — although at first he tried to avoid it — Steve's face looking at him, not with reproach but with pleading, and he remembered what he had said about the heroes in his homeland. He put the revolver back in its holster and snapped down the flap. He knew he must take his pack on his back, and that it would be far heavier than he had ever known it before, that he must get to his feet and shoulder, now and for as long as there was breath in his body, the weight of his failures and responsibilities and an uncommuted sentence to hard labour.

But for the moment he felt exhausted. He needed to rest for a while longer and gather his strength. He put away his revolver and stretched out on the bed in the very hollow where Steve had lain sobbing, with his hands covering his eyes. Now there was more substance to his grief, his mind was more haunted and peopled. He longed to put out his hands to the boy in comfort, in blessing. But he was gone, there was nothing he could do. And in his helplessness it was Steve who miraculously came to bless him. He lay there overcome by memories like bells drifting seaward.... The first time they had met ... when he had been hoping to see the sailor and had been standing in a nimbus of milky golden light, looking this way and that; and as the mist rolled in around them, he had said it would be snowing now in his own country. The Sunday afternoon when they had sat together on the seawall in the warm autumn sunlight and heard the churchbells floating out to sea through a tangle of spires and masts; and he had spoken about how much he had loved Sunday (or was that another time?) when he was a boy at home, with his mother busy in the kitchen and his father playing the cello. His politeness and his old-fashioned turns of phrase: how he had gone "sporting in the forest" when he was a boy; how they would "feast him and make merry" if he should ever return. His way of puckering up his snub nose. The few days he had stayed with him in his room and nursed him and had heard about the town where he had lived — the flower-sellers in front of the church, the crush on market days, the crossing-sweepers with their twig brooms, the statue of the astronomer. What he had told him about the wayside crosses on the country roads ("We used to go out in springtime, Rusty, and gather flowers to put beneath them.") And about the trains: the cold, the stench, the iron doors being slammed to, the bayonets, the cries, the thin soup with fish-heads floating in it, the dying, the dead. And about the camps (where even he for a while had wanted to die): the roll-calls in the open in arctic cold, plunging through drifts to work all day at cutting trees, the bayonets, the weak left to die in the snow, his courage returning to him. At last his courage, his perfect loyalty and courage.

And then, as he lay there, he glimpsed courage of another kind, how Anne, who had needed him, had left him for his ow good, so that she wouldn't be a weight on him. How she ' taken him in with no questions asked, not minding at all that he was a deserter; how bravely she had struggled with her illness, not giving in to it, summoning up resources of fun and high spirits to hold it at bay as long as she could; how courageously in the end she had gone off by herself, not letting him follow but writing to help him find new strength in himself, to put new heart into him.

His honour had left him — and it didn't seem to matter. He didn't know where it was, whether with the self that had been a soldier, or the self that should have returned home, or the self that Mark had tried to appeal to, or the self that had been naked and homeless and had gone down endless turnings. It had vanished, that was all he knew; he didn't know where. What he was left with was only what they had seen in him, Anne and Steve, what they had thought of him, what they had wished for him. With that, and with something of his own that he still shared with them, although he was hardly conscious of it, a deep ultimate animal courage.

The next morning when the landlady came in, he was looking stronger, so much stronger that she reminded him the doctor had said he could venture out now whenever he felt like it.

"I know," he said dully.

But then he looked up. He had hardly noticed her all these past days while she had been looking after him, bringing him food, changing his pillows, making sure that he took his medicine. Now he saw her, really saw her, with her soiled white apron, her gray hair falling over her ears, her chilblained knuckles.

"I can never repay you, you know," he told her truthfully.

"Don't trouble your head about it, dearie," she protested. "If you're getting better, and you are, praise be to God, that's all I care ...ut. But a big strapping lad like you — you ought to get out. ...mise me you'll take a little walk this morning?"

...iled faintly and promised that he would.

...t a little farther. The first morning he walked ... buy himself a paper and a glass of beer. But ...urprised himself by going on until he passed

Dragon's deserted hideout. And before long he was going right into the centre of the city, taking a bus most of the way, it is true, in order to spare his leg, which was still not perfectly strong, but then walking about for a while before he caught a bus back. There were parts of the city he avoided. He didn't go to the market or to the old foreign quarter. But he went to the Plaza again and looked up at the windows of the Ministry and walked under the arcades. He circled the parks without entering them, noticing how, with spring and the leaves all out, they had become again sheeny and liquid like a landscape reflected in water.

Sometimes he caught the smell of spices. Sometimes he remembered how the city had seemed to him when he was first on the loose, everywhere sparkling with adventure. Sometimes as he grew stronger, he saw traces of great wheeling arcs, even of whole spheres, staining the sky, and knew that in spite of everything that had happened they were centred on the few iridescent drops that were still lodged in the passages of his heart; and then he would again want to die, despairing of ever being able to escape from infatuation and be restored to himself and through his own efforts begin breeding order and meaning around him. Or — he wondered — was the only solution to learn to live with it, with the traces and temptations of bewildering, remembered perfection and, without denying its source, try not to be deluded or led astray by trying to recapture it, try, however gradually and painfully, to put it to use? To turn it into something that could be of use here in the city, where the teletypes were clattering, the freighters hooting in the estuary, the transports rolling in with produce for the market, where millions of creatures (all carefully entered in the statistics) were baffled and hungry, prisoners in lock-step, hunted and hunting, lost and wild, in the city so dark, so dark as he knew it now to be, so riddled by chance, so brutal, so full of hopeless longings. That it should be made of use on these strange silted shoals. But now he felt it closed arou
him like a vast, transparent membrane — a membrane with h

showing through. He remembered how Steve had said he was praying for a miracle for him. Sometimes he thought that it was only by a miracle he could ever be freed.

And in the end what came to him was a kind of miracle.

It began one evening as he was rounding the palace and about to make his way back to his room. There had been a little haze all day, but only enough so that when the lights were lit in the globes of the great ornamental lamp-standards, their beams were made to seem more visible and far-reaching. They could even be followed a little distance as they sifted through the obscurity of the park where he had walked so many months ago, in midsummer, and thought about the royal beasts and tournaments and arenas. But for the most part the park was in leafy darkness, swayed and lifted by it, swinging in the breeze like a cage at the end of a tipsy pole. There he would walk no more: tonight it seemed to stand for every paradise from which he was excluded.

But for all that he was excluded, he still was haunted by tell-tale patches of glimmering colour that confirmed his imprisonment in the darkness. Perhaps it was because he had just been walking under the arches in the Plaza and had caught there, however faintly, the savour of his servitude. He didn't know. But it offended him; it humiliated him now, that the intensity of the dark should be qualified by this mocking colour, dear to him though it still was as his own heart. It was a mockery that made him feel immensely tired and burdened, as though all the workings of his body were flooded with death.

He walked on past a sentry. They were wearing their scarlet tunics again, he noticed. He felt outcast and alone, more alone
he would have been even as a roving picket. At the next
two eyes stared out at him from under a shaggy
...ttering with something intensely primitive and
...ly, he didn't know why, he thought of
..., of shaggy hunters returned from the chase,
...ered with furs stripped from the prey they had

captured, but all of them exultant, all of them with eyes glittering like coals; and one of them had come out of the security of the cave to keep watch and to rebuff the night sky. He couldn't help it, it made him think of Brandy and Dragon, of Brandy with his great pelt of black-hair down to his navel and of Dragon like a great sleek stag standing in meadowsweet and nibbling green twigs and shoots. He felt half ashamed to be using this as a brazier, to be warming his hands at the memory of anything so primitive and simple; but in their animal heat was to be found conspicuously the final irreducible particles, random, unpredictable, not to be trusted, but without which nothing could be built, nothing, neither love nor justice nor a city, without which there could be no meaning nor anything but spreading tundra and despair.

And now, inexplicably, he was laughing. And something was tearing and breaking. Films and veils and invisible spheres and membranes were being torn to shreds. The skies were being torn open to their full darkness and distance. And he was laughing and treading exultantly over the lustrous tattered fabrics as they came raining down, laughing in a shower of fading irised crystal. There would always be the taste of perfection in his mouth; he would never be rid of it, he would never recapture the source from which it came; sometimes it might lead him to folly, sometimes it might lead him to wisdom and rare transitory triumphs. He would always be a wild thing with that salt mist in his mouth, as well as a beast of burden.... The wind was rising.... The skies were clearing.... Music was coming from across the park. And not only the crisp bugle-calls that he heard without noticing at retreat and tattoo and lights-out. No, this was something much fuller, larger, although it was no hour for any ceremony that he could think of; side-drums were skirling and ruffling, they were being joined by kettle-drums, by brassy-throated cornets, trumpets, tubas, trombones, by the deep rhythmic fist of a brass-drum pulsing against a leopard's skin. The music was swelling in great rippling chords and bars. A patrol was going out in full array to help bring down those crystal ramparts, with hunting-horns and blood-red standards and, tethered on golden chains, leopards and unicorns and bears and stags. And he was part of the music, he was rising with it and laughing and looking down at himself. He was laughing at his own tenacity and folly, laughing at his own insignificance and worth, laughing in the teeth of death and despair. Laughing and exulting as other voices were joined to his. Now Steve's voice and Anne's were being carried to him on the wind, their courage was being added to his, they were breathing, were shouting, through him. He was uplifted by the vehemence of their breath, he was a trumpet and was helping to tear the last vestiges of illusion to tatters.... And now finally he felt something else tearing and breaking. The crystal vial in his heart that had supported all those circling spheres — the strong muscles of his heart were breaking it at last, the precious iridescent drops were spreading, spreading, were trickling everywhere along his nerves and tissues. Still he exulted. For nothing was lost. Perfection was being broken through his common dying clay.

He went back to his room and slept soundly; and the next morning he turned himself in.